Mountain of Glass

Across Time & Space series

The Eternity Stone
Mountain of Glass
Desert of Fire
Desert of Ice
The Hidden Door
Whiter Than Snow
City of Light

Fairytale Memoirs series
The Mostly Forgotten Memoirs of Rose Red
Viola Sends Her Regrets
Gifted

Standalone books
Breaking the Glass Slipper
Unshakeable
Tyger
Take Me Home
Hereditary

For information on new and upcoming books,
go to **mmarinanbooks.com**

Mountain of Glass

ACROSS TIME & SPACE
BOOK TWO

M. Marinan

Silversmith
PUBLISHING

First published in New Zealand in 2017
This edition published 2023
by Silversmith Publishing

A catalogue record for this book is available from the National Library of New Zealand

Original cover paperback ISBN 978-0-9951108-1-6
This cover paperback ISBN 978-1-99-001420-8
This cover hardcover ISBN 978-1-99-001421-5

Dedication

For my parents:

Mum, thank you for cheering me on all the way.

Dad, thank you for actually reading the draft version of my work, *and* saying nice things about it, *and* meaning them.

I'm blessed to have you both.

Contents

Prologue

The Mountain of Glass

Somewhere, in a space that probably shouldn't have existed, a tapestry ran around the edge of a vast round room. It was made of innumerable black and white threads, carefully intertwined in a way that might make a lovely pattern sometime in the future, but at the moment just looked like a big mass of knots.

But right now, Amaranthus, the maker of the tapestry, was focussed on untangling just one knot. He hummed as he worked, examining the small whitish mass, and as he touched it, tiny images came bouncing out into the air. Three tiny little people with tiny little faces, their thoughts written even more clearly than their expressions.

Unhappy.

"Patience," he told the threads that each represented a single person, "is a virtue."

They didn't hear him, or perhaps they just weren't listening. He'd been expecting that, so he didn't mind. Most of the time people didn't listen. It was their loss.

No, really.

Suddenly the knot released, and the tiny white threads sprang free. They went flying across the tapestry back to where they'd originally been drawn from.

No, further than that still.

Amaranthus laughed, unsurprised. This was going to be *interesting.*

The woman shook her head slightly, trying to clear her thoughts. She was doing something vital, but she wasn't sure what. Or where she was, or *who* she was.

But she knew that she was important in some way. Powerful too – as powerful as…as an elemental god. Was that a real thing?

She was sitting outside a large stone building with an elaborate façade, and the sun shone bright in the blue sky. There was a feeling of relaxation around here, like no one was working and nothing was important.

Next to her sat a youngish man with bland brown hair and an equally bland smile on his plain face. The concern in his eyes when he looked at her seemed real, though.

She could tell what he was thinking: not quite telepathy, but a strong sense of where his thoughts were going. *Middle-aged, unkempt woman; swarthy-skinned with salt and pepper hair; clinging to her past glory.* But his nervousness around her was offset by the fact that he could just tell *them* where to find her, and she'd be done for.

Underneath her confusion was the certainty that this amnesia was temporary. She would recover herself, and she would be as…*powerful*?…as she had been before. A god to fear and revere.

Deias, she was amazing. Shame she didn't know who she was.

The woman gave her keeper a narrow-eyed glare. She could sense he was a little intimidated by her, and that was satisfying.

Just wait, she thought, *just wait until I'm back to…whatever I was before. Then I'll show you.*

FLATMATES

"By the Eternal One!" Anne screamed, throwing herself to the ground. "We're being attacked!"

Ash stopped in the middle of her phone call, turning to stare at the girl now lying on the lounge room carpet. The little redhead looked like an escapee from a period drama in her green velvet gown with its wide skirts, but then she'd go and do something like this, and would remind Ash that she *had*, in fact, been born almost five hundred years earlier. "I told you it's just an airplane, Anne. We're on the flight path from Harthrow airport."

"Death comes from above," Anne moaned. "And 'tis *Lady* Anne to you."

Ash moved to another room with a sigh. "Sorry, Natalie," she said to the person on the other end of the line. "One of my visitors was having an episode."

"A seizure?" her boss asked suspiciously. "Or do you mean a mental breakdown-type episode? I understand if you need to support a family member, but I need warning if you want time off for anything except actual illness-"

"It's not a seizure or a breakdown," Ash cut in, although in truth, one of those might've been easier to manage. Her two uninvited houseguests were so out of place here that they might well be thought insane. And Natalie knew very well that Ash's family was all on the other side of the world.

But how could Ash explain to the very staid office manager

that she was currently sharing a room with two time-travellers, and she'd just come back from her own kidnapping?

She couldn't, and even bringing the other two into work in full period dress wouldn't do her any good. At the moment one of them was watching the TV, enthralled by a toothpaste ad, and the other was whimpering on the floor of the living room, terrified of the Boeling 737 flying overhead.

"As I said, Natalie, they're just very unexpected visitors. Hopefully they won't be staying long, but I can't leave them here alone until I've got them settled in. Two days, that's all I need."

Natalie sighed heavily. "Fine, Ashlea. You may have today and tomorrow off – but I don't want to see these *visitors* interfering with your attendance at work again, understood?"

The woman was one of the few people who called Ash by her full name, but Ash put up with it since she needed the job to pay her bills.

Ash thanked her profusely for the time off, then hung up the phone with a sigh, scrubbing one hand over her tired face and wishing that she didn't have to go back to work *ever*.

The administrative assistant job had paid her bills for the last six months she'd been staying in Angland, but while it was incredibly dull and she'd give it up in a heartbeat, there was nothing to replace it. Her savings barely topped the thousand-pound mark, and if she left the job, all of that would be quickly eaten up by the high cost of living here.

Imagine if she went back home after all this effort, with no savings to show for it!

When the dreaded phone call was over, Lady Anne of Covington looked up from the television. She'd clearly recovered from her fear of the airplane enough to get stuck on the TV along with the other 'visitor'.

The ad had changed from whitening toothpaste (which, without wanting to be unkind, wouldn't have done either of them any harm) to dog food, and the small redhead looked baffled.

"What is this creature supposed to be?" she asked imperiously. "'Tis more like a rat than a dog."

"It's a chihuahua," Ash answered shortly, barely glancing at the TV. "It's a purebred."

Lady Anne (she wouldn't accept anything else from Ash the Peasant) scoffed. "As if the people of your time would know anything about purity. Forsooth, they walk about unclothed half the time. Do they not grow chilled?"

"It's just TV," Ash said dully. "You can't take it seriously."

Oh, Deias. What was she going to do? It was bad enough that she'd had to take these two home with her (not their fault, nor hers, but they were *seriously* uninvited guests). And now she had only two days to settle them into this century and find some way to provide for all of them on her limited income…

…Unless Amaranthus came through with his promise to return them home. Yet that was seeming less and less like a promise, and more like an offhand comment that would never be fulfilled.

Just then the other uninvited guest looked up from the TV. He was a little older than her age of nineteen and a little taller than her height of five-eight, with curly blond hair, a wardrobe straight off Pride and Precipitation, and at the moment, a seriously grim expression.

The Honourable Mister George Seymour cocked his head to the side and studied her face. As if reading her mind he said, "Amaranthus *did* promise to take us home, you know. I have to believe that he will follow through."

Yes, because if they didn't believe that, then they'd have to accept that they were staying here in Ash's time rather than going home to 1556 Tudar Angland for Anne, and 1818 in the Regency period for George.

And they wouldn't be staying here in the height of modern luxury, either. Ash could only afford the basics, because Angland was *expensive*. And that was a ticket to depression for the lot of them.

Ash smiled tightly, resisting the urge to rub at her temples. "Yeah. Sure he will."

The man who'd actually taken them (illegally) to 2155 AD and returned them again (also illegally) had been the scientist Dr Osvaldo Walker, blessed with intelligence and access to time-travel devices, but lacking in compassion.

But the man who'd done them the most good had an almost unpronounceable name, and also may not have been human. Amaranthus was short, balding and bright-eyed, with an uncertain ethnic background and abilities that ran far beyond the norm.

He could also send people through time via an object called the Eternity Stone, which was how most of the trouble had started.

He'd promised he would send the three of them home, but they hadn't seen anything of him after that last battle with Seyen and her Nobles in 2155. So Ash, George and Anne had decided to take Dr Walker's begrudging offer to return them instead. (Some threats and blackmail may have been involved.)

But Dr Walker had the last laugh. He sent the three of them back to Ash's time, knowing that once they were gone, he wouldn't be hearing any complaints.

Ash didn't expect to hear from Dr Walker again. Amaranthus, on the other hand? He had seemed so trustworthy.

He had to come through for them.

Anne knew not how long she had sat on the thin rug, watching the fascinating tee-vee screen with its flickering pictures and many promises. Who knew so many different goods could be bought?

Odd-looking foods, machines intended for one's kitchen that made dreadful noises and turned food into puree, food for animals, animals that *were* food…forsooth, *so* much food. There were also goods such as clothing, furniture, beauty aids-

Suddenly the tee-vee screen turned black. Ash stood beside it, holding the little black bar that controlled the tee-vee's movements, and 'twas clear she'd somehow managed to remove all the images.

"You killed it!" Anne exclaimed in outrage. "I would watch longer. Revive the screen at once."

Ash folded her arms. "You've been watching infomercials for seven hours, Anne. It's almost one in the morning, and George wants to sleep."

Anne looked guiltily to where he lay on the couch, covered by a thin blanket. He was snoring. "He is already asleep, so it harms him not."

"*You* should be asleep," Ash began forcefully, then stopped, mayhap realising how inappropriate 'twas to order Anne about like a child. More politely she continued, "I've made up a bed in the spare room. There are books in there and a lamp if you want to read."

"Books?" Anne brightened. At home in 1556, while printing presses were sometimes used, the most precious books were carefully handwritten and illustrated. In spite of her position as a noblewoman, 'twould be rare to even touch such an expensive item. "What kind of books?"

The spare room was indeed very small. 'Twas lit by another of those glowing glass globes in the flat white ceiling above their heads, and Ash had cleared space for a low, narrow pallet bed against one wall. Next to the bed was a small wooden chest topped with a stack of the aforementioned books.

Anne gravitated to the books with enthusiasm and picked up the nearest. It was unlike anything she'd seen before: large and squarish with a very slender spine. Its luridly coloured cover showed a thin, barely clad woman with big, pouty lips and a dramatic pose. Anne flicked through its pages in growing dismay before checking others in the pile to see they were the same. Her curiosity faded into distaste as she realised what lay before her.

Ash leaned in through the doorway, clad in a patterned breeches and jerkin set she'd called 'pee-jays'. "Everything OK in here?"

"Ash," Anne said carefully, "I am aware that we have become friends of a sort in these last few, trying days. But surely you understand that I cannot and will not expose myself to these…these manuals for harlotry!"

Ash's dark eyebrows shot up. "Harlotry? What are you talking about?"

"This!" Anne pointed at one of the images with righteous indignation, trying not to look at it herself, but failing. "This woman's garb is suitable for only a harlot, and the way she presents herself is as though she would-"

"Be a harlot?" Ash cut in, a smile curving her lips. "Anne, it's an ad selling tennis shoes, and the model's got all the important bits covered. But maybe you shouldn't look at the magazines after all. How about this instead?"

Ash snatched away the brightly coloured harlot-books then handed over a smaller but much fatter book. This one had a plain green leather cover, and crinkled in an odd manner as Anne handled it. "What is this thing?"

"A photo album. It's only family pictures, but I promise they're all PG."

Anne didn't understand the last part of the statement, nor did she know what an 'add' was, but suddenly she wilted. It had been the longest day, following on from a couple more very long days in the strangest surroundings, and once removed from the tee-vee's alluring influence she was tired enough to sleep…but not in this gown.

She turned her back to Ash. "Undo my laces." There was no response, and Anne added belatedly, "Please. I shall sleep in my undergarments."

Ash helped her remove the heavy outer gown, then held out what appeared to be a rough, short shift-dress. "You don't want to wear one of my t-shirts instead?"

"Of course not," Anne replied sensibly, once she realised what the item was. "'Twould show my legs, would it not?"

"Of course." There was a brief pause. "I'll leave you to sleep, then. Don't forget to turn off the lamp when you're done." Ash showed how a little switch on the wall brought instant darkness, then light again. "See?"

"I *do* understand light switches," Anne told her, slightly offended. "You showed us when we arrived, do you not recall?"

For some reason Ash sighed heavily. "Great. Goodnight, Anne."

'Twas on the tip of Anne's tongue to correct the girl's speech – *call me Lady Anne, if you will* – but for some reason she didn't say it. Mayhap because it brought to mind the wicked Nobles, who insisted on being treated like gods and given titles they didn't deserve.

So Anne made a decision. For the few days she was here, she would allow the commoner to call her by her Churchian name only…but in private, of course. In public, all the proprieties must be observed.

"Goodnight, Ash."

"Don't do that!" Ash snapped a bare moment before George stuck a metal fork into the toaster.

He looked up in surprise, fork hovering an inch over the appliance. "The bread is caught between the spokes inside the mechanism."

"The toaster is still on," Ash explained, probably less patiently than she could have – but she'd been having these conversations ever since they'd arrived two days ago. "If you touch it with metal, you might electrocute yourself." George looked blank and she elaborated, "Like being struck by lightning."

He carefully lowered the fork to the table, and a few seconds later the bread popped up out of the toaster, perfectly cooked. He removed it carefully, not looking at Ash while he did so. For the Honourable Mr Seymour, having to make his own Sunday breakfast was no doubt a lowering experience.

Well, at least he *hadn't* killed himself by mistake. It would be hard for Ash to explain a dead body, especially one that didn't match up to anyone born in the last century.

They hadn't heard from Amaranthus yet, but all three were still hopeful that they would soon. In the meantime, Ash had been very busy making the little cottage useable for three people, getting suitable clothing for the other two, and teaching them how to manage in the twenty-first century. Or at least how to use a tap, a fridge and a flush toilet, anyway.

George moved over to the electric jug and flicked its switch.

"Does it have water in it?" Ash asked quickly. "To at least-"

"The minimum line," he cut in. "Yes, it does, as you told me the last three times I used it that if I'm not careful I might start a fire and burn the whole cottage with us in it. And I mustn't touch the oven, nor the mickerwiv, nor leave the tap running, nor change the tee-vee channels to sound only by mistake. I do listen, Ashlea."

Oh. "Am I that bad?" she asked finally, restraining herself from correcting his pronunciation of 'microwave'. She'd been feeling like she had a couple of oversized toddlers in the house, titles and age notwithstanding, and maybe she'd got a little carried away with the instructions…

George paused. "Not dreadfully bad. Just somewhat repetitive and condescending." He looked up at her with a brief smile, cutting through her sudden guilt. "And here you were convinced that we'd be condescending towards you if we stayed. Oh, how the tables have turned."

He was teasing, but there was a vein of truth underneath. She *had* been repetitive and yes, maybe even condescending in trying to teach them how to survive in the wilds of a modern Anglish town. But behind all her explaining was the fear that they'd never get to go home, and she'd be responsible for them for the rest of their lives – or hers, whichever ended first.

"Sorry," she said instead, smiling back. "I'll try to give instructions only once. Unless I think you're really about to kill yourself; then you'll just have to put up with my nagging."

Just then Anne walked into the room. She was wearing the results of yesterday's budget shopping trip: a puffy-sleeved shirt, and a long, floaty skirt with a tight waist. It dragged on the floor, since Ash had bought the clothes by herself and had overestimated Anne's height. The girl clearly wasn't up to wearing women's sizes. Still, at least she'd agreed to wash before changing her clothes. The next step was getting her to wear deodorant or even – shock/horror – *shave under her arms.*

"Oh, are you *still* slaving away in here like a menial servant?" Anne asked George disdainfully. "'Tis hardly your job to make your own breakfast. Ash can do that quite easily for all of us."

Ash felt her face redden with irritation, right to the tips of her ears. "Seems like the tables aren't all that turned after all," she commented to George. "And no, Anne. I can't."

"Of course you can. You did it yesterday. I saw you with my own eyes."

"We agreed to behave as a houseguest in Ash's time would," he cut in before Ash could brain Anne with the toaster (thereby teaching some very bad habits for living in this century). "Besides, I find such things fascinating. It looks like alter-power, but it's merely science. Remarkable."

True. George had hardly been *happy* to be here, but he'd been very polite and cooperative, and unlike a certain redheaded countess, had hardly been condescending at all. Well, just a little bit, but she'd overlooked it for the sake of harmony.

He *did* seem very interested in science and mechanical objects, though. Not the TV so much, because Anne guarded that jealously, but the electric jug, electric toothbrush, mobile phones…

"I have a question," Anne announced.

"No, you can't have an Extreme-Total-Home-Gym," Ash cut in. "I told you yesterday, they're too expensive and we don't have room for one."

Although she *had* managed to get the whitening toothpaste Anne had requested, along with toothbrushes for both of them. Anne had picked a glittery bright blue one, and every hour or so Ash would find her in the bathroom, hunched over the sink with toothbrush in hand, and with her mouth frothing like a rabid squirrel. But hey, it kept her happy, so it was worth having to regularly clean up splattered foam.

"But they fold away most conveniently," Anne muttered. "Anyhow, 'twas not what I wished to say. 'Tis *this*." She held up a large, slightly tattered photo album, held open to display the pictures inside. "This tower. What is it?"

Ash studied the photo briefly. Another surprise had been the way Anne had taken to Ash's photo albums. She absolutely loved the 'excellent miniature paintings' and had been poring over them all morning, finally taking her attention away from the ever-present infomercials. Luckily Ash had actually printed out these photos instead of just displaying them online. "It's the Gustave Tower in Pariss. It's a famous landmark."

"'Tis most hideous."

Ash shrugged. She'd never thought the tall metal tower beautiful, but it was at the top of every tourist checklist for visiting Frencia. "Famous doesn't mean beautiful."

"Famous things ought to be beautiful," Anne countered, seating herself on a rickety chair at the small dining room table.

"Why one would build a tower so ugly, I know not." Her eyes suddenly lit up. "Speaking of ugly, you vowed you would allow us to choose our own garb so we would no longer be forced to wear *these*." She pointed at her floaty skirt with an expression of disdain. "Might we go today?"

Yes, Anne had *really* disliked the clothes Ash had chosen for her, although Ash couldn't see what was so bad about them. Ash opened her mouth to come up with some excuse for keeping Anne and George out of a modern mall, but nothing came to mind. "Why not," she said finally. "Let me just check what time the shops shut, and we can head out."

Two minutes later Ash had her laptop open on the dining room table. She had just typed the instructions into the internet search engine when she suddenly realised she had an audience. George and Anne were both standing behind her, leaning in and staring at the laptop's screen with fascination.

"Sh-oops," Anne slowly read out. "Hoo-uurs. Whuh-"

"Shop hours Whiteside," Ash quickly cut in. She'd figured it was more to do with the style of the font than Anne's reading ability (probably) but the day was only so long. "Yes, well done. I'm looking up the information, as I just said. You two finish your breakfast, and I'll be finished soon enough." She tapped enter, and the list of results appeared on the screen. But while it seemed incredibly ordinary to her, the others hadn't lost interest.

"By Jove," George breathed. "It responded to your command by providing answers. An answering device!"

She looked at him askance. His closeness was getting a bit disturbing, as was the flower-print shirt and stretchy pants she'd found for him. (Hey, they were cheap, and George wasn't supposed to be here long. Don't judge). "Haven't I shown you the laptop before?"

"We thought 'twas a sort of book," Anne cut in. "Besides, the tee-vee provides far more interest." She wandered off to study the photo album further.

"I never noticed it," George said baldly. "So will it give the answer to any question? Any question at all?"

"It'll give an answer, but there's no saying whether it's true or not. It's the internet."

George frowned, bemused. "So this script that claims the shops close at five-dot-thirty, this is not correct?"

So that was how Ash found herself explaining the truth (or possible not-truth) of the internet, and what was dependable information, and what wasn't. "The time is probably right," she explained, "because the shops are the ones that put the information up."

"Very well. What about…history?"

Her eyes narrowed. "What kind of history?"

"Oh…" George looked innocent. "Any kind. Say, lists of notable people who were born in various times, and when they died…"

Ash raised an eyebrow. "Are you asking me to look you up on the internet?"

"No…perhaps…yes. Yes, I suppose I am."

Hmm. She'd been tempted to do so more than once in the last couple of days, but hadn't yet had the courage. "I did look up Iversley," she replied instead. "And it doesn't even exist anymore. All that's there now is a hamlet – a ghost town, really – called Little Meadswell."

There was a pause. "I assume you're afraid that if you research Anne and I, you will find something you don't want to see?"

Basically, but that made her sound like a wimp. Ash looked back down at her laptop, closing the lid decisively. "Maybe later. Shall we go?"

After all, surely a little trip to the mall would be safer than opening *that* can of worms.

Two hours later

Anne pressed her hands up against the perfectly smooth, clear glass, unheeding of the handprints she left behind. Ash and George stood behind her, both carrying large, thin bags full of their recently purchased goods, but her focus was entirely on the wonders before her.

Rows of deep silver trays were piled high with swirling cream in every colour of the rainbow, and the subtle scent that permeated the air was almost enough to bring her to tears.

"Oh," she gasped, and her eyes widened so much they almost hurt. "Oh, what splendour lies before me! What incredible, marvellous riches this place holds! I can barely fathom it!"

Behind the glass the servant girl stood with a silver scoop in one hand, a cone-shaped wafer in the other, and a bemused expression. "You pullin' my leg, miss?" Her manner of speech was quite different from Ash's, but Anne barely noted it, so fixed she was on what lay before her.

"Lady," she replied distractedly. "And I'm sure I would never touch your leg, let alone pull it. I simply wish to- oh my, that one has oranges in it! *Oranges*!" That fruit was extremely difficult to come by in the cool climes of Tudar Angland where Anne had been raised, and she'd only ever seen the shrivelled, imported versions, but she still knew what she was looking at. Her mouth watered at the thought of tasting it.

"Excuse her," Ash said to the servant. "She was raised in a very conservative community. She's never tried ice cream before."

"It's not ice cream," the servant replied with a hint of pity. "It's gelato." She swiped a small, flat stick through the orange-swirled 'gel-ah-tew', then handed it to Anne. "There you go, miss. A tester."

Anne raised the pale gold morsel to her lips with reverence, and as the flavours sank into her tongue she closed her eyes, and then-

Then the cold set in.

"Argh!" she cried in sudden horror. "'Tis *cold!*"

"Yeah," the servant replied flatly. "It's supposed to be."

"But it causes my teeth to ache! And my head feels as though 'tis being clawed by some pestilent imp!"

"You're not supposed to bite it," George said from beside her. "Only lick it." He wore his amusement as openly as his newly purchased garb: plain brown breeches and a white buttoned tunic he called a 'sheert'.

Anne lowered the little stick, lifting her chin even as her cheeks flushed pink. "Do not pretend you know how to eat gel-ah-tew," she retorted coolly. "For you were raised in much the same manner as I."

"Ah, but *we* have flavoured ices at home," he said triumphantly. He nodded to the servant girl. "I shall have the bergamot."

"We don't have that flavour. We've got coffee, tutti-frutti, mango, mixed berry, vanilla, chocolate-"

Anne gave him a sidelong glare (for he was not as knowledge-able as he supposed) and interrupted, "I shall have the chocolate." She had tried such a flavour only once, in the bunker in 2155. It had been a heavenly experience. "Do you have any that are not cold?"

The servant gave her an impertinently pitying look. "No, miss. They're all cold."

Anne sighed. "Then cold chocolate 'tis."

George finally chose the chocolate too, and Ash something called 'tirameesoo'. They sat at one of the small tables nearby to consume the gel-ah-tew, and Anne decided that after the initial shock of its dreadful chill, 'twas in truth quite tasty.

"So," Ash said finally, "all that we need now are some decent shoes, and we'll be done here."

Anne looked down at her expensive chopines in surprise. The

leather-covered wooden shoes with their curved high heels were in fair condition considering the distance she'd walked, but she had not seen anyone else similarly shod. But then free shoes were free shoes, were they not?

"These ones," Anne said intently. Her eyes were focused on the shoes in an obsessive way that made Ash a little nervous, but she was getting used to it by now. That was how Anne showed she liked something – even if Ash wasn't so sure about it.

And so Ash had already bought her the long, silver-shot denim skirt, and the lacy long-sleeved tops (there was a theme there, yes) and even the occasional scarf to tie around her hair – as yet unused. All in all it could have been a lot worse.

But these? "Anne," Ash said carefully, "they're a bit…well, they're a bit bright, aren't they?"

They both looked at the purple, sequinned slippers Anne had found in the children's section. She had feet like a pixie but the fashion taste of a three-year-old.

"They are perfect," Anne said staunchly. "They are by far the finest of all the wonders I have seen today; of all the thousands upon thousands of garments in every size and colour; of all the dozens of shoes in every design; of all-"

"I get it," Ash cut in. "You've seen a lot today."

Anne's reaction to the forty or so shops in the smallish mall had been embarrassingly expressive, but then 'twas (argh! It *was*) probably huge compared to a medieval market. George had been more restrained in his reactions, thankfully, but even he'd been wide-eyed at the range of goods available.

But it was the mechanical side of things that had really caught his attention. Just before, she'd turned to see him walking steadily up the downwards moving escalator, causing a queue as he stared at where the moving steps appeared from the floor.

Ah, well. People had drawn their own conclusions from his (at that point) rather odd clothing and had treated the mental patient kindly. He didn't even seem to realise that he'd been acting oddly – and to be fair, the flowered shirt had been her fault rather than his. But as with Anne's clothing purchases, it could have been worse.

"As I was saying before you interrupted," Anne carried on snootily, "these shoes are by far the most beautiful of all I have seen today, and I *shall* have them. I trow you are hardly the one to comment on appropriate garb, considering your choice for today."

Ash was wearing jeans and a t-shirt, which by Anne's standards still meant she looked like a streetwalker. She sighed, giving in. "Alright. Come on, then."

"Huzzah!"

And that probably meant she was happy. Happy Anne, happy life, Ash thought drily. At least until the two time-travellers found their way back home…

But Anne's choice of shoes was a shock compared to what George had chosen. Ash studied the black rubber boots, usually worn in wet weather, and carefully kept her face neutral. After all, they were cheap, and they wouldn't be used for long.

Right?

But the question kept nagging Ash even once they'd returned home, and finally she gave in to her curiosity. While the other two were distracted – Anne with the photo-album yet again; George with dissecting Ash's old mobile phone – she quietly pulled out her laptop and opened up the search engine.

She typed in the first name, and as the results appeared on the screen, she heard George's voice over her shoulder. "What are you looking at?"

Ash hurriedly clicked out of the webpage, opening her emails, but George wasn't fooled.

He raised an eyebrow. "I may not be able to read this strange writing very easily, but I'm getting better at it," he said mildly. "I can see that you changed what you were looking at. Did you…" He swallowed. "…did you search for my family?"

George waited with bated breath for Ashlea's reply. She stared back at him in silence for a few moments, her light sprinkling of freckles drawing his attention as always. Females in his time thought of freckles as a blemish, and most of them would have skin as white as lilies. Ashlea, on the other hand, didn't seem to care at all. Oddly enough, neither did he.

"No," she replied finally, and he knew she was telling the truth. She wasn't a very good liar.

Ash glanced across to where the petite Lady Anne was still engrossed in the books of family portraits, then changed the device's bright screen to display the information she'd tried to hide from him. 'Anne of Covington', the strange blocky script read. Underneath the name was a list of information, none of which he could read quickly.

A moment later Ashlea clicked the small x at the corner of that screen, returning it to her previous work. It appeared to be some form of letter.

"There are half a dozen women by that name on this history site, but I'm sure none are our Anne," she said very quietly, keeping her head tilted away from Lady Anne. "Mind you, there are plenty of gaps in this society's knowledge. As I said before, the internet doesn't know everything."

George thought about that for a while. These last few nights he'd lain awake on that odd fold-out couch, wondering if he could find out his future…or past, depending on how he looked at it. But he didn't want to know when his family would die, or the things that would happen in his own immediate future.

Very well, he *did* want to know, but he thought it would be extremely unhelpful for his peace of mind.

Just then Lady Anne called over from the other room. "Ash," she said in that imperious tone she tended to use especially for their hostess, "have you ever met Amaranthus? Before future Iversley, that is."

Confused, Ashlea replied, "No, of course not. I would have told you."

"Humph." Lady Anne turned back to her study of the portraits, and George turned back to Ashlea.

"What about me?"

So they searched, but while there were several gentlemen with similar names, George wasn't to be found. "I suppose Dr Walker was right," he said, feeling both relieved and disappointed. "I won't make a mark on history." But that led to his second question. "You said earlier that you already looked up Iversley, but where it is now is just a ghost town. A hamlet with barely a couple of houses, you said, and they've even changed the name."

"That's right," Ashlea agreed cautiously. "I can only think that down the line, someone will rebuild it and decide to take on the old name. You said it looked very different in 2155 from how you remembered it."

George thought back to that two-part town of future Iversley, with its neat little village above-ground, and below-ground, a huge, busy city in a massive cavern. The manors he'd been so accustomed to were nowhere to be seen.

"I want to visit," he said abruptly. "I want to see what it is now." When Ashlea looked as if she would object, he added, "I'm aware that Anne and I are next to helpless here, but we are adults, Ashlea. If you will not help me get there, simply give me a map. I will be quite happy to walk."

She paused, then as if finally seeing the sense of his words, shrugged. "I wouldn't mind seeing it myself. We can take the train."

"What's a train?"

"Oh, it's a sort of locomotive," George said in surprise some time later. "But I don't see any steam. Where's the engine?"

They'd had to walk quickly to catch the next train, Ash having decided it would be more direct than to drive the meandering roads that led to that area. Besides, George and Anne hadn't seemed terribly confident in her abilities not to steer them into a ditch, judging by the earlier drive to the shops this morning.

Ash tried to explain how modern trains worked, hoping George wouldn't notice that she was making up half of it.

Meanwhile, Anne stood owl-eyed, clutching the ever-present photo album to her chest. "Must we travel in the belly of this metal beast?"

Ash gave her a narrow-eyed stare, then decided the girl wasn't scared, just curious. "Yes. Yes, we must."

"Oh, very well." Anne didn't protest further.

The trip to Little Meadswell AKA Iversley went well, all things considered. To get there was a shortish train ride followed by a longish walk, since the few houses left in the area didn't qualify for a proper train station of their own.

As the train ticked along, Ash studied the job section of the newspaper, George stared out of the window, and Anne flicked through the photo album she'd insisted on taking. How many times could the girl handle seeing Ash's distant relatives before she got bored?

"Anything of note?" George asked suddenly.

It took Ash a moment to realise he was talking to *her*. She'd mentioned she was looking for a new job, and he'd clearly paid attention. "More of the same," she replied in disinterest. "But to be honest, I'd rather grub around in the dirt than get more admin work, even if it paid well."

"You want to be a gardener?"

Ash checked for judgement in his tone, but no, he seemed genuinely curious. "I like growing things; it's satisfying. So I suppose yes, I would like to be a gardener."

"You should do it," he said, then turned and looked out the window again.

'She should do it'. Simple as that, right? Ash rolled her eyes, then noticed an ad for apprentice landscapers. Deias, her mother would be unimpressed that she'd travelled all the way to Angland to work as a 'labourer', but that sounded kind of fun. Compared to staring at a computer screen all day, anyway.

There were a few moments of silence, broken only by the sound of the tracks clacking beneath their train's wheels.

Then Anne asked abruptly, "Did you ever meet Amaranthus before?"

Ash stared at her. "No, of course not." And she'd already answered that question.

"Are you *certain* of that?"

"I have no memory of meeting him. None at all. Is that good enough for you?"

"Humph." The redhead looked back down at the photo album.

Ash waited, then asked, "Is there a reason you keep asking me?"

Anne raised her eyebrows but didn't glance up. "No."

Ash was unconvinced, but Anne didn't elaborate, and by then they'd arrived at their stop. They tramped along the hedgerow-lined dirt road in the direction Oogle maps had advised, and not much later they were on the site of Iversley.

They studied their surroundings at length.

"I recognise the area," George commented. "The hills over there. I recognise their shape."

Ash looked around dubiously. She didn't recognise anything, and no wonder. She'd had a fateful walk a few days ago in the nearby woods, but the only time she'd actually visited Iversley was in 2155. That was after a substantial war that had carved up the landscape, and after someone had decided to rebuild a neat little village in this very area. Now, there were some small patches of shrubbery that she could generously call forest, but even that didn't look much like what she remembered. "Do you see your homes?"

"You said Renwick castle was gone," Anne announced, far too cheerfully for the circumstances. "Mayhap 'tis that pile of stone in the distance."

"It could be an old wall," Ash suggested.

They all stared at the piles of grey rock scattered around the grassy slopes of the shallow valley. It could have been *anything*.

"The manors are gone," George said dully, hands in pockets. "There's still the churchyard, though."

The church of Little Meadswell was small and grey and very Anglish. It wasn't the same one as when George had lived here, but it was similar enough to be a sibling.

The graves out the back were all original, though, including what was left of the Seymour family mausoleum. The carved text had faded in the oldest stones, but he managed to recognise the names.

He'd been standing there for some time when Ashlea approached him warily, looking first at him, then at the stone. "Did you know about this?"

"No more than you," she replied. "As I said, the internet doesn't know everything."

George tapped at one of the last names carved on the mausoleum wall. *Hon. George William Seymour. Born May 6, 1798. Died*…and then the text was blurred out by time. "And you knew about this?"

"Whoa. I did *not* know about that! Um…you can't read the date of death, can you?"

"No," he agreed. "But the fact my name's here at all…"

"Means it's likely you went back. Will go back."

"Yes."

There was a long silence, and then George felt a tear roll down his cheek and hit the top of his cheap, uncomfortable boots. He'd chosen them for their shine, but they'd looked rather nicer than they felt.

"Um…isn't that a *good* thing?"

"Yes. But I'm looking at my family's *graves*." Including his father's, and Deias knew that relationship had ended badly. And no matter when they died, the fact remained that they *had* died, and he didn't want to have to see them like this.

Ashlea sighed, then came to stand beside him, putting her arm a little awkwardly around his shoulder. "Congratulations, George. You won't be stuck here forever."

Well, that was the best way of looking at it, wasn't it? "Thank you. I shall remember this moment always," he said drily.

And the funny thing was, he suspected that he would.

Anne sat on a large rock underneath an old willow tree, staring down at the book of images once more. She'd stared at those same images many times. At first 'twas because they were like the most realistic paintings she'd ever seen, but then because she'd noticed something unusual. Not in simply one image, but in many.

Meanwhile George and Ash wandered around the corner, back into sight. The boy seemed a little more settled than he had previously, and Ash had an odd expression on her face.

"We found my grave," he announced suddenly.

Anne paused, taking in what that meant. She smiled at him sunnily. "Huzzah! Did you see the date of death?"

"No, thank Deias," Ash muttered. "Who in Hades needs to know when they'll die? That's incredibly morbid."

"Mind your language," Anne said pleasantly, ignoring the girl's rolled eyes. "Ash, have you ever met Amaranthus before? Have you ever *seen* him before future Iversley?"

"No! For heavens' sake, why do you keep asking me that?"

"No reason," Anne replied breezily. If Ash hadn't taken the trouble to look at these photo-images properly, then Anne wouldn't tell her. Ha.

Oh, this was *fun.* She was going to go home.

Nation of Ciria
circa 4000 BC

In a light-filled, forested setting, a handsome young man wove his way through sun-dappled trees to the nearby river. His skin was olive, his hair and eyes chocolate brown, and he wore only a linen loincloth. The sun was warm enough that nothing else was needed. He came to the river, sparkling clear in the noon light, and bent down to wash his hands.

A head broke the surface of the water. The swimmer was almost a replica of the first man, except for the silvery fish tail that replaced his legs. "Janeus," he called. "Are you coming for a swim?"

The first youth shook his head. "I just came to get you, Tai. Something's happened in the city – the new Sun King is here, and he's *female.*"

Eyes widening in amazement, the merman hoisted himself

out of the water, his tail morphing within seconds into a pair of legs as strong and brown as his brother's. "Let's go!"

Janeus felt the usual stirring of envy as his brother transformed, and he recounted to himself the usual explanation, the one that kept the true envy at bay. *Tai is the elder brother, he gets the gift. If I had been born five minutes earlier rather than him, he wouldn't have envied me.* Besides, Tai might be able to shapeshift, but Janeus was far more popular with girls, and that was just as valuable.

Or at least that was what he told himself.

Minutes later they reached the edge of the city. The largest in the whole region of Ciria, it was a marvel of human ingenuity and teamwork, and of course it would be where the avatar of the greatest god, the Sun King, would arrive for his ten-yearly visit. Always a king – that was the title – but this time he – *she* – was different.

Down below them was the massive stone metropolis with its huge temple and enormous city square and altar-throne in the centre, but today it too was different. Instead of being scattered with a few people hurrying to their duties, it was packed full with a writhing crowd. It seemed that the whole world had come to see her.

She's incredible, Janeus thought. She stood on the altar-throne draped in robes of gold that shone as though lit from within – easily the most magnificent creature he'd ever seen.

"The Sun King," his brother breathed.

Janeus looked at him in irritation. How dare Tai be so affected? He wouldn't have even come if Janeus hadn't gone and got him; he was always flying or swimming or doing something with his powers.

And there seemed something wrong with giving this divine creature the same title as every mortal man before her. She needed her own title. She was a *queen…*

"She came down from the heavens like a falling star," they overheard a dirty farmer say nearby. "Amazing."

And she would go back up to the heavens in smoke, like every Sun King before her. Janeus felt a pang of regret and horror at that thought. The other avatars (that he could remember, anyway) had been so plain and mortal, just handsome youths chosen from among the people. They would be feted for a solid five days, treated like the king whose name they now wore, and then on the sixth day…

That was why it was called the altar-throne, and it was also why as celebrated as the Sun King was, no one wanted to be that person.

Janeus had known the boy who was to be this year's avatar. Serran was the handsome young son of his mother's cousin. He'd seemed happy to be chosen as avatar, but Janeus had thought privately that he must have been terrified, future in the heavens notwithstanding.

But then this morning, when Serran was to come up onto the altar-throne at the beginning of the celebrations, they had all watched as this glowing being had descended. She had leaned into Serran, her glow obscuring him for a moment, and then he had fallen down dead and she had glowed even more brightly.

"Congratulations," she'd said. "Your worship and preparation has served you well. You do not need to provide the gods with a Sun King this year – one has been provided for you."

Her.

Now the two brothers pushed their way through the crowds until they were right at the base of the altar, staring up at her beauty. From here they could see her eyes were green. Janeus had never seen eyes that colour before.

Suddenly Tai darted forward as if to go to her, and Janeus was barely fast enough to grab his arm. "What are you doing? You can't touch her! They'll kill you!"

His brother looked at him in triumph. "But I have the power, don't I? That'll mean something to her."

Janeus looked down to the medallion that his brother wore

around his neck, and had worn since the death of their father ten years before. The birthright of the older son; the power to shapeshift.

"I'll show it to her," Tai said triumphantly.

So Janeus watched as his twin made his way through the jostling crowd towards the temple. That was the first time the ever-present envy in his gut turned into full-blown hatred, and Janeus remembered what their father had told him on his deathbed. Because their father had been the second-born twin, like Janeus – but unlike Janeus he'd carried the same gift Tai did.

See, there was a way to transfer the gift, and it wasn't by taking the medallion. That was only a symbol of the gift that resided *inside* the elder-born twin. No, the transfer would take a little more sacrifice than that…

Whiteside, Leister County, Angland
Mid-2013 AD

Anne sat on the overstuffed couch, reading *Angland: Past and Present* and trying to ignore the argument going on behind her.

There was nothing unusual in either of those activities. Once Anne had grown accustomed to the odd style of the lettering and speech in those history books, she found reading about things that happened after she was born was exciting. 'Twas almost like telling the future.

And as for the arguing…well, with two people from such different times, 'twas not unexpected. Anne was fairly certain they liked each other somewhat, as she'd often see them in deep conversation or laughing at each other's foolish jests. But at times like this, 'twas hard to tell.

George and Ash were truly raising their voices. They'd gone

from their usual ardent debates into full-blown shouting, and over the usual issues.

"How the blazes am I supposed to find work?" George bellowed. "I don't even have proof that I exist in this century!"

"You're standing here, aren't you?" Ash shouted back. "Just show up, act all Anglish and pompous, and convince them to give you a job no matter how young you are! You'd make a great history professor – you lived it!"

That stopped George in his tracks. "Anglish and pompous?"

Ash shrugged, seeming a little shamefaced. "Well, you've got plenty of experience in both of those, too."

George threw his hands in the air, and said in a lower voice, "I don't want to be living off you, Ashlea. It's not right. I know we've been here six months already, but *he* said the Eternity Stone would take us home…"

Now Anne's ears pricked up. Amaranthus had promised that the Eternity Stone would take them back home, and in spite of the time that had passed since their arrival, she still believed him.

"Well, he hasn't turned up, has he?" Ash replied gently, and the tone of the conversation changed. Now Ash would sympathise, and say that he needed to accept that 'he couldn't control when and if he went back, and that was that'.

Never mind that George had seen his own grave in the past. Ash thought that the missing date of death meant 'twas only a memorial, and that in truth he'd just disappeared. At least that was what she had said once, during a heated argument.

Anne knew otherwise.

So that was when Anne lost interest in the conversation. She'd heard the 'find a job' argument a dozen times, and was not quite certain how she felt about it. She liked it here, even though she'd had to put up with Ash's odd behaviour and minimal wardrobe, and practically speaking, she had ceased to use her title. That hadn't been such a loss as she might have thought.

The true loss was her dear half-sister, Elspeth, still in Tudar Angland, as this book called her birthplace- er, birth *time*. But if Amaranthus was slow in fulfilling his promise to return them home, then Anne thought it best to forget her sister for now. Pray for her soul, mayhap, but there was nothing more she could do.

Anne's attitude was in contrast to George's. He had never truly settled into the twenty-first century and seemed to struggle with the absence of his estranged family, home and lifestyle. He'd never said as much, but Anne had seen him on Ash's 'lap-top' searching his family name. He hadn't shared his findings.

True, this society was miles apart from what they were both accustomed to, and it had its distinct downsides like dreadful music and sun-tanning, ugh! But it also had hot showers, dish-washers, cars, chocolate and whitening toothpaste... After brushing three times a day with that wondrous substance, Anne's teeth were as white as pearls.

She much preferred this place to her cold, flea-ridden castle of five hundred years earlier, which was damp in all seasons, and where she had been ordered about first by her late husband Wilbert, and then by various guardians.

Mayhap if George had guardians to order him about similarly, he might change his mind about this era.

Twisting her mouth in displeasure, Anne turned her attention back to her book. She'd borrowed it from the local library where she had a part-time job stacking shelves. The work was under the table, Ash said, because Anne had no 'eye-dee'. Oddly enough, there were no tables involved.

Hmm. In a mere two years – that was, 1558 – Angland would be Protester again! The country kept changing its official religion like a child trying to decide which flavour of sweetmeat it liked best. And the new Queen, Eliza the First, would be a redhead like Anne herself.

Anne resolved that when she got home, she would keep her

new knowledge to herself. She'd be accused of witchcraft otherwise.

From the kitchen she heard Ash exclaim mid-argument. "Oh crap! I'm late!"

Within minutes Ash had run out of the door, off for another day of getting covered in dirt and doing hard labour. Ash called it 'landscaping', but it looked more like punishment to Anne. Still, Ash enjoyed it, so Anne would not criticise her. One must be gracious with one's friends.

Anne marked her page then put down the heavy volume. She got up and wandered into the kitchen. George stood quietly at the sink, looking out the window at their small garden.

"I'll never understand why Ash likes her job so much," she remarked, forgetting her vow not to criticise. "She has become so coarse and brown working out in the sun all day. But then I suppose they seem to like that here, as little as I can understand it."

Unusually, George didn't respond. He just kept staring blankly out the window, which was too high for Anne herself to see through.

Deciding not to take offense, Anne began to make a cup of tea. The small, pleasant ritual was something she had never done before coming here, although 'twas considered quintessentially Anglish in this era.

She pulled down her favourite china cup, the one with the two cats painted sweetly on its side, and which Ash considered overly sentimental. Then a moment later she pulled down a second cup. "Would you like some tea, George?"

She'd been using his first name almost since they'd met. Unusual, but then they'd met in unusual circumstances.

He still didn't respond, and Anne felt a pang of fear. The last time he'd been like this, he'd been under mind control that had almost made him insane. That wicked woman who'd enslaved him so was gone, but they hadn't *seen* her body…

Then he shook himself. "There's someone in the garden."

"Oh. Is it that foolish boy from down the street again?"

George turned to her in surprise. "What do you mean, again?"

Anne flushed a little. Ash had said not to mention it to George, as he might not react all that well, but she'd slipped up. "'Tis naught to concern yourself with," she said casually. "He visited a few days ago looking for his dog."

It had been a transparent effort to meet Anne, which she had to politely rebuff. She was engaged to be married, never mind that her betrothed was an elderly stranger…and five hundred years in the past.

But even if she hadn't been, that boy did not appeal. He'd been wearing strange tight breeches with the crotch halfway down his thighs so that the backside looked like a babe's loaded napkin. Verily, Anne had thought '*twas* a napkin until Ash set her straight.

"Hmm. I might just go find out," George said determinedly, and he strode for the door.

Anne considered going after him, worried about what he might say to any strange-breech'd trespassers, but then decided 'twas not her problem.

A faint sound – or mayhap a change of pressure – made her turn. And just for an instant, out of the corner of her eye, she saw someone move near the dining room table. Then they were gone before she could even gasp in surprise.

But they'd left something on the table. A certain something that made Anne speechless.

She was still standing there staring at the item when George returned.

"Couldn't find the blighter," he said grouchily. "Do pardon my language, Anne. It's as though they never existed."

She laughed: an odd, nervous laugh.

"Are you quite alright?"

But Anne just raised her hand and pointed at the thing on the table.

He saw it, and stared, and stared. "Well," he said eventually. "I wasn't expecting *that*."

HOMEBOUND

George accepted the cup of tea in the end. He'd never admit it to Ashlea, but he actually quite enjoyed the tea bags that were ever-present in this time. Unlike traditional loose-leaf, they didn't leave little black bits in the bottom of his cup.

"Well," he said for what must have been the tenth time, setting the cup down on the wooden table they were sitting at. "This can't be an accident. We were meant to have it."

They were meant to go home. Because why else would the Eternity Stone suddenly appear out of nowhere, where only the two of them would see it?

"Of course we were," Anne agreed, staring at the tabletop, her own cup forgotten. "'Tis what we want, is it not?"

It *was* what George had wanted, but now the change was imminent he felt a strange sorrow. He'd become used to this time, to these people. To a couple of people in particular, as strange as their ways were, and surprisingly it felt painful to think of leaving. But the idea of staying was impossible. He didn't even have a *bed* here, by Jove.

"Yes," he replied finally. "It is what I want."

They could each use the Stone to return to their own times, and that was the least of its power. Whoever held the Stone could travel anywhere in the world, to any *time* in history…and would never again age as long as they held it.

He could do *anything*. He could be like a god – which was exactly what the last bearer had tried to do, and it hadn't ended well for anyone.

Oh Deias, he was going to be sick.

Anne didn't seem to have noticed. She was still staring at the Stone, hands clenched so tightly around her undrunk tea that her knuckles were white. "I should return home. We agreed to, did we not?" She paused. "I'm a *lady*, there. Here, I'm no one at all. But..."

"But what...?"

"But I find I'm freer and happier here than I've ever been before," she admitted quietly. "Except for one thing."

That one thing was quite significant, George saw once she explained it. She'd have to return to her home, at least temporarily.

And then Anne touched the Stone, and something happened.

Because of that something, and because of the possibilities it revealed, *and* because he didn't want to slam shut the door of time travel either, they devised a plan for what to do next.

Then they devised a plan for if the first plan didn't work.

And *then* they just decided to pray if *that* plan didn't work. But it would, of course.

And then George wrote a letter. It was quite long and perhaps revealed more than he intended, but he decided to leave it anyway. Ashlea would decide what she did next...but hopefully she'd agree.

Shortly afterwards, George carefully put the folded letter on top of the small sideboard that sat by the entryway. Then he picked up his hat and followed the plan.

Ashlea would understand once she read the letter. She had to.

Ash bought the weekly groceries on her way home from work. She parked in her driveway, then loaded herself with all eleven shopping bags and staggered up the short path to the front door. Sure, she could've made a second trip to unload the car, but that would've been too much effort.

The door was shut, so she kicked it lightly a couple of times. *Bang, bang.* "George, let me in! I've got full hands."

He hated when she did that. He said it made him feel like a servant, but he'd grown more lenient about it lately. They'd been getting on a lot better than they used to.

Still, when the silence from inside the house stretched out into thirty seconds and the bags grew painfully heavy, Ash put them down with a thump and tried the door handle. Surprisingly it was locked. George must have gone for a walk, she figured, since Anne was off at her part-time job at the library and would finish around five-thirty.

Grumbling good-naturedly to herself, Ash unlocked the door and hauled her bags inside. The wind caught the door and sent papers and envelopes flying off the dresser in the entryway, and she took a few more moments to pick those up before putting away the groceries.

It was a Friday, which meant it was Anne's turn to cook dinner. Ash wouldn't have minded getting started, but the girl had discovered microwave cooking and ferociously guarded her dinner nights as if they were some kind of treat.

But when seven pm arrived and neither George nor Anne had returned, Ash began to worry. George went for the occasional long walk, but never without leaving a note, and Anne would usually be home by now. Perhaps she'd met someone and stayed to chat? It hadn't happened before, but it was possible.

Maybe.

Ash thought about it, then picked up the phone and called the local library. Miraculously someone answered, one of the permanent staff who practically ran the place and who was still around after closing.

"Of course I haven't seen Anne today," the man said irritably. "She called this morning and said she wouldn't be coming in, and wouldn't even say why."

Ash frowned. "That's not like her at all. She's not here either, and hasn't left a note. I'm a bit concerned, to be honest."

"Anne's the one who should be worried about keeping her job, especially if her reason for absence isn't life or death. I do not appreciate unreliable employees."

So Anne *wasn't* at work. Curiouser and curiouser…and that made Ash a little nervous.

After ending the call she double-checked every room to see if she'd overlooked a convenient note, but found nothing to indicate where they'd gone. She did, however, find a stack of overdue library books under Anne's bed (taken out in Ash's name, thanks a lot!), and strangely, a bunch of Ash's magazines under the couch/bed. George obviously had eclectic taste in reading material.

She was starting to wonder if they'd both gone walking and fallen in a ditch when she remembered George's mobile phone. It was her old model and only had call and text function, but he'd grown more confident lately and had wanted to try using it for himself. He'd been quite excited by the idea of being contactable anywhere, anytime.

Ha. Once he'd been pocket-called by acquaintances a few times, he'd lose that excitement.

Ash tried calling his number, but the call went straight to voicemail with her old message. He'd never recorded his own because she hadn't got around to showing him how. So either he had the phone with him and it was turned off, or it had run out of battery and was hidden somewhere around her house.

One last hunt around her small cottage didn't result in finding the phone *or* a note (but she'd pretty much given up on the last part, anyway). But she did notice one unusual thing in Anne's closet-sized bedroom. It was in its usual state of comfortable untidiness, but Anne's little purple shoes were stacked neatly together under the bed…

"She never goes anywhere without them," Ash said aloud to herself.

Ever since Anne had chosen them six months earlier, she'd refused to wear anything else, not even her original 'chopines' – AKA weird wooden clogs.

With an increased sense of foreboding, Ash opened the small closet. Anne's small array of modern clothing was all there, hanging on the plastic coat hangers Ash had bought months earlier. But the chopines were gone, as was Anne's green velvet Tudar gown along with its multiple layers of underthings. Enough fabric to clothe a neighbourhood, Ash had always thought.

Gone. Ash let out a deep breath she hadn't even known she was holding and stared at the empty space for a long moment. Then she went back to the lounge that functioned as George's bedroom and pulled open the wardrobe where he kept his clothes.

His original clothing was also missing. The only things there were his modern trousers and jackets, since she still couldn't get him to wear jeans.

He would have looked good in jeans.

"They wouldn't just leave without telling me. Surely they wouldn't." Besides, Anne would've taken her toothbrush at the very least, and that was still in the bathroom…

Nope. It wasn't. A quick check showed Anne's blue toothbrush and whitening toothpaste *were* gone, although George's yellow brush still sat in its holder. But everything else, every single thing Anne and George had acquired while here in the twenty-first century, remained. Anne had even left her precious photo album on her nightstand, next to the ancient quick-print camera Ash had given her for Ecksmas.

They wouldn't have been able to take them back home, Ash realised. One couldn't just show up in 1556 or 1818 carrying a piece of twenty-first century technology – the local peasants would be calling the witch-finder within minutes.

Well, except that George seemed to have taken his mobile phone, and she was pretty sure 1818 didn't have any witch-finders.

But then what did she know? She would've thought the two of them wouldn't leave without saying goodbye, and yet it seemed to have happened.

And they clearly hadn't been snatched away. They'd had enough warning to get dressed in their original clothing, and Anne had even taken a day off work…

One day. Ash froze in place. If Anne was leaving permanently, she'd have said she wasn't coming back, not that she'd be gone for *one day*. Right? Clearly they were planning on coming back from – from wherever they'd gone, and she just needed to wait.

Cheered at that thought, Ash went and sat down in front of the TV. And for once she didn't have to fight for the remote control.

A month later, Little Meadswell

"You alright there, Ash?" Her boss asked the question more as a matter of habit than from any real sympathy.

Bryce MacIntyre was a solid employer who'd been willing to hire an untrained teenage girl three weeks earlier, but he lacked compassion for what he called 'excuses'. What he was actually doing was pointing out that she'd been standing in the same spot for some time, staring blankly at nothing, and so she jolted to attention with a wry smile.

"Sorry. Zoned out." Ash had been having the weirdest

dreams, and she'd just remembered a scary one from last night. She'd dreamed she was flying again (yes, actually flying like a bird, a plane, or the other option) but this time she'd been flying to escape from these two horrible, mummified *things* that galloped along together, attached at the hip like they were running a three-legged race.

The dream was caused by warped memories from her travels, no doubt. She definitely couldn't fly anymore, more was the pity, and she'd rather not be chased by anything at all, not even a wasp. (She hated wasps, but had always felt that it was cruel to kill them. Hence avoiding the things entirely.)

"As long as you don't fall in that hole you've just dug," Bryce warned.

Ash poked at the dirt-encrusted stones edging what she thought might have been an old well, judging by the vaguely circular way they'd been arranged. "I'll try not to. With a well this old, anything could be in here."

"A well? Could just as easily have been a garderobe."

"A what?"

"You know, a privy. A loo. There was a castle here, once upon a time." Bryce paused. "Or perhaps that was up the hill. Either way, watch yourself."

It might have been a castle. Renwick Castle, to be precise. Anne had once said that her old home was around this location where Ash now helped level the land for a new housing development. The church graveyard they'd visited together was just around the corner from where she stood now.

The memory made a lump rise in Ash's throat. The others were dead of old age by now, and they'd chosen that end when they'd returned to their own times. There was nothing she could do about it, and even grieving was pointless. "I will."

Ash's job was to remove all the good-sized rocks as far as two metres down, since this part of the land was raised and the digger couldn't make it into this awkward space. Any interesting objects she found were to be collected for the local historical society, since this part of Angland had been populated for several thousand years.

In theory, anyway. In practice they'd never found anything that was of interest and in one piece, but the shovels might've had something to do with that. Ash O'Reilly: archaeologist. Finding and destroying ancient artefacts since three weeks ago…

Eh. At least it wasn't admin work. And if all those dead people wanted their crockery preserved for future generations, then they should've stored it better.

But this spot was either a well or an old toilet, and there was nothing to find except rocks. She settled into a steady rhythm of dig, loosen, toss, and her mind began to wander.

Four weeks had gone by, and Ash had finally accepted that Anne and George wouldn't be returning. But she still felt irritated every time she thought of the way they'd left without a word.

At first she'd thought they were planning to come back, but that couldn't be the case, because otherwise they wouldn't have left it so long. At the very least, Anne had screwed up her chances with the local library, and she'd really seemed to enjoy that job.

Fine, so George had clearly been homesick. Ash had found him many times with a sad look in his eye as he watched Regency-era films like Pride and Precipitation – usually right before he criticised some minor detail in the set.

It had been right for him to go. Not because of the movie critique, although that had been annoying, but because he'd been so unhappy. And if she'd grown attached to his stodgy Anglish gentlemanliness, and was sorry to see him go? Well, that was her problem.

And Anne too, of course. Back to the younger half-sister she'd spoken so protectively of, and her upcoming arranged marriage.

Come to think of it, Ash wasn't really sure why Anne had gone back. She hadn't seemed that enamoured of her old life. Ash supposed her sister must've been the deciding factor, but she'd never know for sure, would she?

Clonk. The shovel hit yet another rock, and Ash bent down to loosen it from the dirt. But the texture felt wrong, too soft, and when she picked up the fist-sized lump it fell apart in her hands, revealing a mess of desiccated blue flakes. "Ugh."

She moved to throw it aside, but a hint of something shiny caught the light. Someone's old jewellery, perhaps?

Curious, Ash gently worked on the remaining stuff until she got to its hard centre: a small, mud-encrusted item the size of her thumb. She rubbed at the mud with one finger, and she'd exposed a half-inch of shimmering black before realising what it looked like.

She sucked in a shocked breath. Time seemed to slow, and trembling, she checked around her to see if anyone was watching.

Ash met the eyes of one of her coworkers, James. He was staring at her, unmoving, as if he knew what she'd found even before she really did. She clutched the filthy object to her chest, staring back defensively for a moment before realising James wasn't moving at all.

In fact, none of the others were moving. There was an eerie stillness about her whole surroundings, and even the tree branches were rigid: not a single leaf fluttering in the gentle breeze that had been there a moment before.

"Oh my Deias. Oh, my Deias…"

Then Ash lifted her thumb from the object, and like pressing play on a paused video, suddenly everything was back to normal.

"What's that there?" James asked curiously. "Something interesting?"

Ash swallowed awkwardly, her mouth so dry she could barely reply. "Uh…kind of looks like plastic."

Well, it *did* look like plastic, although it was infinitely more valuable.

He inspected the object for about two seconds before shrugging. "Bin's over that way. Don't leave it in the dirt."

"I won't."

But when James turned away, Ash shoved the whole thing into the pocket of her windbreaker, dirt and all.

The local historical society wouldn't be getting *this* particular artifact.

It felt like the longest work day in history, but finally they were done, and Ash practically ran to her car. She drove along the country road until she found somewhere secluded enough to pull over, then lifted the filthy bundle out of her pocket with shaking hands.

Thank Deias for leftover fast food restaurant serviettes, because with every rub, the object was becoming clearer and clearer.

"It can't be," Ash said aloud, her voice tight enough that it almost squeaked. "It can't be that much of a coincidence."

What were the chances that she'd find the Eternity Stone in a lump of mud in the remnants of an old castle?

She'd have to test it.

Ash closed her trembling hand around the Stone, scrunching her eyes shut, and thought of her kitchen table as she'd left it this morning.

Then suddenly she was there, surrounded by those familiar things and sitting in an awkward half-squat in the empty air. At the other end of the house, she heard a door slam a moment before she fell on her backside.

She jumped up and ran to the front door to see what had made the sound, then saw through its small glass window an odd sight. There was a dark-haired girl in jeans and a red jacket, running to the car parked out front. She looked strangely familiar, and Ash knew exactly who she was.

Herself, from the rarely seen back view.

"I was late," she said in dawning amazement. And she'd been extremely close to running into her future self, not that she'd known it at the time.

She had the Eternity Stone.

She *had* the *Eternity* Stone!

Ash danced a jig right there, then added in a few happy cheerleading moves. She could do anything, go anywhere! Europa – South Amyrica – Ancient Reme!

She could even go see George and Anne, the ungrateful so-and-sos, and ask why they'd left so suddenly. And if she did, she would be very gracious and not give them the slap around the ear that they clearly deserved for their rude departure, and then when they apologised as they surely would, she'd forgive them…especially George.

Ash dismissed that idea with difficulty. She'd already checked half a dozen times for some kind of goodbye letter before finally accepting that they'd just chosen to go. It seemed out of character enough that she'd wondered if they'd been snatched away – but if that was the case, they wouldn't have taken their clothes like they had. And if they didn't care enough to say goodbye, she wouldn't go chasing them.

Just then her eyes fell on a tiny, spiral-bound book sitting on the shelf with the DVDs, where she'd put it some weeks earlier. It was Anne's album, bought second-hand for 20p out the back of someone's car boot.

It was so small that even the quick-print photos Anne had taken had to be cropped to fit on the pages, and to make it worse, someone had already scribbled nonsense all over the thing. They'd also glued on random, ugly snippets from magazines and newspapers.

Ash thought that if someone wanted a really unattractive photo album, then that was the way to go about it. She had never understood why Anne had liked it so much, but she'd treated it like a treasure.

But now things had changed. Ash had found the Eternity Stone in the remnants of Anne's old home, and maybe, just maybe, there was something worth seeing here.

She picked up the album, flipping past the cover patterned to look like an old newspaper, and something caught her eye. On the front, on that 'fake' newspaper, was a tiny image of a man smiling. It was set up like those editor's pictures in modern newspapers, and he looked familiar. Kind of like Amaranthus at a glance.

Unnerved, Ash looked at the first page inside. There was an old, wrinkled page out of some book pasted in place, something about Grecian gods or similar. Past that, Anne had begun to stick in her quick-print photos, one per page.

But she'd missed the point of photography. When Ash had told Anne she should do a photo album of her own, she'd meant of entirely new photos, like normal people would take.

But Anne was hardly normal, and so she'd gone through Ash's old albums, magazines and books, and had taken photos of whatever appealed. Yes, Anne had taken photos of photos; and a really strange variety, too.

See, here was a photo (of a photo) of Ash on her eighteenth birthday, when she'd gone to a bar with a few friends back home in the Southern Isles to celebrate being a legal adult.

Nothing much to see there, especially for Anne who wouldn't have recognised anyone in the picture besides Ash, grinning and shiny-faced in the dim lights of the bar, complete with party hat. Someone had scrawled on the empty page beside the photo, and it looked like there was highlighter on the photo itself.

Ash dismissed that and flicked over to the second page. Here, Anne had photographed an old family picture, again of Ash, but this time of a picnic in the botanical gardens when she was about ten or so. There she was with her family, squinting in the sun. Again, nice for Ash, but meaningless for Anne.

The third page held a black and white photo (of a photo) of Ash's mother when she'd been young. She was in the foreground smiling, her face at an angle that made her look lighthearted and lovely. The old picture had somehow sneaked its way into Ash's more modern album.

Like the others, this copy had been scribbled on. There was a blob of yellow highlighter in the corner of the image, and on the other page beside it was scrawled in black pen: '*When are you going to see?*' That text had been there already, Ash knew, and it was quite different from Anne's own style of handwriting.

"Very meaningful," Ash said sarcastically. But then her eyes fell again on that blob of highlighter, and she finally looked at it properly.

Anne had highlighted a tiny figure in the background of the photo. It was a little bald guy smiling straight at the camera, a hand raised as if waving. And it really *did* look like Amaranthus.

"No way. It *has* to be a coincidence."

Just like finding the Eternity Stone?

Ash froze, but no other quiet little thoughts crept in.

She flicked back to the previous page with the family picnic. This photo was also highlighted over a figure in the background of the scene, who was almost hidden by a lady walking her dog. It was a little bald man, smiling at the camera and with one hand lifted as though he was waving. The text on the spare page read, '*Surprised yet?*'

Deias, yes! Her jaw had dropped so far she could have comfortably swallowed a tennis ball.

But the first photo, the one that she'd glanced over so many times, held the biggest surprise. There in the foreground was Ash, smiling with her arm around her old school friend Talia.

And behind them at the bar was a little old bald guy, vaguely Asien-looking, with a bright smile on his face and wearing a party hat. He was pointing at something – the reflection in the mirror behind was of Ash's birthday banner. *Happy Birthday*, it read.

Ohhh.

Ash's lip trembled, and she stuck it out in a fierce pout to stop herself from crying. It *was* her birthday today, but she hadn't told anyone because she was embarrassed that she didn't have any plans to celebrate.

If George and Anne had still been here, they probably would've had takeaways and cake, and maybe watched a movie…

Oh, who was she kidding. She'd still have those things; she just planned to do them pathetically alone. Her family was lovely, but they were asleep on the other side of the world, and they'd sent a parcel that had arrived a couple of days earlier. That was their birthday duty done.

"Thank you," she told the book-Amaranthus. "Your photo-stalking is very meaningful."

But it really *was*, and it meant a lot today of all days.

Ash finally did cry, just a little. Then she went through every single photo Anne had taken, all twenty-two of them in that stuffed-full little album, and found Amaranthus in the background of every. Single. One. It started to become funny – being photobombed so many times – and Ash finally knew why Anne had asked her those annoying questions about whether she'd met the man before 2155.

"Could have just *told* me," Ash muttered, but her mouth curved into a smile.

Suddenly she felt so, so much more valued than she had this morning. She hadn't been forgotten after all.

Happy birthday to her.

Nation of Ciria, circa 4000 BC

Tai reappeared two days after he'd first wangled his way in to meet the Sun King, leaving Janeus jealously behind. With a daft smile on his face, Tai swayed his way to the workshop where both brothers were supposed to build idols for the sixth-day sacrifice.

But Tai, of course, had something better to do.

Janeus heard him come in but ignored him. He lowered his head and focused on pressing gold leaf onto the finely carved surface of the miniature Sun King – or Sun Queen, as Janeus was privately thinking of her.

"Janeus."

"What?" Janeus finally turned his head to look at his brother. Tai looked slightly woozy but very pleased with himself, and that satisfied expression – along with how Tai hadn't been apart from *her* in two whole days and nights – meant that Janeus's envy intensified. He had to grip the table to stop himself punching his brother in the face.

Tai didn't seem to notice, launching into an excited speech. "She's incredible, brother, like you wouldn't believe. I think she might actually be a god. But whatever she is…" His voice faded off, and he smiled into the distance.

"I get it," Janeus said sullenly. "She's perfect." Then a touch of malice made him add, "Is she better than Ziane?"

Referring to the last girl Janeus had stolen from Tai didn't even shake the latter. He simply nodded, playing with his medallion, then said contemplatively, "I wouldn't go near her though, if I were you."

"What, because I might steal her from you too?"

"No. Because she eats people."

Janeus's eyes shot wide open and he stared at his brother. "Are you serious? That's…" Disgusting. Unlawful.

"No! I don't mean consuming their flesh," Tai explained hastily. "I mean what she did to Serran. She…I don't know, drank his life force. That's what the priests told me it looked like. But they didn't tell me until after I'd already gone to see her."

A prickle ran down Janeus's spine. That was what their father had told him about, long before. The power to shapeshift wasn't in the medallion; it was in the person. The medallion had another use.

He asked hoarsely, "Did she try it with you?"

"She did. The very moment she got me alone and realised I had power, she tried it," Tai agreed. "But she couldn't take it from me. She couldn't touch me, and that was when she decided to take me as a lover instead."

"Lucky you."

"Yes, lucky me," Tai agreed with that same dopey expression. "But you mustn't go near there. She's killed at least ten people, and no one tries to stop her. They think it will be a better sacrifice, and they don't want to displease her."

"And you keep sleeping with her, unafraid of being harmed?"

Tai shrugged a shoulder, looking both guilty and proud. "She is a god, Janeus. Who am I to say what she can and can't do? Besides, she can't hurt me. She thinks it must be my innate shapeshifting power that protects me."

"Like playing with an adder whose mouth has been tied shut. It must be a thrill indeed," Janeus observed drily.

But his thoughts were fixed on what Father had said about the medallion.

Tai was wrong: it wasn't the power handed down from oldest living son to oldest son that saved him. No, that was what had drawn the Sun King – Queen – to Tai in the first place.

Instead, the medallion was what kept Tai safe when he slept next to someone who'd suck out his life force if they could. It held a different sort of power to anything else that Janeus had felt or heard of before, and its origins were unknown.

Father had told Janeus the horrible secret on his deathbed – of how he had taken the shapeshifting power from his own older brother Terr when they were just youths themselves. He'd learned from a sorcerer how to steal life force, how to put your hands on the chest of a dying man and breathe in the power that had made him more than just flesh and blood, and feel yourself grow in strength as you did so, taking on any unusual abilities the person had.

Father had tried it with Terr one night as he slept, and he'd had a vision of the medallion being like a golden shield over Terr's body, keeping him safe from supernatural attack. To get the gift, he'd have to first get the medallion.

So Father had wheedled and begged until finally Terr had agreed to 'let him try the medallion on, just to see how it felt'. And the moment he had, Father had turned on him and killed him. Then he'd set his hands on Terr's chest and felt the shapeshifting ability flow into him.

He'd told the family that Terr had died in an accident, that he'd fallen off a cliff into the river, and his body had never been found to prove otherwise.

Janeus had been horrified to hear that his father was a murderer, a kin-slayer. And the old man had died soon after, so he never had the chance to tell anyone else.

Janeus hadn't told anyone either. He'd just tucked the awful knowledge of that murder in the back of his memory, only taking it out to examine in very quiet times where he would wonder exactly *why* his father had told him, the younger son, about how to steal the birthright…

"So if you didn't come to gloat over how wonderful she is and how only you can be safe around her, then why are you here?" Janeus asked, pushing aside that other horrible thought.

Tai yawned, stretching, then grinned at his brother. "I need sleep. I wouldn't have come otherwise, but I'm absolutely shattered. Haven't slept in two days, if you know what I mean."

Rub it in a bit, why don't you. Janeus just grunted, his attention fixed back on the gold leaf.

True to his word, Tai was snoring in the back room within ten minutes. Janeus waited a few minutes longer, then rose to look at him.

The small, dull brown medallion sat comfortably against Tai's chest on its thick leather thong, and Janeus couldn't help himself. He reached out to touch it, picking it up gently, then gave it a little tug when Tai didn't stir. Truly, he was sleeping deeply.

Janeus decided in an instant. He picked up the nearby sharpened blade, then set to work.

The road off Little Meadswell, 2013 AD

Amazing. Amaranthus was in the background of every single family photo Anne had so carefully collected.

Every single one.

Ash couldn't believe she hadn't noticed earlier. She'd feel a bit stupid if she wasn't so excited.

Those were the family photos, though. Anne had taken others: strange sketched images of ancient Turkiye, or old paintings that she'd presumably liked. Their presence didn't make sense, but Ash thought perhaps they would soon.

Ash's car was still at the side of a country road where she'd left it, and probably unlocked, too. So she tucked the little album under her arm, then took the Eternity Stone in one hand and focused on the moment she'd left.

In a blink, she found herself back in her car. With the Stone, any moves across time and space were gentle and smooth, but the sky was now a little dark – her timing wasn't quite right.

Buzzing with excitement, Ash quickly set the Stone and the album on the seat beside her, then turned on the engine and headed off towards home. This place wasn't terribly far from Whiteside by train, but the lack of decent roads meant that driving to and from the site took a good twenty minutes longer than it should have.

The wheels kicked up gravel as she went, trying to focus on the now darkening road, but so, so caught up in what she'd found.

She had the Stone! She could do anything, anything at all. She could go home to the Southern Isles for the evening – except then she'd have to explain the short trip to her parents.

Or here was a better idea: she could go to another century, and not have to explain the trip to anyone! As Anne or George would say, 'huzzah!' Except *this* time when she came back from wherever she was going, she'd make sure to arrive at the same time she'd left, and without any uninvited extras.

Suddenly, a huge, pale shape appeared in the dark beside her window, right up against the glass. Ash caught a glimpse of white features and colossal black eyes and shrieked in fright, automatically swerving the car away from the thing.

But the roads weren't built for sudden swerves, and as though in slow motion, her car juddered for a few long moments on the edge of a deep ditch before flipping on its side with a horrible screech.

Or maybe that horrible screech was Ash. The whole world was moving around her, the precious Eternity Stone went flying from its place in the passenger seat, and the album spun into the air before hitting her temple with a thump. The Stone landed with its string of beads hooked over her outstretched hand, and then suddenly there was silence.

Ash couldn't move. She couldn't even groan. Out of the corner of her eye she could see something horrible approaching from above/beside her; something white with big round yellow eyes and a man-like body, and fear shot right through her.

Deias, I wish George was here-

Renwick Castle, Iversley, Leister County, Angland
1556 AD

"You've not been acting yourself, Anne. Is marriage to that pig truly so dreadful?"

Elspeth asked the question so plainly – as though 'twas without a doubt that Edgar was a pig, and so not to be seen as an insult – that Anne laughed aloud.

Lol. That meant laugh-out-loud, and 'twas a phrase used in the early twenty-first century, although oddly in written form only. One would think that 'twould be used aloud, but then mayhap one could simply *laugh* instead…

"Anne? You did not answer the question." And now her half-sister looked truly concerned, lines of anxiety creasing around her pretty green eyes. She was only six months Anne's junior, although with the dark hair that so resembled Elspeth's mother. Anne resembled her own mother.

"Forgive me," Anne said finally, realising she was giving an excellent impression of a madwoman. "My thoughts were elsewhere."

"Back in fairyland, I'd vow," Maura muttered as she trotted into the light-filled upstairs room, arms laden with linens in need of edging. As the ladies of the castle, 'twas their job to sew for the household.

Well, *Anne* was a lady. Elspeth, although the dearest person in the world to Anne, was not…quite…legitimate. 'Twas more of a social handicap than her twisted left foot.

"Fairyland?" Elspeth asked, brightening. She loved any tales of the supernatural, although Anne hadn't mentioned a word of her own long travels. A full three weeks had passed since her return. "What do you speak of, Maura?"

The servant sniffed. "That cursed two hours I spent trying to find my lady, that's what. Where did she go, I don't know, but I doona like feeling a fool. And you made the veriest fool of me, my lady. They say you were with a man in the woods. A man!" When Maura was upset, her old Scots accent would show itself.

Anne gave a heavy sigh. "As I told you before, I wished for some time alone. I was not meeting a *man*. 'Twas not prudent to leave for so long, but it has been done now and cannot be undone." In truth, she'd been gone for far more than two hours. More like six months. But she would not share that information with Maura.

Maura sniffed again, then mercifully left the room, leaving the two girls alone. Anne picked up one of the linens and began to inspect it for a good place to begin sewing, thinking of the machines back home- back in *Ash's* time that could do such a task in mere minutes. 'Twould take hours here, stitch by painstaking stitch.

Anne sighed again, heavily.

"You never answered my question."

Oh. Elspeth meant Edgar – was marriage so dreadful? "Not as such," Anne replied honestly. "He ignores me most of the time, and that is as I wish it."

He was more tied up with his own importance as the new Earl of Longford than with his new bride, and – thank the Eternal One – spent his nights elsewhere.

Elspeth stared at her wide-eyed. She opened her mouth once, twice; but did not speak.

"What is it, Bethie?"

"I should not say it," the girl blurted out, "but I pity you above all creatures, sister, because you must lie with that ancient, odious beast. Do you wish to die when he visits you at night?"

Anne's jaw dropped, and a few moments passed before she could even answer. Partly because she hadn't expected Elspeth to ask *that*, and partly because the answer gave her mixed emotions.

Three weeks ago, Anne had arrived home from her lengthy time-travel adventure on the very date on which she'd left. With her people having no idea what had happened, they'd promptly wed her to Edgar LeSpenser, a favourite of Queen Marian, and the new earl. (The previous earl, Anne's husband, had been recently executed for heresy.)

Seeing no other option, Anne had gone through with the marriage. Then, on the night of the wedding, Edgar had announced that he did not wish to consummate.

At first she hadn't believed her ears. Had she wanted to hear those words so much that she'd imagined them?

To Anne, who was fresh from the twenty-first century, Edgar seemed small, smelly, and unpleasantly bossy. He was also old enough to be her own father. Unlike the people of Ash's time, Anne did not believe one must feel an overwhelming attraction for one's spouse, but surely 'twas better not to feel disgust?

"As appealing as that sounds," Anne had said, "I must ask why. 'Tis dangerous to leave a marriage incomplete, for if anyone was to find out, it could be annulled."

"Why should anyone find out?" Edgar had retorted. "You have been wed before, so our word will be enough. Will you agree?"

Most certainly! Anne had spared a few moments wondering *why* he did not wish to bed his new bride, then decided his advanced age must be the reason. He was simply incapable.

Oh, happy day! Her plans with George would have been quite damaged had she become with child.

"Indeed I agree," she'd said enthusiastically. "And fear not; I shall not tell a soul of your…condition. Your reputation is safe with me."

Edgar had reared back, appalled. "You misunderstand, Lady Anne! I am most fit and capable, I assure you! I already have a son from my first marriage, and my own lovely mistress is about to grant me yet another. Why should I give my attention to an unwanted bride? Any children of *yours* might also have hideous red hair!"

Anne remembered every word he'd said that night. Hideous red hair, indeed! Plenty of men in the future had found her attractive. Well…at least two had. And she'd also been forced into this marriage. Under other circumstances, she might've found herself penniless or in a convent along with other unwanted widows.

So she'd told him what she thought of him, and he'd told her to burn in Hades.

Here, that was about the worst insult one could use. It had

shocked them both into silence – but at least it had ended the argument.

Since then, Edgar had been passably polite in front of other people, but otherwise completely ignored her. She'd returned the favour.

Anne checked no one was in earshot, then replied in a whisper to Elspeth's question. "Edgar has never visited me. In truth, we never consummated the marriage, and I am glad for it!"

"Oh! Is he too old?"

Ha! Even innocent Elspeth thought as much. "One would think so," Anne said smugly, "but he says no. He says his interests lie elsewhere, and he does not like the colour of my hair."

"And you truly do not mind? Not his lack of attention; rather that the marriage is incomplete. Are you not afraid someone will find out and you will be cast aside?" Elspeth's brows lowered anxiously. "I do not know what will become of me without you."

"Never fear; I have a plan for both of us. A plan for a safe and exciting future." Although, she would've expected to see some progress by now…

Elspeth didn't seem appeased. "What sort of plan?"

Anne ought to tell her. She'd wanted to wait until the very last moment, but mayhap Elspeth's peace of mind was of more import. And in truth, Anne desperately wanted to share what had happened in those 'two hours' in the woods.

"Bethie," Anne began, putting down the needle and thread neatly beside her and taking a deep breath.

Then she told her everything.

BIRTHRIGHT

Nation of Ciria, circa 4000 BC

"My wolf, you've finally returned."

The welcome that the Sun Queen gave to Janeus startled him. Her wolf? But instead of letting his surprise show, he smiled widely in that way Tai did, then stepped fully inside the inner temple, closing the door after him.

She was standing under the skylight in the centre of the room, illuminated gold and glowing like she had been when she first arrived. But then she stepped out into the artificial light from the torches set in the walls, and he saw that she was just a woman. A beautiful one, but with skin and flesh like any other.

Well, not quite like any other. She seemed to have pale traceries of silver marking the skin of her arms where it was exposed by her sleeveless dress, forming the shape of a delicate twisting vine around her biceps then disappearing under the fabric of her dress.

Her hair was darker than his, her skin much paler, and her eyes a jade green made sharper by their expression. The gold dress, made of an unfamiliar shiny material, fell smoothly to the floor, and under her flowing hair he caught glimpses of strange earrings, rather like bunches of grapes. A small black object was tied around her neck with a thin, strong-looking cord.

The Sun Queen regarded Janeus for a long moment. Then she

said in a voice like melted gold, "Are you going to speak or just stare at me like a fool? Because if it's the second, then you may as well go home to sleep like you said you would."

That startled him, and he found himself answering like he would have any other woman. "But you like men staring at you in awe, don't you? Don't scold me for doing what I know you really enjoy."

There was a frozen moment where they just looked at each other, and Janeus waited for lightning to strike.

Then the Sun Queen tipped her head back and laughed. "You're right, of course. Is there anything else you want to say? An ode to my beauty, perhaps?"

"You know you're beautiful." Janeus looked her up and down, silently agreeing with himself. *Oh yes, she was.* Then he said, far too casually since that was the way he'd always dealt with women who looked like her, "That's a nice dress, but I think you'd look better in red."

Another long stare, and this time the Queen walked right up to him, not touching him, but moving closer until she was barely a handspan away from his chest. They were almost the same height, and she looked intently into his eyes until he couldn't help himself and glanced away in submission.

"You are not my wolf," she stated gently. "You took that knife, and you left my wolf lying still on the rough bed in the back of your workshop. Why are you here, brother of my wolf? Do you wish to take his place?"

Janeus swallowed with difficulty. He knew she'd find out, but hadn't expected it to be so fast. He knew she must have taken the knowledge right from his mind, but rather than scaring him, that excited him. What else could she do?

"You make it sound like I killed him rather than just taking the medallion while he slept," he replied. "He'll be fine. I'll put it back and he'll never know."

"Hmm." She finally stepped back, and he let out a deep

breath he hadn't known he was holding. "Then why are you here, brother of my wolf? Just to stare and play word games?"

"I did want to see you," Janeus admitted. "All our lives, Tai has had the best of everything, the first, because he had the luck to be born a few minutes before me. He even has the shapeshifting power, but you already know that. I mostly don't care about those things, but I didn't want to miss out on this. On you."

When she didn't answer, he added quickly, "I don't expect anything from you, not at all. But you're different, you're something that I've never met before, and perhaps never will again. A chance to widen my world, to be something more than a…a statue-maker! If I hadn't taken this chance, even with its risks, I never would've forgiven myself."

Her feelings weren't evident on her face, but Janeus felt a softening in her attitude towards him. Then she gestured towards the low table off to one side, laden with rich foods and surrounded by furs. "Come, sit with me."

She didn't talk much, his Sun Queen. He had to fight for every scrap of information he could get from her, and he sensed that she enjoyed the battle.

He did find out several things, though. She hadn't been sleeping with Tai, no matter what he'd said. Instead, she'd had him turn into wolf form and sit by her while she ate and petted him on the head like a dog. That made Janeus feel much better.

He asked if Tai had told her that the youth killed on the first day, Serran, was their cousin. Apparently he hadn't, because she turned to him with slightly widened eyes and asked if he was angry. Janeus answered quite honestly that he wasn't, because Serran would have died anyway, and at least this way it hadn't been painful.

Now that got a response from the Sun Queen. She paused, then very slightly widened her eyes again in a way he now could tell meant surprise. "Explain what you mean by that."

Ah. So she *didn't* know. "This is the third day of celebrations,"

Janeus explained, helping himself to a peeled grape. "On the sixth day the Sun King is always sacrificed by being cut into quarters while alive, then sent up in smoke to the gods. But of course, you already knew that."

It was clear by her reaction that she hadn't known. She went very silent, then finally, deliberately shrugged. "It makes no difference to me what you people do." She reached for her goblet of wine, and Janeus stopped her. She looked down at his darker hand on her pale one. "I could strike you down for daring to touch me."

"The wine," he said instead. "It's drugged to make you compliant."

She looked at the goblet for one long moment, then withdrew her hand. Then she turned and looked him in the eyes again, and whatever she saw there made her relax. "You know."

"That you aren't really the Sun King? Or Queen, as I've been thinking of you? Yes."

"Why haven't you told anyone?"

Now Janeus was the one to laugh. "You can teach me how to read minds, how to make people think I'm a god. Why would I give away that opportunity?"

"You think I'd teach you?"

"If I ask very, very nicely." He smiled at her again. "I don't expect anything from you, like I said. But I would very much like to know how you've become what you are."

"You already know," she replied flatly. "The way your father took the power from his brother, and I have done it many times over. There are other ways, but that is the main one."

He hadn't even been thinking about that. "So you can read memories too."

She shook her head. "I read what's close to the surface. I don't yet have the power to read all memories, but I will. You've been thinking a lot about what your father said, even if not consciously. You wonder why he told you such a thing."

"I won't kill my brother," Janeus said adamantly, as much to remind himself as to inform her. "He's my twin. I love him."

She raised an eyebrow. "Do you? That's very loyal of you, considering how little Tai cares for you."

"What's that supposed to mean?"

"Only that he's terribly jealous of you and always has been. That's why he insinuated we were lovers. He wanted you to envy him."

Janeus sat bolt upright, shaking his head. "Why? That doesn't make any sense! He's the one who has the birthright. I have nothing he could want!"

"Not true," she corrected. "You have popularity and charm. His conversation was so dull that when he turned into a mute animal it actually made him more interesting. And let's face it, you're better-looking. Just a little, but it's enough that he would notice."

"Oh." Janeus had always known these things, and had mocked Tai about them often enough. But only because he thought that Tai always had the upper hand, that the birthright more than made up for everything else. Clearly Tai thought differently.

He didn't know what to think about that, so he changed the subject. "What are you going to do about the sacrifice?"

"Leave the way I came, of course." For a moment her hand stole to that strange black necklace, then dropped again. "Do you want to come with me?"

His heart leapt in his chest. "I don't know," he said casually. "Are you going to suck out my life force the moment I fall asleep?"

"Not while you're wearing that medallion. But I would teach you how to become like me, as you wanted."

Janeus pointed at the silver designs on her arms. "Can you show me how to do those? They're powerful, yes?"

"They're a way of siphoning someone's alter-power – their life force – without having to kill them immediately. They just sicken and die. And no, I can't show you, since it takes a tremendous amount of power to do, and you'll never have it."

Janeus agreed. He'd never killed anyone at all, but hypothetically: "If I took the alter-power of say…a thousand people, surely that would be enough?"

She sighed, and touched her earrings. She likely didn't even realise she was doing it. "No. Not for you. Only I can do that."

Ah. So it *was* something to do with the earrings. Perhaps they contained power themselves?

She clearly guessed what he was thinking, because she turned on him and snarled, "If you try to touch these, I will kill you so painfully and slowly that you will have plenty of time to regret it!"

"I won't try," Janeus said honestly. "In fact, I think I should go now. Tai will wake up soon, and I don't want him to find out I, er, borrowed the medallion." As he spoke, he realised that by letting this woman know that Tai was now unprotected, he might have given her the chance to go and kill him. If she took Tai's life force, would she gain the birthright too?

"I would gain the birthright," she replied to his unspoken thought. "But I won't do it."

He studied her uneasily. Tai might be jealous, but he was still his brother, and Janeus would hate to be responsible for his death. "Why not?"

She gave a little half smile. "Because you would never forgive me."

"What do you care about what I think?" he asked. "You'll leave, and we'll never see each other again." He'd said aloud what he'd been thinking the whole time. Having power the way she did sounded wonderful, but he couldn't take it. He had never killed, never would. Not even with Tai when he felt like there was so much to gain. So as wonderful as going with this woman to wherever her home was sounded, he couldn't do it.

She studied his face, then frowned. "I care. I don't know why, but I do."

He didn't know what to say to that, so he just turned and headed for the door.

"Janeus."

He turned.

"My name is Seyen. Not Sun King, not even Sun Queen. Just Seyen."

He let out a short laugh and bowed politely. "A pleasure to meet you, Seyen."

Then he left.

Tai was waiting for him on the road outside their house, his face taut with anger. As Janeus approached, Tai stuck out his hand, palm upwards. "Give me my medallion, Janeus."

Janeus reached up to his neck where the cool metal sat, then hesitated. Was it really true that Tai envied him? "I don't know," he said slowly. "You've had it for years. I think it's fair that I borrow it just for a day or two."

Tai swore. "It's mine! If you wanted to borrow it, you should have asked!"

"And you would have said no," Janeus replied simply. "So I didn't ask."

He walked past his brother towards the entrance to their home/workshop, then abruptly changed his mind, swerving towards the river. There were too many people around here. He couldn't think, and he needed to think.

Tai followed. "You went to see her, didn't you?"

"Yes."

"She would have known you're not me. You can't shapeshift!"

"She knew," Janeus agreed.

His placid tone infuriated his brother. Halfway down the path to the river, Tai grabbed him by the shoulder, turning him around. "Give back the medallion right now, or I'll shift and take it from you," he threatened. "You think that little scratch on your chin is a scar? I'll give you far worse this time if you don't give it back."

Janeus lifted his hand to his chin, touching the mark in question. They'd both been eleven and had been fighting over something stupid – who got the last raisin cake, perhaps? Janeus had grabbed it, sticking his tongue out at his brother, and Tai had changed his hand into claws and swiped at him. He'd cut Janeus's chin right open, and that had been the last time Tai ever used his powers against his brother. Until now.

"Why haven't you taken it already?" Janeus asked curiously.

Tai reached out towards the medallion, his hand coming within inches of it, then pulled away again. He looked furious and afraid. "I don't know. Just…just give it to me, Janeus! Don't play games!"

Tai might be angry, but suddenly Janeus was angrier. But he kept his appearance of outward calm, doing what he knew hot-headed Tai couldn't stand. "If we were playing games, I would win," he said mockingly. "She told me how jealous you are of me because I'm better at everything. Let's face it, the only thing you have that I don't is the birthright. Maybe that's why you were born first. Maybe the gods felt sorry for you, knowing that otherwise you'd be worse than useless."

Why he did what he did next, Janeus would never know. But it was something which he would think on many times in years to come, knowing it had been the point of no return.

Janeus gave the small, round medallion a strong tug, freeing it from the cord, then he tossed into his mouth and swallowed. It was too big, sharper than it looked, and it scraped all the way down into his stomach, but still he managed to give Tai a triumphant smile tinged with nausea. "Guess I'll be keeping it, then."

Tai snarled in fury, shifting his whole head and shoulders into that of a scaled, massive-fanged beast. He threw himself at Janeus, knocking him to the ground, and then his jaws were snapping at Janeus's face, his clawed hands scrabbling for the now empty medallion cord.

Whatever self-control had held Tai back was gone. One claw hooked on the soft leather and pulled, almost choking Janeus, and they grappled for a few hard moments, rolling until Janeus finally got the upper hand and shoved his brother hard against the ground, knocking his head against the base of a tree. Tai roared at him again and got a hand free, gouging a burning trail down Janeus's face and neck, then swiped again.

With his entire world reduced down to fear, anger and pain, Janeus grabbed for the nearest rock and hit the beastman hard, right in the side of the head. Tai jolted, eyes widening, and Janeus hit him again.

Then finally he was still, and the scaled visage melted back into Tai's familiar features, but this time with a trickle of blood winding its way down the side of his head. He didn't move again.

Shocked by what he had done, Janeus sat straddling his brother's body, staring down into the blank face. "Tai?" he called weakly. "Are you alright?"

It was worse than stupid to ask that. Janeus could feel it the way his father had described: the life force that made Tai truly Tai was draining away. Soon the only thing left would be a lump of human-shaped meat and bone.

Shaking with fear and horrified excitement, Janeus set his hands on either side of his brother's chest. He could feel the tingle, the warmth of the power that rested there, and then like taking a deep breath in, it began to flow through his hands, into his arms and then his entire body. He felt the deep gouges on his neck seal together, his eyesight sharpen, and it was like a glass of water to a man dying of thirst. It was life itself, and he felt wonderful.

Physically, that was. The rest of him – his mind and emotions – felt sick. The medallion sat heavily in his stomach like it was made of stone, like it was fighting the power that had made Tai live. So, so wrong.

A small sound nearby made Janeus turn. It was a girl child, perhaps eight or nine years old, clutching a woven basket in her small hands. She was staring at Tai's body with an expression of utter horror on her face. The moment she met Janeus's eyes, she turned and ran for the city, throwing the basket aside and screaming the whole way.

Murderer. Kin-slayer.

That was what they would call him, what Janeus was already calling himself. Shaking, unsure of what to do, he mentally ran through the different people who would help him if they knew what had happened. The list came down to only one name.

Seyen.

But how to get to her? If she was still there, she'd be inside the temple. If he could outpace the screaming child, he could run and beg for sanctuary. She, out of everyone, would understand.

What was he thinking, outpace the child? He had the birthright now. He focused on the one animal form that he'd envied Tai having the most, and felt the change come over his body.

She should just go, Seyen told herself. The power that came from these people's worship was less than inspiring, and even less so now she knew they were planning to sacrifice her.

As if she'd let them.

But if the wine really was drugged, and she didn't doubt Janeus on that, then perhaps she would've been too dopey to fight properly.

Janeus. Now she'd admitted the real reason she was still here in this place. She was hoping he would come back. He was handsome, yes, and that wasn't very special. She'd met plenty of handsome men in her travels. Taller ones, too.

It was something more than his appearance. It was the way he looked at her, the way he spoke to her, the way he knew how she gathered her power and still hadn't judged her. He could be a good companion, if only he could get past his concern over the less than ethical alter-power harvesting method…

Suddenly she heard the sound of beating wings, and an enormous eagle came flapping through the skylight to land awkwardly on the stone floor.

A half second later, it morphed into that familiar male form. "Seyen!"

"Janeus?!"

He nodded, his crouched posture one of fear and defeat.

She managed a smile. "I'm almost disappointed. I never thought you would actually do it."

"It was an accident," he burst out. "We fought, and he shifted and tried to tear out my throat. I hit him with a rock…"

"And killed him," Seyen finished. "Why would he attack you? And where is the medallion?"

Janeus's response was so unexpected she almost didn't take it in.

"What did you say?"

"I swallowed it," he repeated defiantly, meeting her eyes. She heard his unspoken thought: *Now I'll always be safe from you.* That was followed by a flood of guilt and horror, and a small amount of pleasure at his new ability, then more guilt over that pleasure too.

Well, well, well. Seyen hadn't expected *that* – but she wasn't sorry. "The first is always the hardest," she told him gently. "And for you even more so."

Janeus shook his head. "I can't…I didn't mean to. I don't want to do it again." But even as he spoke, she knew he was remembering how it had felt to drink up the life force, and she knew that he would do it again.

She would make sure of it.

Seyen moved over to him and cupped her hand over the side of his smooth jaw, ignoring the still-wet blood smeared down his chin and neck. As she did so, she sent a tiny burst of power into him. He wouldn't even feel it now, wouldn't realise what she'd done until the mark grew enough to be noticed, and by then she'd have bound him as securely as a pet dog was tied to a steel post.

"Don't worry," she repeated. "I'll look after you. Be loyal to me, and I'll see that you never need to worry again."

Then with her other hand, Seyen reached up to touch her most treasured object of power, and visualised *home*.

A moment later the sanctuary was empty – they'd have to find someone else to sacrifice this year.

Mountbatten Manor, Iversley, Leister County, Angland
1818 AD

A house party. One of those loved or hated gatherings of the unemployed beau monde, depending on whether you enjoyed the constant company of at least half a dozen acquaintances.

In truth, it wasn't George's favourite way to spend a week. But he'd gone to the trouble of getting back here, and he was damned well going to grit his teeth and appreciate all the various trappings that came with this lifestyle.

One thing he was *not* appreciating, though, was the way a gentleman could be obligated to marry some silly, scheming chit just because they were sly enough to be trapped in a room with him.

Even worse, it was *this* scheming chit who'd thought to throw herself at him while making sure that her father, George's mother, and various others were in earshot. Then they'd been 'accidentally' discovered in an embrace, and not one he'd initiated.

He wouldn't. Not after the way she'd left him last time.

There would be no second chances for Clarissa.

George looked down at the girl (ashy blonde curls, big blue eyes, trying to look winsome), and then at her father (not at all winsome), George's mother (shocked but not entirely displeased) and whoever that was with the feathers in the background (gleefully shocked), and made a decision to lie.

"I cannot marry you," he said firmly. "Not even if we'd been caught nude in the village square."

"Why not?" the girl gasped.

"Why not?" the father roared.

And here was the lie. A big, fat, lovely lie to save him from Miss Clarissa Margate's matrimonial clutches…again.

George said, "Because I'm already married."

Considerably later that evening, the fuss finally died down. Then it was just George, his mother Lady Eleanor, and his brother Edward, Viscount Morley, in the side parlour where he'd almost been tricked into marriage.

His mother gave him a gimlet-eyed stare, her posture ramrod stiff. She wasn't tall, but she'd been the one to gift him those arched eyebrows, and they added a whole new level of displeasure to her angry looks. "That was not well done, George. Not well done at all."

George slumped into one of the well-stuffed armchairs. If she wasn't going to sit, then that was her choice. "What would you have had me do, Mother? Marry the girl?"

"Not humiliate her in front of everyone!" Lady Eleanor exploded. "The only reason Miss Margate was invited was because of you, George, and then you reject her so openly? And stand up when I'm speaking to you!"

George practically leapt to his feet, that particular tone getting a prompt response, but his automatic reaction just made him more annoyed.

It was strange how he'd spent six months wanting to be back

here. Yet now he'd been home less than three weeks, and some of the local habits now seemed odd and rather silly – like not sitting in the presence of a lady who was standing, even if the lady in question was one's mother. "I did *not* ask for her to come. You did that all on your own. Nor did I ask for her to throw herself at me the moment we were left alone!"

"I say, old man," Edward said lazily. He was several years older than George, a little shorter and a little fairer, and his relaxed tone hid a deeply conventional soul. "You should know better than to be in a room alone with a marriage-minded lady, especially one who has *expectations*. Wasn't that whole fuss last year over this Margate chit anyway?"

"It was," their mother agreed, not giving George time to respond. "You wished to marry her, but your father believed her connections were too low. Not even a baronet among them – *and* her great uncle was a Walsh coal-miner. But if your father had known that you would leave us as a result of his refusal, no doubt he would have allowed the marriage rather than lose you as he did." She paused. "As we all did. Have you changed so very much in these last twelve months that you would marry without even informing your own family?"

Actually it had been more like eighteen months, if you included the six hidden months he spent in the future. And yes, George supposed he had changed that much, because he would have chosen to marry had the right person shown up.

But whatever Mother and Edward thought they knew of Clarissa, they didn't know the full story.

"Father paid Clarissa Margate not to marry me." George's tone was weary and quiet. "I'd heard she married a solicitor in Cairnwall straight afterwards, although that appears to be a lie as well. If I'd known of your misapprehension, I would have corrected you and saved us this scandal."

There was a long silence in the room, broken up by the entry of a servant with a tray of tea and scones. Another joy of the nineteenth century was having someone else to bring food and drink, but it also brought the constant danger of eavesdroppers.

"It wasn't very much of a scandal," Lady Eleanor admitted once the maid had left. "I won't tell, of course, and neither will the Margates. Mrs Coutts, however…" That was the lady with the feathers who'd been standing in the background. Her lips tightened. "I will impress upon her the importance of remaining silent, but I can make no promises for what she will say or do. She is known to gossip."

"It'll do more harm to the girl than to you," his brother suggested, taking a scone. It reminded George briefly of the time he'd eaten the same meal but in a very different location, and of the people he'd eaten with. "Unless you weren't truly married, of course. Then you'd be seen as a scoundrel of monumental proportions."

Argh. George supposed he must be, somewhat. It all seemed so unfair, because when his family had come to him two days after his return to this time period and had offered to reinstate his allowance, he'd not imagined *this* would be in his future. And just when he'd promised no scandals…

Lady Eleanor sighed, taking a seat. Her sons followed suit. "So tell us of this Ashlea Hamiltyn, George."

"Isn't that a man's name?" Edward suggested. "I've never heard of a female called Ashleigh before."

George just about choked on his mouthful, because when he'd first met Ashlea he had actually mistaken her for a boy. It had been down to the breeches and hat, really, because he couldn't imagine making the same mistake now. "Ah….where she's from, they use the name for both male and female, although the spelling is different."

"And where is that?" their mother asked impatiently. "Who are her people, her connections? Not the *Eirish* Hamiltyns, surely? Where is she now? When is she coming to visit?"

By Jove, were they Eirish? He'd specifically made up the name

Hamiltyn because it sounded so Anglish – and also because it was Ashlea's hometown back in the Southern Isles. Or so she'd said. "I don't know," he replied finally.

"Don't know any of it?" Edward asked suspiciously, a hint of a smile playing around his mouth. "Are you sure this girl actually exists?"

"Oh, she exists," George replied. "She's tall with dark hair and hazel eyes. She's from the Colonies originally, although she was living in Leister County when I met her six months ago. We were thrown together almost from the very start. Like fate, really."

Lady Eleanor sucked in a deep breath, almost turning purple. "*Colonies*? Is she gently bred, George?"

He thought of the soft beds, the automatic dishwashers, the machines that washed your clothes and dried them again, the foods that you could prepare just by pressing a couple of buttons, and the bathing facilities that didn't require a single servant to draw water.

Then he purposely ignored the arguments about women's rights, the odd accent that grew strangely appealing the more he listened to it, and the dreadful dress habits.

"She has had a very gentle upbringing," George replied, mostly honestly. "Most couldn't compete with her privileges, although it is, as you say, new money."

His mother let out a heavy sigh, closing her eyes briefly. "Well, there's nothing that can be done now. When is she coming to stay with you?"

"I am expecting her arrival any time," George replied, and this part *was* true. It had been almost four weeks, and he was truly surprised she hadn't come by now. She'd said more than once that she'd like to visit both their times, although didn't seem to under-stand how very different it would be.

But since she *hadn't* come, perhaps something had gone

wrong with the plan. Perhaps something went wrong at Anne's end, or Ashlea couldn't work out how to use the gateways…

Four weeks, they'd agreed. Four weeks, and if there wasn't any contact, then George would go back himself to find her. Anne too, of course. He'd been travelling each day over to the border of Damien's estate, to the same place he'd come through with Anne, trying to see if Ashlea had arrived yet. She hadn't, and he was beginning to worry. Now he added to that worry the knowledge that he'd just seriously complicated his future here, and more so with every single lie he told.

"Very well," Lady Eleanor said. "Once she arrives, we shall introduce her properly." Her expression – and Edward's – clearly said, *don't embarrass the family.* But it seemed a certainty that he would.

Oh Hades, he was in such a mess.

What a tangled web we weave, when we first practice to deceive…

Renwick Castle, 1556 AD

"And then the wicked giants all vanished," Anne said with great animation, "but for the dead ones, of course. But the Eternity Stone had also vanished, so we could not yet return-"

Elspeth had been listening with growing incredulity ever since her sister began the tale. Elspeth had simply asked what kind of plan Anne had in mind, and instead of a proper answer, was given this tale of- of- being stolen away by elves.

Or people who were not elves, as Anne was insisting, although their powers resembled such. People who could move through time just as easily as gypsies moved their homes from place to place. And then Anne spun a tale of flying, and about true giants in every colour of the rainbow…

Elspeth's lips tightened. Her poor, poor sister. Although Anne was the elder by less than a year, and the legitimate child that protected Elspeth with her position, Anne had always had a streak of whimsy that contrasted with her otherwise practical nature. She'd accepted from a young age her lot in life, but it didn't stop her from hunting for fairies when they were aged eleven and twelve, too old to be doing such things.

Elspeth had been blamed for that one (since the bastard daughter of a milkmaid was an easy scapegoat) but she'd remembered it. Anne had the idea that she could reach the fairy realm if only she knocked on the right tree trunk. Instead, all she'd got were bruised knuckles and a scolding.

"So Ash flew after Dr Walker and shouted at him and made him return us, and he vowed that he would-"

"Ash is the oversized yeoman, yes?" Elspeth interrupted. "Who was given a flying potion. By the walking doctor."

"Yes to all of those. By the by, she-"

"But if he had a flying potion," Elspeth interrupted again, "why did he not use it to free himself?"

Anne looked startled by that question, then dismissed it. "I'd vow he had some reason. But 'tis not the point of the tale, Bethie. Then the next day I said goodbye to handsome Islo, and that cod's head of a doctor sent us all back to Ashlea's time rather than each of our own! He knew we could do nothing to stop him, for once the change was done, 'twas done."

Elspeth felt that the tale was growing worse and worse, and she couldn't bear to hear it any longer. "Can you prove the truth of this tale?"

"Of course," Anne replied simply. "I have brought several items of value. Small ones only, you understand, as I do not wish to be caught and considered a witch. Some of the things available in Ash's time are so wonderful. Oh, Bethie! You would love it there! They might even be able to fix your foot!"

A pang of pain shot through Elspeth at that false hope – pain in her heart, not her foot. 'Twas impossible for her to be anything other than what she was, and she knew it well. "The evidence," she repeated gently. "If you will."

As if suddenly realising that her tale wasn't believed, Anne stood abruptly and ran from the room.

Was Anne so very offended? A little unsure, Elspeth picked up a linen sheet to begin hemming it, accidentally jostling a wound on her leg as she did so. She grimaced. The wound was just above her knee on her bad leg, only two inches wide and not very deep, and had been caused when the rusted edge on an iron-trimmed water barrel had sliced her clean through her skirts.

'Twas not healing well. Saints' teeth, it hurt worse now than it had before, and the poultices she'd applied were not drawing out the infection. She might even have to *show* someone.

Anne came running back into the room, almost stumbling over her wide skirts as she did so. "Hades, these gowns are too long!"

"They seem the same as always to me," Elspeth pointed out, distracted from her own small pain. "And Anne, you *swore*."

"Did I?" For a moment the girl looked startled, then shrugged. "'Tis not considered a foul word in Ash's time. I fear I forgot the manners of our home. But now see for yourself, Bethie. Here is my plas-tik toothbrush," – and she held up an unnaturally bright blue stick with one bulbous end – "and here is the Eternity Stone."

Anne held out her other, cloth-draped palm. On it was a small black item rather like a little hourglass, with a short string of beads extending from one end. Odd, but hardly magical in appearance. Still, it could be worth something. Elspeth reached out as though to touch it, but Anne pulled her hand back. "Oh, you mustn't. You might use it by mistake, and 'twould be a dreadful thing."

Suddenly the small amount of belief Elspeth had gained

drained away. "Why is that?"

"Because…" Anne looked down at the little object, frowning. "For to use it carelessly would cause all manner of trouble, and the kind that cannot be fixed."

Four

THE OTHER WAY TO TRAVEL

Erus Province, 2900 AD

Janeus lay on the secluded couch, staring blankly at the slightly peeling plaster on the nearby wall. Seyen was sleeping beside him, her hand splayed possessively over his bare chest, and that was all he could feel. Her hand on his skin, the buzzing in his ears from the overdose of power they'd both just taken…and his eyes fixed on that stupid peeling piece of plaster.

He frowned, pointing a finger at it, and a spark of something goldish burst out to cover the wall. "And now it's perfect."

"What's perfect?" Seyen raised her dark head from the pillow, staring muzzily at the now flawless patch. She didn't need him to answer the question, as he knew she would already have plucked the information from his mind. "Oh."

"Sorry, thought you were asleep."

"I'm never really asleep. Perils of carrying so much power." She tapped her fingers on the tiny red rosebud tattoo now marking the middle of his chest – matching the one she'd created on herself. He hadn't asked for that kind of permanent link, but Seyen wasn't the sort to wait to be asked. "How do you feel?"

"Buzzing," Janeus answered, still not taking his eyes off the wall. He couldn't. The alter-power he'd gained in their last little gathering attempt – one of many for her, but his first intentional one – meant he felt like he could do anything…or else explode into a million pieces. "I didn't think it would be so intense." Although, there was still the lingering moral question as to how he'd gained the power.

"Just the first few times," Seyen answered casually. "Partly because you still don't know how to hold the power. You'll learn." She was still tracing that same pattern on his chest. He didn't have a problem with being touched, especially by a lover, but it made him uncomfortable the way the rose tattoo grew larger with every touch. "What's the problem?"

She'd picked up on his discomfort, although hadn't yet worked out the reason. Carefully controlling his thoughts, Janeus replied, "Just thinking about that old man."

It was a deliberate misdirection, but it worked.

Seyen made a moue of distaste. "You did him a favour. I mean, how old was he? Had to be at least a hundred, and so ugly. Besides, if those monks didn't want someone trying to gather from them, they shouldn't keep so many objects of power around. It was them or us, Janeus."

"Yeah," he agreed half-heartedly, thinking that deliberately breaking into a monastery to steal the valuables was hardly a necessity. "He *was* old."

"And gathering like that hardly hurts at all," she continued. "I can tell. They spend about a second being surprised, then they're gone. You don't feel *guilty* about it, do you?"

Janeus sighed, finally managing to blink and break that blank stare. "Maybe I do, just a bit. It takes some getting used to, Sashy."

He'd used the pet name deliberately, because it softened her up every time. In the months they'd been together, she'd grown more and more lenient with him – probably because she didn't have anyone else. She moved through time constantly, gathering power and objects of power, but without a set home. This was the closest she ever got to her own home time, but even her grandmother hadn't been born yet.

"And that's why I love you." Seyen kissed him on the neck.

"You're so sweet. Just don't be too sweet. After all, we can't be gods if we don't demand sacrifice, can we?"

She laughed, and Janeus made sure to laugh with her.

The problem was that she actually wasn't joking. She knew she was only human, but she *did* want to be treated like a god. Even now she was talking about establishing herself in some unfamiliar land where multiple gods were worshipped.

I'll be the queen, she'd said, *and you'll be my consort.*

Janeus didn't need to be the king. He *definitely* didn't need to be a god. He could handle being the consort to the world's most powerful being, though, since that was the way Seyen was headed. It was a world away from being a metal worker in Ciria, and it was a life he never could've imagined he'd live.

Shame Tai had to die to bring it about.

Seyen caught his thoughts that time. "No more grief," she told him, sending a burst of power in through his chest.

It hurt and felt good at the same time, and suddenly the grief was gone. Janeus just felt alive, and he smiled at his lover. She was beautiful and fascinating and yes, terrifying; and he was going to make the most of this new life.

"No more grief," he agreed. "Just fun."

Renwick Castle, 1556 AD

Anne had said it so simply. To use the Eternity Stone carelessly would cause all manner of trouble, and of the kind that could not be fixed. But 'twas not precisely what she'd been told.

Four weeks earlier she'd been in Ash's home (or five centuries later, depending on how one considered time) and she and George had found the Eternity Stone sitting on a table. Anne had seen someone place it there; had seen a flash of colour as they moved too fast to be identified, and there 'twas.

But once she'd picked it up, the strangest thing had happened.

George had still been present, unmoving in the corner of her eye, but 'twas as though Anne had been taken into another room. The room had been round and vast enough that the distant sides almost faded out of view, and all along the walls had been a black and white tapestry made of billions of miniscule threads.

Anne had recognised it immediately even as she'd understood she was visiting it only in her mind. Ash had told her of such things: the tapestry where each thread represented a single life and how it tangled and wove in with others.

More than just a representation: changes to the tapestry also meant changes to people's lives. That was because of the person who'd made it. But Anne hadn't been alone in the room…

"Amaranthus!" she'd cried, and the man over by the distant wall had turned to smile at her.

She hadn't seen him move, but suddenly he'd been standing right beside her. "Hello, Anne. What brings you here?"

He had, hadn't he? She was there because she'd found the Eternity Stone.

"You've been *given* the Eternity Stone," he'd corrected. "Did I not promise you would return home with it?"

"I was not expecting the six months in-between," Anne had said tartly, and he'd laughed.

Do you wish you hadn't had those six months? Amaranthus had asked directly into her mind.

Anne hadn't even had to consider the answer. She regretted them not at all, except that her half-sister had been left at home alone and helpless. 'Twas a dreadful fate to be a young girl, crippled and unmarried and parentless, without the dignity of legitimate birth, and with no one to watch over her. *Anything* might happen to Elspeth if Anne didn't return.

"And yet you may return to the very moment you left," the

man had said aloud. "So Elspeth won't even know you were gone."

That thought had made Anne's spirits plummet, for 'twas as though all this precious experience she'd gained mattered not at all. But then a wonderful thought had occurred. "Do you want the Stone back after we've used it?"

"I will send someone to retrieve it in good time. Use it to return home first."

"Yes, but-" The desperate thought had nagged at her, the one she'd clung onto at night in her little bedroom. "Could I not bring Bethie to Ash's time? They might heal her twisted foot. I'd vow they'd not even mind she was born outside of wedlock."

Amaranthus had turned away from her, focussing on some tiny details of the tapestry in front of him. Tiny images flickered as his hand played the threads like the strings of a harp, making some pattern evident only to him. Then finally he had answered. "The Eternity Stone frightens you, dear, because you know all the possibilities for help and for destruction. This means you have some wisdom. Would you like some more?"

"Erm…yes, please."

She'd thought he might have given her one of those tiny bottles that had contained flight, but instead he had said, "Use it quickly, use it seldom, and keep moving until you find a place of safety to stop. There are those who are attracted to the use of the Stone, and who do not have your welfare in mind."

"A place of safety?" Anne had echoed.

"You'll know it when you see it."

"But if we use the Stone," she'd persisted, "then we'll move through time. How might anyone follow us? It does not seem possible."

Amaranthus had crooked a finger. "Come, see this." He'd pointed her towards a tiny, tiny white thread where it disappeared into the finely knit fabric, appearing an inch or two further to the right. Anne knew not how she'd picked that out amongst all those threads, but mayhap 'twas the magic of the room. "See how this thread isn't like the others. They're close knit together, but this one has some movement about it, see?"

He'd moved the thread, and Anne had realised that there was a hole left behind where it had moved. Then suddenly he had moved his hand back and forth, and the same thread had doubled back and forth, back and forth between the two holes, perfectly following its own path, and while the lines of thread grew more numerous, the holes never seemed to grow any smaller. "The Eternity Stone leaves a hole in the fabric of time as it moves," he explained. "A gateway, perhaps you might call it, and one that moves in time along with the user. Very few people know how to sense such gateways, and even fewer know how to use them."

Anne's breath had caught short. "Who can use them?"

Then he had smiled, and 'twas like knowledge had been imparted in that very expression. "Only those who have already used the Stone, of course."

And suddenly the vision had gone and she was once more wholly in Ash's tiny dining room. George hadn't even noticed that she'd left, but he had believed what she'd told him. Then they'd tested it, and once they'd realised the gateways worked, they had followed Amaranthus's instructions. *Use it quickly, use it seldom, keep moving.*

Oh, but they'd left a letter for Ash, of course. So she'd know too.

"And that is why we chose as we did," Anne finished telling Elspeth. "Because of the gateways between times. They truly work, Bethie, but for you to use them as we do, you must first travel with the Stone-"

"Travel?" her sister interrupted suddenly. She was pale-faced, with bright pink spots on her cheeks that Anne had first taken for excitement but now wondered if showed some kind of distress. "Travel between realms, sister? As you have?"

"But of course," Anne replied, baffled. "Was that not what

I've just told you?"

Elspeth went very silent, looking away.

The silence dragged on until Anne couldn't bear it any longer. "Do you disbelieve me, or does it frighten you, what I have said?"

The younger girl still didn't turn, but her reply was low and quiet. "You say that you mustn't use the Stone, because 'twill bring trouble, and that mayhap some villain would follow when you do. Who is the villain, Anne? And you say *I* must use it, when you just said that we mustn't. And you say we must keep moving until we find a safe place-"

"This place is safe enough," Anne cut in soothingly, realising how her words had been misunderstood. "'Tis our home. Verily, Amaranthus must have meant that we should not stay in unknown places. As for those who would follow…" She wrinkled her nose. "Mayhap any of those who'd followed the Queen and still hold some power, I know not. But 'twould seem a miracle if any would find us now. As for you, Bethie, you must use it just once along with me, so that we might use the gateways forever more."

"I'll shall tell Maura that we're leaving, then."

Had Elspeth not understood? "No, you mustn't!" Anne burst out, horrified. "Don't you realise no one must hear of this? 'Tis our secret, Bethie. Not Maura, not a soul."

"I understand," Elspeth replied gently. "I truly do. But mayhap we shall save the travelling for another day? I do not feel quite myself."

Anne relaxed, smiling at her sister as she wrapped up the Stone. She'd been keeping it hidden in a secret place, because she'd feared she might use it by accident if 'twas kept on her person. "I shall wait another three days as we promised Ash in the letter. If she does not come by then, we shall go to her."

"How wonderful," her sister said weakly, and Anne smiled again.

Wasn't it just?

It mattered not whether Anne's tale was true or false, Elspeth thought as she quietly crept along the corridor away from Anne's bedroom. It mattered that 'twas dangerous. And she now held the evidence of that tale: the blue toothbrush and the Stone, both hidden in the deep pockets of her plain skirt.

It had taken her less than a day to find where Anne had hidden them in the hollow end of her wooden bedhead, as though Elspeth hadn't known of this hiding place since they'd first arrived in Renwick castle.

In truth, Elspeth did not disbelieve Anne when she'd told her tale. Not wholly, anyway, but she'd known that such things as 'time travel' and 'power' and 'supernatural gifts' must never be spoken of here in this place, not if one wished to live. Anne had spoken as though she might be able to hop back and forth through time, her speech and manners changing along with every movement, and popping up with new, odd objects every few days.

Anne should *not* have those items. She should not, because 'twas not safe for a woman to set herself apart as strange in this time.

And more so, she should not speak of them. Meeting men in the woods, fixing Elspeth's foot – 'twas more likely they'd both end up hung as witches or burned as heretics. Either way, dead. Both crippled bastards and disgraced redheaded nobles must tread carefully, and with the way she'd spoken to Elspeth, Anne was not being careful enough.

Elspeth was so caught up in worried thoughts that she ran full into the lord of the castle, bouncing off his padded chest with an apology.

The new Earl of Longford curled his lip when he saw who had struck him. "The milkmaid's whelp, is it? Where is your lady?"

There was no point saying that she wouldn't answer to such an insult; she'd been called worse. Elspeth bobbed a curtsey, not meeting Anne's husband's eye. "I know not, milord."

"Are you not Anne of Covington's shadow? I always see you following her around."

Now that was rude, but probably true. People were kinder to Elspeth when she was with Anne, because Anne defended her so fiercely. "I last saw her in the herb garden, milord."

'Twas true that Anne had been in the herb garden…yesterday. Now 'twas more likely she was in the kitchen or speaking with the steward, but Edgar did not need to know that.

"Humph." There was a moment when Elspeth could feel his eyes fixed on her bowed head. "What has you in such a hurry?"

She couldn't tell the truth, so she went for a believable lie. "I do not feel well, milord." She glanced up at the garderobe door just five feet to their right, and he understood her implication.

"Ugh. Hop along, then." He turned and strode away, his footsteps echoing on the stones of the hallway.

Elspeth felt a pang of nerves twist her stomach. 'Twas true that she did not feel well, but 'twas less to do with possibly rotten food, and more to do with that festering cut on her leg…and the knowledge that she was about to upset her sister very, very much.

Although it had not been her original plan, she turned and stepped quickly into the nearby garderobe, taking a deep breath first as was her habit. Although the privy would be emptied out and filled with straw (by very, very unlucky servants) once full, it always held a distinctive pong that meant no one would search it. And unlike some of the other garderobes, this one did not empty out into the castle moat.

Then when Elspeth stepped back out into the corridor a minute later, her pocket was significantly lighter.

Two days later

"My lady!"

Anne froze in the middle of her search, trying to act as though nothing was amiss. "Yes, Maura?"

The servant stopped at the doorway to Anne's room, looking at the open chest suspiciously. "Why have you spread your gowns all over the floor? 'Tis well and truly time for the rushes to be replaced, and the cloth may be soiled."

'Twas true, but at this moment Anne did not care. She was more concerned about the missing Eternity Stone. No one, not a single soul should have known where it was, and yet 'twas gone from the hollow bedhead where she'd hidden it. The toothbrush was gone too, but *that* was replaceable. "I am reminding myself of what I own," she replied, teeth gritted. "What do you need of me, Maura?"

"'Tis that...*girl,*" the servant replied sniffily. Unlike most, she'd never got into the habit of openly acknowledging Anne and Elspeth were sisters.

Anne's late father had not been discreet in his adultery, but he had been good enough to claim his younger daughter after her low-born mother's death, twisted foot and all. Mayhap 'twas *why* he'd claimed her, out of kindness. Or so Anne liked to think.

"What about Elspeth?"

Maura huffed. "She's not getting out of her bed, my lady. I'd say 'twas mere laziness brought about by bad blood, but the cook thinks she has a fever."

When Anne went to check, she saw that Elspeth *did* have a fever: a dreadful one. Her skin was hot enough to scorch Anne's hand, and her gown soaked in sweat. Anne felt a pang of intense guilt – she'd been so distracted by her search for the Stone that she'd not stopped to check on her sister, who was the purpose of the whole venture.

"My poor dear," Anne gasped. "What has brought this on?"

Elspeth didn't answer at first, blinking too-bright eyes and whimpering. "'Twas my sin, sister. I have done this to myself."

"The sweating sickness!" someone cried behind Anne's shoulder. "It has struck the weakest of us first!"

"'Tis not the sweating sickness," Anne retorted grumpily, but in truth she wasn't sure. She knew from her time in the twenty-first that her own people didn't always deal with illness well, but she didn't know which illnesses, nor what she should do otherwise.

To her sister she said, "And 'twas not your sin, either. Being born out of wedlock doesn't make one ill, Bethie. Have you eaten something overly spiced?" That usually meant the cooks were trying to disguise rotten meat, and while Anne didn't know if 'twould bring on fever, she wouldn't be surprised.

But Elspeth just groaned.

"If she's got the sweating sickness, she must be contained," the cook said authoritatively.

"What's going on here?" the steward said from behind her.

"William, my sister is ill," Anne told him. "I shall need her taken to the solar, and…ale. Plenty of cold ale, and some clean water." They could set her up in the smallest spare room up in the family's quarters, the one currently occupied by some of the maidservants.

He didn't move. "Don't know where y'can get clean water around here, my lady."

"Then whatever you've got!"

"Wife!"

Oh Hades, now what? Anne turned and smiled sweetly at her husband, but mayhap it didn't come out so sweet, as he stepped back in alarm.

"What is the trouble here?" he asked.

"The sweating sickness," Maura replied. "The bastard has it."

Ooh, Anne could have struck the woman. "She does *not*! She simply has a fever, and I will tend to her."

"In her own room, nonetheless," Maura said with a sniff. "You'll be tainted, my lady. You'll grow ill yourself, and then where will you be?"

Probably covered in leeches and dropped in the castle moat, if she wasn't careful. "I will be fine," Anne clipped out. "William, call the men to carry Elspeth to the solar at once."

"My lord, tell her she cannot tend to a fever," Maura beseeched the earl. "If 'tis the sweating sickness, then milady might also be killed. There might be an outbreak."

Anne would have argued that one fever did not an outbreak make, but something suddenly gleamed in Edgar's eyes. "Oh, no, I could not take my wife away from her beloved Bethie. You will tend her, lady wife, until she is well. And see that the contagion does not spread beyond her room."

Somewhere in the background the cook let out a heavy sigh. "I'll bring the herbs."

'Twas a festering wound, Anne finally saw once they had some privacy. She'd checked for buboes hidden around Elspeth's torso – the black plague was a real fear, although hadn't struck this area in her lifetime – and instead found the true cause of the fever.

"I told them 'twas not the sweating sickness," she said with satisfaction.

Not that Elspeth mightn't die of it. Fevers could be fatal, even from such a small wound. This one wouldn't become a plague, though, in spite of how Edgar had liked the idea of removing his unwanted wife so easily.

"My sin," Elspeth moaned, and Anne patted her head with the damp cloth.

"No, 'tis not, my girl. Just wait, once I find the Eternity Stone I'll take us both somewhere they can treat your illness most effectively."

In the meantime, she'd brought out another of the tiny, helpful things she'd stolen- ahem, *borrowed* from Ash's home: a little vial of sickly-sweet pain medicine that also reduced fever. She'd kept these few, small items under the large mattress in her room, and they'd been exactly where she'd left them. "Not as good as antee-bots, but along with the herbs to prevent contagion 'twill be enough for now."

"Antee-bots?"

Ah, so Elspeth *was* listening. "Might be anti-botties," Anne correctly thoughtfully, trying to recall the exact word for those twenty-first century medicines that healed infections. "I'll be back."

Anne quietly exited the smoke-filled room where her sister lay. They'd made the room's usual occupants sleep down in the hall instead, this whole upper area usually being a private place for herself, Edgar and their immediate servants.

But Edgar was standing there in the hall, and as though he might catch some disease, he stepped back as he saw her.

"'Tis not contagion," Anne told him with satisfaction. "'Tis but a cut. I will find a- a poultice," she quickly lied, "and all will be well."

Even if she had to use the remnant gateways herself, and bring back anti-bottiks. Botties. The closest gateway was just on the edge of the woods outside the castle wall, and while not the ideal choice, she'd do it if the Stone wasn't found by tomorrow morning.

It might have been her imagination, but her husband looked disappointed. He quickly covered it, though. "Not contagious. Oh. Verily, 'tis…good."

"You'll need to find another way to dispose of your unwanted wife," Anne said lightly. Mayhap the smoky herbs were going to *her* head. "'Twas a jest, of course," she added upon seeing his shocked expression.

"Of course," Edgar echoed. But she could still feel him watching her as she left the room.

Mountbatten Manor, 1818 AD

George pulled off his mud-covered Hessian boots and collapsed onto the armchair in his bedroom. He'd spent most of the day riding (the horse was on loan from his brother, and *not* afraid of squirrels, which was an excellent quality for a horse to have) and trying to act as expected.

Clarissa and her father hadn't run off in embarrassment, as Mother had somehow managed to keep the last eavesdropper Mrs Coutts from telling anyone what she'd heard. About Clarissa, anyway. Instead, she'd been given permission to tell about George's 'marriage', and he'd never been congratulated so many times on anything.

It was going to be remarkably awkward if the truth came out. Perhaps George would need to stage his 'wife's' death the same way he'd introduced his marriage, because if he admitted now that the whole thing was a lie, he'd be absolutely vilified.

Perhaps that was why he'd in fact spent most of his day riding around the area bordering his brother's and neighbour's estates, lingering around the shimmering patches of air that marked the remnant gateways.

That's what he'd decided to call them, anyway. Amaranthus had told Anne of this new way to time travel: a far safer and more restrictive way to move between two or three time periods without the awkward confusion of wondering how long you'd been gone.

Anne and George had created this set of gateways four weeks earlier (his time). They were practically invisible, and he only knew where they were because he'd scratched an 'x' into the closest tree. He could feel it, feel the power like a faint buzz when he got too close, and if he looked out of the corner of his eye, he could see it shimmer like air over heated rocks.

If he walked into *that* gateway, and thought very hard about seeing Ashlea, he'd find himself in her tiny back garden, four weeks from when he'd left her time.

And if he walked into *that* one, he'd find himself in the woods outside of the ancient lump of rock Anne called Renwick Castle.

Hades, it would be so, so tempting to just walk back through to the twenty-first century, to ask Ashlea why on earth she'd taken so long to visit. They were friends, were they not? As a matter of fact he'd thought them quite good friends, and barring little Anne, he'd never spent so much time with a female who wasn't his relative. Certainly they'd had their arguments, and perhaps she'd been offended that they left so suddenly…

But he and Anne had decided they would allow Ash twenty-eight days to come through to either time. Twenty-eight days, and then they would go back through themselves. And now George would have to find a way to explain why he needed a 'wife' to come visit. By Jupiter, that'd be an interesting conversation.

Twenty-eight days was tomorrow, and that was why George hadn't walked through that remnant gateway yet. He'd kept his word, and he'd waited, and he'd come back to this house all alone.

It was strange how the manor he'd grown up in seemed so incredibly different now he'd spent so much time away. He'd spent time away before, when he'd rented a little townhouse in Lunden and tried to make a go of it himself, but not out of the time period. And now everything seemed enormous and ornate and fussy and perhaps a little bit grubby, although that was hardly the servants' fault for not keeping it clean enough. It was simply that he'd grown accustomed to shiny vinyl surfaces, and all they had to offer here was old wood and stone.

George sighed, considering ringing the bell for refreshments.

Just then, Edward walked into the room without knocking, a habit he'd had since they were children. "My word, man. Are you still up in this little room?"

Evidently. This attic room George now occupied had also been his own childhood bedroom, since they'd already given all the proper bedrooms to the two dozen 'dear friends' attending the house party. The manor was full to the brim.

On the bright side, it was bigger than the little room he'd shared with the tee-vee in the twenty-first, and at least he had peace and quiet. Hardly anyone came up here, since the stairs were too daunting for most.

George didn't answer the question, instead raising his eyebrows amiably at his brother. "Dinner's not 'til eight, I thought."

"I'm not here to call you to dinner." Edward rolled his eyes. "I've barely seen you these past few weeks, and less still before that. And here we are both leg-shackled, old married men…"

"You might be old," George retorted lightly. "I'm barely twenty-one."

Edward laughed, leaning back against the open door. "So this wife of yours must be something if she'd make you settle down before you even reached your majority. Did she bamboozle you into wedlock?"

"We needn't talk about my wife," George replied, desperately hoping for a change of subject. "Yours is lovely. I only saw her at the wedding, but she's a looker, isn't she?"

"A what?"

Oops, that compliment was from the wrong time period. "I meant she's beautiful." And his sister-in-law *was* attractive in that slender, delicate way that was so popular here in 1818, pale curls and all. A little like Clarissa, in fact, although it seemed that George's tastes had changed somewhat.

"Oh. You might have said that, and of course she is, and as sweet-natured as she is lovely. Would you see me with a shrewish plain Jane?"

George half smiled. Although his brother was five years older, he had always found his way to the most attractive girls. Edward was the better-looking of the two of them, or so George had been told once or twice by less than sensitive acquaintances. "Of course not."

"Although my current light o' love," and here Edward's voice dropped low, "now *she's* a beauty. Had to haggle something awful, though, since the old Duke of Scarborough wanted her too. Her name is Alice Bonney, and she is indeed *bonny*. Perhaps when we're next in Lunden I'll introduce you."

There was a long silence.

"I didn't realise you had a mistress," George said finally.

"It's not as though you were around to ask," his brother pointed out. "Have you got one? Or are your pockets to-let?"

"I don't… Lack of money has nothing to do with it!"

"Then why?"

Edward seemed genuinely clueless, and George realised with some surprise that his time in the twenty-first had affected him after all. Perhaps not the attitudes on tee-vee – but the things that Ashlea had said, perhaps.

"Well," George said slowly, "the Good Book says we oughtn't to commit adultery. So I figure that if the Eternal One dislikes it enough to write it down, we should probably listen. At the very least we'll avoid illegitimate children and nasty diseases."

Edward started to smile, but it faded when he realised George was serious. "The Eternal One, really? When did you get so uptight, George? It's not as though I'm visiting light-skirts night after night. It's just one actress in a little house in the city, who knows well enough to avoid breeding. As for my wife – what she doesn't know can't hurt her."

It was a common way of thinking, but now it stuck in George's craw. "I confess I'm disillusioned, Edward. I thought it was a love match between the two of you."

In a society where marriage was often for money and convenience, he'd been pleased that his brother had found something more. But perhaps he hadn't after all.

Edward opened his mouth, but another voice spoke. This one was young and female and shaking with emotion...because the door had been open, and they weren't the only people in this part of the house.

"I thought it was a love match too." George's sister-in-law was standing white-faced in the doorway, her hands fisted at her sides.

Oh, *no*.

"Livvy. I didn't realise you were there," Edward said numbly. He shot George a look of complete horror, which George returned. He hadn't thought anyone was nearby to hear – the woman must walk as quietly as a cat.

"Evidently not." There was a pause, and Olivia took a deep, shaky breath as though she wanted to speak, but instead her face crumpled and she turned and ran. Somewhere down the hall a door slammed.

"Damn it to Hades, George!" Edward hissed. "You might've told me she was there!"

"I didn't know she was there!" George insisted, but his brother turned and stalked off, presumably to try to make amends with his wife.

Hades indeed. So much for a brotherly conversation.

Edward would need more than pretty words to fix this misstep. Even with George's limited experience of marriage (i.e. none), he could see that the trust between them had been broken, and no amount of promises or jewels would put that back together.

The irony was that Edward probably did love Olivia, and George would bet ten to one that he fully expected her to be faithful to him. Here, the upper classes often expected the woman's fidelity only until she had borne a couple of sons, but that tended to be for the marriages of convenience.

George suddenly felt very sad, and something Ashlea had said once came to mind. They'd been arguing over differences between their times, and he'd said how in the twenty-first marriages seemed to be started and ended as easily as he'd buy a horse, and held as much value.

And *she'd* said that most people just wanted to feel loved and valued by their spouse, and sometimes weren't able to fight past the difficult times, or they'd go hunting for that feeling elsewhere. It wasn't right, she'd said, but it wasn't any worse than a marriage in name only, when both parties' hearts and bodies were elsewhere.

What he wanted was the best of both worlds. The kind of marriage where neither would even consider leaving, but the kind where they both felt loved and valued by each other. A small miracle, perhaps, but probably possible. If he wasn't already 'married', that was.

By Jupiter, he'd really shot himself in the foot this time.

"One more day," George muttered, getting up to look for a change of clothing for dinner.

One more day, and then he'd have a whole new kind of challenge to work through.

Mount Olympas, Grecia, 650 BC

"Consort."

The man didn't turn, seeming to be focussed on staring at some image in the scrying pool they'd set up at in the centre of the palace. And while *she* was talking, too…

"CONSORT! Janeus!"

Janeus finally turned to look into Seyen's irritated face. "Oh…sorry, darling. My mind wandered."

Her lips tightened. He seemed to be doing that more and more lately, and she thought it had more to do with his *will* than any distraction. He just wasn't as interested in her as he used to be. "Pay more attention next time."

"Of course," he agreed smoothly. "What did I miss?"

Seyen paused for a moment, then recounted the discussion – whether they would settle permanently on Olympas now the Grecians were becoming a people worth subjugating, or whether they'd keep moving round, gathering objects of power and followers for her pantheon.

Well, she called it a discussion – it was more like allowing her seventeen followers to think they had a choice in the matter.

And they did, sort of. They could go along with what she decided, or they could leave. For most of them that would mean an immediate return to old age and/or death, so basically not an option at all.

Seyen held the Eternity Stone, and she shared its power freely with her followers. She was their queen and complete ruler, and they were her pantheon. The little humans down below thought of them as gods, and that was exactly what Seyen intended.

She'd picked up most of her pantheon in the same way she'd found Janeus. She'd been travelling, collecting power the way she knew how, and dazzling the mindless peasants. She would only go to places and times where there were peasants to be dazzled, of course.

The others were far less gullible. Generally, once you got past about 2700 AD, the spread of alter-power was so extensive that everyone knew where her power had come from, and knew that it was nothing special. Anyone could have it, if they had the guts to take it.

And then there were the Creatures who were ever-present after that time. Dangerous, powerful and supernatural; they didn't like competition. Better to stay far, far away from that time period.

But enough about that. They would all stay on Olympas, and Seyen would send off one of her trusted aides to find others. She could sense more objects of power across this time period, and she'd squeeze the power from every last one, sending perhaps Aegus or Lorcan to fetch them. Not that she trusted those two completely, but they knew that if they displeased her, she'd cut their connection to her power, and again…old age and/or death. So they would please her.

Unlike Janeus, the one she loved the most and trusted the least. He was such a smooth talker, so handsome and charming, and he had this way of looking at a woman… That was why she'd taken him on almost fifty years earlier. Even when she'd seen that he'd freshly killed his own brother over that shapeshifting 'birthright' and sensed grief but no real regret, and known that if he'd do that, then there was nothing he wouldn't do, she'd still chosen him. Perhaps she'd felt him to be a kindred spirit, but certainly she'd believed that she could continue to fascinate him the way she had in the beginning.

She'd been wrong. She knew she didn't fascinate him anymore. But he *did* know that she was the source of the power, and that was why he stayed by her side. He knew that he'd die without her, and he knew that she loved him so fiercely that she would never give him up.

And that was why he kept pushing, and pushing, and seeing how disinterested he could be, and making little comments about how he *so* wanted a child; what a shame they hadn't had one even though they'd been together so long; perhaps she was too old…? A child was the one thing her power hadn't yet brought her.

The irony was that Seyen suspected he didn't really need her. Oh, she definitely buoyed his power up considerably, but it was as if that medallion he'd swallowed many years before had been forgotten.

It was still there in his belly. She could sense it because it wasn't of her power. It was different, wrong. Not that she would let him know, of course. He might take the risk to leave her, and she couldn't have that.

He'd been seen in the company of one of the local women again. Nothing could be proven…but with him, he could take any form; look like any person. If he hadn't even bothered to shapeshift a disguise, then perhaps he was telling the truth, and he had been faithful after all. But perhaps he hadn't, and she was a thousand times a fool.

No. As long as Seyen could possibly believe good of him, she would. She wished so much that she could trust him implicitly, but she couldn't, and it twisted her up inside. And that was why Seyen hated him as much as she loved him.

But he was right about one thing. She would never let him go. All over her body she wore faint tattooed flowers, each linked to a single soul, living or dead. Those marks gave her power over the person: power and a connection that would last as long as they did.

Janeus's flower was the only one to still hold colour. It was a red rose, right over her heart.

She wouldn't let him go, and he wouldn't be able to leave her. Not really, not forever, because she'd always know where he was.

Always.

FROZEN

Mountbatten Manor, 1818 AD

George stood in the otherwise deserted library, flicking through a little-used volume on the history of Leister county. It went as far back as the Normen conquest, but had precious little useful information. Such as, for example, what happened to a certain red-haired Anne of Covington.

It seemed Dr Walker had been right when he'd said they wouldn't make history. All the easier to borrow them for time travel experiments, George supposed.

Although, he'd at least imagined he'd see Anne in someone's family tree. There were at least six Anne of Covingtons recorded, and two or three that could have been in the right time period. None seemed to fit, though.

George set the book down on the small round table nearby, almost knocking off his snifter of brandy while he did so. He'd barely had a sip so far. The drink was more for appearance than anything else. In truth, he needed a reason to be standing in the manor library at eleven at night, away from the rest of the party who were still dancing in the small ballroom.

Tor his mother, reading was *not* an excuse to leave ladies unaccompanied in a ballroom, but she hadn't found him yet, and he couldn't bear another inquisition about his imaginary wife that he was certain to get if he did appear to socialise.

"Use it quickly, use it seldom," he muttered to himself.

It was a phrase he'd memorized after that conversation with

Anne. And they had: they'd used the Stone quickly to get here, had used it only to create pathways between each of their times, and then had set it aside.

Or Anne had, rather. George had pretended he was being a gentleman by allowing her to hold it, but in truth he'd not trusted himself not to misuse it.

Not really interested in any of the books now that he couldn't find his friend, George wandered over to the nearby world globe that seemed to exist in every decent library that he knew of. He found Angland near the middle-top as always, then spun the globe around until he found a tiny group of islands at the bottom of the southern hemisphere, as far from Angland as could be. The Southern Isles was a rather literal name, but had an odd grace to it-

A shift in the atmosphere made the hairs lift on the back of George's neck, and he realised he was no longer alone.

He slowly turned around.

I wish George was here, Ash had thought in one moment of terror, and the world around her changed.

Suddenly she wasn't lying in a flipped-over car, in the dark, with something not quite human looming in through her window. Now she was lying on her side, on carpet in a darkened room, with a definitely-human shape just in front of her, their back filling her vision.

She knew those broad shoulders, those tan trousers, and that wavy blond hair.

George!

Ash tried to call out but her mouth wasn't working. She tried to move from the cramped, half-sitting/lying pose, but it was as if she'd been set in glue – she couldn't move a muscle.

For Deias's sake, he was still playing with that silly globe, humming away to himself as he spun it. Then suddenly he stiffened, and slowly turned to look at her.

He stared for a long time without blinking, then blinked rapidly several times in quick succession. Ash stared back. She still couldn't move, and if this wasn't so shocking and so awkward, she might even find it funny.

"Erm…Ashlea, why are you lying on my carpet?!"

She still couldn't speak a word. All she could do was breathe and blink, and even that was a struggle.

"Ashlea?" George finally seemed to realise something was wrong, quickly moving to help her get up. He propped her into a sitting position against the base of a couch, but the moment he let go, she fell sideways again. "By Jupiter, you're a mess. Is that blood on your head?"

Ash couldn't answer, and George grew understandably agitated. *She* was agitated. "Why won't you answer me, Ashlea?"

Because she felt like she was a statue. At first she'd thought it was simply shock, but shock didn't hit as hard as this, did it?

Help, she thought. *Help!* She tried to show her panic through her eyes, but still couldn't open her mouth.

Suddenly his gaze fixed on something below her chin. "What's this, then?"

She felt his hands gentle against her skin, and then he was lifting something over her head, something like a necklace, and suddenly she could move again, every last inch of her.

She was so relieved she almost cried. "Oh Deias. Oh, Deias."

"No, just George, although I can understand the mistake," he quipped, and even through her distress Ash laughed.

"What in Hades just happened?"

"If you don't know, then I hardly do either," he replied frankly. "I'm very pleased to see you, of course, but this isn't quite what we recommended, is it?"

Ash just stared at him, feeling confused and shaky and still somehow happy. She hadn't meant to come here, but she couldn't be sorry. "What did you recommend?"

"Oh, perhaps a nice gown, hair up in curls, arriving with a suitcase from the gateway at the edge of the estate…just like in the letter."

Instead he got muddy sweats and gumboots, an old windbreaker, and a bloodied forehead. Ash couldn't even focus on what he'd said about some letter.

She thought about the last two minutes of her experience, and then she did cry, just a little. "George, I was just in a car crash."

It took some time to straighten out what had happened. Once they got past the whole issue of why Ash even had the Stone – because that upset George quite a lot as it meant Anne *didn't* have it – he kept saying that they'd written her a letter, and wondering why she hadn't got it.

Then when Ash asked what the letter said, he'd flushed a little and mumbled something about gateways. She had also told him about the weird owl-like face in her window, and they'd come to a few conclusions.

"It's a good thing you used the Eternity Stone when you did," George said staunchly. "It's evident that there's someone in your time who knows how to sense such things, as Amaranthus warned. That must be why we must use the Stone seldom. You found it in the ruins of Renwick Castle, you say?"

"You've been there," she replied. She wasn't crying anymore, although she still had the gash on her temple. George had given her his handkerchief to hold against it. It hurt, but it was a side issue. She'd time travelled again – to *1818*. "There's not much left at all. But yes, it was on site that I found it."

"Hmm." George studied the cord he'd pulled off Ash's neck. It was a loop about twice the size of a dinner plate, like a very fine yellow plait with the two ends perfectly connected together. It didn't look like much, but she was certain it had prevented her moving. He hooked it over one hand, wiggling his fingers. "It seems harmless. Are you so certain it wasn't just fear holding you in place?"

"I was shocked more than scared," Ash retorted, irritated. "And I literally could not move. But it was over my head, not my hand."

"Hmm."

She sighed, looking away to study the room. It was as predictably old-fashioned and Anglish as George himself, and even had a fire burning low off to one side. She felt as out of place as a vegan at a steakhouse. "Whatever it was, I'm sure that I can't stay here like this. If you didn't fit when you first arrived in my time, I'd be even worse off. I'd probably be run out of the house as some kind of tramp. I'll need to go back home, at least to get a change of clothes."

It could be fun here, right? Once she was properly dressed, it'd be like walking on set for one of those old movies, except that everyone had to always act in character.

But from George there was a strangled noise, and then a thump as he fell sideways, frozen in place with his arms by his sides.

"George!" Finally Ash got the cord off from over his head – it had tightened a little, but not so you'd notice – and he managed to sit up. "Just had to test it out yourself, did you?"

"At least we now know it *was* the cord," he said darkly, rubbing at his neck. "Hades, it *was* like being frozen."

"Told you so." And yes, that was just a little smug.

He gave her a narrow-eyed glare as he rubbed his unmarked neck, but there was no anger in it. "We know what this means, though. Someone *did* attack you, perhaps intending to steal the Eternity Stone. It's clear that you mustn't go back yet. No doubt they'll be waiting for you on the other side, and will be attracted once more to the Stone's use."

It made sense, but the idea made Ash nervous. 'They'. This mysterious 'someone', who might have made her crash her car…

"Who do you think it is?"

George shrugged. "Dr Walker proposed that the Nobles might have been returned to their own times once the Queen's power had gone. Who's to say that one didn't live in your time and felt the use of power?"

"Oh, Deias," Ash groaned again. She quite liked the idea of a time-travel holiday, but not the kind where you couldn't go home for fear of power-stealing royal wannabees…again. Most people went through their whole lives without having to dodge death threats, but Ash had managed to turn several people homicidal before she'd even turned twenty. It was quite an achievement.

And then there was her car, all by itself at the side of the road with her house keys inside. But hey, at least her insurance was up to date. "Please don't tell me I'm going to lose my job for not showing up."

"Hopefully not. But we have a more immediate problem than whether you can go home or not." And now George looked strangely guilty.

"What might that be?" she asked suspiciously.

There was a long pause, long enough that her suspicion jumped to epic levels.

"It's a funny story, really," he said in a too-hearty voice. "You recall I mentioned my former fiancée Miss Clarissa Margate?"

"Yes…" Ash remembered that story. She was the one who'd left him once the money dried up. And she even had an unlikeable name – 'Clarissa' was for poncey Anglish girls who attended private schools, or perhaps for expensive, fluffy cats with squashed faces.

"Well, she came to visit on the invitation of my family, who I'm afraid didn't quite realise the full extent of the…happenings between us. I was foolish enough to agree to speak with her alone, and she was sly enough to arrange for her father to burst in on us while we were embracing."

"George, you didn't!" Ash gasped in horror and more than a

little disappointment. "I thought you didn't like her!"

"But I don't! We were simply talking. She was making apologies which I, quite frankly, had no desire to hear, and she leapt on me at the last moment. Simply leapt on me, Ashlea, right in time for her father to open the door along with several others, making it appear that I'd compromised her, when in truth I had simply moved too slowly to push her away."

"What a little tart," Ash muttered, wondering grumpily if he'd actually been as disgusted as he made out. By the sound of things this girl was quite pretty, or he'd never have been interested in the first place. "So what does this have to do with me?"

George smiled awkwardly. "And there lies the rub. You see, my only way to escape marriage to her was to claim I was already committed. So I'm dreadfully sorry, but I need you to pretend to be my wife."

All the thoughts of isn't-this-exciting and I'm-actually-in-a-Jean-Austen-novel fell out of Ash's head, and her jaw dropped. "You're joking, right?"

He shook his head. "I'm afraid I'm quite serious. Deadly serious, in fact. You see-"

Just then there was a tap on the closed door, and it opened to reveal an older woman in a plain long-sleeved dress with a white apron over top. She was holding a tray of what might have been tea and scones (Lord, George had a fixation on those things!) and her eyes barely widened to see Ash sitting in her full gardener's glory on the fine couch.

But the servant barely skipped a beat, moving inside to place the tray on the nearby table. "I didn't know you had visitors, sir. Would you like a second cup?"

"Er…yes, Adams. And do bring my-" and George's voice almost squeaked, "…my *wife* a dinner tray, if there's anything left. She's not yet eaten."

There it was. George had gone and said it, and it was out there. Adams' eyes almost bugged, although she was well practiced enough to quickly control herself. The whole household had been waiting with bated breath for 'Mrs Seymour' to arrive, and here she was. Sort of.

"Of course, sir. Shall I inform your mother of the arrival? Retrieve any… baggage?"

"Neither of those will be necessary," he answered quickly. "But do see that a room is made up, and a bath."

The woman curtseyed, and the moment she left the room Ashlea turned on him, eyes wide in horror. "What on earth are you thinking? You can't seriously mean for us to go through with this!"

"I'm not asking for you to stay here for thirty years and bear my children," he pleaded desperately. "I just need one day, Ashlea. One day to get all this sorted, and so that I don't end up married to a gold-digger or run out of the county as the worst sort of scoundrel. I've only just made things up with my family," excepting the fact he'd just alienated both his brother and brother's wife earlier this evening, "and I can't bear for this to go bad again so quickly, not when I've only just got home."

"But look at me," she said in a low voice. "They *can't* see me like this, George. I'm a mess, even for my own time. And even if I wasn't, how I am supposed to pull off being your wife even for a day? The only things I know from this time period are from watching old films and…well, *you*."

"Be shy," he suggested. "Very, very shy."

"Keep my mouth shut, you mean?!"

"It probably wouldn't hurt."

Ashlea looked as though she was deciding whether to be offended, and fortunately settled on the side of depressed humour. "So what if I did go along with this mysterious plan of yours, just for one day. I pretend to be your very shy wife-"

"From the Colonies," George cut in. "I hadn't stated which,

but perhaps Amyrica?"

"I won't lie more than I have to," she said staunchly. "So I'll be your shy, Colonial wife for a day, and I'll do my best not to humiliate you or myself. But I can't do it like this. I've got no clothes. Let me go home and hire something-"

"With some villain waiting for you in your own time, waiting for the Eternity Stone to be used so that they might steal it?" he retorted. "I think not, Ashlea. We'll borrow something." He looked at her critically. She wasn't plump, but she was tall and didn't have the carefully corseted figure that would be required to wear most garments here. For women, that was. "Not from my mother. Nor from my sister-in-law…"

"I can't borrow clothes from here," she said again, looking almost panicked. "I just can't. They won't fit, either, since I've never worn a corset in my life. You know that. I'll just use the Eternity Stone-"

"Not yet!"

"Fine, the remnant gateways then!" Ashlea snapped back. "Whatever those are. No one really knows I'm here yet, anyway. I've got time."

"I hate to disappoint you," George corrected. "But everyone will know within the hour. One of the downfalls of having servants, unfortunately. As for the gateways… Ashlea, they are essentially passages through time that never change size. The one out on the border of the estate is always a hundred and ninety-five years before your time, and leads to your own back garden in *your* time. This one here in the library – well, I presume it must go back to whichever road you just came from. What date is it back home for you?"

"June 13, 2013."

"Oh. That's the same time difference, then. It's been four weeks for you?"

"About."

That was lucky. He said slowly, "Perhaps we might be able to reach the gateway at the edge of the estate tonight. We could fetch you something wearable, perhaps an item or two, and even bring your car back to your house, then come back here as soon as possible. Anne might still come through, you know, and we must be here for her."

It was a good plan. In fact, Ashlea looked as though she'd actually agree, except for one thing. As predicted, Adams had told someone…who'd told someone, who'd told his mother.

"Who would have thought there'd be clothing to fit *me*?" Ashlea commented later that evening when they were finally alone in his room.

She was wearing an ancient nightgown that covered her from ankles to wrists to high neckline, and shouldn't have at all been appealing. It somehow was, though; perhaps because it was a nightgown and she was in his bedroom. There hadn't been a spare room even in the servants' quarters, and under the circumstances they hadn't tried to push for one.

George deliberately looked away, studying the mirror on the far wall. But that just showed another view of Ashlea, and so he studied his feet instead. "Don't sound so surprised. You're hardly a colossus, no matter what Anne might have said at times. Simply tall and well-built."

"Why thank you, George. I'm flattered." And she sounded like she meant it. "And your mother was far nicer than I expected her to be."

It was a backhanded compliment, but true. "The fact that you cried probably helped with that. I've never seen you cry like that before."

Ashlea reddened. "I wasn't faking. I was just really embarrassed, and it's been a big day what with car crashes and time travelling and so on."

Lucky. Now they knew that Lady Eleanor had a soft side: soft enough to overlook any confusion over the exact circumstances of

Ashlea's 'carriage accident' and why she had no clothing whatso-ever. *And* why she was dressed as a male in the first place, and a poor male at that.

George's mother had also made a point of smuggling 'Mrs Seymour' up to George's room, promising that she could be intro-duced to everyone in the morning. Ashlea had barely even spoken a word.

"And the good news is that as they think you're a clueless Colonial, they'll overlook any number of social gaffes," he said thoughtfully.

"Gee, thanks!"

"What did I say?"

Renwick Castle, 1556 AD

"I'm sorry," Anne told the sleeping figure on the bed beside her. Elspeth lay as still as the dead under one thin blanket, her dark hair spread over the pillow, and her too-thin cheeks flushed red with fever. 'Twas not right that someone should grow thin so very fast – it had only been two days. "I haven't found the Stone, and so I must leave you for a while to find some medicine that will truly aid your healing."

She'd decided to use the gateway back to Ash's time, find some kind of antee-bottik that would help her poor sister, and then be back within the hour. Mayhap two, if needed.

"Privy," Elspeth groaned.

Anne dipped a cloth into the bowl of water she held on her lap and dabbed it over the poor girl's forehead again. "You've already been to the privy, dear." Poor thing, she was delirious. Kept saying 'privy' and 'garderobe' over and over, when clearly there was nothing left to expel.

"Privy," Elspeth said again. "My sins."

Forsooth, she *still* moaned about that? Anne let out a heavy sigh, checked the leg wound one more time as though 'twould have miraculously healed in the last five minutes (it hadn't), and then kissed her sister on the forehead. Ugh, wet. "Not your sins," she countered yet again. "I shall return anon. If anyone should ask, tell them I'm getting herbs."

But no one would ask, because no one wanted to risk getting the sweating sickness – no matter how many times Anne had insisted 'twas a fever from infection only.

Pulling on a plain brown hooded cloak she'd borrowed from Elspeth, Anne quickly headed out of the castle grounds. She'd almost made it through the main gateway when one of Edgar's knights spotted her.

"Milady, where are you going?"

"To fetch herbs for my sister's sickbed," she replied, steeling her face in the same way she had ever since she was a child, and realised that acknowledging a bastard sibling meant some kind of censure.

This knight's expression barely flickered, and she remembered that he wasn't unkind. A younger man with a round face and a prickle of new beard on his chin; he looked at her quizzically. "Is not the herb garden at the back of the castle?"

Hades, he was right. "I need another sort of herb," she improvised. "One I hope to find *this* way."

"What kind of herb?" he persisted. "Mayhap one of the cottagers has it already."

"Er...horehound."

The knight's brow furrowed in confusion. "Is that not for head colds?"

Anne coughed awkwardly. "Um. Sometimes. But I cannot tarry, sir. The longer I linger here, the longer my sister is alone."

"Yes, milady." He paused. "Do you not need a basket, milady?"

Saints' bones, he was dedicated! And now she'd need to

actually bring some herbs back with her. "I have deep pockets. Good morrow."

"Good morrow," he called after her, and she quickly sped away before anyone else noticed she was leaving and tried to be helpful.

Heavens above, what had she and George been thinking, making the gateways so far from the castle? If anything they should have made them in a back room in the castle so that she might have come and gone without a soul seeing her.

This way, she may as well have announced to the world that she was sneaking off, and the comment Maura had made regarding meeting 'men' in the woods wouldn't help that at all.

In truth there had been just one man. She and George had used the Stone together to reach his home in 1818, in a leafy place that reminded her rather of the woods around Renwick castle.

They'd ensured they'd come to the right location, and then went *back* to the place they'd arrived in, and travelled to Anne's own time of 1556, arriving just in these very woods…in the place where she'd hidden from Maura so long ago. She'd thought they'd been unseen, but clearly she'd been wrong.

They'd practised using the two new gateways once or twice between 1818, 1556 and 2013; and then once they were convinced that they worked, had made an agreement. As planned, they would allow four weeks to each settle back into their own times and make whatever arrangements were required.

By that time Ash should have arrived, as per the letter they'd left for her, and they would make new arrangements. Anne was almost certain that Elspeth would wish to come to the twenty-first, at least to see what 'twas like, but she hadn't accounted for unexpected illness…or the loss of the Eternity Stone.

See, that had been the last step of the plan. After twenty-eight days, had Ash not arrived in Anne's time via George's time, Anne would use the Stone along with Elspeth and create a new gateway back to Ash's garden, straight from 1556. Then there'd be three gateways, and they could *all* travel as much as they liked, even Bethie.

As it stood now, Anne was following the second-best option. She reached the area where they'd created the gateways and closed her eyes, trying to recall how she'd found it last time. And there it was in the darkness behind her eyelids, like a glowing gold-red line in the air. She walked towards it, eyes still closed; then took a deep breath and stepped through, feeling the faint buzz of the gateway surround her.

Mayhap thirty minutes later Anne stepped back through to 1556, pockets somewhat fuller. She'd spent all of thirty seconds in 1818, just enough to find the second gateway and move on.

She'd appeared in Ash's garden (which in hindsight also wasn't the wisest choice; they ought to have made the gateway in the house) and quickly found the key hidden as ever in the empty flowerpot by the back door.

The house had been empty, and she'd helped herself to a pile of items from Ash's medicine drawer; anything which might help Elspeth heal. That wonderful antee- oh, *antibiotics*, the odd text appeared to be saying. Those, anyway, some kind of cream in a tube and some tablets which Ash had never used, as well as a host of bandages and four more packets of painkilling tablets.

Then, fearful lest she overdose Elspeth as Ash had warned was possible, Anne put half the painkillers back and scribbled a quick note for Ash should she notice the lack. After all, she could always come back for more...

Although at this point, Elspeth couldn't come with her, and that rather defeated the whole point of Anne returning home at all.

Back in the woods of 1556, Anne looked in vain for something resembling horehound, realising too late that she'd never actually seen the herb before. She grabbed a few handfuls of a plant that smelled like mint (so not horehound, then) but would at least support her tale that she'd gone out searching for herbs.

By some miracle she made it back to the castle without being questioned, and then she arrived back in the small, smoky room at last.

"I'm here," she sang. "Are you alright?"

"Sorry," Elspeth mumbled. "My fault."

She was like a banging drum, making the same sound over and over. Anne ignored her nonsense, applying the antee-*antibiotic* cream to the wound, then covering it with those lovely clean bandages. Such a waste of their thin paper wrapping, though; she had to shred it and hide it in the mattress.

"Urgh."

"Yes, I know the medicine tastes horrid all ground up like this," Anne said gently, "but 'twill make you well." Hopefully.

"Med'cin?"

Anne realised with a start that medicine was a twenty-first century word. "Er…physick, I meant."

Elspeth didn't take that in, falling back on the bed and closing her eyes. Time, Anne told herself. They needed time for the antee-…whatevers to work.

"Lady Anne." 'Twas Blanche, the maiden sister of Anne's first husband and unfortunately, still present and in one piece in Renwick castle. She stood outside the bedroom door, her lined face twisted in its perpetual sneer of disapproval. Odd to think she was but four and thirty, for that lemon-sucking mouth made her seem a decade older.

"Yes, Blanche?"

"The fourth earl requires your presence."

Truly? That was a first. "Did he say what he-" Oh bother, she'd already gone.

Anne sighed. Whatever Edgar had to say, she ought to find out. "Ten minutes," she promised the sleeping Elspeth. "I'll return anon."

Cubana, 1826 AD

The twins were beautiful. A boy and a girl, only three months old, and as golden-haired as Seyen's most common 'costume', as Janeus thought of her illusions.

She finally had her children. It was a shame she'd had to kill someone else to get them.

She had named the girl Jenessa after him, although they were already calling her Jenni, and the boy Troilus after her own father, who was either long dead, or three thousand years pre-birth, depending on how you looked at it.

The girl being his namesake could also be good or bad, depending on how he looked at it. It might be that Seyen was honouring him as her consort and the children's father, or it might be in memory of him… As in, she was going to have him executed.

She was very, very angry.

His last view of the twins was of them being held up in front of Seyen, looking very small and helpless, and him wondering how they could be his, although he knew they were. There was no doubt, not in this case.

That was unusual. The power of Seyen's pantheon must have damaged their fertility, since in all the time they'd been here on Olympas – easily three hundred years – there'd been only half a dozen children born, and all to outsiders, normals. All of those children who had shown potential had been brought into the fold, of course.

Not like Janeus. He'd been kicked out…again. He'd never seen Seyen as angry as this. The other times he'd been suspected of messing around with women, she couldn't prove it, or a couple of times the women had 'disappeared'. Bad luck for them.

He hadn't felt guilty, exactly, but he'd got sneakier, and he'd thought that the time with Aleda had been very sneaky indeed.

It had seemed like it was worth it, too. The Esparten princess was very beautiful, and never questioned that she was blessed by being visited by the king of gods, as he was styling himself then. He'd had the affair then left, not looking back.

That was until the silly girl made a sacrifice, thanking the wonderful king of the gods for gifting her with heavenly children (had she really thought that? Ha!) and of course Seyen had heard about it. The 'queen of the gods' did not allow a foolish female to claim what she herself couldn't have. The results were no surprise, then. Poor, silly Aleda.

Except for Seyen's anger at him. Now that was a surprise – this time he'd really thought she was going to kill him. And he knew that when she'd sent him away and told him to never come back, she'd meant it, and he'd taken it seriously. That's why he was sitting quietly on a beach in nineteenth-century Cubana, pretending to be a humble fisherman but really just relaxing. Getting a tan, flirting with the ladies…

Funnily enough, his power hadn't been cut off. Was it even hers at all? And what would happen to those twins?

He wished he cared more, but all he could think of was his own fear of Seyen, his relief at being away from her…and freedom.

Mountbatten Manor, 1818 AD

"What concerns me," George said thoughtfully, "is the fact that you found the Eternity Stone at all. It makes me wonder if something happened to Anne so that she never came through as planned."

"One more day, you said," Ash pointed out. He'd explained the whole 'plan' to her, and while it mostly made sense, she was still irritated that she'd spent four weeks thinking herself abandoned. The infamous letter must have blown off the desk in that wind gust when she was bringing in the groceries. "Maybe she would have used the gates. Maybe she's already travelled with her sister."

"Perhaps," he agreed half-heartedly.

But they'd still made an agreement together. In the morning he'd ride out to the gateway first thing, and if Anne wasn't there, they'd make plans to go find her and see what happened.

Deias, it was so exciting and nerve-wracking. She was actually time-travelling on purpose! Well, kind of.

"I don't have any weapons," Ash realised aloud. "Not even my pepper spray."

George grimaced. "I could do without seeing that stuff ever again."

"Sorry." She'd apologised repeatedly for their first meeting, where they'd both just been snatched away from their own times and hadn't yet realised it. They'd met for the first time in the woods, had argued, and she'd felt threatened enough to pepper spray him right in the eyes. She didn't *think* he was holding a grudge. "Well, at least we have that binding cord thing."

"Could do without that as well," he said, but seemed cheered by it. "And what about that book you brought, Ashlea? What's in that?"

She'd almost forgotten about Anne's little photo album with all of its unexpected extras. It had hit her in the head when she'd crashed, and had somehow managed to travel along with her. It might have been what had bloodied her temple, actually.

She showed him the pages that she'd noticed, skipping past the odd little snippets of magazines and books that made no sense, and finished with, "I ended up looking at the first page last. See, here's Amaranthus wishing me happy birthday. And so I knew that he was still involved somehow."

"But it's August," George pointed out. "Your birthday is in June, isn't it?"

"June 13 is the date back home." Ash realised with some dismay that she'd managed to miss part of her birthday, then dismissed the thought. Time travel was a decent birthday present, especially when she hadn't made plans for anything more than takeaways and a movie. "Well done, you remembered the date."

He seemed startled. "Of course I did. We celebrated Anne's birthday in your odd little way, and would have yours and mine also had the Stone not returned to us."

By 'odd little way' he'd meant a cupcake with seventeen candles sticking out of it 'til it looked like a hedgehog, and yes, takeaways and a movie.

"It's funny, isn't it," Ash mused. "We celebrated Anne's birthday because it was January in my time, and yet she comes back to 1556 and it would be like no time had passed. She'll feel like she turned seventeen twice."

George let out a heavy sigh. "Deias, time travel is weird."

It was such a twenty-first century thing to say that Ash laughed. "I've had some influence on you after all, George." Either her, or all the Amyrican sitcoms he had watched during the day.

"Hmm." He smiled just a little, that nice smile that made him look so very likeable…and more than a little handsome. "I do believe I would have enjoyed your time far more if I'd known that it would be a temporary change, even accounting for all the differences. Perhaps you might have the same attitude to your time here?"

"It's only for a weekend, so I should consider it a holiday?" Ash smiled back, putting on her best upper-class Anglish accent. Thanks to her inbuilt translator, it worked rather well. "I do believe I could do that."

"Hades, don't talk like that! On second thoughts, do talk like that, but whatever you do, don't slip up."

"I shall endeavour not to," she agreed in the same accent, and he grimaced again. "That bad?"

"No, excellent, actually. But you sound rather like my mother…or Clarissa."

"Really?" Ash had heard snippets about the infamous gold digger over the last couple of months, and was curious to meet the girl who'd broken George's heart. "I can't believe that little witch tried to actually trap you into a marriage. What could she have been thinking?"

"It's a sort of sport here. Bachelor-catching."

"But if you'd given in, then you'd always know that she had forced you into it. You'd always have that resentment against her! How could she want to enter a marriage like that?" She barely paused, then rattled on, "Besides, I didn't think you'd be such a good bet. Didn't you say you were the black sheep of the family, disowned or something?"

"Oh, stop with the flattery," George muttered sarcastically. "And I was, yes. But I've been welcomed back into the fold, allowance reinstated and everything. Unless Edward decides to punish me by tossing me out again, of course."

"Why would he do that?" Ash asked curiously, but George only looked awkward and didn't answer. "Oh, well. We should get some sleep. I don't know about you, but I'm wasted."

"I'll make up the couch."

Ash paused, looking over the generously sized bed, then at the tiny, awkward little embroidered couch with its spindly legs. It wasn't exactly a fold-out comfort item. "You don't need to do that. Let's just share the bed."

"Ashlea, I'm not certain that's a wise idea-"

"Sounds a darn sight wiser than some servant walking in and finding you on the couch. Wouldn't do well for our story, would it? Besides, I promise not to jump on you in the night."

It had been meant as a joke, but George just got this odd look on his face. He gave in, though, and went into his side room to get into his PJs – which looked rather like her nightgown. Ash had seen him in nightwear a hundred times when they'd shared the house, so she kept her mouth shut and just leafed through Anne's little book while she waited.

The Eternity Stone sat in the narrow draw of her side table, hidden from sight but within reach. In fact, it all seemed nice and normal until George finally got into the other side of the bed, very distinctly not looking at her as he settled in. In fact, he'd been doing that ever since they'd reached the bedroom.

But then it *was* awkward, wasn't it? Maybe it would have been less so if he'd been old or ugly, or if she hadn't liked him quite so much.

"Just like an old married couple," Ash quipped to cover her own unease, "except this is the first time we've slept together."

"Deias damn it, Ashlea!" he shouted, so suddenly that she actually dropped the book on the covers. "You mustn't say things like that!"

"I was just trying to lighten the atmosphere," she said defensively. "I mean, it's not like we're attracted to each other-"

"Who said we're not- I mean, *I'm* not?"

There was an awkward pause as she tried to take in what that meant. "But we're not each other's type." She meant *she* wasn't *his* type. She'd discovered long ago that she had a soft spot for well-spoken Anglishmen, not that she'd let him know it.

"Maybe my type has changed," George said quietly. His cheeks were red and he was frowning ferociously, but he was finally looking at her. "Did you not notice, Ashlea, in all that time we lived together, that I was…interested?"

"Only that you seemed scandalised by every other item of clothing I wore." And she was genuinely shocked, but a warm feeling of pleasure was turning her cheeks pink too.

He *liked* her.

"Well, they were generally quite scandalous." After a moment George admitted, "Although not much in comparison to daytime tee-vee, was it?"

Ash was still shocked that he'd liked *that*, too. "I've always thought you were good-looking," she said finally. She'd admitted that to herself ever since the first few days. "But we seemed so different that there was no point in even trying for anything. It seemed like you thought…*think* that I'm beneath you."

There was another thoughtful silence. "Well, perhaps I've changed in that way, too. I do very much admire you, Ashlea, although I don't agree with everything you do."

She felt her cheeks turn from warm to hot. She looked down at her hands, twisted on the covers and wearing one of George's rings. He'd given it to her earlier to fit with their story, and it hung a little loose on her finger. "This isn't a marriage proposal, is it?"

He shook his head. "You're right. We are too different – but I don't want to be treated like I'm a eunuch. It's not fair."

"Fair enough. And I am sorry."

"Forgiven."

They turned out the light, and Ash resolutely tried to sleep, pushing aside all the swirling thoughts of what *he'd* just said, on top of everything else that had happened today.

But then George asked, very quietly, "What if it had been a proposal? What would you have said?"

She stared at the dark ceiling. "I don't know."

MUSHROOMS AND DOPPELGÄNGERS

When Ash awoke the next morning, she had a moment of complete disorientation. The weak morning sun was sneaking in through a gap in the curtains, and she had no idea where she was.

Funny wallpaper, strange bed, antique furniture, boy in an old-fashioned outfit about to head out the door…

Then it all made sense, and she almost had to close her eyes again in shock. That was right; she'd time-travelled again.

Yay!

"Ashlea, you're awake," George whispered. "It's only six-thirty, and I thought you might want to sleep longer. I'm going to ride out to the gateway at the edge of the estate to see if Anne has come through yet."

Oh, she *was* tired. "I'll sleep longer," she agreed muzzily, deciding she could be more excited later. "When will breakfast be?"

"Any time from eight or so. I shouldn't be long."

Presumably he left then, but she'd fallen asleep again and when she woke the room was quite bright. Someone was opening her curtains – a teenage girl in a long dress, white smock and a funny little hat.

"Good morning, missus," the girl said brightly. "I'm Constance. I'll be your maid while you're here, unless you've got another one coming?"

The last was said a bit desperately, and Ash remembered something she'd read once, that the position of lady's maid was considered better than just a general maid. Except Ash wasn't a lady, and she didn't have a thing to wear…

"Uh…no one else is coming," Ash mumbled, not comfortable with strangers in her bedroom when she'd just woken up. See, *this* was why you didn't have servants – no privacy.

"I've brought a selection of clothing from Lady Eleanor," the girl continued. "To see if anything fits- suits you, missus."

George's mother had been a fair bit shorter than Ash, with grey-streaked brown hair tied on top of her head, and a tiny waist that Ash *knew* wasn't natural. Nature had never gifted a fifty-year-old woman with a wasp waist, and Ash sure didn't have one even though she was only twenty. "The nightgown fit because it's loose," she said carefully. "Anything else-"

"These used to belong to her grandmother who passed away five years ago," Constance said brightly. "She was a larger lady herself. Almost as tall as you, missus. Would you like to see?"

And that was how Ash ended up wearing the clothing of a three-hundred-year-old dead woman. It wasn't too bad, actually; she had a choice of either gray or light purple, both dresses having long sleeves and high, slightly frilled necklines. It wasn't what Ash had seen on TV (or on the often-viewed Pride and Precipitation DVD) but it wasn't ugly.

The only downside was the underwear. Ash had wanted to wear her own, but quite simply, the gowns wouldn't fit without the corset.

Yes, George's great-grandmother had worn a corset, right to her death, apparently – or 'stays' as Constance called them. As in, 'stay there, you can't move'.

First Ash had to wear a long white nighty thing called a chemise, and then a hellish contraption stiffened with whalebone that squished her from her armpits through to her hip-bones. It shoved her bosom into her collarbone and meant that breathing deeply became a luxury.

"There you go," Constance said with satisfaction once the lavender dress was finally buttoned into place. "No more men's clothing for you, missus. You're safe now."

Ash shot her a startled glance. "Sorry?"

The maid seemed clueless. "I don't mean to be impertinent, but they say you was in dreadful condition when Mr Seymour rescued you last night. Covered in blood and dirt, wearing *trousers*… Was the attack so very dreadful?"

"Attack…?"

"You don't need to talk about it if you don't want to," Constance said quickly, although Ash sensed she was a little miffed at the prospect. "I was just saying that you're safe now. It's a good family, this one."

Ash finally understood what the girl meant, although clearly it had all been blown out of proportion. She was about to say that there hadn't been an attack, but realised that there actually had been. Somewhere – probably in George's pocket – was that binding cord as proof.

She touched the little cut on her forehead tentatively. It still ached, although it wasn't nearly as bad as she first recalled.

"I'm sure I'm safe," she said slowly, trying to remember to keep her well-bred accent in place. It was hard when the maid spoke in a distinctly more casual way, and Ash was tempted to mimic her. "In truth I don't recall much of last night. Just darkness…and the accident…and then Geo- Mr Seymour."

There, she hadn't even told a lie.

The maid seemed happy enough with that, and she chattered cheerfully while she fixed Ash's hair into a loose twist on the back of her head. Ash allowed it, knowing it would be bad-mannered to go down with hair loose around her shoulders.

Deias, history was weird.

The house seemed different in daylight. It was bigger, definitely fussier, and it was certain that Regency Angland had no concept of minimalism. The room she'd shared with George was at the top of two flights of polished wooden stairs, and while the wallpaper was ornately detailed, the further downstairs you got, the more packed-full of knickknacks the rooms became.

They tended to have high ceilings, and the walls were full of paintings all the way up: of fruit or people in old-fashioned clothing, with just a single landscape in the whole place. Ash vaguely recalled that landscapes as art didn't come into fashion until several decades after this time period.

And no shiny vinyl furniture here either. Everything was carved wood, sometimes gilded, or tapestried until there wasn't an inch of empty space. Even the floors were covered, and she couldn't decide if it was beautiful or overwhelming.

Ash was staring into a medium-sized room with a piano in one corner when she heard a gentle cough from behind her. It was a man wearing a slightly plainer version of what George had worn, with the colours in muted dark grey, but with that posture and deadpan expression he could only have been the butler. "May I assist you, madam?"

Oh Deias, George had a *butler*. Ash was struck again by the difference between their living situations and forced a smile. No wonder he'd had trouble settling into her little two-bedroom cottage. "I'm looking for the breakfast room, please."

"Follow me, madam."

There were already others eating when she finally arrived in what had to be the dining room. The walls were light yellow, not that you'd notice underneath the myriad paintings, and people were taking food from a buffet sideboard then sitting to eat at the long table. Maybe about six or seven so far, and all seeming like they were in fancy dress with their old-fashioned clothing and hairstyles. They barely looked up as she approached.

Phew. Ash took a deep breath to help her relax – which turned into a shallow one because of the stupid corset – and told herself that she could do this. But the initial thought that she'd been unnoticed disappeared when one person turned to face her…then everyone did.

There was a silence, then a middle-aged woman in a dark blue long-sleeved dress stood, a pleasantly curious expression on her face. Reluctantly the two men in the room followed suit. "We have not been introduced, but might I venture to guess that you are Mrs George Seymour?"

Right in that moment Ash resolved to do everything she could to speak the truth while still maintaining their story. "Call me Ashlea," she said instead. "Are you one of Lady Eleanor's friends?"

"Isn't that a man's name?" someone muttered off to the side, and the lady in blue tittered.

"My, you Colonials *are* refreshingly forward! I am Mrs Coutts, and I am indeed a dear friend of Lady Eleanor's. It appears that all the family has already breakfasted or is still abed, so it falls to me to make introductions. This is Mr Farnsworth," and here an older gentleman with a sizeable moustache nodded to her; "Mrs Parsenne, Miss Parsenne and Miss Elizabeth Parsenne," and here was a thin-faced older woman, along with two young girls dressed in white who had to be her daughters; "Lord Ellesley, Baron Flitwick," a ginger-haired young man of about twenty-five, who studied her with cool politeness; "and…oh, where is Mrs Woolsten?"

"Disappeared as soon as she arrived," one of the Miss Parsennes said. "No doubt she'll be hiding away in that side parlour again."

"Such a shame," Mrs Parsenne murmured. "I do believe you would have liked her, Mrs Seymour."

Maybe that was true, but Ash decided within a few minutes that she didn't particularly like any of the others here. No one was overtly rude (not counting their refusal to use her first name, an apparent faux-pas on her part), but most completely ignored her.

A couple asked questions that were gently worded, but

showed clearly that they were trying to work out her place in the world, and they didn't think much of her even if she *had* married the Honourable Mr Seymour. Well, pretended to marry him, anyway.

"A Hamiltyn, were you?" Mr Farnsworth asked, a touch too loudly considering he was sitting right next to her. "Any relation to the Lords of Mar?"

"No, sir." Because she was an O'Reilly, and not related to the Lords of anything.

Ash smiled at him, then turned back to her heart-attack on a plate. It was no wonder the Anglish had a reputation for being uptight when they didn't seem to have a single morsel of fibre on the breakfast table.

There was what looked like coddled eggs, something that was probably once fish but now resembled soggy boot leather, ham, sweet rolls and jam (thank goodness) and was that *steak* for breakfast? It explained why George hadn't been happy with a bowl of cereal and a cup of coffee in the morning.

Mr Farnsworth seemed to accept that answer, but a moment later she felt a hand squeeze her knee through that lavender gown. She stifled a gasp, then dug her fingernails into the hand until he was the one squeaking.

Now *that* wasn't good manners, sir! She wondered how long she'd have to sit here before she could escape.

But Ash played the part of the shy Colonial bride anyway, answering each question simply and with a bit of fudging as required. She thought she'd survived the inquisition intact until she heard the redhead (Lord Baron something or other) murmur in Frencine to one of the girls beside him.

"It appears our dear Mr Seymour has a yearning for the mud, considering his choice of bride. I can see why he kept her a secret."

The girl tittered then whispered back, also in Frencine, *"La, that hideous morning gown! It's twenty years out of date, and her damaged skin- Mr Seymour has more than a yearning for mud, my dear baron. I'd say he also enjoys…mushroom soup?"*

There was snigger from more than one of the others at the table, showing that Ash wasn't the only one to understand Frencine. She put down her coffee with cream (breaking an Anglish stereotype that they only drank tea; it appeared it was just George with the hatred of coffee) and said calmly in Frencine, *"I can't comment on my husband's tastes for mud or mushrooms, but even this hideously dressed Colonial knows that to speak as you just did is very ill-bred."* She switched back to Anglish, adding as she stood from her seat, "Please excuse me. I find I've lost my appetite."

The two men also stood abruptly, showing they hadn't lost all politeness, and there was silence as she left the room…until she heard someone mutter, "My apologies. We should have spoken in Italien."

"Parlo anche Italieno," she called back through the doorway (*I also speak Italien*), then fled before it could become any more ridiculous.

But she still heard, "I say, how many languages does the girl speak?!"

An infinite number, considering that Ash had a translation device somewhere in her brain, as did George and Anne. She hadn't yet come across a language she couldn't understand.

But the way they'd insulted her in Frencine – a language that was extremely common here in Regency Angland – showed that those two at least had no respect for her intelligence or breeding. Not that she had any breeding, but that wasn't the point. It had been rude, and she was more upset than she'd let herself show.

How could people be so *mean*?

Ash made it as far as the first hallway, unsure of where she should go next, when George came into view. He ambled towards her, an intent gleam in his eye.

She was too upset to take in much except that he'd clearly made it back from his morning ride. "There you are, thank Deias. I think I've just alienated myself from all of your visitors with my low class – except at least now they know I'm multilingual low-class. Did you find Anne?"

"Anne?"

"At the gateway," she enunciated. George was looking rather vague although quite attractive in a dark grey suit rather like the butler had worn, and with his hair neatly swept back. Not what she'd imagined him wearing for riding, but never mind. "The remnant gateway on the edge of the estate, the one you told me about last night."

"Ah…" He looked around as if to see if they were alone, then indicated to a nearby doorway. They stepped inside what turned out to be a small room filled with couches, shelves and books, and he closed the door behind him. "The gateway."

"Yeees," Ash repeated, feeling her upset turn into irritation. "You haven't had a mind-wipe since last night, surely?"

George didn't answer. He just looked at his feet for one, two moments, then did a very odd thing. Quicker than she could follow, he lifted his hand and cupped her cheek, using his other hand to push her back against the wall.

She let out a startled *oof*. "What the- George!" He'd made those comments last night about not being a eunuch, but this was getting *weird*. "What do you think you're doing?"

"Just a moment," he murmured, voice low and a little hoarse. His warm blue eyes were fixed on her mouth, and she could just see that he had something in his other hand-

That was when they both heard the little cough. George stepped back abruptly.

"Ahem. Excuse me." The youngish woman sat quietly in the corner of the room, looking rather embarrassed. She held an open novel, and an empty plate sat beside her on the couch, still scattered with crumbs.

"Oh, sorry," Ash exclaimed, feeling her face flush hot from the neck upwards. "We thought this room was empty." She turned to George, but he was already disappearing out the door.

"What on earth…?"

"He ran out while you were looking at me," the woman said with a small shrug. "He does move fast, doesn't he?"

Ash stuck her head out into the hall to find George was nowhere in sight. "He certainly does," she agreed bemusedly, pulling her head back into the room.

What had *that* been? Was he playing his part of the besotted husband? It wasn't like he'd known there was anyone to see them.

"Don't be embarrassed," the woman said with a smile. "It would be nice if my husband had that sort of passion for me still."

Realising what she had thought – and perhaps what *had* happened, since Ash truly had no idea – Ash's face went even redder, if that was possible. "Oh, we're not-" she began, then realised she'd almost given the game away. She considered vacating the room out of embarrassment, but decided against it as there was nowhere else to go. This woman seemed to be the nicest person by far she'd met in this whole time period, and Ash could do with a kind face right now. "Can we pretend that never happened?"

"What never happened?"

"That- oh. Good." Ash laughed. "Do you mind if I join you?"

"Please do."

Ash sat on the opposite couch and just enjoyed the quiet for a moment. Then she realised that she hadn't introduced herself; yet another misstep. "I'm Ashlea O-Seymour," she corrected at the last minute. "George- uh, Mr Seymour's wife." The lie slipped out a little easier than she'd thought. It was calling everyone 'Mr' that caught her short.

"Mrs Frederick Woolsten," the woman replied.

Ah, so this was the Mrs Woolsten who'd not been there to be introduced along with the others. Brushing aside the urge to ask the woman's first name – that seemed to be rude here – Ash smiled at her. "I was told that we might get along well. Very nice to meet you."

"And you, Mrs Seymour." She paused. "Who said that we might get along?"

"Uh…Mrs Parsenne, I believe."

"Ah." There was a meaningful silence where Mrs Woolsten studied her face. Then she said carefully, "They're usually more amiable when the family is around. Lady Eleanor is a stickler for politeness, and her late husband was a friend of my own husband. She often takes her breakfast abed, but I'm surprised that the viscountess wasn't there."

Ash worked out she must mean George's sister-in-law. "So perhaps no one would have mentioned mushrooms or a *nostalgie de la bouie* if they'd been there?"

Mrs Woolsten gasped. "Certainly not. Who said such a thing?"

"One of the younger girls. Uh…I know that a mushroom is an edible fungus, but what does it mean when it's used as an insult?"

"Well, if you overheard it in the breakfast room in reference to a person, then I daresay it means someone who tries to climb above their station in life. An interloper."

"I see," Ash murmured. Now she understood what the quip about 'mushroom soup' was, she could almost appreciate the humour. Almost, but not quite. "Can't have any fresh blood to liven up the upper-class gene pool," she added a little sarcastically, then saw the shock on the other woman's face. "No offense intended to you. I've just had a rather…interesting morning, and I'm not feeling very gracious right now."

The older woman nodded in understanding. "I know exactly what you mean. I'm not considered good *ton*, even though I married Mr Woolsten more than a decade ago. They never let me forget that my father is a wine merchant."

Ah, a kindred spirit. "I don't see a problem with actually doing something with your life," Ash said honestly. "I've been raised to respect hard work and ambition. I just don't understand this disdain of gainful employment. It doesn't make sense to me."

"I've always believed it leads to dissipation," Mrs Woolsten agreed in a confiding tone. "Some of the atrocities these young bucks get up to – I say that if they had employment, it wouldn't be a problem. They wouldn't have the time or energy to use on vices."

It seemed perfectly sensible, but Ash knew enough of the time period to know that it would be considered a radical opinion here. She was about to tell the woman how much she agreed when George meandered in.

He was looking rather flustered, but he smiled widely when he saw the two of them. "Oh, good morning, Mrs Woolsten. I was told I could find my wife in here." To Ash, he added, "There you are. And decently clothed, I see."

Wife. Ha. And as for the clothing… Ash said dryly, "Considering you left me in here not three minutes ago, I'm surprised you had to ask for directions."

George stared at her blankly. "What do you mean?"

He seemed like his normal self again, but Ash was still annoyed at him for leaving her alone. Perhaps the breakfast fiasco wouldn't have happened if he'd been there. "I mean that you told me you wanted to talk to me in here, then bolted like the hounds of Hades were after you. Have you forgotten so fast?"

He shook his head, eyes wide. "I beg your pardon, but I haven't seen you all morning. I just got back from the stables. Morning ride, as we discussed."

That would explain the messy hair and the flush on his cheeks, which hadn't been there earlier. Growing more confused herself, Ash looked at the other woman in confirmation, then scanned George up and down. He was dressed differently than before in his usual beige trousers and dark blue jacket, and in his trouser pocket she could see the outline of what could only be the rolled-up binding cord.

"A fast ride then," Mrs Woolsten commented dryly. "Perhaps you have a secret doppelganger, Mr Seymour? Or perhaps we've been talking at cross-purposes."

"Must be," Ash said as casually as she could, but a sense of panic was rising in her. Doppelganger. Someone who looked like George, but wasn't…

She'd dealt with that before in future-Iversley, with a Noble who'd made themselves resemble George enough to almost capture her. But that person's eyes had been grey, and they hadn't been able to hide it. *This* other George's eyes had been blue – the correct colour.

But his voice hadn't been quite correct, and neither had his actions.

Swallowing with difficulty, she forced a laugh. "Never mind any of that. Actually George, I would like to talk to you. Urgently."

His eyes flickered to Mrs Woolsten still ensconced comfortably in the corner, and he nodded. "Of course. Might I just change into something a little tidier? We're supposed to be making an excursion into the village this afternoon, and I shouldn't be wandering around in my riding clothes."

He looked fine to Ash, but it was an excuse to get out of the room. Getting up to follow him out, Ash said genuinely to Mrs Woolsten, "It was really lovely to meet you. Will you be coming into the village?"

"I wasn't planning to, but perhaps I will after all."

Ash said her goodbyes, then turned to where George was standing. They began to walk towards his room, and she asked what she really wanted to know. "I need to get this straight. Did you or did you not ask to speak with me privately in that parlour we were just in, shove me against the wall once we were in there, then run away when you saw Mrs Woolsten?"

There was a long silence. Then, "Shove you against the wall?"

Ash stared at his familiar face with those blue eyes, messy blondish hair, and the good-natured expression she was used to seeing. "You were wearing dark grey, rather like the butler. And your hair was different. Your brother's not your twin, is he?"

"A twin that's five years older? And no. He doesn't look much like me. But even if he did, he wouldn't lay his hands on you!"

Ash's heart sank. Suddenly the dark wood and ornate finishings of George's family home felt a lot less safe than they had this morning. He was thinking it too; she could tell in the way he glared at every servant they passed as if they might be an intruder in disguise.

"Looks like your time isn't as safe as we'd imagined," Ash said finally. "And like we're dealing with another enemy who can use illusion."

"Damn it to Hades! I do beg your pardon, Ashlea, but I thought we were through this. I thought we'd left it all behind!"

"I agree with you completely," she said in a low tone. "But if it's people that have used the Eternity Stone who can travel through gateways, then all of the Nobles can use them, if they can *find* them. And weren't you the one to say that the Nobles could only sense the Stone when it was being used?"

"So we don't use the Stone. We should use the gateway on the edge of the estate to go find Anne, because I *know* that something has gone wrong if she hasn't come through with her sister, and if you've found the Stone-"

"Sister?" And then remembering something else, something worse, Ash shook that off. "Never mind that. George, I told the fake you where the gateway was, when I thought he was you. I asked if you'd found Anne, and he just repeated what I said in this hoarse voice, and then he ran off when he saw we weren't alone…"

"Hades," George swore again, and this time he didn't apologise. She didn't ask him to. "Hades and perdition. Ashlea, we must go to Anne at once. Perhaps this is why she never came through – perhaps this is why the Stone ended up in your hands, in some dreadful kind of cycle. We must use it to go to an earlier time, before the gateway was created, and to bring her through."

"And let the fake you sense it being used?"

"If he's already used the gateway to 1556 then he won't sense it," he pointed out. "And please don't call him the fake me."

"The Noble, then."

"Right. The Noble." George paused thoughtfully, then his eyes lit up. "I have an idea…"

It might not be a perfect plan as George saw it, but it was better than waiting here for some illusion-using enemy to make the next move.

The plan was to quickly use the Eternity Stone to detour through some random destination just for long enough to cause confusion, and then to head back to 1556 to a time *after* Anne had returned from her travels, but *before* the twenty-eight days would have passed.

"And we'll be back in time for that excursion to the village," he pointed out helpfully. "You can experience some more of my home. I'll introduce you to everyone here at the manor – I'd meant to do it already, but hadn't expected that you'd come out of our room this morning."

For some reason it seemed important that she meet his family and get on with them. He didn't think too deeply about why that was.

"Uh…" Ashlea looked awkward, then glanced away. "Meet the locals. Why not."

"Only we'll need to find you something more appropriate to wear," he mused. The lavender shade she wore now was half-mourning – worn after a bereavement when black was too grim, but other colours too cheerful.

"What, you don't like your great-grandmother's dress on me?"

"By gad, no. It's a morning gown, of course – and a *mourning* gown. A bit dated, perhaps, but pretty enough I suppose to wear casually at home. But for any public outings you'll need to dress up. And for dinner, of course, not that you would be expected to know that."

"Of course not," she echoed, looking a little stunned. "But if we're going to find Anne, shouldn't we get changed again? I mean, I'm barely dressed for 1818, let alone Tudar Angland."

"I think we'll just have to accept that we won't look quite right. And move quickly, of course. Now, I've got the binding cord, you have the Eternity Stone…"

"And Anne's photo album."

"…And Anne's photo-album," George agreed. "I suppose we could take that with us in case it proves useful. Now, all we require is a detour location."

They were sitting together on the small couch that was a recent addition to George's childhood room. Ashlea flipped open the little book that Anne had so treasured, revealing an image of an old painting. It depicted a desert scene, complete with palm trees and a sun-bleached town in the background. It made George think of the stories he'd heard about seraglios full of scantily-clad women…not that he would dwell on those thoughts, of course. But it made him think.

"Let's go here," she said, "walk for ten minutes, and go home."

Simple as that. "Very well," George agreed, feeling his heart race like it did every time he thought about time-travelling. There was a fear he'd be trapped away from his home, never able to return…and a fear that he'd be trapped *in* his home, never able to leave again.

He held out his hand, palm up. "Shall we go?"

Ashlea put her hand in his, the Eternity Stone's cord looped around her middle finger almost like a ring. She held the little album in her other hand, open to the page with that exotic location. "Why not. Think of deserts, George."

So he did.

The smell was the first thing George noticed. It was an unfamiliar one he couldn't quite place, like dust and spice and something unpleasantly sweet.

A split second later the heat hit him: a dry heat, but overwhelming. It was like stepping from the chill of winter into a room with a roaring fire. He turned around, eyes wide, taking in their surroundings.

In the near distance were the walls of a city, almost blending into the landscape with straggly, stick-like trees lining the road towards it. Dry, dry, dry, was how it looked, except for a few sparse patches of green.

To his far left was a slope down to what looked like a gorge. Most of the greenery was in that direction, and even a few more trees were growing. He could just hear running water.

By Jove, it truly did look like that image from Anne's little book. Shame, because he'd rather have had the seraglio.

"Always wanted to visit the near-east," he commented happily. "Hot though, isn't it?"

She didn't answer.

"Ashlea?"

But when he turned to look, she wasn't standing next to him. In fact, she wasn't anywhere to be seen.

He was completely alone in this place, without even the Eternity Stone for help.

A HOP, SKIP
AND A JUMP

City of Lilluania, 1422 AD

Jenessa heard the commotion long before she saw it. The mother of all dragons sat huge, black and smug on the curved dome roof of the Central Municipal House, its wingspan as wide as the building beneath it, and a self-satisfied smirk on its reptilian face. The expression said, *Yes, I'm causing trouble again…and I love it.*

Or perhaps that was just how Jenessa interpreted it, since she'd known this particular dragon a very long time, and she knew how it thought.

Really. They would come here to this little city centre in the corner of the world, at the end of the dark ages, a hop, skip and a jump through time and space away from their own home, just for what? A power trip?

The dragon spread its massive wings to their full capacity, then gently closed them again, rather like a butterfly preparing to alight from a flower. But these wings were no butterfly's – they sent up a gust of wind that knocked over a nearby orange cart, the vendor long having fled.

The irony was that as big as the dragon's wings were, it could barely get off the ground. It was simply too heavy – not that it cared. It just liked to keep the humans in their place.

They came to visit every six months or so…you'd think the people would be used to it by now. But no, it was the same every time. Jenessa and her twin brother Troilus would wander in looking like their normal selves, wearing just enough illusion to fit in with the locals. They'd have a bit of fun, perhaps play tricks on people, but the dragon…

Every single time it was the same. Transform secretly, roar into view, blow some illusion-based flame, then plunk itself on the highest point of the city, glaring balefully at anyone stupid enough to come out of hiding.

Unsurprisingly, the thrill of this wouldn't last very long, only a few days at most. Troilus had no patience for it; he'd stopped at the previous gateway (actually the distant future) where he indulged his love of virtual reality to the maximum, with no one to scold him. She'd save that for on the way out.

It was silly that he should spend all his time in his mind, when out of the two of them, he was the one to have inherited Janeus's shapeshifting ability. Unlike Jenessa and her mother Seyen (AKA 'The Queen', as she'd been called for many years) Troilus could *truly* transform. He could become anything he wanted, anything larger than a butterfly or smaller than an elephant. But he took it for granted, thinking it wasn't anything special.

He was wrong. It was very special, but all of Jenessa's haranguing couldn't convince him of that. Stupid man. *She* should have been the one with the ability, not him.

Oh, well. At least she wasn't Seyen's favourite, like Troilus was. Jenessa knew that her mother loved her 'in her own way', but after many decades of blatant favouritism, she'd come to see that it was better to be ignored by that particular woman.

Just look at her father, Janeus. He was a fool to be sure, apparently thinking himself immortal. If not for Seyen's intense, unshakeable loyalty, he'd have been let go centuries before.

But every time Seyen banished him, she'd simply go back and

get him again, and cling even tighter, be even more controlling. Then he'd sneak around behind her back, like he was doing now, and she'd find out and get angry and banish him again…

Currently they were in-between banishings, although the way things were going, Jenessa knew one would be coming up anytime. She just hoped *she* didn't get pulled into it. Seyen would be furious that Jenessa had known about the remnant gateways and not said anything.

A startled roar caught Jenessa's attention, and she saw that there was something wrong. Instead of fleeing in fear as usual, this time a ring of armed humans had climbed the roof and were surrounding the dragon. They were armed with all manner of sharp-tipped weapons, and they didn't look nearly as frightened as they should. The dragon opened its mouth, pouring out a column of blue-hot flame, but they barely shrank back.

That illusion had been the last, most effective weapon past its physical bulk, and it had always worked in the past. Unlike the dragon itself, the flame was fake, but it looked so very real. But now Jenessa saw the fear in those black eyes. It'd have to fight its way out.

Jenessa swore emphatically. This wasn't the first time they'd been in such a situation, but usually Troilus was there to help. Now it was up to her and her alone. With the minimum of effort, she closed her eyes, stepped forward, and let her own less-than-impressive red dragon form spill out. The illusion surrounding her wasn't nearly as big as the black's, but just as dangerous.

Distraction. It would have to work.

Up ahead she saw that the ring of armed humans had now backed off, making way for one man. Taller than the others (but who wasn't? Medieval midgets, all of them) and dressed in thick leather armour, he held the leash to a huge, snarling dog in one hand and a sword in the other. He looked very professional and very unconcerned.

Jenessa hadn't yet been noticed.

"Go for 'im, Dragon-slayer!" one of the nearby men called out, and the black dragon's strong tail flicked out, sending him flying off the low roof into a nearby wall. It might not have any true flame, but it was still strong.

A dragon-slayer. Great.

Jenessa knew exactly what that meant. Either that armoured man was a prancing, boastful faker who was about to be painfully killed…or he knew what they were. There were no *real* dragons in this realm, and not really in the Other one either.

Up on the roof, the proud black dragon was reluctant to give up on the methods that had worked for so long. It spread its wings again to their full, impressive span, spurted flame, and stomped its clawed feet until cracks appeared in the stone roof.

The men quaked, but held firm.

Enough. Jenessa raised her head and roared, sending the illusion as far ahead of her as she could, swooping down on the nearest men. They ducked and swore, but the dragon-slayer turned his cold grey gaze on Jenessa, looking her right in the eyes. Her real eyes, not the eyes of the illusion, and she knew then for certain what he was. Yet another opportunistic power gatherer, looking for easy pickings.

These certainly weren't easy, but if he took down this shapeshifter, he'd have gained more than enough power to make it worth the risk. And she saw the excitement in his expression; the love of the kill. He'd killed many, she guessed in that moment, and he'd enjoyed it.

But the dragon-slayer wasn't as smart as he thought he was. Turning his attention away from the black dragon, even for a moment, had been enough time for a shape change of sorts. The huge creature had lumbered off to the side, almost falling off the curved dome of the roof, and knocking a few more men off onto the ground.

Then showing none of the grace this shapeshifter was known for, the dragon clumsily began to shrink, its wings disappearing until it was like a man-sized lizard creature, panic and confusion still evident in its eyes.

No longer dragon, it turned and ran for the edge of the building, leaping off just as the dragon-slayer turned back and saw what he'd missed. He ran after the fleeing figure, and Jenessa ran to intercept. Using her red-dragon illusion just enough to frighten and distract the other humans, she reached the stumbling lizard-man and shook him.

"Shift, damn it!" she roared, the illusion turning her words into almost garbled nonsense. But he would understand. "We've got to get to the gateway!"

They'd found out the hard way many years before, that to travel through one of the almost-invisible gateways left behind by the Eternity Stone, they had to be in their true form. Being shifted could leave them powerless for a long time, or even damaged mentally.

"Can't..." the lizard-man whimpered. He was moving weakly as if he bled from some invisible wound, and genuinely frightened, Jenessa began to drag his heavier form towards the nearby gate anyway.

"You've got to," she insisted. "The dragon-slayer is a power-gatherer. He wants you-"

They'd reached the gateway now. Jenessa could feel it with her other senses, tingling right in front of them. Making a last-minute decision, she let go of the lizard-man, closed her eyes, and stepped through.

There was the feeling like a cold wind blowing over her whole body, then she was standing hundreds of years in the future, not far from the primitive virtual reality machines that characterised this particular era.

It was the middle of the night here, and there were few people using the machines. They reminded her of coat racks, tall and narrow, with tentacle-like fibres running down to touch the ground. Or in this case, to wrap around the still bodies of those utilising them.

Of course, further into the future VR was far more sophisticated, the illusion permeating the very air rather than needing to be physical. But those places were harder to get to, and this was on their way anyway.

As always, Troilus had leaped right in, and she could see his distinctive shoes sticking out from one of the bundles. 'Space Adventure', the label read. How foolish. If he wanted a space adventure, he just needed to go a little further into the future.

But of course then he'd need Seyen's permission to use the Stone to go that far, and that ruined the fun of it. Half the fun was simply that Seyen didn't know about the gateways. No one did; no one except her, her brother, and their father.

Jenessa heard him come through a bare moment after she did, and turned with a sigh of relief. Phew. He'd followed after her, and in his true form. She wouldn't have wanted to explain *that* one to her mother – why she'd let her father be killed by some leather-wearing barbarian, or had let him go crazy. Worse, she'd have to explain why she hadn't told Seyen about the remnant gateways.

"You left me," Janeus said, but his tone was more resigned than accusing. He knew where her true priorities lay.

"You were playing with a damned power-gatherer," she retorted, letting her fear and frustration come out in her voice. "I was going to get Troilus and bring him back to help you. You know my illusions aren't worth much." She strode towards the machines, and Janeus followed her.

Her father stared down at those still, tentacle-wrapped feet, and he gave one a kick. "Chaos-damned Troilus and his VR. *He's* the useless one. He doesn't appreciate the power that he has, spending all his time wrapped up in these illusions..."

"We all spend our time wrapped up in illusions," Jenessa countered, even though she knew he was right about Troilus. He *didn't* appreciate what he had. Not the way she would have.

"Mine aren't illusions. I can truly change."

"Yeah, I know. But you're even more twisted. Why do you so often take inhuman forms? It's just weird."

Janeus shrugged, pushing a hand through his longish dark hair. His handsome face fell into that same neutral, slightly bored expression that she so despised...and had copied many times. "For interest's sake, I suppose. But it doesn't matter. After that fiasco, we've lost any power we had over that city. We can't use that gateway again."

She knew what he was talking about. That particular gateway would be no good now, not for their kind of fun. Those people wouldn't be fearing dragons anytime soon. "It was risky anyway. We were gone too long. If Mother finds out about this..."

"She won't," he snapped back. "Not unless you tell her."

"Or unless someone *sees* us," she argued. "We've been doing this for almost thirty years, and our luck has to run out sooner or later."

"*I've* been using the gateways for hundreds," Janeus countered arrogantly. "Ever since the first time she banished me and I didn't want to spend my time wandering that damned sand heap she left me in. She hasn't found out in over two hundred years; why would she find out now? If she did, it would only be because of you two."

Troilus and Jenessa had followed their father once twenty-eight years ago, wondering exactly where he went. When they'd found out, he'd sworn them to secrecy, and they'd decided to go along with it. It *was* interesting, and it was nice to know something that the all-powerful Queen didn't.

"I told you, I haven't said a word, and I won't. But if you go down, we do too."

It was true. Jenessa hadn't told anyone yet, and she wouldn't, not until it suited her to do so. It took a certain level of power to use the gateways, but most of the Queen's pantheon would be able to do it. She just didn't know if she wanted them to.

She still thought her father an absolute fool with no sense of self-preservation, but perhaps that was because he had lived so long. Three hundred and fifty years of time jumping, or so he claimed. It was only fifty or so less than Seyen herself, but then he was the first that she had collected rather than killed.

He'd started a trend. Jenessa understood the loneliness of longevity that could make people do foolish things, but she still thought that in Seyen's place, she would have just gathered power. Collecting live people rather than their life-forces took too much work.

"And what was with you not shifting?" Jenessa asked. "After all that you've told us about the gateways."

If there was one thing he'd hammered home over and over again, it was that you never, ever went through a remnant gateway in shifted form. The damage to mind and memory could be irreparable.

He looked as though he would answer, but that was when she saw the new figure come through the gateway. There was a shimmer in the empty air, and then the dragon-slayer was standing there in front of them. No dog this time, but his sword – really a long spear with a sharp blade on the end – had come through fine.

She gasped in panic, but this time Janeus was ready. He spun to face the intruder, and Jenessa ran to get Troilus. The moment she bent down and touched the cloth-like fibres wrapping him, they rushed up and enveloped her, momentarily pulling her into his virtual reality session. A glowing creature rather like a jellyfish rushed at her face, and just beyond it was her brother, who was doing something dubious with a six-legged creature.

He looked up and saw her. "What?" he snapped.

"We're being attacked," she snapped right back. "Get out, right now!"

With the force of her will, Jenessa disconnected her mind from the virtual world, pulling off the cloth fibres that clung to her and created the sense of the unreal. She could see Troilus twitching, trying to wake himself, but for someone who'd spent more than moments in VR, waking could take some time. He had to do it on his own.

Janeus was still dodging the dragon-slayer's weapon. He'd picked up a piece of machinery, a long, metal pole with wires attached, and was using it to fend off the strikes. It was clearly a part of the VR machine, and sparks came off it with every blow.

Drawing together all of her energy, Jenessa sent a lightning-like strike of alter-power towards the dragon-slayer. It hit him in the back of the head, knocking him to the ground, and he rolled out of the way just in time to avoid the rest of the machinery as it came down hard to hit the floor.

There was the sound of something breaking, and then the dragon-slayer was on his feet again, facing the now weaponless Janeus with a grin and half an eye on Jenessa.

"Kill him and you'll seal your own death in a way you can't imagine," Jenessa warned the man, putting more confidence into her voice than she truly felt. Troilus was still wrapped in VR. Janeus wasn't shifting. He was still weak, it seemed. By now he should have turned into something vicious and poisonous and killed their attacker, but it hadn't happened.

The man laughed. "From you, you mean? You've used up everything on that weak little lightning strike. You're practically helpless."

"Not from me. From my mother, Seyen Johannis. Although you might have heard of her by another name."

He shrugged, his gaze still darting between the father and daughter, measuring when to strike.

"Hera. Junaper. Queen of Olympas and every other worth-while polytheistic belief system," Jenessa said coolly, watching as Janeus edged towards the second gateway, the one which would lead them to Olympas and safety, and where this upstart would get his just deserts.

The dragon-slayer laughed again. "You think I'm going to believe that your mother is an antique goddess?"

Jenessa scoffed. "Of course she's not a real goddess, but she's managed to convince the entire Grecian empire that she is. She's the most powerful, feared power-gatherer across history, and trust me, we've checked. Anyone who goes up against her either swears allegiance or is killed. And that man you have in front of you – that's her consort. I'm her daughter. If you hurt us, there won't be enough left of you to bury."

With the word 'bury', she saw Janeus reach the second gateway and slip through it. The dragon-slayer jolted as if to go after him, then turned back for her instead.

That was when Jenessa felt Troilus finally break free of the VR sleep and climb to his feet, beginning to shift.

She didn't wait. She darted for the blaster she knew Troilus kept in his pocket, grabbing it from him, turning and shooting in one smooth movement. The dragon-slayer jolted once, then fell, a round burn mark on his exposed forehead.

Troilus stopped in a furry half-shift, then melted back to his human form. His fine features were curled into a scowl, as if he was put out that he hadn't really had to fight.

Just then, the sparks that had been coming off the broken machinery ignited. Within seconds, all the VR racks were engulfed in flames. The twins stepped away from the blaze, exchanged irritated glances, then headed for the gateway.

"Nice one," Troilus scoffed. "You ruined my favourite pastime."

"It was Janeus, not me. And if you're really going to be fussy about it, it was the dragon-slayer's fault for following us through the gateway."

"Dragon- what? He followed us through?" Troilus sounded horrified, and rightly so. *No one* else was supposed to know about the remnant gateways, let alone use them.

"He's dead now, so don't worry about it," Jenessa told him.

In the background there was a *whomph* of heat as the flames caught hold of another set of VR machinery, and without looking back they moved through the next gateway. She remembered then that there'd been others in the VR sets, even at night time. They certainly couldn't have got away in time, not when it took so long to extract oneself from the machines even on a good day. Mentally she shrugged. It wasn't her problem.

On the other side of the gateway, it was twilight. Time moved evenly on both sides, so since they'd been gone a full day, a full day had passed here on Olympas as well. The dim light of the setting sun glowed off the white stone buildings arranged neatly on this mountain top...and silhouetted Seyen Johannis where she stood in front of the gateway.

Uh oh.

"My children," the Queen said without a hint of a smile. "Where have you been?"

Her 'children' were two centuries old, but they'd always be her children. And now they were very much in danger of being grounded, or worse. Whatever the 'worse' might be.

Troilus, the favourite, stepped forward with a rueful smile. "Mother," he began, but she held up a hand and his mouth opened and closed soundlessly for a few moments before he realised what she'd done and stopped trying to talk.

"You lied to me." Seyen's voice was cold and calm. Too calm. Her anger raged hot: that it should be so cold was a very bad sign.

"We never lied," Jenessa said quietly.

"Omitting the truth is the same thing when it comes to me," Seyen bit out. "You knew what you were doing when you hid these gateways from me, and you knew the consequences. Now tell me everything! Where have you been?"

"Eastern Europa in the early medieval period," Janeus said flatly. He was still cradling his arms around himself, looking shell-shocked.

"Straight to Eastern Europa?"

There was a silence, and as little as Jenessa wanted the Queen's attention drawn to her, she found herself answering. "But to get there, we had to go through Erastus in about 2600 AD."

Seyen's voice was sharp. "*About* 2600?"

"2614," Janeus muttered, and there was a distinct, pregnant pause where he looked up and met Seyen's eyes.

She looked at him for a long moment, looking almost *hurt*, and then shook her head. "No. No, you've betrayed me for the last time. This time, Janeus of Ciria, there will be no forgiveness."

Seyen only called him by his full name when she was very angry. Otherwise it was 'consort', as if by using the title she could hold the man.

It hadn't worked so far.

Her father bowed his head, but Jenessa could feel the defiance coming off him. Yep, he had a death wish all right, or else he truly thought himself irreplaceable. Guess they'd find out soon enough.

Seyen looked again at Jenessa, and then she frowned. She lifted a hand and Jenessa couldn't stop herself cringing – that was never a good thing – but nothing happened, and Jenessa realised that they were all staring at something over her shoulder. Both her parents and the whole assembly that had accompanied them, all staring at something behind where Jenessa stood.

She turned slowly, and standing right behind her with his burning hand outstretched, barely two inches from the back of her neck, was the frozen figure of the dragon-slayer. Where the fatal wound should have been on his forehead was simply smooth skin, and the only movement was his grey eyes twitching from side to side furiously, then focussing on her face.

"I see you brought us a visitor," Seyen said dryly. "He doesn't seem to like you very much."

God of death, his arse, Janeus thought with scorn later that evening. That dragon-slayer might have found some clever trick that enabled him to survive otherwise fatal wounds (since Jenessa had sworn that she'd left the man unmoving with a hole in his head) but that didn't make him an actual *god*.

OK, *and* he'd managed to do something to temporarily stop Janeus from shifting back in Lilluania, but that didn't make him a god either. It just meant he had enough power that the rest of them should be wary.

Of course they'd all claimed to be gods. As Seyen always said, what made a god except that they were worshipped? Seyen and the others (including Janeus himself at one time) had been worshipped, ergo they were 'gods'.

But they didn't really believe it. Janeus was sure they didn't. They – the whole pantheon of powerful, morally dubious people that he and Seyen had collected over the centuries – enjoyed the power that being worshipped gave them, but they didn't take it that seriously. Not like this 'Mortimer' did.

He'd said that his name meant 'Lake of Death', since apparently 'Hades' was too clichéd. Seyen had laughed as if the man was actually amusing. Perhaps he was to her, although Janeus thought it more likely that Seyen both considered Mortimer a novelty and wanted to make Janeus jealous.

The second was futile. At this point Janeus was well past any kind of jealousy. They'd been together so very long, and except for the first few years he'd spent most of that time simultaneously despising and fearing Seyen. Not the best recipe for the sort of love she thought she deserved.

He couldn't leave her. If she cut off her power from him completely – or rather the power that came from her collection of objects – then he'd die, and he didn't want to die. After what had happened with Tai... Well, Janeus didn't know where he'd be going after death, and he suspected it wouldn't be very nice.

He'd killed so many people while power-gathering with

Seyen, and he wasn't certain that death meant a true ending. If it didn't, then they'd be waiting there for him, ready to give him his just deserts for speeding up their own transfer through the veil.

If it wasn't for Janeus's fear of death, of what lay beyond death, he would quite easily let himself die. Or at least he thought he might.

Once upon a time when he was young and stupid, he'd imagined that living forever would be a wonderful thing, but now he knew better. Perhaps in some universe immortality would be a gift, with every day a new joy.

But this wasn't that universe. His life could be terrifying, sickening; but mostly it was just dull, dull, dull. So much so that he'd found himself doing strange and perverse things for amusement. Shifting to a female or animal form was the least of them. Not that he particularly wanted to be female or an animal, but it lightened the tedium of the years upon years of *sameness*.

Some of the things he'd done… It constantly amazed him that Seyen still kept him as consort. He wouldn't, if he was her.

But she didn't kill him. Instead she would rage at him for his faithlessness, banish him, order him to come back, plead with him, take other lovers to make him jealous…

It looked like this 'dragon-slayer' would be Seyen's new favourite. She would pick a handsome young man every now and then and make a point of showing them favour – as long as Janeus was watching, of course.

Seyen would particularly like how this Mortimer had already titled himself a god. To her, it would mean he had the right mindset to be a part of the pantheon. He'd already accepted the position.

God of death. What a fool.

Then it dawned on Janeus that while Mortimer might be a fool who truly believed himself immortal, *he* wasn't the one who'd just lost everything; whose position and even his life (especially his life!) was in terrible jeopardy.

Mortimer wasn't the one who'd managed to get himself outmanoeuvred by a bunch of regular humans, get stuck in his shifted form, then almost drain away all of his collected power in some unknown disaster. Janeus still didn't know exactly what had happened, but it wasn't good.

2614 was the year that Janeus had sworn to Seyen that he'd never go back to. He'd meant it at the time, too, knowing how important it was to her after what had happened there.

But then he'd worked out how to use the remnant gateways, and he'd found that if he just went through that year, just very briefly, he could get to a lovely part of the Dark Ages where he could scare the blazes out of everyone to his heart's content. What she didn't know wouldn't hurt her, right?

But what Seyen *did* know would hurt *him*. He'd lost that gateway now. There was no sense in going back to Lilluania; they knew what he was now. He didn't have the power to hold up a form like the dragon again anyway. In fact, he felt incredibly weak, like he could perhaps make one more shift. Just one more.

Janeus glanced out past where the group of people acted as a barrier. The road down the very steep slopes of Mount Olympas was behind them, and so was the same gateway they'd been using. There was no way for him to leave.

Or so they thought.

Seyen was very obviously ignoring him, talking to Mortimer and the others, impressing him with her power. She'd likely bind the man to her with an oath swearing allegiance – more than just words; those oaths had power. Mortimer, once the oath was spoken, would literally be unable to turn against Seyen. Janeus was the only one who'd ever been able to, perhaps the reason for her ongoing obsession with him.

It was a good thing. For Mortimer to be controlled, that was. Janeus was no angel, not by a mile, but the other man… His hands burned and stole power with a mere touch, and that was before he'd ever joined the pantheon. He had the coldest eyes that Janeus had ever seen, and he'd seen a lot of eyes in his time.

Janeus had killed exactly eighty-seven people including Tai, but he had never enjoyed killing the way this Mortimer clearly did.

Seyen should watch her back. They all should.

Just then Seyen turned towards Janeus. He snapped his most bored expression into place, careful to conceal his tension behind slack features and a relaxed pose. They were still talking, or rather *she* was talking and they were all listening, but her cold glare was fixed on him. Oh how, how had he got himself into this?

He shouldn't have gone back to 2614. He'd known better. Any other time – any other *place*, and she could have forgiven him. But something told him that this time was different. This time, he'd really done it.

But now wasn't the time for recriminations. He could either wait and see what his punishment would be, or he could flee, take the one path that he knew would lead to freedom of a sort. He'd never considered it before, but now that kind of oblivion seemed like a blessing.

He needed to escape.

Janeus waited until they had dispersed a little on their set duties, and then a little longer so they'd grow lax in watching him. Then the moment Ajax (that suck-up) turned away, he leaped to his feet and threw himself onto the slick mud path leading down the forested mountain side.

Someone had originally created it as a joke, he knew, because none of them had to bother with paths if they didn't want to, let alone wet, filthy mud slides like this one.

But it worked. None of them were expecting it, and all he heard was, "Hey!" and then he was out of sight. Speeding up, faster and faster, until his butt hurt and a tree was looming…

He threw his power into the air, his body shimmered into that old familiar form, the gateway opened just in front of that tree – and he was gone.

Somewhere unexpected...

Ash had held George's hand, the Eternity Stone pressed between their palms, and thought of deserts. And it had worked, sort of. They weren't in the same place they'd been before – his little room up in the attic of his family's manor.

So hooray, they'd time-travelled!

But they sure weren't in a desert, either, so Ash didn't have nearly as good a grasp on using the Stone as she'd imagined.

They appeared to be in the corner of a walled garden, filled with birdsong and with a water feature right in front of her. The air was warm and scented with something rich and unfamiliar. It was lush and lovely…and again, not a desert.

"It could be worse," she commented to George, feeling satisfied excitement over the change of scene. "It's quite pretty, isn't it?"

He didn't answer, and she realised that her arm was feeling rather empty – as in not holding onto anyone else.

That wasn't a good sign. Either she'd left him behind, or they'd been separated during travel.

"George…?" Ash called out querulously. She heard the hum of voices from around the corner, and froze.

A few seconds went past and the voices moved away, and Ash breathed a sigh of relief as deeply as her corset would let her. Glancing down at the small open book in her hand, she saw that the scene displayed wasn't the desert she and George had been expecting. Instead, it was this walled garden in full, 3D Technicolor.

She turned the page to reveal the desert sketch, then baffled, turned it back to the garden one. She must have switched the pages by accident.

"What an idiot," she muttered to herself. She barely remembered even seeing this garden scene in Anne's book at all.

Just then something small fell out of the book's pages to land on the gravel path with an audible clunk. It was a tiny little glass pot, only about a quarter-inch high and the size of an old Southern Isles fifty-cent piece. Except for its shape, it resembled the vials that had once given her flight and prophetic abilities. Scrolling text on its lid read *Healing*.

Well, well, well. That didn't look like much of a coincidence. There was no doubt it had come from Amaranthus (because there was *no way* it could have fit in that book and Ash not have noticed) but it made her worry what might be coming that they'd need healing for.

Still curious, she unscrewed the fine lid. Inside was a small shiny pool of clear gel. It smelled lovely, like fruit and flowers, and she gave in to the urge to stick her nose right inside.

Phoof. A burst of light and warmth puffed out into her face, dazzling her for a moment and then leaving only a sense of wellbeing. Suddenly her head didn't hurt anymore, and when she felt the wound tentatively, there wasn't a bump or a scrape there anymore.

Wow. Instant healing wasn't as amazing as being able to fly, perhaps, but a cancer patient might disagree. The pot had just a little less gel in it than before, and with a new sense of wellbeing and anticipation Ash carefully tucked it and the book into the deep pocket of her borrowed purple gown.

All she had to do now was see if George was nearby. If he was, then they'd take the Stone and go – holding hands a bit more tightly this time. If he *wasn't*, then she'd use the Stone to leave, focusing on his location and hoping like crazy that it would work properly.

Ash didn't trust herself to take the second option now, since judging by her lack of success so far, she could end up even further away from where she'd intended to be.

She slipped the Stone into her pocket along with the other items, then poked her head around the corner towards where she could hear those voices. "George?" she whispered hoarsely. "Is that you?"

In hindsight that wasn't her best move. Around the corner the voices quietened abruptly, and she heard a curious female voice say, "Did you hear that?"

Footsteps sounded, and a moment later, a girl came into view. She was small and plumply pretty, with pale skin and black hair and eyes, and wearing some kind of floaty trouser-vest outfit that reminded Ash of Arabien Nights.

Definitely not George. Damn and double damn. Where on earth was he?

Ash smiled awkwardly. "Uh, hi."

The girl stared at her bug-eyed, then ran away shrieking, "Intruder! There's an intruder!"

That was an overreaction to a friendly smile. Ash actually felt quite offended. But being the loyal person she was, she still had to look for George.

Following the girl around the corner, Ash found herself at the wide entrance of what looked like an oriental-themed building. To either side, the garden extended until it reached walls in both directions. There were also guards – men with curved swords – who were now running towards her from both sides.

George, unsurprisingly, was nowhere to be seen.

Too late Ash tried to fish in her pocket for the Eternity Stone, but it seemed to be lost in the depths of her clothing, and her constant movement wasn't helping.

One moment. She just needed one moment to grab it out, so she hiked up her ancient purple gown and sprinted for the nearest doorway.

TREES

Ash ran through the nearest open door. Inside, the large, open-plan building was richly embroidered and decorated in intense red, gold, and purple down to the very walls. It was beautiful in a near-eastern sort of way, with the decorations implying that the owner had a 'more is more' philosophy, and probably a good deal of money.

There were also dozens of women scattered around the rooms. Most of them were dark-haired and dark-eyed, fairly attractive in a round sort of way, and dressed in an unfamiliar style of robes. It almost looked like a harem scene from some cheesy historical film, but far less sexy.

Still no George. Ash was starting to think she'd left him behind.

Ash and the harem girls stared at each other for a second or two. Most of the girls wore expressions of horror or dismay, or perhaps a little curiosity.

Then one of them screamed, "Ahmed! There's a man in the harem!"

How rude. Ash had been mistaken for a man before, but this time she was wearing a dress!

The doors right next to Ash burst open, and a couple more of those enormous men wearing loose trousers and robes and carrying sizeable swords rushed in, spotting her immediately. "Stop! Intruder!"

Ah…no.

Ash ran for it, dodging chubby white limbs left right and centre. Who knew that harem girls tended to be plus-size? All that lounging around eating grapes, most likely, and no exercise past the occasional excursion to the Sultan's boudoir.

Eek! Ash dodged one man's slashing blade, grabbing a nearby cushion and throwing it at him as she did so. It caught around his face and he lost precious moments pulling it away. Then she jumped over yet another screaming, reclining girl and ran through a doorway towards daylight.

Beyond that was an outdoor corridor. Ash dashed through, then took the first room she saw. It was empty and dark, with only the outlines of a few beds on the floor, so she slumped against the wall, breathing a sigh of relief. She put her hand in her pocket to feel for the Eternity Stone, but instead her finger stuck in something gooey. The lid must've come off the healing pot.

Cursing, and preparing to see if she could scrape it back in (waste not, want not, especially when it had such limited uses) Ash was completely unprepared for one thing. She was not, in fact, alone in that dark room.

From then it seemed to happen in slow motion. She realised that one of the beds was occupied by a male-female combination. Before she could squeak out an apology or turn to leave, the extremely large male leapt up with an oath and slammed her back against the wall, one huge hand pressing against her throat.

"What is your business here?" he growled, looking very large and menacing and…large, still. He wasn't fat, but he had to be one of the biggest, most solid men Ash had ever run into.

"Accident," she managed to squeak, struggling to make him let go.

He ignored her efforts, simply gripping her tighter around the throat. He wasn't quite choking her, but it certainly wasn't comfortable.

"Hold on, Hasan," his companion exclaimed. "It's a girl!"

Startled, Hasan stepped back a little and looked at Ash critically. He must've been relieved by what he saw, because his grip on her throat loosened and he let her slide back down to the ground, although didn't let her go completely.

"You are not unattractive," he rumbled. "Although your skin could do with being kept out of the sun, and your clothing is unappealingly foreign. This is one of the more inventive ways of catching our master's attention, but it was very dangerous. Don't you know we could have killed you?"

"She could be a thief," the girl suggested.

"Too well-dressed for a thief," Hasan countered. "Look at this cloth. It's quality."

Ash tried to regather her dignity. Hard to do when she was still pinned against the wall by one of the largest men she'd ever seen, and panting from the unexpected exercise. "I assure you, I'm not a thief, and I wasn't trying to get anyone's attention," she wheezed, then gave the man a solid kick between the legs.

To her horror, he barely flinched.

"He's a eunuch," the girl pointed out helpfully, looking Ash up and down from behind Hasan's shoulder. There was something in her tone that indicated she was disappointed with this state of events, and for the first time Ash noticed that her captor wasn't bad-looking, in an enormous, thick-browed sort of way.

Ash stared at him with wide eyes. "Eunuch? Really? I would've thought you'd be more…girly-looking."

Hasan frowned, relaxing his grip slightly. "I was taken when I was already a grown man."

"Fascinating," Ash said. Then she lifted her hand – the one holding the little healing pot – and stuck it rather clumsily against his mouth.

Phoof. A puff of light briefly blinded both of them, and by the time Ash had recovered enough to try to escape, she could hear sobbing. Not the girl – the man.

"I'm sorry," Ash told him sincerely, desperately trying to find the Eternity Stone in her pocket. She was still holding the pot, and here was the book, but she wasn't feeling anything else except empty cloth. Inside her head she let out a panicked scream at its loss (*nononononono!*), but outside, barely kept it together. "Whatever I did, I'm sorry, I just need a minute so I can get out of here-"

"No, no," Hasan was saying. He dropped his hands away from her, tears streaming down his face as he sobbed in...joy? "I'm a man again. Nerah, I'm a man again."

"It's not possible," the girl said in disbelief.

"But it is. *Look.*"

Argh...oh Deias, at least he had his back to her. And now Nerah was crying too, so it seemed likely that there were...unexpected extras down there.

Ash was too dumbfounded to be embarrassed by sudden nudity. Restoring lost body parts was a bit more dramatic than just healing a cut forehead, but it didn't help her more serious issue.

She couldn't find the Eternity Stone.

She took a few deep breaths, pushing back the fear and panic that threatened to overwhelm her. After all, she'd been in this kind of trouble before, and she'd got home. Eventually. "Ahem." She waited until she had the couple's attention, then smiled apologetically. "So, I helped you, you help me, right?"

"But you didn't help us," Nerah sobbed. "By some miracle you have restored Hasan's manhood, but now they will say I was unfaithful to my husband, and they'll kill us both. At the very least Hasan will be castrated again, and I'll be beaten. This is *worse.*"

Talk about ungrateful. Ash could have pointed out that Nerah had already made a good attempt at being unfaithful to her greedy, greedy husband (because who needed that many wives?) at least in spirit, but held her tongue. A hopeful idea had come to mind, of her *asking them to bring her the Eternity Stone...and never seeing them again.*

No, she quickly ditched that idea, because it was too possible that if they knew what it was, they'd be gone without a trace. How about asking them *to lead her to the walled garden again where she could retrace her own steps, and make sure another soul never touched the Stone while it was here…?*

And then the thought got a little crazy, as thoughts sometimes did, and she dismissed it. But it felt kind of like far-sight had, where she'd see the consequences of any actions she was considering, except the future results of this just got *silly*. Crucifixes, really?

But she went with the initial idea anyway, because she was feeling more than a little desperate. "Not if I help you escape. And all I need is one little thing…"

"No way," Ash said emphatically ten minutes later. "I'm not wearing that." She hadn't gone out with her belly showing since she was about two years old, when chubby was considered adorable.

"We can't lead you out there dressed as you are," Hasan pointed out impatiently. "They'll see you straight away and want to know what you were doing all that time, and you'll never find your necklace."

That was the story she'd given them, not wanting to reveal what she was really looking for.

"Or perhaps you lied to us," Nerah said tearily, unknowingly touching on the truth. "Perhaps you can't really help us escape at all. We're all going to die here."

Ash would have scolded the girl for being overly dramatic, but in truth she was scared of the exact same thing. But then she *saw herself putting on the stupid two-piece, and it wasn't as bad as she'd thought because it meant she was finally free of the torturous corset. They stuck a veil over her face and then she walked casually via a back route into the walled garden, and there was the Eternity Stone, sitting at the bottom of the fountain where she'd unwittingly dropped it.*

Wow, that really *had* felt like far-sight then. A pang of excitement ran through Ash at the idea that any of her old gifts might be returning, as if this day wasn't exciting enough.

But there was still the outfit…

"Fine," she gritted out. "But I'm going to need a cloak."

Somewhere not too far from Ash geographically, although a few centuries away chronologically…

George looked around frantically for Ashlea's distinctive dress or any sign that he wasn't here alone. Then he heard, very faintly, what sounded like his name being called. He turned in the direction the sound had come from, and there in the far distance was a tiny figure in purple.

Oh, thank Deias. Ashlea!

George practically ran to meet her, but as he drew closer he noticed something strange. "Er…hello there. You appear to have changed your clothing."

Ashlea blushed and scowled at the same time. Her hair remained in its neat nineteenth-century style, but she was now wearing some kind of loose, gauzy trousers with a vest that was slightly too short to cover her belly, the style strangely familiar. To top it off, her purple morning gown was wrapped around her shoulders like a cloak. "Hello to you too. And I'm dressed like this because I took a detour that you wouldn't believe. I think I was in a harem! Oh, and apparently castration is reversible."

George blinked. She'd made several improbable statements, but he focused on just one. "Harem? Do you mean a seraglio?"

"I don't know. Is that a place where a bunch of women lie around uselessly while guarded by giant eunuchs with swords?"

That was a very unappealing way of looking at it. "Er…yes."

"Then yes, I was in a seraglio." Ashlea shook her head in a sort of amazed dismay, pulling out Anne's little photo-book and showing it to him. "I somehow managed to get *here,*" – here being a faded image of yes, some sort of garden that might be a seraglio – "rather than *here,* where you are now. It's the strangest thing, because I was focussing so hard on the desert scene. I've no idea how it happened. Did you come straight here?"

"Indeed I did." And with a flash of guilt, George realised why she might have ended up in the wrong location – it had been his thoughts, not hers. Oops. But he kept that to himself. "Did you say something about castration being reversible?!"

In line with their original plan, the two set off down the road for the distant town, wanting to move well away from their original arrival points before travelling to Anne's time. While they walked, Ashlea told of how she'd found yet another alter-powered object – a substance that caused remarkable healing to the point of restoring lost, um, *limbs* and other assorted body parts.

"I have to admit I'm envious," George commented, then realised how it sounded. "Not of the healing! I don't require… I simply meant it's very likely Amaranthus gifted you that item. You also were given those two vials by Dr Walker, but I'm yet to find even one."

Ashlea looked surprised, then held out the little glass pot to him. "You have it, then. I've got the Eternity Stone."

"Oh, I couldn't. It was given to you."

"I found it, and that's not the same thing. Take it."

She was practically shoving it into his hand, so George took it, quietly thrilled that such a thing even existed, and honoured that he might have even temporary possession of it. Of course, he'd thought his time with supernatural objects was over, so he'd actually taken an extra little item home from Ashlea's time. She didn't need to know about *that,* though.

"I'll just hold it for a while," he said graciously. "It has limited uses, you say?"

"Looks like it," she agreed. "I used it twice, and it's less full than it was before. Maybe there'd be half a dozen more uses?"

Then they'd have to save it for something really important, George decided as he studied the road to the town up ahead. It was lined with straggly trees, but now he was closer, he could see that perhaps they weren't really trees after all...

Ashlea continued her story obliviously. "And so I realised I'd dropped the Eternity Stone, and I was having what might have been far-sight. Wouldn't that be wonderful if I had that back? Anyway, I thought that if I just sent the couple out to find the Stone for me, I'd never see them again. I figured they'd run off with it if they knew what it did, or even just by accident. So they agreed to take me to the garden, but they said I couldn't go outside in my gown. They put me in this, and we managed to get back to the garden and I found the Stone in the fountain."

"Splendid."

"I had to leave the corset back there," she rattled on. "I hope your mother doesn't mind – I'll try to replace it. I've still got the dress, at least, even though at least one of your houseguests thinks that it's hideous. So I used the Stone to take Hasan and Nerah to one of the other photos in Anne's book. The one that looked like an old caravan, you know? And the note next to it said, 'head north', so I just took a guess and told them to head north. And then I came here, and got the location right this time." Ashlea finished with a triumphant smile.

"How startling."

There was a silence. "Are you even listening to me?"

"Yes," George replied, but his eyes were still fixed on those 'trees' that were quickly showing themselves to be another kind of wooden structure: a rather less natural one. By Jove, could they really be what he thought they were? "You escaped from a seraglio. Well done."

"I thought you'd be more interested, that's all," she commented impatiently. "Um...what are you looking at?"

"I think I know where we are." George lifted a finger to point at the distant shapes. "Some time during the Reman empire."

"Oh? Why would you think that?"

"Because I don't know of anyone else who'd line their famously straight roads with crosses, that's why."

"Crosses?" Ash burst out in horror. "You mean…crucifixions?" That was something that only happened in horror movies or perhaps in the art of traditional cathedrals. She hadn't expected to *see* it.

"They might be empty," George suggested hopefully.

They looked up at the tall structures that were now almost close enough to recognise as 't' shapes, and she accepted it was unlikely they were anything else. And the two of them could have just used the Eternity Stone right then; left before there was any chance to see anything unpleasant, but they didn't. Instead they kept walking on that straight, straight road, the rise temporarily blocking out their view of the maybe-crosses. Morbid curiosity perhaps, but Ash didn't even try to suggest that they move on without an answer.

"Have you ever heard the story of the Remans' origins?" George commented suddenly (and also irrelevantly to the rest of their conversation). "About the twins?"

"I can't say I have."

"Well, I studied Classics at Combridge, so I know a few tales about the Antique Remans and Grecians and so forth. Anyway, there were supposedly these twin boys, Romulus and Remus, born in the usual dramatic circumstances in which heroes are born, and ending up abandoned in the wilderness."

"That is cheerful indeed," Ash said drily, interested in spite of herself.

"Shush, I haven't finished yet. So these twins were rescued by a humble shepherd or a wolf or something equally unusual, and they were raised to adulthood. Then being intrepid young men, they decided to found a city on a mostly uninhabited group of hills in the middle of what we would call the Italien peninsula. But they couldn't agree on exactly where to build."

"There were two of them, and they were going to build a city?" Now those were men with ambition. "Must've been a different idea of what a city was back then. But what happened? Did they build two cities?"

George shook his head. "Not at all. In fact, they argued so badly that Romulus ended up killing his brother, and then he felt so guilty for what he'd done that he named the city in Remus's memory. And that's why we have the city, and now the empire, of Reme."

"Makes sense. But it sounds a little familiar. Twins killing each other out of jealousy or such…" It reminded her of an old story or two. "Maybe twins have to love each other or hate each other. Nothing in between."

"Too much competition," George suggested. "Or too much time spent together."

Ash gave him a sideways smile. "And yet we got through six months in that little cottage, and all three of us are in one piece."

"Or perhaps-" George began, but then they came up over the rise and he fell silent.

The road to the town stretched out in front of them, lined with those strange leafless trees which were not trees at all. And then the smell hit…

"Deias," Ash blurted out, trying not to retch. "I see dead people."

They both saw dead people, and while George had known what was coming, he hadn't expected it to be so very…*ugh.*

Crosses. Dozens of them, scattered along the side of the oh-so-straight road to the town. Most of them were occupied.

Roads weren't the only thing the Remans were known for.

George couldn't speak. The closest crosses clearly had been there a while. The bodies on them were well decomposed, and birds of carrion flapped away as he and Ashlea approached.

He put his arm around Ashlea and moved her to his other side, away from the horrible sight, and wished they'd never come here. Wished they'd left as soon as he suspected what lay before them.

"Don't look," he ordered. "Get the Stone, and we'll go. These are well past any help."

His words came out all choked and strange. Deias, just the idea of it made him want to vomit. He'd seen the dead once or twice, at funerals or on the street perhaps: in winter, with those faceless piles of clothing covered in newspaper, it was hard to tell.

But here? So close, so public, so *naked*.

He sneaked another glance. So, so undignified. The few paintings and wooden crucifixes he'd seen in churches didn't show the true horror of this execution. They made it look almost romantic, like the death of a tragic hero rather than a violent, bloody ending.

Next to him, Ashlea had gone very still. "*They're* still alive," she whispered. "Over there. We can't go yet."

George looked over to where she was pointing, to the next set of crosses closer to the town. Around the tiny figures he could see a couple of others on the ground, but even as he squinted, he couldn't see any movement. "How could you possibly know?"

"Far-sight *has* come back. It really has, George. I'm sure of it now." Stone-faced, Ashlea slipped out from under his arm and began to move briskly towards the distant group.

He scrambled to catch up. When she'd mentioned that ability earlier, he hadn't taken it too seriously. After all, if his abilities had worn off after two days, so hers must have too. It was only fair.

"Far-sight? That would be very helpful, but I thought that wore off months ago!"

"I thought it had too," she agreed. "But I've been having the craziest dreams… Maybe it's got to do with time travel, because I had what *seemed* like visions of the future, back when I was in the harem. I saw myself helping that couple escape, and then coming here and finding you. And I *saw* the crosses, and I saw the people on them, and I saw-" and here she swallowed – "I saw us taking them down and healing them. I saw them running off into the town, about five of them."

Well, *that* was a sweeping statement, George thought in amazement. And if it was true – then all hail George and Ashlea, the miracle-workers.

They'd passed the first lot of crosses now, the overwhelming smell either having faded or his nose having given in, and the next lot were just a hundred feet away.

"They're criminals," he said, feeling his eyes were almost painfully wide and his throat dry, but he didn't stop walking. "Crucifixions were to punish all kinds of crimes, to show everyone what happened when you broke the law."

"Christos was crucified," Ashlea said in a small voice. "You've heard of that, I know. And they say that was just politics. He made the wrong people angry. What if those ones up there are innocent too?"

Well, it wasn't like George was going to ask if they thought they deserved to be crucified. He'd always thought of himself as a fair man, that crimes should be punished because it was justice, but seeing anyone in this kind of suffering made him think again.

He decided in that moment that he would help them, if he could.

He could hardly make it worse.

Now George was closer, he could clearly see there were five men on the crosses. Ashlea was right; they didn't look dead. They looked alive, and he could hear them moaning in pain, and all five of them stuck like butterflies on a board.

An armed soldier stood at the base of the crosses, while a robed woman cried from a distance. George quickly recognised the soldier's uniform from his studies. It *was* Reman. The helmet didn't have the red brush George would have expected, but there was a shield, a spear, a metal breastplate and so forth.

The soldier turned to look at them as they approached. His face was set like stone.

George's belly twisted, and he put a staying hand on Ashlea's arm. By Jove, this was *not* a place for a lady, but he most certainly wasn't going to turn and run.

"What are you going to do?" she asked.

He straightened his shoulders in new determination. "Just talk to them."

Seriously? Ash thought in dismay. He was going to *talk* to them? And say what?

But George was already striding towards the soldier, his nineteenth-century clothing seeming very bizarre next to the skirt-like clothing of the soldier and the long robes of the crying woman. Ash just watched as the ridiculous scene unfolded.

"Good day," George said briskly in Anglish. "I was wondering if you could answer a question for me."

Ash could make a guess at the answer – they didn't speak Anglish, and wouldn't understand a word he'd just said.

"I don't speak that language," the soldier said stolidly, the words quickly translating in Ash's brain. "Just Laten and Arameic."

"Laten and Arameic," George repeated brightly in the language the soldier had just spoken. "Which are we speaking now?"

The soldier stared at him like he was an idiot. To be fair, that was how he'd sounded, even though Ash had an idea of where he was going with this. "I don't have time for stupid questions from idiot foreigners. Move on, or you'll feel the edge of my sword."

Ash stepped forward before George could say anything else that would have *him* needing the healing pot. She blurted out in the same language, "What do you mean, you don't have time to talk? What are you doing out here by yourself?"

The soldier gave her a scornful glance. "And I won't answer questions from a trouser-wearing harlot, either."

Ash's eyebrows shot up. This wasn't the first time she'd been called a harlot for her clothing choices. Maybe there was something wrong with her translator.

Then George stepped forward, quicker than Ash knew he was capable of moving, and suddenly the soldier was twitching and convulsing, falling to the stony ground as though electrocuted.

Oh. He *had* been electrocuted. A taser's hooks were still attached to his loose collar where they'd struck him.

"Couldn't have him talking to you like that," George said, sounding equally pleased and defensive. "And he was speaking Laten, I'm sure of it. I *knew* this must be somewhere in the Reman empire. He said the other language was Arameic – we might even be in the Holy Land, do you think?"

"Never mind that. George, where did you get a *taser*?" Ash asked in amazement.

"From your time, of course." George shrugged sheepishly. "I found it in the same car boot sale that Anne bought her album."

Ash had given them both a couple of pounds to spend that day, neither having any income at the time, but she hadn't known what George had bought, or if he'd even bought anything. "They were selling a taser at a car boot sale?!"

"Apparently."

Then he'd got a bargain at less than two pounds.

"How long do you think the effect lasts?" he asked.

"I have no idea," Ash answered. "So we better move fast."

Yes, they were actually going to do this thing. They were going to get those men down off those crosses and heal them, for better or worse. Far-sight had said so.

"Certainly," George agreed promptly. "Ah…did the far-sight show you *how* we were going to do this?"

And that was where it got a little vague. But while Ash was debating how to interpret the images that had flickered full-speed through her mind, the robed woman approached them.

"Were you sent to help us?" she cried. "My brother Eli is not a criminal! He's a patriot who stands against the wicked invaders who occupy our land, but he's going to die a criminal's death."

The woman was younger than Ash had first supposed, probably about her own age, with light brown skin and large, tear-swollen dark eyes.

"How long have they been up there?" George asked.

"Just since this morning."

Just then the soldier began to move, trying to push himself to a sitting position. George casually shocked him again with the still-attached taser probes until he stopped moving, then turned back to Ash. "The Eternity Stone," he said decisively in Anglish. "We can use it to move them down and leave the nails behind, and to Hades with any danger. Then we can heal them."

Ash wasn't sure about that because *she'd* always managed to bring things with her when she'd travelled with the Stone, but she shrugged. Something was going to work, and soon, even if not this. "Let's do it."

The soldier started to make a moaning noise, and as if suddenly remembering he held it, George pulled out the binding cord. "Just a moment. There, it works, doesn't it? I could have done that the first time and saved the taser battery."

Ash shot him a startled glance. He'd clearly learned more from her own time than she'd realised, if he knew how batteries worked.

The binding cord worked just as well on random Reman

soldiers as it had on the two of them, and together they dragged him to the side of the road. As they finished, she could hear the girl saying tearfully to one of the men on the crosses, "The strange, unclean foreigners are going to help us, Eli. They must be celestials in disguise."

"I say," George muttered. "Probably cleaner than that lot."

One of the other men shouted, "I'll believe it when I see it!" therefore destroying Ash's illusion that being crucified also affected one's vocal cords.

"Ignore them," Ash said briskly. "Two steps, as quick as we can. I'll do the Stone; you do the healing."

She took a deep breath and moved up to the nearest cross, pushing back her revulsion over the sight. Yes, the nails did go right through the limbs (yuck, yuck, yuck), and were held with rope to make sure they didn't pull through (extra yuck!). It was disgusting and violent and clever and cruel, and she had to tell herself that it wasn't real before she could put her hand on the man's leg.

Pretend it was a game. A fake nail, a fake leg, with fake blood…

She had the Eternity Stone in the other hand, and she looked at the ground three feet away and thought: *there.*

As always, there was a disconcerting moment when it felt like the world had moved around her, but there she was, and there the man was, standing on the ground naked and bloody and thankfully minus metal attachments.

Hooray! It had worked! But then he moaned in pain and collapsed, and George rushed over, the healing pot with its lid off. "Up to the face, you said?"

But the puff of bright light had already emitted, and the man stopped moaning, now blinking awkwardly where he lay on the ground.

"He's fine," Ash said briskly, her tone hiding the incredible sense of achievement she felt. (Yeah, sure, she did this kind of thing all the time!) She pulled her purple gown/cloak off her shoulders and dropped it over the man's lap to give him some dignity. "Next."

It worked. Incredibly, wonderfully, it worked for every last one of them. Within three minutes, the crosses were empty and their victims were all standing or sitting on the stony ground, George's great-grandmother's gown having become multiple purple loin-cloths.

"Thank you, thank you, thank you," one of the men kept saying, and the woman just kept crying and hanging off him.

Ash hated to ask, but… "Aren't you afraid they'll just do it again? Crucify you, that is?"

"That's why we've got to leave immediately," one of the other men replied decisively. He wasn't a man – more of a boy, really, with a scrubby brown beard and skinny cheeks – and Ash wondered again what he possibly could have done to merit such an execution. She hoped they hadn't just rescued a bunch of murderers.

George must have been thinking the same thing, because he said, "Well, good luck with everything. Go, and sin no more, and all that."

They gave him an odd look, and some began to run for the gates of the nearby town, leaving something white fluttering in the air behind them. The last couple of men lingered. "Do you need anything? Food, drink?"

"Celestials don't need to eat," his friend whispered. "You might be insulting them."

"They could eat," the first argued. "If they wanted to."

"Actually, we should be going," Ash said before the conversation could get any sillier and they had to admit they were not, in fact, heavenly beings hiding their wings. Besides, she felt like she'd only just had breakfast.

Annoyingly the two men looked to George for confirmation,

and he nodded. "We must go immediately. But thank you for your kind offer."

"As we must also," the first man said, giving another thankful bow. "But if you need anything, anything at all, ask for the home of Simon bar Judah! He is most gracious in entertaining strangers, and we will tell him what you have done!"

They disappeared off into the distance, and George sighed. "All the more reason we should move on. There's probably only one more use left in that little glass pot of yours, and just think of all the invalids there must be in that town."

"This pot of ours," Ash corrected happily. She walked over to pick up the desolate petticoat from the shredded morning gown, left behind when the men fled. "I should probably put this on before we go see Anne. But we'll have to make that quick too – I can't be seen like this."

"Mm," George said, but it was obvious he wasn't paying attention. He was practically beaming. "By Jove, that was amazing, wasn't it? I don't even mind that they called us unclean foreigners."

She turned to him, grinning. "Yeah, it was amazing. We make a good team."

"And all we need are a couple of improbably supernatural objects."

Ash would have made some joke in return, but suddenly a series of images flashed through her mind. They told of danger: serious, and scary, and soon. "Behind you!"

George turned too slowly, but just fast enough to dodge the sword strike of the no-longer bound Reman soldier. The soldier stumbled, his heavy sword pulling him forward, and George stuck out his foot and tripped him, then pressed his taser directly against the fallen soldier's shoulder.

The man twitched and went still, and Ash ran forward to grab the sword. It was short and heavy and not at all beautiful, but hey, it was a souvenir. Besides, if she had it, then he couldn't use it.

"Deias, that was too close," she muttered, still shaking from the suddenness of the failed attack. "But that binding cord doesn't last for long, does it?"

George was standing at the side of the road, looking over the slight rise to where they'd originally left the soldier. "Yes, it does," he answered, and his voice sounded thin and strange. "Because that's not the soldier we bound. Look here."

Behind the rise, almost exactly where they'd left him, lay the body of the soldier. The yellow binding cord was still wrapped around his neck and shoulders, and there was no doubt that he was dead. Live people weren't usually that shade of grey.

The elation of a moment earlier drained away as George and Ashlea looked at the soldier's body with shock and horror. Yes, they'd walked past multiple bodies in different, disgusting stages of decomposition, but this man had just been *alive* and arguing. Now he was decisively dead.

Ashlea said a word that George had never heard from her mouth before, and then as one they turned back to where he'd left the false-soldier on the ground.

But even as they watched, the man's figure changed and began to morph into a black flapping thing. It formed within seconds into a large carrion bird, which staggered to its feet and awkwardly took to the air, hovering a moment before disappearing off into the desert.

The two travellers stood there for a long, numb moment, watching it go.

Then George said, "Bother. I should have thrown a rock at it."

"Forget that," Ashlea countered, still watching the space where the shapeshifter had vanished to. Her face was white and eyes wide. "I think I know who that is, and it's not someone we want following us."

THE THRONE GATEWAY

Renwick Castle, 1556 AD

Anne leaned against the wall, tapping her fingers impatiently against its rough stone blocks. From here on the top of the bailey wall she could see across the busy courtyard to the outer wall of the castle, all the way to the nearby river and the dozens of cottages scattered across the estate, and right to the forest she'd so recently been 'lost' in.

All was much as it ever had been here at Renwick Castle, except for one thing. Edgar had commanded her presence…and up here, in this strange place?

Edgar had asked to speak to *her*. Considering they only spoke when they were forced to, 'twas most odd that he would want to speak to her at all, much less privately. And that he'd sent Blanche to fetch her…?

Shivering slightly at the chill air, Anne wrapped her arms around herself. She hadn't brought her cloak, but then Edgar's summons *had* come quickly. She knew not why he didn't simply come to her, but mayhap his fear of the non-existent sweating sickness stopped him. That might explain why he'd chosen such an odd meeting place.

Could it be bad news? Mayhap he wished to reject her as his wife; to have her put away in a little house all on her own…

No, that would be excellent news! Then she might take her

sister and return to 2013, and they'd never know the difference. But 'twould be too easy, too neat an ending for their fractious relationship.

And then Edgar arrived, and put an end to her musings.

"Lady Anne," he greeted her. As usual, he was wearing his beard trimmed into a neat goatee. It reminded Anne of a villain from a children's film in Ash's time – but in that one, the heroine didn't find herself wed to the villain.

That last thought was probably unfair, Anne corrected herself. Edgar was an ass in typically 1556 ways, but he hadn't shown any true villainous tendencies.

"My lord." Anne curtseyed politely. "You wished to speak to me?"

"Yes. Yes, indeed." He turned away, running an agitated hand through his hair. "I wished to speak with you."

"Yes," she replied patiently. She was already clear on that. "On what matter do you wish to speak? Are you sending me away?"

"What? No. I mean, yes. Sort of. You might say that."

Anne frowned at him quizzically. He really did look out of sorts; almost nervous. "Well, what is it? I'm away from my sister's sick bed to be here."

He scowled back, suddenly less nervous. "Heaven forbid you take a mere ten minutes to speak to your lord and master. What happened to promising to honour and obey?"

"What happened to promising to forsake all others?" Anne snapped back before she could stop herself.

Edgar's face went red with anger, then he smirked. "You're a mouthy little wench, are you not? I shall not be sorry to say this…"

"What? Come out with it. My sister may be dying as we speak." Hopefully not true, but better than slapping him in the face.

That same smirk, and then he looked nervous again. "I must

show you." He gestured towards the wall a little further down from where she was standing. "Over here, come see."

Puzzled, she did so, craning her head out over the wall where he was pointing. "I don't see anything amiss. What am I looking for?"

"No, on the base of the wall itself, right in front of you. What do you see?"

The wide wall hit her at mid chest, and to see whatever he referred to, Anne practically had had to go up on her tiptoes. The stone she now leaned on shifted unpleasantly. "Ugh, the stone is loose, and I see nothing."

"Look again."

Sighing in irritation, she leaned so far over the wide, loose stone wall that her toes left the ground. She studied the base of the bailey wall before them. "I still don't-" she started to say, but then Edgar planted both hands on her back and pushed *hard*.

The loose stone fell away and she stumbled out over the gap, for a moment hovering between falling and catching herself. She screamed.

"Oh no, watch out!" he called loudly, and then he pushed her again, sending her over the top and plummeting head first towards the hard, hard ground.

Her last coherent thought was *I can't believe I fell for that…*

At the foot of five empty crosses, Reman Palestine

"Janeus," George echoed. "What makes you think it's him instead of any other of the two dozen Nobles? They've all used the Eternity Stone when they travelled with Seyen Johannis."

"The eyes," Ash replied firmly, willing him to believe her. "The fake-George at the manor looked just like you, right down to the eye colour. Back in 2155, the Noble that looked like you couldn't get the colour right, and if you think on how that fake-soldier thing just changed into a bird – that wasn't illusion, George. It looked like a real change, and Sam was always telling me of how his Noble, Janeus, was the one *real* shapeshifter."

"Sam said a lot of things."

"It doesn't mean he wasn't right about this one," Ash argued. "Janeus was sent away somewhere. Banished from the others, yes? Maybe he wasn't impacted by the others' power loss. Maybe he felt the Stone was freed from Seyen and came after it. Came after *us*."

She flicked open Anne's photo album to one of the pages she previously hadn't understood – the page from a book about Grecian and Reman myths. *This* page showed the many loves of the king of the gods, who by rights should have been in prison on assault charges. He had changed into eagles, bulls, even clouds of gold in his pursuit of 'romance'. What a lecher.

"That's a lot of maybes." But as George stared at that odd little picture, she saw the moment where he believed her. "But it does makes sense. You do realise, though, that it doesn't matter who's following us. What matters is that someone *is*, and as you said, it's not someone we can trust."

Ash slumped glumly at that reminder. Yes, they were again being pursued by homicidal maniacs. Again. "So what can we do?"

"The only thing there is to do. Fetch Anne and her sister…then go to find Amaranthus."

It was the only thing to do that made any sense. Amaranthus's little flying house had felt as safe as a mother's womb, and probably hadn't even existed in the normal realm. Of course, they wouldn't know *when* to find Amaranthus, but as George agreed, it most likely wouldn't matter. The man had an excellent grasp on time travel, and whenever they showed up, he'd be expecting them.

They hoped.

They'd decided this time that only Ash would hold the Eternity Stone to avoid confusion over their destination. George still held the healing pot and the recovered binding cord. The open photo album displayed an image of an old castle on which Anne had carefully written *Renwick Castle,* and scrawled on the blank page next to it were the numbers *10.10.1556.* They had a location and a date.

"Think of Anne," George instructed half a second before she'd been about to do that exact thing. "No, wait, don't. If we appear right next to her in a public place, we'll be in a dreadful spot. Focus on somewhere quiet, secluded."

"Like a toilet?" Ash asked sarcastically.

He didn't seem to notice. "Like a storage closet, perhaps."

"Storage closet it is."

And then because they really couldn't wait any longer, they gripped hands, and Ash tried to focus on that castle sketch, Anne, and the year 1556. Oh, and maybe a storage closet too…

A fraction of a second later, Ash and George were crammed together in a small, dark space. It felt like a closet – Ash could feel clothes pressing in on her side – but it smelled like a toilet. A very well-used toilet.

Next to her, she heard George make a retching noise. "Damn it to Hades, Ashlea! I said *not* a toilet!"

"Shush," Ash breathed, cupping her hand protectively over her nose and mouth. "I hear voices."

They froze. Two women's voices – accompanied by footsteps – became louder for a moment, then moved away. They appeared to be speaking Anglish, but then so did everybody when their speech was automatically translated.

After a minute, George said, "Do you think we're in a closet? I can't see a thing."

Ash swung her arm out experimentally. It connected with (ouch) a stone wall, and-

"Ouch!"

…found George's head, and far lower down than it ought to be.

"What are you doing down there?" she hissed.

"I think we're in a garderobe," he whispered back.

"What's that?"

"A water closet. Where they keep the privy."

"George, there are clothes in here. It can't be!"

"I can feel the seat."

Ew.

There was a creaking noise as he clearly found the door, and a thin vertical ribbon of light widened, briefly blinding Ash. Once her eyes adjusted, she saw it revealed a hall.

George stuck his head cautiously out of the gap. "I can't see anyone."

"Then let's get out of here! It stinks!"

They tumbled out of what was revealed in the light to be yes, a privy. It also appeared to double as a well-stocked wardrobe.

"That's disgusting," Ash complained, shaking her borrowed robes as if she could shake off the smell. "Why would anyone put nice gowns and furs like that in what smells like a portaloo? The clothes would reek."

George was looking both ways down the narrow stone hall. Thin windows were scattered down one side, interspersed with tapestries and unlit wooden torches. "That was the idea, I think. The smell scared off any moths."

"Would scare off anybody," Ash muttered. Good grief, no wonder Anne had smelled a bit fragrant the first time they'd met, if this was what she was used to.

"I think it was a medieval practice," he commented as if Ash hadn't spoken.

She perked up. If they'd got the timing right, then they were now in 1556, home of big poofy skirts and Shakespear (or that might be too early, she mused) and court jesters and funny collars and the bubonic plague... "Now we just have to find Anne!"

Just then they heard more footsteps approaching. George quickly moved down the hallway and opened the first door he came to, checking inside. "It's empty."

Ash followed him into the dimly lit room. It was stuffy with an odd, almost incense-like smell to the air, and was dominated by a high four-poster bed with long swathes of fabric falling right to the floor.

"Well, it's better than the garderobe," she commented quietly once the voices had gone. "What do you think we should do now?"

In the semi-dark she saw him, a mixture of amusement and dismay evident on his face. "Do you mean to say you don't know?"

"I *never* know. If I gave you the impression that I ever knew what I was doing, then sorry. Because I don't. I just show up..."

"And deal with things as they come along," George finished. "Well, *someone* in this castle will know where to find Anne. All we need to do is ask."

It showed he was an unusual male, if he'd even consider that. But perhaps this wasn't the same as asking for directions when driving. "And hope that the person doesn't run off screaming about intruders," Ash said dryly. She sighed, a deep heartfelt one right from her core. "I've had enough running for today. I'm just tired. It feels like it's been a very long day."

"Centuries," George quipped.

Ash smiled at him, then moved to sit back on the high, lumpy surface of the bed. But no sooner had she sat down than she felt a strange firmness underneath her, and leapt up with a yelp. "There's something here!"

"Someone, rather," George said, looking over her shoulder at the still figure, whose arms appeared to be crossed over their chest under the draped cloth. "And I'm pretty sure they're past help. They only put them in that position when they're...well, deceased."

Slightly repulsed, Ash still couldn't help herself from bringing the cloth back to reveal a familiar pale face, and George's horrified gasp just confirmed what she already knew.

"So that's why Anne never came back with the Stone," she croaked, her throat tight. "She's dead."

"I can't believe we're too late," George said in disbelief. "You pictured her alive, did you not?"

"Of course I did! But the Eternity Stone doesn't always work the way we think it will," Ash despaired. Then an idea occurred. "Wait, all we need to do is go back a day or two. It'll be fine!"

"You can't change the past," he said in a low voice. "We can't go back to stop something happening. Don't you remember?"

"I remember that we stopped Sam from dying back in 2155," Ash retorted. "He sure as Hades didn't deserve it, yet we still did it." Although to be fair, it hadn't been the intention of them going back in time. They'd only wanted to avoid the incredible destruction, and Sam had been a side effect. Maybe that was the problem – if they tried to go back in time to change one single issue, it wasn't possible, but if it was for a different issue…?

But they'd never actually seen Sam's body.

George made a strange groaning noise, no doubt from the grief.

"Don't worry," she told him, firmly pushing back her own tears. "We'll make this work, or none of it was worth it. What's the point of time-travelling if you can't go back a day to save a friend's life?"

"*Nnnt ddd-d.*"

"Speak up, I didn't hear you."

"That wasn't *me*," he said in surprise.

They both turned towards the bed, from where the occupant now stared at them with wide eyes in their pale face.

For a half second Ash was tempted to scream about zombies, then she realised the open eyes were a good thing. "Anne! You're alive!"

"*N-t a-hn.*"

Whatever that meant. "Don't worry," Ash told her joyfully. "We'll get you sorted out in a jiffy, and then you can talk as much as you like!"

The healing pot was hastily pulled out and pressed up against Anne's mouth with the customary blinding flash of light, and within moments they saw the colour return to her cheeks.

"How do you feel?" George asked breathlessly.

"Saint's bones, I feel much, much better," the girl replied with growing animation. "And I vow, you must be celestials to have healed me thus, but why is it that you would make such a simple error?"

George was frowning at her, and Ash stared in increasing realisation.

"What do you mean?" he asked.

"Why, that you have mistaken me for my sister," the girl said simply.

"She's not Anne," Ash said flatly. Now she wasn't panicking over Anne's supposed death, she could see that this girl was perhaps a little younger and had darker hair, although their bone structure was remarkably similar. The room's darkness had caused the confusion.

"Indeed I'm not. I am Elspeth, although Anne calls me Bethie at times. And sometimes just Beth. But that is because I have given her permission to do so." She briefly looked anxious. "But you must call me Elspeth, whoever you are, because although you did just heal me, we are not friends. I'm sure you understand."

"She really is Anne's sister," Ash repeated, her mouth beginning to curve in a smile. She'd never met anyone else who could be so carelessly, earnestly insulting.

"Wonderful to meet you, Lady Elspeth," George said sincerely. "We're friends of your sister. I'm the Honourable Mr George Seymour, and this is…" He and Ash exchanged glances as they struggled to work out exactly how they would introduce her. "…My friend, Miss Ashlea O'Reilly."

"*Ohh*," Elspeth said knowingly. "She's your mistress."

"I am not!" Ash exclaimed just as George said, "She is not!"

"She is my betrothed," he corrected, and while Ash shot him in a glare, she didn't say otherwise. The story would make their lives easier.

"Then why did you not say so in the first place?" Elspeth didn't wait for them to answer, rattling on, "And I'm not a lady. I'm just Elspeth, although my sister Anne *is* a lady. And I can't think how you would ever have met her. She has been very sheltered despite all the trouble of the past few years, none of which was her fault, of course. But she rarely has more than two minutes alone, and I've never seen any of *you* before. Your garb is most odd. Except…"

Elspeth stopped abruptly mid-speech, everything Anne had said suddenly making sense. The last period of time had been a mess of heat and sweat and confusion, and although she now felt as sprightly as a spring hare, 'twas only beginning to come together.

George… Ashlea… Some device called the Eternity Stone…

"Saint's bones," she muttered desolately. "Anne was telling the truth."

And Elspeth, in a well-meaning fit of fever, had dropped the valuable item down into one of the nastier privies.

"She told you, then?" the dark-haired girl asked. "Of course she would. Did she tell you everything?"

Elspeth nodded dolefully. Everything. Anne had told her every last detail, and she hadn't been sure whether to believe or not. "I saw the blue plas-tik toothbrush."

"By Jove, not the toothbrush," the boy muttered. "Do you know where she is now?"

Elspeth was about to shake her head, but vaguely recalled familiar shrill tones asking for Anne's presence. "With her husband, the earl. I know not where."

"But it's been barely a month," George burst out, looking horrified. "She can't have been married already."

Elspeth looked at him pityingly. "A month is more than enough time to be wed. A day is more than enough time, if you've a fat enough purse to speed the way." They hadn't even called the banns for Anne's wedding – when 'twould be announced in church for the three weeks prior to the marriage. Queen Marian's orders had been enough.

"Never mind that," Ashlea said. "Can you take us to Anne?"

In that garb…? Elspeth thought not. "I will bring her here," she said instead. "You cannot leave this room dressed as you are. 'Twould be a scandal."

"Then I'll go," George suggested. "Bring her back here."

"Both of you can't leave this room," Elspeth repeated. Did he really think his overly fitting garments were any better? He might not have a thin line of belly showing as the girl did, but he wasn't wearing a codpiece as any decent man would.

Enough said.

Elspeth ran down the empty halls faster than she knew she had energy to run, ignoring the chill stone on her bare feet. Unusually, all the main rooms were empty, and she could hear some kind of chatter from outside.

The kitchen, she decided. The cooks always knew who was where. But when she burst in, that room was empty too. Even the roasting spit had been abandoned.

She followed the noise to the outer side of the inner bailey: the inner courtyard of the castle where most of the day-to-day action took place. It seemed like every other living soul in Renwick castle had the same idea. They were all crowded around one location where *everyone* seemed to be shouting. 'Twas only by chance that she heard a snippet of her sister's voice, and she knew Anne was right in the thick of it.

"My lady!" But Elspeth couldn't get through the crowd. Finally she nudged one of the farmhands eagerly watching from the edge, who was also considerably taller than her. "What's going on?"

"Milady fell off the bailey wall," the boy answered without even glancing at her. "An' she's accused his lordship of pushin' her."

Elspeth felt the blood drain from her face. "Fell off the wall? Is she harmed?"

"Not at all, 'tis the miracle of it. Fell right from the top and landed on rocks, and is up and shoutin' at the earl just fine." The boy finally turned to look down at her. "Hey, you're milady's base-born sister. Ain't you s'posed to be dying of the sweatin' sickness?"

"The sweating sickness?" the man next to him asked. "Who?"

"This one here."

"I never had the sweating sickness," Elspeth snapped. "'Twas but a festering cut. As you see, I am quite well. But I need to speak-"

But the man had already covered his mouth with the dirty sleeve of his jerkin and was shrieking, "Contagion! This girl here has the deadly sweating sickness!"

"I do not!"

But people were starting to pay attention, and it didn't look like anyone was interested in listening to what Elspeth had to say.

"Clumsy!" Anne shouted. Her face was hot with anger and shock, and her wimple had long since fallen off her hair. Her bare head made her think of 2013, and she cared not. "'Twas not my clumsiness but your own villainy, you bewspawling cumberground! As if I would take myself up to that wall for the sake of the *view* when my dear sister lay so ill?"

She'd said it a dozen times since finding herself abruptly at the base of the wall rather than at the top, and it seemed the more she insisted, the less people believed her.

'Twas a miracle, they all admitted, that she had fallen such a long way and now stood before them, but the reason *why* she fell was still being loudly debated.

Standing between the two of them looking rather panicked was Sir Robert, the castle's long-time steward. He was trying to maintain some kind of order, but 'twas all Anne could do not to run over and slap her murderous husband in his lying, wicked face.

"As though I would sully my hands with such low works!" Edgar insisted, his hands held dramatically to his chest.

"You would! You did, to be rid of an unwanted wife!"

"Wife! You are hardly a wife, woman, and well you know it. With the threats you made me should I do my husbandly duty, 'tis by necessity that our marriage remains unconsummated. I could have been rid of you at any time, and I chose not. I am no murderer!"

It seemed the entirety of Renwick's population was here, and now every last one of them knew that Anne's marriage was unconsummated. And Edgar was placing the blame squarely on Anne's head. 'Twas a distraction from the true problem, but a clever one.

"Just one moment," Sir Robert said, bewilderment turning to anger. "Your marriage is not a true one, and by your doing, my lady?"

Well, 'twas true that Anne hadn't precisely insisted, but that was an unfair assertion that she'd *threatened* Edgar should he try to consummate. She opened her mouth to argue (and to direct their attention back to her attempted murder) when a scuffle at the edge of the crowd caught her attention.

The crowd parted as though from a rabid dog, and there in the gap stood Elspeth, bare-headed and barefoot and looking vibrant with good health.

"Bethie!" Anne exclaimed in sudden joy. Her throat was almost sore from such exclamations, but there was room for just one more. "Oh happy day – the anti-botiks worked!"

"I know not what that means," the girl said, looking worried at all the eyes fixed on her. "I merely came to tell you that you have visitors, but these fools all think I have the sweating sickness. They won't believe 'twas but a festering cut. Did you truly fall from the bailey wall?"

"Festering cut?" someone shouted. "If 'tis but a festering cut, then why won't she show us?"

"Because 'tis in a place not for your eyes to see," Anne snapped at the unknown accuser. Then to her sister, "I was pushed from the wall, not that anyone seems to listen. And what visitors could I have?"

"Two foreigners. The Honourable George Seymour, and Ash-"

"Ashlea O'Reilly?" Anne finished. Her heart leapt – they were here, finally! – and she barely waited for her sister's nod of agreement before she lifted her skirts and began running for the castle wall, leaving behind the stunned crowd.

Her friends had surely come in through the gateway in the woods, and 'twas the Eternal One's mercy that they'd met Elspeth first and not another of the servants.

Anne had made it quite some way before realising that she didn't know where Ash and George were, and she ground to a halt. "Well? Where are they?"

"In the solar," Elspeth replied. "But-"

"Visitors?" Sir Robert was saying in bafflement somewhere behind her. "What foreign visitors do you have, my lady? You have not left this castle in nigh two years."

"Ahh..." Anne was lost for an answer, then she shrugged,

uncaring. Her day had quickly gone from dreadful to marvellous, just like that, and all their other troubles would surely work themselves out too. "Very unusual ones. Excuse me. Bethie! Come at once!"

George and Ash sat awkwardly on the hard bed in the smoky room, George tapping his fingers on his knees. Ash was still holding the Reman sword, so she entertained herself by tapping the heavy blade on the ground in unison. *Tip…tap. Tip…tap.*

'Wait for me to return', little Elspeth had said, and so they had. And they were *still* waiting.

"I can't believe we're in 1556, and we're stuck in a stuffy little room," Ash exclaimed finally, dropping the sword on the floor. "I want to *see* something."

"Look out the window."

She'd already tried that, but with the angle of the very narrow gap, there was nothing to see except stone and sky. "I'll just check the hall," she said a few moments later, expecting George to disagree, or to at least say that they should stay out of sight.

But he must have been as bored as her, because he jumped up off the bed. "I'll come with you."

Excellent.

The hall was the same one they'd just come in by, but earlier they hadn't had a chance to really look at it. Now it seemed less like a hall and almost like a long, thin room, complete with chairs and shelves and tapestried walls. Ash didn't think much of the style of the tapestry, but if she had to create everything by hand, maybe she wouldn't be so fussy.

The floors were covered with a kind of woven mat, and the faint smell of herbs emitted with every step. At least it smelled better than the garderobe.

"Just think," George commented, looking around him with

interest. "These buildings are remnants from a much bloodier time, when the strength of a castle determined the inhabitants' safety. You can see the outer windows are too narrow to allow attack, although of course it means the whole thing is rather dark. Odd to think that it'll be gone within two hundred years."

It was odd, but Ash was realising it was just part of time travel (or life, actually). While jewels, for example, could last centuries, the really important things were all gone within two hundred years. Like people.

Suddenly the door at the end of the hall burst open, so fast that they didn't have time to run and hide or even to apologise for not staying in one place. And there was Anne, wearing a green and grey dress in a similar style to what Ash had last seen her in, with a big fat skirt, long tight sleeves, and a bodice that would crush the average rib cage. Her cheeks were pink and her hair loose and flustered, and when she saw them, her face lit up.

"You came!" But then her face fell again. "But I've lost the Eternity Stone and so Elspeth can't come through the gateway and I can't very well leave her here alone! And I can't stay either because Edgar's just gone and told the whole world that we had a white marriage, and 'twas after he pushed me off the bailey wall, that canker-crusted warthog, *and* now Sir Robert wishes to *speak* with me, as though the whole thing were my fault alone!

"But I'm most relieved that you're here. Although Ash, what *are* you wearing? Did I not explain to you the expected garb for 1556?"

Anne had said the whole thing without pausing for breath, and Ash was still catching up. "Ahh…"

Behind Anne appeared another, similar figure, except the hair darker and the clothing plainer. The not-lady Elspeth – and that was a question Ash would like answered too – closed the door behind her. "They healed me," she said. "With light like the noon-day sun. So who cares what they're wearing."

Hear, hear.

"It wasn't quite like the noon-day sun," George said a little sheepishly, looking pleased. "But it was rather impressive. Definitely alter-power, just like the vials, Anne. We found them in your little book, with all the instructions."

"So 'twas not the anti-botiks?" Anne frowned. "And what little book do you speak of?"

"Your photo album, of course," he replied. "Although I'd like to know how you lined up the instructions so very well."

"There were no instructions," Anne said blankly. "I simply took photographs of those images with Amaranthus in them, and set them in the empty spaces in the book. What else was in there?"

George and Ash exchanged a puzzled glance. That *really* wasn't what they'd been thinking, and it seemed that they might have put their trust in something that was purely coincidental.

"Other pictures…" Ash replied vaguely. "But I can see we've got a lot to catch up on."

Just then the hall door burst open again. In flooded at least half a dozen people, including a thin woman with an expression like curdled milk, wearing a rather lovely dress in shades of orange and gold, and a youngish man with a scrubby beard and a nervous expression, and what might have been a sword at his side. He wore tights and a funny bulging jacket with a snug waist, almost like a dress. To top it off was a horrendous, fascinating codpiece perched like an oversized cricket cup on the outside of his clothing. There were others too, but those were the ones Ash noticed the most.

"Oh my Deias," she whispered to George. "They're so *medieval*."

"Technically I don't believe 1556 counts as medieval," he whispered back. "It's early Renaissance period."

"But you told me it was medieval when we got here!"

"Yes, but then I considered it further, and I'm quite certain it's early Renaissance!"

Their whispered conversation came to an end when the new

people began to speak.

"So these are your visitors, are they?" the woman in orange announced shrilly. "Why have they been sneaked into the solar as though they must hide themselves, hmm Lady Anne? And why did you run from Sir Robert as you did? There will be a reckoning!"

"Later, Blanche," Anne snapped, causing Ash to secretly cheer her on. "We must go to the woods at once. 'Twill be a most brief visit – I've left a *most* valuable item there." She gave Ash and George a meaningful look that took a few moments to decipher.

"You can't leave!" Blanche shrieked. "Did you not hear what I just said?"

"My lady," the younger man said a little apologetically to the shrill orange person, who apparently held a title, then to Anne, "'Tis true, Lady Anne. Sir Robert is even now speaking with your husband, and desires to speak with you also once he has finished. You cannot leave this castle, not at this moment. Not alone nor with visitors."

He frowned at George and Ash, his eyes almost bugging when they landed on Ash's too-short vest. Ash flushed in embarrassment and more than a little irritation. Codpiece man could hardly talk about modesty.

Anne opened her mouth to speak again – and possibly to make the situation worse in her tactless way – but then Ash realised what Anne was trying to achieve. A gateway in the woods…

"We have the Eternity Stone," Ash burst out, and suddenly all eyes were on her. "Anne. We have the Stone already."

"How on earth do *you* have it?" Anne asked, baffled.

"What's she saying?" the annoying orange Blanche snapped. "What pagan language is this, Anne of Covington?"

"Countess," Anne snapped back at her. "And none of your damn business, woman, if you can't understand it."

There was a collective gasp from around the room, and Ash

took another step back. "I thought I was speaking Anglish," she said apologetically. "But we can leave any time you want."

"'Tis but the accent," Elspeth said quietly from behind Anne. "But as for why the Stone is in other hands, sister, 'twas my own actions. My sin."

"Oh, shut it about your sin, Bethie! 'Tis not *your* sin to be illegit-"

"Not that," the girl snapped back, finally showing she also had a temper. "I meant that I threw your little black stone into the privy when I had a fever. 'Twas wrong, but I did it."

Anne's jaw dropped. "The privy?"

"The one just there," Elspeth explained, guiltily pointing to the door Ash and George had arrived through. "'Twas meant to be for your own good."

"Bethie!"

The pieces of the puzzle suddenly clicked into place for Ash. The Stone had been dropped into a privy – garderobe; whatever they called it – and had languished there for half a millennium, safe in a pile of…

Urgh.

"So that's how you found it in the ruins, Ashlea," George commented happily, showing he'd been thinking along the same lines, but apparently less concerned about the hygiene of the thing. "But as entertaining as this is, we *do* have some pressing matters to attend to. Might we have two minutes of your time to speak *privately*?"

Anne moved to open the nearest door, revealing what a storage room filled with bolts of cloth and stacked baskets. "In here."

"My lady," the young man said warningly. "I do not believe that going into rooms with strange men-"

"Sir Jasper," Anne retorted in much the same tone, "I do not know what you believe Mr Seymour will get up to with myself, my friend and my sister, but I do not appreciate the insinuation."

Sir Jasper flushed deep pink. "I did not mean such, my lady, but I have been instructed that you are not to leave."

"I say, we're hardly leaving," George interjected in a blatant lie. Of course they intended to leave the country and the time period as soon as possible.

"And I do not know *you*, sirrah," the man retorted. "So forgive me if I will not take your word either."

"By the Rood," Anne said in exasperation. "We shall speak in that storeroom for two minutes. What is it you fear we will do: open a magic door to fairyland the moment we leave your sight?"

It was a clever thing to say, Ash thought, because it was very close to the truth, but it sounded so unlikely that the man was certain to disagree.

Sir Jasper fell for the bait. "Of course not," he stammered, stepping back out as though to distance himself from the idea. "You may have a few minutes, my lady."

Anne nodded at him loftily, lifted her chin, and led the way into the small room with Ash, George and Elspeth following close behind. Then she slammed the door decisively behind her, looked at the three of them, and burst into tears.

"I do apologise," Anne said several minutes later. Her eyes and nose were red, but otherwise she looked a lot more cheerful. "'Twas all of it happening at once, you understand."

"I'd probably cry too if my husband tried to kill me," Ash soothed.

They'd each summarized what had happened in their time apart, and why they were now here together, and Ash had to say that Anne's version was slightly more dramatic. Especially the part where she'd fallen from the castle wall and landed softly on the ground. Anne had said it had felt like she'd floated at the last moment, and that sent a pang of wistful excitement through Ash. Maybe, just maybe, there was a little bit of flying left in each of them...

"I promise I won't try to kill you," George said jokingly. "But you've got to let me hold the TV remote."

Anne's head shot up in surprise as she connected the two statements somewhat incorrectly. "You two were wed?"

"No, we're not wed," Ash gritted out, feeling her cheeks heat. They hadn't yet discussed *that* part of the story, instead focusing on how Ash had found the Eternity Stone (for which Elspeth appeared to be in the dog box slightly with Anne, what with throwing it down the toilet where it lay for five hundred years) and the not-so mysterious attacker following them. But George was implying that he'd come back to her time to hog the TV, and she found she quite liked the idea. "It's a long story, but just remember that there's no such thing as a white lie."

"Ashlea has unwittingly rescued me from the dreaded fate of a forced marriage," he added jokingly. It fell flat when they all realised that Anne had hardly escaped that same fate.

"I do not see that 'tis such a bad idea for the two of you," Anne said to all of their surprise. "After all, who else could understand what we've been through?"

"On that reasoning, George may as well marry you," Ash countered, feeling that her blush hadn't faded. "At least you're nobly born." Anne had made a point of emphasizing their different classes from the day they'd met, and although she'd quietened about it in the last few months of living together, Ash hadn't realised her opinion had changed so much.

Anne waved a hand dismissively. "Ah, but we would not suit. But now, about this threat to our lives…"

"Janeus," George interjected. "The Queen's missing consort from future Iversley."

Anne frowned. "Are you certain 'tis he?"

"There was a page in your little book that talked about the king of the Grecian gods taking different forms," Ash pointed out, showing her. "And we know that Seyen Johannis's pantheon was filling in their places, and that Janeus was a shapeshifter. Who else would it be?"

Anne sighed, shrugging. "'Tis well enough, I suppose, that it happens now. I believe I have burned my bridges with this place, what with knowing that Edgar can no longer be trusted." Her eyes lit up suddenly. "Unless 'twas not Edgar at all, but 'twas Janeus in disguise?"

That would be a neat theory, Ash agreed, except the details didn't fit. Edgar had stayed to argue his side, which indicated the real earl himself had attempted murder. All the various shapeshifter doubles had always fled the scene. The fake-George had acted quite out of character, too, and his voice had been wrong.

"If 'twas not Edgar, then you have just accused your husband falsely before all the people of Renwick," Elspeth pointed out meekly. "And besides, all now know the true state of your marriage."

Anne sighed again, but seemed surprisingly upbeat considering the circumstances. "Ah, well. My true husband or not, we *are* in danger. You are quite right. We shall have to leave anon."

"Now?" Elspeth said in alarm.

"Now," the others agreed in unison, and then laughed.

Ash laughed too, but she was wondering how they were supposed to find Amaranthus when they'd struggled to even find Anne. Then suddenly a series of images flashed into her mind.

The door *slammed open, pushing Elspeth hard into the wall. There was a middle-aged bearded man in a very Tudar outfit, with blue tights and a big, fat, fur-trimmed jacket; righteous anger all over his face. He had a sword, and there were others behind him just the same, including the annoyingly shrill Blanche, a gleeful expression on her face.*

"You dare hide yourself away in here?" he accused. "Your dark actions are coming back to roost, Lady Anne!"

There was a scuffle, and someone ended up with a bloody hole in their belly...

"You've just had a vision," Anne announced. "You had that

odd expression as though you're passing wind."

Elspeth giggled, her hand over her mouth, and Ash scowled. Did Anne have to use that same joke *every* time? "Does this door lock?" Ash asked.

"From the outside, yes."

"Not good enough." Ash found a large barrel and began shuffling it over to block the door, but it was heavier than it looked. "Help me, someone. We're about to have company, and it won't be good."

LIONS AND
TERRIBLE LIZARDS

Anne watched blankly as Ash fumbled in the deep pockets of her odd, billowy trousers. What she searched for, Anne knew not. None of the others had moved in spite of Ash's last pronouncement, mayhap from shock or confusion over the odd request. But then 'twas a most strange situation.

"What are you doing?" Anne asked finally.

"Trying to find the Eternity Stone," Ash replied, frowning in frustration. "But these pockets are too deep. And someone, please hold the door!"

George rushed over to brace his back against it, and Anne did the same. "What is it, Ash?" she asked.

"People will believe your husband when he says the fall was an accident, and the people will turn on us," Ash replied succinctly, still rummaging through those pockets. "They'll say your good health was witchcraft rather than a miracle, and even your sister's healing will be suspect."

'Twas the very scenario Anne had feared, and she did not doubt the truth of Ash's words. "By the Rood, I was right. Well, don't wait. Let us leave at once!"

"I'm trying to! I just don't know why all of these pockets have to be so deep yet so tight…and why I've got so much rubbish in here!"

The sound of many footsteps echoed off the flagstones outside, and 'twas all Anne could do not to open the door to see who approached. But then she did not wish to die this day.

Just then someone tried to open the door from the outside. Anne squeaked in alarm as she realised that this *was* a most serious situation, and she and George leaned against the door with all their combined might. "Have you found the Stone yet?" she asked Ash.

"Nearly!"

"Lady Anne," Sir Robert's voice came from outside. He didn't sound the sort of man to set up a flaming stake, but how could she know? "Open the door. We must speak with you."

"One moment please!" she called back. Then to those inside, "Whatever you would do, do it now."

Ash now had the Eternity Stone in her hand. "Hold onto each other," she ordered, linking one arm with Elspeth's. George held the girl's other arm, and indicated towards Anne. "Don't let go whatever you do!"

"Do what she said," Anne ordered her sister, feeling excitement and alarm thrum through her veins.

The younger girl nodded, wide-eyed. "But what about you, Anne?"

Well, Anne was just trying to reach George's arm, but her whole weight was back against the door, and 'twas all she could do to hold the handle closed.

"Wife!" Edgar barked from outside. "I forbid you to be alone with those people!"

"Anne, grab my hand," George ordered.

"But I'd have to let go of the door," she said in dismay.

"On the count of three," Ash announced. "One-"

There was another rough knock on the door.

"Two-"

"Lady Anne, you let us in!" The door was forced open a crack, and a strong man's hand grabbed for her. She turned and dug her nails into the skin as hard as she could. There was a scream of pain – her husband's, hopefully – and she was released.

"Three!"

Anne reached for George's arm and Elspeth's, and then the door flew open and Anne was bowled over by a heavy body, knocked away from both of them right onto the floor in a huddle of cloth and flesh. Elspeth was screaming, and George was bellowing, "I don't have her!" then, "Take my hand!"

But Anne didn't know where his hand was. Someone's strong grasp reached out and grabbed her wrist, and in an instant the crush was gone, and then…

…there was light.

A moment after the light came the heat. Wet heat this time, and clearly different to the dry heat of the desert land George had visited with Ashlea. But like the last time, the group had been split up in the journey.

George panicked briefly when he realised he was no longer holding any of the girls, then relaxed when he saw Ashlea and Anne both less than ten feet away.

"Where are we?"

George looked down to the source of the voice. It was Anne's little sister, Elizabeth. (No, that wasn't right. Agnes…?) She was so far below his line of sight that he hadn't noticed her until she spoke, but now she was staring in awe at her surroundings.

George did a bit of staring himself. This place was as green and fecund as any rainforest, and he could hear the sounds of unfamiliar wildlife screeching unseen around them. High above them the sky was a deep blue, with not a cloud to be seen from horizon to horizon.

"The Indies?" he suggested tentatively.

Ashlea walked over and stood close to him as though his presence brought her comfort. "I don't think so. Look at the size of some of those plants." She pointed at a flax plant that was large enough to hide a small army.

George frowned, irritated by her knowing tone. "Have you ever been to the Indies, Ashlea?"

"Well, no. But I've seen pictures, and-" She stopped speaking abruptly and shrugged. "Oh, I suppose it could be. It's a sub-continent, right? I just don't think we're there. Gut feeling."

He couldn't argue with that, could he? He turned to take a better look around, and that was when he saw Edgar.

The man was huddled into the side of a nearby, massive tree, clutching a dagger and white-faced with fear. Luckily he'd dropped his sword. When he realised George had seen him, he went on the offensive. "Witches! Sorcerers! Fie on you gleeking, half-faced mold-warps! You will return me at once or I shall see you all dead, child or nay!"

Oh, *bother*. Edgar must have been touching one of them when Ashlea had used the Stone, and of course he'd come through. But now he had all their attention.

"Hades," Ashlea said flatly. "Who brought the party pooper?"

And what was a mold-warp?

George stepped defensively in front of the women. "If you kill us, then you will never get back." Quietly he murmured to Ashlea, "Did you bring the Reman sword?"

"I left it back at the castle."

Damn. "We could just move on and leave him behind." It would be the easiest option, and really, the man deserved it.

"Not until I know where we are," Ashlea countered. "We could be *anywhere*. I didn't have time to really focus on destination. I'd just been thinking of going somewhere far away from that castle, somewhere with no people…"

It seemed she'd achieved that, George thought.

Anne stepped around George and confronted her husband furiously. "You weren't supposed to be here! You should have just let us go, you murderous, paunchy boar-pig! And to call *us* mold-warps? You, sirrah, are nothing but a villainous, toad-spotted rats-bane!"

Amazing. George knew she was speaking Anglish, but it may as well have been gobbledegook for all he could understand it.

Ashlea murmured in his ear, "Do you think she's in danger?"

But Edgar looked more taken back than angry, and Anne kept on railing at him. "I wish to the Eternal One and all the saints that I'd never laid eyes on you! You tried to kill me! Why? Why?"

"I don't really think so," George said hesitantly to Ashlea. Edgar looked to be the one in danger from Anne.

Just then Edgar gestured at Anne half-heartedly with the dagger, and she knocked his arm away. "An eating dagger? You cannot harm me with that puny thing. Much in line with your manhood, isn't it?"

Ouch, George thought. That had to hurt. He kept well out of it.

Anne was right in her husband's face now, red with fury. "Tell me why you tried to kill me!"

Edgar gasped and mumbled something. George didn't catch it, but he heard the last word and it sounded like 'witch'. That word was being used more often than George would like, because it was often followed up with piles of firewood and someone striking a match.

Anne screeched, *"Your harlot is with child!? So what?!* Every other man has bastard children, but no, the great Edgar LeSpenser must *marry* his harlot. So naturally it followed that you had to kill me rather than have our marriage annulled?"

"She's not a harlot; she's respectably born but in reduced circumstances! I wish to marry her. My son must be legitimate, and I dare not displease the queen-"

"And how do you know 'twill be a son? You can see through the flesh of her belly?"

Edgar recovered some of his manhood, snapping back, "I wouldn't get any decent child on you, that is certain. Any son you bore would be undersized and devil-touched, with your blood running through his veins!"

Anne suddenly deflated, and George stepped forward. "That's quite enough," he snapped at Edgar. "As you can clearly see, you won't be harming Anne or any of us. If you do, we'll leave you here to die."

The man thrust his chin up defiantly. "And where is here? In the land of the elves? You've created by evil powers some cursed doorway into lands forsaken by the Eternal One, and I am but a pawn in your plan!"

Ashlea tapped George urgently on the shoulder. "We're in a worse spot than that, I think."

George followed her finger to where she pointed through a gap in the foliage, and they all turned to look.

"Z'wounds!" Anne swore rudely.

"What are they?" Elspeth whispered. "Dragons?"

Through the gap George could see large green and brown shapes – *very* large. They were the biggest lizards that he'd ever seen or imagined. Huge. Colossal, even.

Their tiny heads on the top of long, elegant necks were taller than George's childhood home, and that was three levels high. But they were familiar, somehow…

"I've heard of these," he murmured, memories from history documentaries in Ashlea's time coming back to mind. He'd hardly believed them at the time. "Their name meant terrible lizard…"

"Dinosaurs," Ashlea said decisively, eyes wide. "This is like one of those old movies come to life."

Indeed it was, and the creatures were fascinating. They were so enormous that George knew they could crush him as easily and carelessly as he would step on a beetle, and that made him want to avoid them like the plague.

At the same time he wanted to move closer, to take pictures with Anne's little quick-print camera (left in 2013, unfortunately), and to feel their hides and see if they were rough or smooth.

Even the younger girls didn't seem as nearly as afraid as they ought to be. Elspeth had moved a little closer into Anne's side, but apart from that they all just stood and stared. George assumed their lack of fear was because it didn't feel real. In spite of the warmth and the wetness of the dirt below and the smell of the creatures, they were far enough away that it seemed like viewing a fascinating museum exhibit.

Maybe that was why Anne crept forward towards the gap in the foliage.

"What are you doing?" Ashlea snapped. "Stay back here with us!"

Anne looked over her shoulder, wounded. "They do not appear dangerous. I simply wish to see a bit better."

Nevertheless, she moved back to stand with the others, and that was when they heard a roar from nearby. Ashlea paled. "I *really* wish I hadn't seen all those dinosaur films. It's not those long-necks we have to worry about!"

Through the gap in the trees they saw the long-necked giants move off. In their place was something smaller (but still a lot bigger than the humans) with a big, tooth-filled head and solid legs, but tiny little arms.

It roared and charged after the long necks. Though larger, George doubted they had a chance. That thing had jaws the size of his whole body. A second big-headed beast followed it, pausing in the gap not fifty feet from them.

Just like small prey in the sight of a predator, they'd all frozen into place as they'd seen those monster lizards.

George forced his mouth to move enough to say, "Ashlea, I do believe it's time to move on."

She nodded, her face so white that all her faint freckles stood out clearly on her skin. "Oh, yes." But she didn't move, her eyes still fixed on the monster.

And then they saw something truly strange. Looking terribly out of place, a large, maned, sandy brown cat had appeared at its feet. "What on earth…"

"'Tis a lion!" Elspeth squeaked. "I saw one in a menagerie once. Do you think the lizard will eat it?"

"That has to be Janeus," Ashlea said in disbelief. "There shouldn't be any lions here at all. But how did he follow us?"

As if realising its surroundings, the golden shape of the lion flickered and stretched, and there was yet another lizard-monster not fifty feet away from them. The newcomer and the originals faced each other off, and then the new one opened its massive hinged jaws and breathed fire on the originals, which turned and ran like terrified chickens. Giant, toothy chickens.

"By Jove," George swore. It was clear which was the shapeshifter, and even the terrible lizards had been afraid of it. "The Stone, Ashlea."

"He breathed fire," she replied vaguely, but for some reason she still wasn't moving.

The Janeus-monster was. It looked around and spotted them almost immediately, and unlike Ashlea, it had no fear paralysis. It opened that big mouth and roared again, then lumbered towards them, covering ground at a shocking speed, and she still didn't move.

A moment later George realised what had happened. She was so frightened she *couldn't* move, and she'd probably put the Stone away in her stupid, too-deep pocket. They really ought to have taken the Stone from her after the ridiculous scene in the storeroom. Now she held both hands loose at her sides, empty. He swore again, then looking around desperately, spotted a cleft in the rocky cliff edging the clearing they stood in.

"Everybody, get in that cave!"

They didn't have to be told twice. All except for Ashlea who still stood there, mouth open as the thing lurched towards them, its powerful hind legs covering the ground in seconds… Could it hear them? Smell them?

George grabbed her by the arm and manhandled her through the narrow cave entrance, then scrambled to pull the Eternity

Stone out of her pocket, ignoring his upbringing that screamed that one *did not treat a woman like this* and knowing that as a shapeshifter, the small entrance to the cave wouldn't hold back Janeus for long.

But all of a sudden Ashlea unfroze and hurried to help him, pulling the Stone out of her deep pocket and holding it with shaking hands. "I'm sorry, I'm so sorry," she kept saying, and he brushed it off, linking an arm through hers and holding the Stone, and then reaching through to grab hold of both Anne and Elspeth in a tight tangle.

"Never mind that now!" he shouted. "Just think of Amaranthus! Go!"

And Ashlea must have done it, because over the screaming in his ears the world around them began to change.

He felt the others being pulled out of his arms, and…

…Oh Hades, they'd forgotten Edgar.

Belleview Special Patients Mental Hospital,
Rys-on-Leeds, Angland
2430 AD

The woman shook her head slightly, trying to clear her thoughts. She was doing something vital, but she wasn't sure what. Or where she was, or *who* she was.

But she knew that she was important in some way. Powerful too – as powerful as…as an elemental god. Was that a real thing?

She was sitting outside a large stone building with an elaborate façade, and the sun shone bright in the blue sky. There was a feeling of relaxation around here, like no one was working and nothing was important.

Next to her sat a youngish man with bland brown hair and an equally bland smile on his plain face. The concern in his eyes when he looked at her seemed real, though.

She could tell what he was thinking: not quite telepathy, but a strong sense of where his thoughts were going. *Middle-aged, unkempt woman; swarthy-skinned with salt and pepper hair; clinging to her past glory.* But his nervousness around her was offset by the fact that he could just tell *them* where to find her, and she'd be done for.

Underneath her confusion was the certainty that this amnesia was temporary. She would recover herself, and she would be as…*powerful*?…as she had been before. A god to fear and revere.

Deias, she was amazing. Shame she didn't know who she was.

The woman gave her keeper a narrow-eyed glare. She could sense he was a little intimidated by her, and that was satisfying.

Just wait, she thought, *just wait until I'm back to…whatever I was before. Then I'll show you.*

She decided to start then and there with a little illusion, throwing an image of herself up into the air as though she was floating, and then cloaking her true self in invisibility where she sat on the ground.

It looked as though she'd up and flown away, and the keeper fell for it hook, line and sinker. He got up, a bored expression on his face, and began to follow the floating illusion.

The woman sent it as far into the distance as she could manage, then when she felt the power begin to fade, stood up and followed quietly afterwards.

Oh, but I must be careful, a quiet little thought popped in. *They'll be looking for me. They'll sense my power.*

We already know where you are, a different voice came directly into her mind, an unwanted, familiar one. The memory of *them* followed with it – a young man and woman, golden-haired and fair-skinned and even-featured enough for true beauty. They were familiar, but again she didn't know how. But they were also untrustworthy.

The woman paused in place. In the distance her illusion flickered and almost dropped, and she saw the keeper throw his hands up in irritated despair as he realised her ploy.

But she was more focused on that voice, those people who were speaking to her in a way that no one else could hear. *No, you don't know where I am*, she thought carefully to the unknown *them*. *You're trying to trick me, and it won't work.*

"We totally do know," came the young man's voice, right next to where she still stood invisibly. "We're right here too."

And there he was, solid and exceptionally handsome and oozing with an odd mix of arrogance and self-doubt. Not too bright, perhaps, and reluctantly aware of it?

The woman picked up all of this in less than a second, as well as noting the second figure a step behind the young man's. His twin sister, who was quieter to speak, but probably held the brains for both of them. The girl's negative opinion oozed off her. She thought the woman was unkempt and old, and had never been lovely…and perhaps something about an unwilling familial connection?

"Oh my Deias, Troilus, seriously?" the girl said with rolled eyes, but the woman had already panicked.

Forget the illusion. This time she pulled together the last of her power, the last of that knowledge that said she could in truth become something other than what she was born to be, and changed.

Now she was big, oh so very big, and black and winged and terrifying. The new dragon reared up on its hind legs, swiping with clawed paws at the golden twins, wings beating the air in an attempt to drive them away. Nearby a couple of lounge chairs were blown over sideways in the wind gust, as well as an unwitting waiter with a tray of drinks. An umbrella went flying to smash through a window, scattering a few screaming residents, but the dragon didn't care.

"You'll never catch me!" it hissed out of reptilian vocal cords.

"I'm a god, and my power is beyond you!"

"Chaos, Jenessa," Troilus muttered, taking a bite out of the food he was holding. It looked like meat twisted around a stick. "He really has lost his marbles. He never actually thought he was a god before."

"Then we'll find them for him," Jenessa snapped impatiently. She looked up at where the dragon hovered just above the ground, those wings still not big enough to gain any decent height, and there was nothing but a mild disgust in her eyes and something golden-bright on her lips. "Come on, *Dad*. Come back down."

Dad. The word hit the dragon like a stone falling into a still lake, the power that the girl had attached to it hitting its mind and sending ripples of unwanted change, of *memory* right through. But still it resisted, turning and trying to flee. Maybe it hadn't been a god after all. But it knew that its power was an intrinsic part of its identity, and people had known. It had been *respected*.

He, the thought came quietly. *Not she, not it. You're a man.*

Oh.

That quiet thought hit hard enough to stop the dragon in its tracks. Had it truly forgotten that basic part of its identity?

But it- *he'd* paused too long. The twins threw a binding cord over his neck, and suddenly frozen, he fell to the ground and began to take his true form. The binding cord wouldn't allow any shapeshifts to remain.

It was a slow change, and painful, and just as painful were the memories pouring back in. He knew they were his, but they were so disconnected that it felt like they had to belong to someone else.

So many things he'd done; twisted things in the form of animals and other people, that had alleviated the boredom briefly but had left others hurt. Women, sometimes, and he wondered what had been wrong with him that he hadn't minded what he'd been doing...

Dimly he heard the male twin say, "How long is this going to take? I can feel my power weakening already."

"Two more minutes," the girl replied. He heard the displeasure in her voice. "Too long. Troilus, help me carry him to the gateway. We'll go through as soon as he's shifted."

"I don't have enough power left for levitation," the boy whined.

"Then shapeshift and carry him!"

There was some kind of movement around him, but that was the moment where the change completed. With a heavy sigh the twins' father accepted his true form, and with it his memories and the unwanted guilt that came with them.

Janeus lay on the grass staring up at the blue sky, still frozen in place by that binding cord. Two faces appeared in his vision – his daughter, Jenessa, and what looked like a large golden horse. A second later the horse's figure blurred, and there was his son Troilus, shaking off the aftereffects of his own change.

"You may as well get up," Jenessa told Janeus, lip curled. "We're not going to carry you when you can walk yourself."

Surprised, Janeus pushed himself into a sitting position. He could still feel the binding cord holding him in this one form, subject to his captors' will, but he could *move*.

"It's a new sort of binding cord," Troilus told him. He'd found his meat-stick again and was chewing while he talked – a habit that Seyen had hated, but hadn't managed to break him of. "We mixed the old ones with alter-power. Now we control you."

"Your movement, anyway," Jenessa corrected. "Now come on. Walk."

And Janeus did. He got up and began to walk quickly in the first direction he saw, towards the nearest building. A few blank-eyed patients sat around, unbothered by the fuss he'd caused, and one was laughing at someone no one else could see.

Jenessa let out a huff of disgust. "Not that way! With us."

Janeus found his feet stopped quite independently of his brain telling them to, and he turned and swerved back the other way, to where the twins were walking.

Ah, so he did have some control over this thing. He had to follow the letter of what she said, but not the spirit of it.

"I suppose you're taking me to Seyen for my execution," he said glumly as he trudged along in that plain, torn Belleview uniform, too big now for his leaner male form. "You could have some familial loyalty."

Another scoff, this time from both of them. "Our loyalty is to Mother," Jenessa said succinctly.

"Did you really think you'd get away from her?" his son asked.

Janeus rubbed at the cord where it sat tight against his neck. This body – now this one was his. He'd missed it, unsurprisingly. He'd missed it even when he hadn't known what he'd been missing. Young man beat middle-aged woman for energy any day.

Well, if his old lover was going to kill him, he would at least spend his last moments in his own body. "Actually, yes," he replied. "I figured that if I skipped through time enough and hid myself well enough then she'd give up. That's why I purposely went through in a shifted form, trying to lose my memory. It didn't last, I see, if you two are here.

"So how is Seyen?" he asked casually. "Sharpening the knives?" He tried to sound uncaring, but the thought of what she'd threatened to do the last time she'd seen him made certain parts of his anatomy try to crawl inside his body.

"She's decided to forgive you and rescind your banishment," his daughter replied. "Again."

Janeus tried not to let his disbelief show on his face. His estranged wife wasn't known for her graciousness. It would be more accurate to say that when she held a grudge, she never let it go. Ever. Before that business with the twins' mother, there had been a few others, and that damned goddess beauty competition that eventually led to the Trojen War.

Janeus didn't know if there had ever been any *real* gods, but if they were anything like Seyen's pantheon, then they weren't the sort that ordinary humans should have anything to do with. It almost always ended in tears.

But what was a god except something that was worshipped and had the power to back up their boasts? He did know something that fit that particular definition, but those…those were very, very nasty Creatures. Even Seyen hadn't dared run into them after one occasion in her youth that had damaged her terribly. Even in their best days together, she still wouldn't tell him all the details, but it had been enough to keep him from travelling in the Other realm more than absolutely necessary.

The crowd melted away as they stepped through the first remnant gateway, away from the hospital and into the busy streets of an old, clay-walled city. Without missing a beat they used illusion to match their clothing to the locals', continuing walking towards the second gateway.

At least the twins were walking there, and Janeus had to go with them – this wasn't a place he was familiar with. "So what's the plan?" he asked casually. "What does she want this time?"

"How is it that you haven't aged?" Jenessa asked with a distinct lack of curiosity, not answering his question. Knowing her, that meant she really *was* curious. As a matter of fact, so was he. In that shifted state where his memory and identity had faded away, his true form hadn't changed a bit. "I didn't think you'd been gathering in this time period. You should have started to wither by now."

Janeus shrugged. "Don't know."

"You know that true immortality only comes from one place. How did you get it?"

He turned on her. "Are you suggesting that I've been involved with the old enemy, Amaranthus? Because I haven't. You know that he's so bloody black and white that you're either for him or you're against him, and my involvement with Seyen has meant that I'm quite definitely against him. He'd kill me rather than give me anything, I know it."

Troilus scoffed. "Perhaps your centuries of power-gathering might have something to do with it as well, hmm? You know how *he* feels about that sort of thing."

"That's only because *Amaranthus* doesn't need to do it to stay immortal," Janeus countered. He might be a little wary of the man himself, but he wasn't afraid of using the name. "If he faced aging and dying helplessly rather than borrowing years from someone else, maybe he'd reconsider it."

"You're preaching to the choir," Jenessa snapped. "Besides, there are a few things you don't know."

"Like what?"

She studied his face slyly. "I bet you don't even know what year we were just in. How much do you remember of your life?"

He decided to be honest, to a point. "The year doesn't matter when you're a time-traveller, you know that. As for my life, I remember centuries of back and forth being banished and then ordered to come back again. I remember being chased through the gateways from Lilluania back to Olympas with that damned dragon-slayer Mortimer behind us, and losing my power and not being able to shift properly, and Seyen finding out about the gateways. And of course she was furious, so I took a risk and left."

He shrugged. "Since I travelled through the gateway in shifted form, when I got through I didn't know who I was. Someone came and got me and took me to this mental hospital for people with…special abilities."

"Yes," Troilus said. "That's what happened. But what we want to know…"

"…Is why you would take the risk of using the gateways when you were shifted, even knowing that it could take your mind," Jenessa finished, barely missing a step. "Mother had been angry at you before, but this time you decided it was worth your sanity to get away. Why?"

"There's angry," Janeus replied, "and then there's *angry*. You saw her."

"We did see her," his daughter agreed calmly. "And she was *angry*. We've never seen her like that before, and we want to know why."

"What happened in Lilluania that you were never supposed to go back there?" Troilus asked.

The two of them both stared at him dispassionately and expectantly, and Janeus felt his gut sink. As always, there was no affection for him to be seen, but since that went both ways he didn't really care. But as for Lilluania…that wasn't even the problem.

It had been Erastus, the gateway between the two other times which they'd accidentally left on fire in their last hasty visit. Erastus had been the scene of Seyen's greatest failure and humiliation, and her first face to face encounter with Amaranthus. The two were inextricably linked.

"I swore I'd never tell," he said, "and I won't." At least not while Seyen still lived.

"You swore many things," Jenessa countered. "That never made a difference before. Tell us."

"This is different." It really was. Besides, he didn't like being intimidated and manipulated. He got enough of that from Seyen, even if he hadn't seen her in…how long?

"A hundred and fifty years," Troilus said, answering the unspoken question. "But we estimate that you've only lost around ten years, fifteen at the most."

Janeus was stunned at that information, so stunned that he laughed aloud. So Seyen really had been furious. A hundred and fifty years worth of furious, and she had never once tried to get him back. He would be glad, except that he himself had only got a decade of peace. "I suppose you're older than me now," he said, covering up his shock with a cocky grin. "How many fathers can say that?"

The twins just stared at him until his smile died, and in that moment they both looked just like Seyen, in spite of having no shared blood with her. But she'd raised them, hadn't she? After many decades of life, of course they would be in her image rather than his.

But now, seeing it in their expressions, he felt chilled.

"Side effect of time travel," Troilus stated casually. "And I'd hardly say you're our father. You're more of a…"

"…Sperm donor," Jenessa finished. "As I said before."

"That's the second time you've finished each other's sentences," Janeus said flatly. "How cute. Now what does Seyen really want from this particular sperm donor?"

"You're not entirely foolish if you know there's more," his daughter replied. "So here's the thing. Seyen doesn't want you back out of love and devotion. No, she needs something from you…"

Ash opened her eyes to see desert. Desert in every direction, not sandy desert like in that ancient place with its hideous crosses, but flat, hard and dry; like earth that hadn't seen water in a long, long time. The only visible green was far in the distance, past a range of hills, and piles of what looked like ruins were scattered randomly across the flat earth.

This sure didn't look like home. Or *any* place she'd seen before, actually. She'd seen the Great Sandie Desert in person, she'd even seen the Shahara (via television) – but this just seemed…off. It was like the sky was too purple…or something, and the atmosphere felt wrong. She felt lighter than normal, but at the same time more solid. And that didn't make sense, Ash knew, but that was how it *felt*.

She was alone. And unlike the last time she'd found herself alone in a desert, there were no small figures waving frantically at her in the distance, no locals to screech at her or even to give her directions to the nearest town.

"Damn it, damn it, damn it again. I *hate* being lost!" And with time travel, getting lost could go to a whole new level. If it wasn't for the Stone, she might end up dying of old age in a time long before her home nation even had a name.

Just then the memories of the last few minutes came rushing in, and she felt a hot wash of shame. When that toothy dinosaur had come charging at her, she'd frozen uselessly in place. It was like she actually couldn't move, and she knew there was nothing magical about it. It had simply been fear.

George had hauled her to safety, and then they'd scrambled to pull out the Stone from her pocket, and which of them had used it? She didn't remember.

The horrible thought came to her that perhaps she hadn't been touching the others and had left them behind by mistake, but then she shook that off. No, she distinctly remembered George grabbing her and shouting for everyone to hold on, and his tight grip on her arm.

That was right. He'd must have had the Stone. Still had it, hopefully, because Ash sure didn't. She looked around her one more time as though she'd spot any of the others in a corner she'd missed before, but she was alone as she'd ever been. For a moment she was tempted to cry, but instead she sighed heavily. If they'd split up, it could be a good thing, because then Janeus-or-whoever would have multiple people to follow.

Unfortunately, she also didn't have the binding cord. All she had was her randomly occurring far-sight and the faint hope that other supernatural skills would fall into her lap at just the right time.

She screwed up her face in that way when she wanted to cry and there was no one watching to judge her, but it just made her feel worse. So instead she sighed, slumping her shoulders where she stood.

"Did you hear that, Amaranthus?" she told the empty air. "We came looking for you. Don't forget us."

Just then Ash remembered Anne's photo album. She still had *that*, by some miracle, in the very deep pockets of these rather comfortable harem-style trousers. She pulled it out and opened it eagerly. Inside, near the end, was a newspaper cutting of a T-Rex in a jungle scene, drawn in the style of 1950s comic books.

She vaguely recalled seeing it before, but there was *no way* that she'd even been thinking of it when they'd used the Stone to escape from 1556. Absolutely no way – and that meant they had even less control over the Eternity Stone than they'd imagined.

Was it rigged, she wondered in a panic, or was someone hijacking the destinations?

But then she saw there was more handwritten text on the other page. It read, *Don't panic.*

Too late. Ash had already panicked. That was probably why she'd been separated from the group.

Underneath the first sentence appeared another line: *Really, don't. Accidents aren't always what they seem.*

Ash stared at it for a moment before her face creased into a relieved smile. This had Amaranthus written all over it, although she had no idea what he thought he was doing. Or what *she* was doing. But 'don't panic'…so she wouldn't panic.

Feeling her heart rate go back to normal, she flicked through a few more pages curiously, trying to find anything else that looked familiar. But no more pithy phrases popped up beside the random photographs, and finally she snapped the book shut.

That was when she saw what was written on the back cover. Spiralling out around a silver sticker that reflected her puzzled face were the words, *Water is life. All green does not mean growth. A gift once given is never rescinded.* And there was a little shape like a crudely drawn bird in flight.

Nope, still puzzled, but she hoped that at some point it would make sense. So far, so good, right?

With another sigh Ash put the now-precious book back in her pocket, then turning towards the nearest set of ruins, began to walk.

"Ashlea? Anne?" George looked around wildly, then even up and down as if they might be crouched by his feet or hovering in the sky above him. "Elizabeth…?"

It was to no avail. There was no one else in sight: simply dry, grey dirt for a long way in every direction, broken only by round pools of water every few yards. Just in case one of the others had fallen in, he studied one of the pools more closely.

It was flat as glass, completely opaque, and reflected the purple-tinged sky. There wasn't a chance that anyone had fallen in, even if the water had been deep enough and if they'd been unlucky enough. The dirt around the pool was also very dry, without a hint of splash.

It was then George noticed what was wrong with the scene: that exact detail. The dirt around the pools was extremely dry, the water not having soaked in even an inch around the edges. And from what he knew of water, that was not normal behaviour. Perhaps it wasn't even truly water?

Curiously he picked up a dry twig off the hard ground and poked its end into the surface of the pool. It made a hissing noise and a small puddle of vivid green appeared around the twig where it hit the water.

He pulled it out and saw that there was nothing left. The 'water' had dissolved the stick almost instantly.

Ugh. George stood hurriedly and backed away, fervently grateful that he hadn't tested it with his finger. It wasn't fresh water at all – more like some form of powerful acid. The even more dreadful thought sneaked in that anyone who fell in one of those pools wouldn't have a *chance* to climb out. What if the girls…?

"Hades, no," he swore. "No. No."

No, he decided then and there. It wasn't possible that such a dreadful thing would have happened, especially not when they'd come seeking Amaranthus.

He'd touched the Eternity Stone with his left hand, he vaguely recalled, and surely Ashlea had been touching it as well. They'd been separated, that was all, and one of the others now had the Stone. He didn't have it any longer. All he needed to do was get somewhere safe away from the gateway he'd surely just created, and wait to either run into the others or until they came to find him.

George shook his head decisively to discard the lingering fears that it was all going dreadfully wrong, then set off in what looked like the most sensible direction; the vague haze of green hills in the distance.

OOF! Anne's breath left her in a rush as she landed hard on her belly, something strange underneath her. It felt both soft and hard, and 'twas moving slightly.

With an apology, she climbed off a slightly stunned Elspeth and helped her sister to her feet. Her *bare* feet, and in that moment Anne noticed something different.

"By the Rood, Bethie. Your foot – 'tis no longer twisted!"

"I told you before, your foreign friends healed me," her sister replied with a pleased smile, lifting her now-straight foot and wiggling her toes. "Did you not hear me? 'Twas a flash of light, bright-"

"As the noon-day sun," Anne finished, staring at the appendage in amazement. "But I thought they'd healed only the fever. And they're not foreigners, Bethie. George at least is Anglish-born." She stared at Elspeth's foot again. It had been the bane of the girl's life, for many took it as yet another sign of the Eternal One's displeasure at her for being born out of wedlock. And now 'twas healed. Healed… "By the Rood," she breathed again. "How marvellous."

"Yes, 'tis, quite," Elspeth agreed happily, then jumped a few times in place as though to prove the point. "And it has not pained me since."

"But you are not shod," Anne pointed out. "George, Ash-" 'Twas then that she realised her two friends were nowhere to be seen. "Where on earth are they?"

She searched around carefully for the familiar blond curls or wild, dark hair that belonged to her friends, but she could see neither. She seemed to be alone with her sister in the middle of a wide, painfully dry valley. In the distance, where the two hillsides converged, was a small dusting of green. Slightly closer Anne could just make out a sprawling farmhouse, the same sand-coloured materials as the landscape and looking very much like it belonged there.

"Z'wounds," Elspeth said, but she looked interested rather than upset. "They've left us behind. Is this elf-land, then?"

Anne gave her sister a very grown-up look. "Elves don't exist, Bethie. This will simply be another time we're not familiar with."

"Mayhap," Elspeth said cautiously, "but there is something amiss with the air of this place, do you feel it? As though I cannot breathe one moment, and the next as though I'd cough up bubbles."

'Twas a most odd way of phrasing it, but Anne understood what she meant. The air felt like…like *power*, and 'twas not a thing she'd experienced since leaving the Queen's presence in 2155. Queen Seyen Johannis, not Queen Marian Tudar, that was. 'Twas almost like they still stood in a remnant gateway.

Anne took her sister's arm, pulling her away from where they'd stood. "I know they would not leave us apurpose. 'Twas surely a simple mistake. Once they realise what has happened, they shall return anon, for they have the Eternity Stone."

"You said we might travel the gateways ourselves, though. Might we not return back to find them?"

Anne shook her head decisively. "They've surely gone to another location close by. 'Tis as 'twas when George and I travelled together the last time; we arrived several feet apart."

"Several feet?" Elspeth said doubtfully, looking at the miles of surrounding landscape. "I see them not at all."

"They'll be somewhere," Anne replied airily, convincing herself of it as she spoke. "And I shall not return through that gateway, Bethie. Did you not see what would be waiting for us?"

Elspeth shuddered. "That dragon-creature. Surely 'tis feasting on Edgar's corpse as we speak."

"Beth!"

"What?" she asked innocently. "You saw he was left behind. And surely you do not mourn his loss."

Anne thought about it. "Mayhap not," she admitted. "But I would rather not have disappeared from a storeroom and taken my husband with me. I shall never be able to return home now...and neither will you. Mayhap we shall have to live with Ash once more."

Elspeth slumped briefly, then brightened. "Will there be plas-tik tooth-brushes? I vow your teeth are as white as pearls."

"As many as you like," Anne offered grandly. "You may even have a pink one, if you wish." Elspeth had always liked pink.

"I do like the sound of that."

And so 'twas with stars in Elspeth's eyes, and a determined confidence in Anne's heart, that they set off for the distant farmhouse.

Eleven

THE THIRTEENTH GATEWAY

Somewhere in southern Canadia...maybe

After the sixth or seventh gateway Janeus began to protest. "This is just getting stupid. There's no way I made it through this many gateways when I was out of my head."

"You didn't," Jenessa replied. The twins walked on either side of him like jailers through the small, lonely town that was growing steadily whiter under the heavy snowfall. Based on the last few gateways, they wouldn't be here for more than ten minutes. "We're taking another route."

Not back to Olympas. From what they'd told him as they walked, they hadn't lived in that place in a long, long time. They'd gone from Grecia to the seven hills of Reme, then to Northern Europa where they'd pretended to be Norse gods. But that didn't last long. Seyen had lost interest in ruling a backward and super-stitious population (their words, not his) and she'd fixed her eyes on a new era.

Post-World-War-Three Europa. That had all the comforts of technology, and if she played it right, she would have the alle-giance of many millions. To start off with, anyway. And of course that era had just discovered time travel (the only era in history to do so without alter-power, in fact) and although they had quickly banned it, she wanted to have control of such a thing. Seyen had the Eternity Stone, and she wanted to be the *only* human who could manipulate time. Amaranthus and his ilk didn't count, not being precisely human.

The isolated underground city of Iversley in the mid-twenty-second century seemed perfect. It even had its own water source, easily tainted so that the inhabitants would become susceptible to mind control. It would be a starting point for Angland and then Europa, and then the world, because what megalomaniac didn't want world domination? (Janeus's words, since the twins seemed quite keen on world domination, as long as they were the ones doing the dominating.)

But to Janeus, Seyen had overstepped by trying to rule a more modern culture, especially one that was already aware of time travel. Mind control could only go so far. But then even more than that…

"So she lost the Stone, did she?" His neutral tone covered up his intense shock. "How?"

"We still don't know," Jenessa replied grimly. "But it doesn't take a genius to figure out who might have been involved, and the time travellers who ended up with it were too stupid to know to use it. So we couldn't find it for ages."

"What time travellers?"

"Some dumb kids brought in by a local scientist," Troilus said around a mouthful of food. He'd managed to find yet something else to eat – had probably stolen it as they'd passed by a food stall or someone's window. "And then they stole all the rest of Seyen's power, too."

Jenessa shot her brother an evil glare, but Janeus's jaw had already dropped. "Stole *all* of her power? *How*?"

"Dumb luck. They finally figured out how to use the Stone, then took her earrings." Jenessa said flatly. "It hit us all hard. It's had to be a fresh start, for all of us."

"But *I'm* fine," Janeus said in bafflement. "I didn't notice a thing."

"You were out of your head," his son commented, voice still muffled. "Of course you wouldn't know. Anyway, that's why Mother-"

His sister turned on him. "Must you always be eating?"

"Food tastes better out here," Troilus countered defensively. "In the Other it never tastes right."

"We're going to *the Other realm*?" Janeus exploded. He set his feet in the snow-covered ground, trying to stop walking for even a moment, but of course the binding cord overrode that. So he kept moving with the other two, his head spinning with new information. "Seyen swore she'd never go back there. Why now?"

There was a silence broken only by the sound of their footsteps through snow, and then *schwoop*, through another gateway into a pleasantly warm beach. They didn't miss a step, but Janeus was putting it together. Seyen had lost her power, then. Had *really* lost it.

"So she didn't get the Eternity Stone back," he said in sudden realisation. "That's the only reason that she'd ever choose to go back to the Other. By the suns, she must look *ancient*! But why didn't she just start gathering again? That would have halted the aging enough to find the Eternity Stone and get back on with her wonderful plans."

"Yes," his daughter said.

"So something's gone wrong with the gathering," Janeus mused. "Because I can't see that she'd have a change of heart and just stop doing it. So that's what she wants me for, right? To find her the Eternity Stone, so everything can start over."

Jenessa let out a sigh as they stepped through the next gateway – the eighth he'd counted so far. "We already know where it is. The same time travellers have it, and they've been using it, too. It's just getting it that's the hard part."

"They use the Stone to get away once you find them, right?" Janeus said knowingly. "But why not just follow them through the new gateway?"

"No time," Troilus replied. "We stay away from the Other too long and we start to get wrinkly, no matter how much gathering we do. It's not enough to keep us out for more than half an hour, and sometimes we have to go through a dozen gateways to reach anywhere. By the time we find the bastards, time's almost up, or they move on."

The girl added, "And the gateways those travellers produce aren't right. They're hard to find and they don't take you to the same place, and so when we follow through we're always split up."

They went through the ninth gateway, and then the tenth rapidly afterwards, while Janeus took that all in. "Outwitted by a bunch of primitive kids, huh? Sounds like you've dropped your game."

"They've got help," Jenessa hissed. "And watch what you say. Remember *we* have the power here."

He grinned, shaking his head. "Seems like except for this binding cord, you need me far more than I need you."

In unison the twins stopped, pulling Janeus to a sharp halt between them, then turned and stared him right in the face. Troilus had been right, they *had* got wrinkly, but it wasn't the usual lines of age. It rippled right across the previously smooth skin of their faces, almost like a crumpled piece of paper, and there was nothing in their eyes but dislike. And something more…

Jenessa tapped him on the chest, her nail feeling far sharper than it ought to. "So you say," she said in a soft, ominously cold voice. "Yet Seyen still wears your rose right over her heart. She holds you just as surely as we do with this binding cord, and you *will* do as we desire. And if I were you, Kin-slayer, I would keep myself sweet. Keep myself *alive*."

Troilus echoed that with a dispassionate glance, and then suddenly they were pulling him forward again, towards the eleventh gateway. Janeus could see it just ahead, shimmering over the black tar road of whatever time this was.

But there was something else he'd seen, something that he hadn't imagined any of Seyen's pantheon would ever stoop to.

Behind Jenessa's eyes, in that last cold glance, that icy voice, had been someone else. Some*thing* else.

Creature.

Jenessa remembered so clearly the changes that took place after the failure at Iversley. It had been a series of disasters, starting from the disappearance of the Eternity Stone right after their arrival.

Then, she'd known their gathered power would only last so long before all the avoided years came crashing down on them. Jenessa estimated she'd been about two hundred and seventy at that point, but they'd had time to sort it, right? All they had to do was find the Stone, and they knew it still had to be in the same time period. Seyen would have sensed its power if it had been used.

Jenessa didn't know how long it had been since, but she *did* know that the worst of it came when the time travellers stole Seyen's earrings. They'd been like tiny, potent bunches of grapes, looking far too heavy to be comfortable, but they'd held the ability to do anything from reading minds to growing apples from a peach tree. Mostly to do with manipulating people, but still, power.

With those earrings gone, suddenly the fact that Seyen's power was leaking from some malformed tattoo didn't matter, because barring those life-stealing tattoos, it was pretty much all gone.

And then the earrings went who knew where, and suddenly the Nobles were all being slingshotted through what felt like a hundred gateways, all the way back to their original times.

Not that Jenessa would remember that era, of course. She'd lived with Seyen since she was less than three months old. But the twins had found themselves in Esparta of about 200 BC, haggard and rapidly ageing and feeling weaker than it seemed possible to feel.

They'd gone on a gathering spree to refresh themselves, taking all that they could before moving on to the next town; then when they'd found the first gateways, gone through those too. The locals thought some kind of dreadful plague had swept through when people never woke up from a good night's sleep – but no, it was just the twins recharging their low power levels.

It had been entirely random that Troilus had found Seyen some time later in that quiet desert town. She'd been so ancient and decrepit that she was almost unrecognisable. In fact, if it hadn't been for the faint mental link they still had, he never would've known her.

Troilus had been in the form of a dog at the time, and with one of the quirks of time travel, what might have been months for the twins had been only a few minutes for her.

Seyen had mistaken Troilus for Janeus at first and had been quite sentimental. Apparently losing everything could make someone that way. But once she'd got over the disappointment of Troilus merely being himself (Jenessa understood that; she faced it almost daily) Seyen had begun making plans. She seemed to think that if she could only find the Eternity Stone then everything would go back to how it was before.

But it turned out that unlike the twins', Seyen's ability to gather power was greatly reduced. The tattoos that covered her body still remained, but now no longer silver, they were all a strange pinky-copper that meant any gathered power quickly leached back out into her surroundings.

It seemed that with the loss of the Stone, *and* the loss of all the other collected objects of power, she'd been broken. Like a smashed vase that couldn't hold water any longer, no matter how much you tried to glue the cracks.

Jenessa wouldn't have cared, really, except for how it affected them.

See, *they* were connected to her just as Janeus still was, and their ability to gather and keep power had also been based on Seyen's. So Seyen's plan to settle temporarily in the Other while searching for the Eternity Stone was also a good one from the twins' point of view.

But of course things hadn't worked out as they'd expected. Once they'd settled in the Other and made that damned agreement with the Creatures that lived there, they'd found they couldn't leave for any decent length of time. Not Jenessa – that made sense considering the bloody pact that had been made regarding her – but not Troilus either.

It was frustrating since they'd finally found the Eternity Stone back in the hands of the same time traveller who'd first taken it. They'd felt its movement from the scrying pool in the old city, and Jenessa had gone out like a shot to find it, rushing through seven gateways to reach it.

She'd taken one of those new binding cords with her, and she'd managed to frighten the girl into crashing her primitive fuel-run vehicle. Jenessa had even got as far as putting the binding cord on the girl when she'd used the Eternity Stone to escape. Jenessa would have followed her through the new gateway, but then that infuriating thing had happened; the one where the power from the Other pulled her back, pulled her into weakness.

So she'd gone back to the house to recuperate and Troilus had gone out instead. He'd taken a soul-drinker with him – a device that Seyen had been using to great effect since the events at Iversley – and had been *so* close to killing the girl and taking the Stone when he'd been frightened off by some bystander.

Jenessa was still angry at him for that one. He should have just killed the other one too, not run off and hidden until his own power ran out.

So, it had been back to the Other, back to recuperate for him too. Seyen in her grand wisdom had then decided that Troilus should continue to go out because he had the 'gift', and Jenessa had only a decent working brain. But this time, it was two time travellers he was following, and the gateways had split enough that he'd taken some time to catch them up in yet another dry, antique location. And *this* time he'd-

That wasn't my fault, Troilus's angry mental voice cut in. *I almost had them, but they had some kind of electrical device, and then I ran out of time again.*

She hadn't realised she'd been thinking of the past so clearly. *Just like you ran out of time with the dinosaurs.*

Yes!

Oh, he shouldn't be so sensitive. All Jenessa had been thinking was that they'd done their best, but in the end they'd realised they had to try something new. And they'd found Janeus ages before but hadn't gone to see him-

Because he's a codweed, and we don't like him.

Because he was a codweed, Jenessa agreed. But because he had some weird ability to stay fresh *and* hadn't got the same strong links to the Other, they thought he'd be able to complete what they weren't. Hopefully.

Definitely.

She felt Troilus's vindication at his own failure; to be fair, she'd been unable to complete it either. And here she kept her thoughts much, much quieter...that if it didn't work, they could always just kill Janeus and take his power. Seyen was just too sentimental to think of doing it sooner.

They bumped their way through gate twelve, heading through the gates of an old farmer's field that held the very last gateway to the Other. Their father was trudging between them with that cocky half-grin that Jenessa found so annoying; the one that said he didn't really care what happened to him or to the world. He had always been reckless, like a train driven too fast, constantly risking derailment.

At least he looked better now than he had before when they'd seen him, cocky and confused in the guise of a particularly ugly middle-aged woman just like their old servant from back in Grecia. Then of course they'd recalled that Janeus had always had a thing for changing gender, and that it would be very much like him to disguise himself so.

They had quietly approached the woman's handler, a bland young man who hated his job and was happy to do whatever they wanted in return for payment. After explaining that they were the woman's children, the handler had explained that the Special Patients Mental Hospital took on those who had…particular abilities.

Often madness caused the sufferers to believe themselves superheroes, but some of these actually were. They were people who'd dabbled too much in the alter-power of the Other realm and had found themselves with new abilities and without sound minds, and here they were looked after by people who knew how to.

"I still can't believe that Seyen's staying voluntarily in the Other realm," Janeus said for what must have been the fifth time, shaking his head in disbelief. "Madness."

Jenessa didn't see what was so surprising about it. Seyen would always do what was best for herself, and she'd said that in this, she'd had no choice. Her whole unnaturally long life she'd siphoned power from the Other. That was where all alter-power came from; that realm that overlaid the normal one like a layer of paint, yet most people weren't able to access it.

It bubbled with power – no, it *was* alter-power, and so were the beings that lived in it. The Creatures, as most of them were known, couldn't ever enter the normal world. Bad luck for them, although they had their other methods of interfering in the normal world without actually being present in it.

"And here you can join in the madness," Jenessa said,

stopping at the side of the path where a tall grey boulder sat alone in the dust. She gestured at it. "Here's the gateway. It leads straight to our house in the Other."

Janeus studied it suspiciously. "You think after I've spent a lifetime avoiding the Other realm – on Seyen's advice, by the way – I'll now just waltz in to have coffee with her like it's just another time period?"

"Yes."

"It's a quiet part in the middle of the Other desert," Troilus said, trying to reassure him. "We've never seen any Creatures around our house. I don't think they even know it's there. They're beasts, really, too stupid to do more than maul if you ran into one."

"And what if you did? You couldn't kill them."

Janeus was right, unfortunately. Creatures were immortal, and some of them were technically already dead…but only technically.

Anyway, as usual Troilus had it wrong. Sometimes he was so thick Jenessa couldn't believe they were related. "The beasts that you're talking about, Troi, they're not the danger. They're like the vagrants of the Creature world. The real ones, the real dangers, they *do* know we're there," she said impatiently. "But they choose to leave us be for their own reasons."

"What reasons?" Janeus asked.

"None of your business," she snapped. That was something she didn't even like to think about, although it was an ever-present reality. But Seyen had negotiated that her beloved 'son' be left alone, so Jenessa carried that burden. "Now if you've got any objects of power, hang onto them tight. Things tend to slip away as we move into the Other."

"I don't have anything."

Funny, because she'd felt like he did…

Losing patience, she slapped her hand flat against the boulder, then simultaneously focused on their destination and took a step forward.

Moving into the Other wasn't the same as using the other gateways. It made her feel ill, the feeling of leaving her body behind, then being slammed back into it at full-speed. Troilus said it wasn't like that for him, lucky beast. But then he did get all the luck, didn't he?

There was a faint sound of discomfort behind her as her father came through (apparently she took after him) and then they were right outside the sheltered front door of their little Other house.

Janeus didn't think he'd ever been so nervous in his whole, long life; not even right after he'd accidentally killed Tai and had known his own death could be imminent.

Maybe it was the atmosphere of the Other, buzzing with power like having a hundred mosquitoes in your room at night, but also with the feeling that if you tried to tap into power from this location, it'd suck you dry.

Perhaps it was a good metaphor in relation to Seyen. The closer he got to her, the more he could feel the connection she'd created so many years ago with that red rose tattoo, given when she'd cupped his bloodied cheek mere minutes after Tai's death.

But when Janeus saw her standing in the doorway to the house, he still did a double-take.

Finally she said coldly, "Yes, I'm old. Well done for noticing. Come in before you bring anything else with you."

The three moved inside and the door shut solidly behind them.

"Could be worse," Janeus said finally, having found his voice.

Seyen just gave him another cold look, but he could feel that she agreed, and that she too was thinking of Erastus. There they'd seen worse...*worst*. Here, she had salt and pepper grey hair pulled back at the nape of her neck, and her once strikingly lovely features were as loose, lined and liver-spotted as the average seventy-year-old woman. But he'd seen various former lovers die of old age, and really, she could be uglier. Could be *older*.

But then he was walking unwillingly down a short hallway into a sitting room, and found himself plonked without ceremony onto a chair made of hard, yellowed wood. Or maybe not wood…

"The Creatures graciously allow us to take advantage of this home," Seyen said flatly, moving to stand in front of him. "The walls and doors are strongly warded on every side. No one goes in or out without permission."

"Your permission or theirs?" Janeus said it like it was a joke, but he was actually serious, and she knew it.

She just stared at him, eyes narrowed. "I thought the birthright was the real gift you carried. But it seems that it was something else indeed. You've not changed a bit, lover. Not on the outside, anyway."

Whereas she hadn't changed a bit on the inside. Not from what he could tell. Janeus swallowed, trying not to look away from those eyes that could be either murky or bright green depending on the light and her mood. "I hear you left me for a hundred and fifty years," he said instead, tone light. "And you've called me back now. How can I help you, Sashy?"

There was a long, tense silence, and Janeus felt something he hadn't felt in many years – she was drawing on that connection between the two of them, the one she'd created long before with the original rose tattoo. She'd planted it on him, then on herself, and had siphoned his power ever since.

Now she was drawing on it, and he felt an answering pull on his own heart. Not emotions; his literal heart, and it *hurt*. It felt like if she could, she'd take everything from him.

But she'd been right. The birthright wasn't the true gift, not in regards to his own unnaturally long life. It was the *other* thing he'd stolen from his brother so long before.

"You can start by not calling me Sashy," she said coolly.

"Uh-" Because his chest still hurt....

"Oh, for flark's sake," Seyen said in disgust, tapping him on the head with her forefinger. "Sleep."

Sleep…

The twins had left on Seyen's instruction. Jenessa to check in at the scrying pool in the old city – and check in with the Creatures, who always insisted on it every time they moved through the gateways – and Troilus to do who knew what, as long as he was out of the way.

Not the brightest bulb, that one; unfortunately like his birth mother. Or fortunately, because perhaps if he'd been smarter Seyen wouldn't have loved him so well. Unlike his father or sister, he wasn't clever enough to consider turning on her.

That was why Seyen was so hard on Jenessa. She'd known right from the start that blood aside, the girl was just like her. A competitor, not a cherished pet. Still family, though.

Seyen studied Janeus's sleeping figure, intentionally distancing her emotions. It had been a very long time. Perhaps not quite the hundred and fifty years that he'd said, but something close to it.

Even after all that time she'd still felt her heart leap a little on seeing his familiar features and form. Not quite as classically handsome as Troilus, and with those large, dark, black-lashed eyes that reminded her of a deer (or a cow; the more unflattering the comparison, the better). He was as clean-shaven as always. He could never grow much of a beard, this man.

"I hate you," Seyen told her unconscious ex-lover.

She hated him for the way he had made her feel: out of control and needing to grab tighter, and a little bit desperate for his full love and attention, and knowing she wasn't getting it. There was so much remembered pain, and then she'd reached the point where it hurt too much, and she'd almost shut down.

That was why she hadn't pursued him after he'd left that last time. She'd known that it wouldn't stop hurting until she didn't see him or hear him or even think of him, and she'd tried to replace him with a dozen others, but just ended up frustrated.

Seyen scratched irritably at the red rose marking her chest. She wasn't especially sentimental (or hardly at all, really) so she knew that this stupid, enduring connection came from something more than just hundreds of years of shared experience. It was alter-power, and she'd caused it. She'd break the connection just as easily if she could (and killing him was the easiest option) but…well…she couldn't do it. Just couldn't.

She didn't love Janeus anymore. She hadn't loved him for a long time, and finding out about the gateways and his travel in Erastus had simply snapped that last thin thread of affection. Loving him had caused her pain, like a direct link was sewn from her heart to his hands and every move he made *hurt*. Leaving that behind had been a blessing.

But there was still…*something* there. Soul ties, she'd heard it called, where two could be lovers for so long that even when the love left and only indifference or even hatred remained, they would never forget each other. Never.

And Janeus had been with her almost from the beginning, and that was a lot of years to build soul ties.

Outside the closed door, Jenessa curled her lip. Seyen thought she held her own thoughts in so very closely, but at this point Jenessa had more than enough power to tap in and hear all except the quietest ones.

Eugh, the sentimentality was sickening. How could Seyen still care for Janeus after how unfaithful and disloyal he had been? She hadn't even seen him in fifteen decades!

Jenessa didn't even see what was so good about him. Yes, he was handsome enough, but he had a slightly weak chin which thankfully hadn't been passed on to his children, and he was too slender for her tastes.

But she supposed he had his uses. With a silent, resigned sigh, Jenessa left for the old city.

Time to check in with the Creatures…again.

Seyen waited until she felt her daughter's presence recede for real, and let her actual thoughts spill to the surface.

She couldn't kill Janeus for quite another reason than what the girl had been thinking, and it was all about that ancient medallion that he'd swallowed so many years before. You'd think he would have passed the thing through by now, but apparently unlike the Eternity Stone (which from memory tried to scramble out of your hands the moment you arrived in the Other realm, trying to get back into the normal) it was happy to sit inside his belly, keeping him safe from gathering. Keeping him alive.

Ironically Seyen realised it was probably keeping *her* alive too, that and her connection to the twins, who didn't have a single issue with gathering at all, but who would surely die of old age if they stayed in the normal realm for any length of time, Creatures notwithstanding.

Seyen wasn't stupid, and wasn't as naïve as the twins might sometimes presume. She knew that her pantheon had followed her because of the power she gifted, not because of any loyalty to herself personally. And she knew that the twins had been taking every chance to pick off those old Nobles, former friends regard-less, whenever they found them in their travels. ('Oh, *you two* are still alive-*ghhk.*')

And, she knew that without the Eternity Stone or something of similar power, she didn't have a chance of returning to what she'd been before, or even of leaving this Deias-forsaken place.

Right now she was a purse with holes in the bottom. Any gathered power would just fall right out again. She needed to be fixed before she could seriously think about her next move.

She took one last look at Janeus's smooth, sleeping face, and tapped her fingers on her knee thoughtfully. What kind of persuasion would it take to get that medallion?

This desert was an odd place, Ash decided. It wasn't hot at all, and there wasn't a drop of water to be seen, but one moment the air would be as thick as ninety percent humidity (and she'd struggle to breathe) and then the next the air would be as thin as on a mountaintop (and she'd struggle to breathe).

Not like she had asthma or was about to pass out, but more like she'd just stop suddenly and take an extra deep breath.

Odd.

But speaking of odd, the 'ruins' Ash had been heading towards were now showing themselves to be a collection of buildings – solid of structure and with the sense of incredible age, but with the untidiest architecture she'd ever seen. It was like the people who'd lived here had added onto them every few hundred years to keep them fashionable.

It hadn't worked.

Around the buildings were actual ruins. Ash stopped beside a fallen pillar to inspect the style, but couldn't place it. The carving in the stonework was incredibly intricate and unlike anything she'd seen before; just shapes and lines that didn't quite make a picture.

It was beautiful, but also disturbing. She thought she could *almost* see horrible monsters, but the lines stopped just short of completing them. If she was more fanciful, she would have said that the intent of the makers was to create something horrid in spirit but hide it in abstract patterns.

Or maybe that was just lack of oxygen messing with her head.

Near the base of the pillar, a large section of the stone had been chipped away to reveal a second carved layer underneath, like someone had decided to remodel and had concreted right over the original.

These hidden carvings were different. Maybe the lines were smoother, maybe there were more curves, but somehow that hidden layer seemed so much more pleasant. Perhaps it was true that the soul of the artist could be seen in the work, but if it was, then that second sculptor, the one whose work had covered the original, was one sick person.

Ash turned away from the pillar with a little shudder and continued towards the still-standing structures in the centre of the ruins. She could hear noises as she approached, the sound of business and industry, although she couldn't see anybody.

She reached a low wall encircling the main buildings. It was made of pale stones square-cut and set into a sturdy barrier, but it was only four feet high. Clearly to mark territory rather than actually keep anyone out, then. She stepped over it without much difficulty.

Inside the low wall was a complex of well-made stone buildings in the same off-white stone, but again very old and worn-looking in spite of their almost modern design. There were no windows in the walls, but she could definitely hear voices now.

Ash followed the white wall around two sides before finding an entrance to the nearest building: a colonnaded walkway leading up to a high, square doorway. People were walking in and out, barely sparing her a glance. Gathering her confidence, she moved towards the nearest person, a woman in pastel green, and tapped her on the shoulder.

The woman in green looked at Ash with irritation. "Yes?"

"Could you tell me where I am, please?"

"You're standing outside the doorway."

Gee, what a revelation. "I know that," Ash said politely. "I meant where this place is. This…country."

Oops. She hadn't meant to let slip that she was so out of her way she couldn't even point to her location on a globe, but it was out now. Besides, her clothes would tell the story even if she didn't.

Clearly agreeing, the woman ran her eyes up and down Ash's body dismissively. "You must be a new worker. Take the first left inside the doorway and ask for Bera. She'll tell you where to go." Then she left.

Ash was left a little stunned, watching the woman's retreating back in surprise. But then she should be used to rudeness after her recent experiences, and anyway, it could have been worse. She *still* didn't know where she was, but judging by the woman's clothing it was at least somewhere that had heard of zips.

She followed the instructions anyway, taking the first left into what looked like a small-scale factory. It was a large, plain room, filled with men and women working at tables arranged in rough assembly lines. Ash could see bits and pieces coming together into what looked like children's toys, except with an edge. The occasional puff of coloured light would emit from them as they moved along the lines, and Ash felt her hair stand on end as she realised that it was alter-power. Alter-power, just out in the open.

On a tabletop close by she could see what looked like an old-fashioned wooden doll, the sort with loose joints. It was being cheerfully painted in multiple colours. As she studied it, the doll's purple, painted-on eyes flicked towards her.

Ash gasped and stepped back, smacking into someone.

"Watch yourself," the man said irritably. "You just stepped on my foot."

Ash flushed, but she still couldn't forget the way that doll had looked at her…or if it even had. Perhaps she'd imagined it. "Sorry. I was sent in here to find Bera."

"You'd be Gerak's newest, then. Over there." He pointed at an older woman working at a table nearby: grey-haired and round and friendly-looking, thankfully. "Talk to her."

"Right. Thanks."

Bera looked up as Ash approached and smiled welcomingly, making her look even more like the stereotypical friendly grandmother, minus any trays of freshly baked goods.

Ash smiled back in relief. "Hi, Bera? I'm Ash-"

"A new worker? Excellent. I'll show you how we do things around here, and you can get started with Geoff on the hand mirrors." She stood, and taking Ash's arm, began moving over to the other side of the large room.

Ash dug in her heels. "I'm sorry, there's been a misunderstanding. I'm not a worker; I'm actually lost in the area and I've just stumbled across this place by accident. No one would answer my questions, so I was sent to you."

Bera raised a silver eyebrow. "That is unexpected. People rarely find this place by accident. In fact, I've never had anyone come here except who was sent. Ever."

Ash looked awkwardly at her slippered feet. "Well, I get around a bit, and don't always know where I'm going. Could you just give me a pointer, though?"

"Sure." The other woman sat back down and patted the bench next to her. "It's been a long day. I don't like to stand if I can help it."

Ash sat, wondering why Bera hadn't commented on her odd clothing. Bera herself was wearing a similar outfit to everyone else here: light-coloured trouser and shirt sets, looking like they just needed a bob and a set of pearls to fit in a twentieth-century country club. Very casual, normal even, except for the fact everything was the same colour.

It reminded Ash uncomfortably of Iversley, with Queen Seyen's nobles and everyone's colour-coded uniforms. "Er – what year is it, please?"

The woman seemed unperturbed by the odd question. "We're

in the Other, dear. Time hardly matters."

"It doesn't?"

"Only a very little. You might say that it's just around the start of the third millennium AD, as that's where these items will go once completed. But really, without days or nights, who can really tell time?"

Ash was growing increasingly baffled. It sounded like it was about the year 2000 – which meant she wasn't too far off home, and she *thought* Bera was speaking Anglish, but… "What kind of place has no days or nights?"

"The Other, dear. I just told you that."

There was an awkward pause where it became very clear that Ash still had no idea what she was talking about. "

You really did stumble across this place, didn't you? And that's not so easy to do. Ash – that was your name, right? Let me tell you a few things."

THE OTHER

"I'm sorry," Elspeth finally blurted out.

Anne turned to look at her in surprise, almost tripping over her long skirts as she did so. The farmhouse had turned out to be further than they'd thought, and the path down to the valley not an easy one, but that wasn't Elspeth's fault. "What for?"

"For throwing your Stone in the garderobe. 'Twas not my place to do so, and it has caused all manner of trouble."

Anne thought about it. "No," she said finally. "If not for you, I would not have returned to Renwick Castle at all. You do understand that, do you not? And Edgar still would've made the same plans to kill me. So with or without the Eternity Stone, the castle was no longer safe. It matters not how we arrived at this place, but I am only glad that I was able to bring you with me this time."

"Except now we are alone in the middle of a desert without even your friends to aid us."

True, 'twas something of a problem. "Fear not, Bethie," Anne declared staunchly. "'Twill not be long before help comes."

"I'm not afraid," Elspeth said, and she looked at Anne with those light green eyes so much like her mother's. "I think this must be the most interesting day I've ever had, and I wish 'twould go on forever."

What an unlikely wish. "Why not?" Anne replied cheerfully.

"But look, our help might be at hand."

She pointed to a figure up ahead, not far from the farmhouse. 'Twas a man on a horse, and he'd definitely seen them, as he'd begun to move in their direction.

They scrambled their way to the bottom of the rocky slope just as he reached them. Closer up, Anne could see he was old and white-haired, seemingly baked as dry as his surroundings, and the shaggy, weather-beaten horse was just the same. They appeared amiable enough, though.

"Gudday," the man called. "What brings you two little lassies here?"

Well, that was the question, was it not? "We've misplaced our escort," Anne replied with a little curtsey. "Mayhap you might have seen them."

"What language were you speaking just then?" Elspeth asked in a loud whisper. "'Twas not Anglish."

Honestly Anne had *no idea*. But that was the thing about the translating nano-somethings that scientist had given them months before. When they worked and she understood or spoke another language, she could barely tell she was doing it. Unsurprisingly, this bothered some people. "'Twas just another gift I gained while I was away," she mumbled. "'Tis not witchcraft. 'Tis simply…"

"Like the flying?"

"Like the flying," Anne agreed, although in truth 'twas not the same thing at all, and not from the same source. To the old man, who was watching them curiously, she said, "My apologies, sir. My sister speaks only Anglish. Have you seen a tall couple of about twenty years old, the boy with fair hair and the girl with dark? They should not be far from here."

The man stared at them with what might have been sympathy on his lined features. "Can't say I have. Don't see many around here at all, no, not at all. Been left behind, have you? Abandoned?"

"Certainly not," Anne replied staunchly, pushing down the

thought that mayhap she *did* feel a little abandoned, although 'twas not at all George and Ash's fault. "A simple mistake, that was all. Then mayhap you might direct us to the nearest town?"

"Weeell...there is a city over that way." He waved vaguely towards the other end of the valley, where a shadow of green hovered where the desert and horizon met. "It'll be a long walk for you though. At least four days, looking at the length of yer legs. And there's no water, either. Not in this desert."

Wonderful. Just...*wonderful.* Anne's feelings must have shown on her face because she felt her sister touch her arm, and Elspeth murmured worriedly, "What was that? What did he say?"

"I'll tell you in a moment," she answered. Then she said to the man, feeling the change at the back of her throat as she switched to his tongue, "Do you know how we can get to the city, then? By a path that does have water?"

The old man paused, a blank expression coming over his face for a long moment. He turned to look back at the house, and enough time passed that Anne began to wonder if he'd had a brain bleed while standing there.

"Weeeelll," he said thoughtfully. "I was thinkin' that you girls should come back to the house, and my wife could look after you for a day or two, then we'll pass a message on to the next trader that goes through here. Should be two, three days at the most. He'll be goin' to the city, and you can hitch a ride with him."

"Three days!" Anne exclaimed. "That's far too long!"

"What did you say, Anne?" Elspeth hissed frantically next to her, but Anne shushed her.

The old man shrugged. "Up to you. Thought you'd not want to be wanderin' the desert, is all."

Of *course* they didn't want to be wandering the desert. But Anne hadn't met this man before in her life, and she really *was* expecting Ash and George to show up at any time...

Just then a voice spoke into her mind, so clearly she couldn't have missed it. *Go with him. You can trust him.*

Anne leapt on that. Oh, thank *goodness*, she'd really had no idea what to do, and Elspeth was depending on her too. Hearing from Amaranthus, through that voice in her head, was perfect timing.

Hoping her delayed reaction hadn't been noticed, she recalled her manners. "Thank you very much. That's very kind."

"'Course it is," he replied, sounding disgruntled. "I'm a very kind person."

"Yes, I can see that."

"I'm Tray. Yer?"

His speech, already hard to follow, had become so strange that it took Anne a moment to realise what he was saying. "Oh. I'm Anne, and this is my sister Elspeth."

"Nice t' meet yer. Now if ye want a ride to the house, get on the horse. If ye want to walk, then walk."

"A ride would be lovely, thank you." Then ignoring her unsettled nerves, she turned to her sister and quickly summarised the conversation in Anglish.

"On that horse?" Elspeth said doubtfully. "I've never been on a horse before, you know that. And this one smells like someone died. Are they supposed to smell so foul?"

Anne had noticed 'twas a particularly stinky horse, but had been too polite to say so. But really, they weren't going to wander this desert until they ran into George and Ash, especially not when Elspeth wasn't even wearing *shoes*.

"Never mind the horse," she said firmly. "Amaranthus says all is well, so we shall go."

"I know where they are," Jenessa had announced upon her return from the old city, face pale and rather grumpy. And then Janeus, who'd been in some odd kind of sleep where he couldn't move but could hear what was going on around him, had been shaken awake by Old Seyen, as he was now thinking of her.

"You heard the girl," Seyen told him. "Go and get them. Get the Stone."

"What if they don't have it?"

"Then find out who *does* have it, and kill them," she said impatiently.

"But what about-"

"We'll deal with it," Seyen snapped. "You go, do what you were told. Now."

And just like before, Janeus found himself propelled to his feet and flying towards the portal that Seyen had opened. This one wasn't a gateway, but instead a connecting point within two parts of the Other. He thought about arguing and saying he couldn't find them, but didn't bother. They both knew that wasn't true – he was an excellent tracker, and would feel the Stone's movement from a mile away.

There was another jolt as he moved through the portal, which felt worse than the gateway into the Other had. That time Janeus had almost vomited from the disorientation it brought, but this time he actually did vomit. There was a flash of light and bright colour (because even regurgitating in the Other had power to it) and afterwards he felt worse, not better.

He shook off the feeling, struggling to draw on the power around him to do so, and set off in the direction he'd been sent.

George sat down on the large rock with a sigh. He'd been walking for hours, figuring that if he just kept going in one direction long enough, he'd eventually reach civilisation…or at least something green.

Perhaps an incorrect assumption. He felt as though he could walk until he dropped from thirst or hunger or exhaustion – which seemed more of a possibility than he would have liked –

and still not reach anywhere useful. He couldn't see where he was going, and while he'd reached some low-lying hills, they hadn't proved high enough to get a good view of the area.

George had even half-heartedly tried to fly, to get more height and a better view. He'd thrown himself off a moderately high rock to see if the fear of falling would renew his ability as it had once with Ashlea.

Regrettably, the bruises from that landing showed that to be incorrect.

George leaned forward, resting his elbows on his knees, and pondered. When he'd heard about Anne's miraculous fall from the castle wall, he'd thought – hoped – that she'd unknowingly flown rather than fallen. And of course if Anne still had the ability to fly, then he would've too.

But if Anne hadn't actually been flying, then how did she survive? That thirty-foot fall should have killed her, or broken her back at least.

Who knew? Perhaps it *had* been a real miracle.

He wondered again where the ladies were, and if they were well. Everything had been going ever so fast since Ashlea had shown up in the library, that he'd not had a chance to sit and simply think things over. It seemed that something needed to change in his old life, but he didn't know what.

Sighing, George hauled himself to his feet and continued walking up the hill, taking the easiest path amongst the dry dirt. While not a proper road, the wide path had clearly been travelled more than a few times, with the dirt trampled firm in the middle and rocks pushed to the outside. So there must be other people around here somewhere, even if he hadn't met any yet.

Then, as if to prove confirm that idea, George spotted an old coin lying in the dirt, dull from age but largely dust-free. Clearly someone had dropped it recently. He pocketed it just in case it turned out to be useful.

There were a few trees here too, tired, dry-looking pines with their needles stiff brown, and the gentle path wove its way around them as it moved up the slope. But then at a sharp curve the path turned steep and George stopped, trying to decide if he should keep going, or head back down to flat land again.

With a shrug, he decided to keep going upwards. Maybe if he got high enough, he could see civilisation. Climbing a hill to get that vantage point wasn't nearly as much fun as flying would have been, but it was his only choice.

"Pssst."

The soft voice made George jump. He looked around in confusion and hope, but didn't see anybody. Shaken at what seemed to be his imagination, he resumed walking.

"Pssst. Down here."

This time he couldn't stop himself cursing, the voice had given him such a fright. But he shook it off and looked down. There, standing not three feet away from him, was a little…creature. Small, brown and furry, it reminded him of a tailless beaver, except it had a snout like a hog. The only thing was, this…rodent-hog was wearing a woolly green jacket, and was looking up at him expectantly from bright brown eyes.

"Excuse me?" he said incredulously.

"You're excused, then," the thing said, its words translating in his head into a strong, low-Anglish accent. "I come to talk to you cos I need to go up that there hill, and can't make it on my own. Legs too short, see?" He gestured down at his stumpy, furry hindquarters. "So, I was wonderin' if you wouldn't mind cartin' me and the missus up that there hill to our home. Seein' as how you're goin' up there anyway."

It smiled in a way it no doubt thought was endearing (and perhaps might have been had the thing not strongly reminded him of a creation of taxidermy, complete with glass eyes) and George turned to see a slightly smaller version standing next to it, in a red dress this time. Off to the side was a small hand cart, just big enough for the two of them to climb into. And that was exactly what they did.

Then the male one looked at him with bright eyes, and said, "Come on, then. Aren't you gonna take us up the hill?"

George looked at them in their child-sized toy cart, and then looked at the hilly path. "What…what…?"

The one in the red dress frowned and poked a furry claw at him. "Go on then. If we don't move then the big ones will come out, and where will we all be? Lunch, that's what."

"Lunch? Big ones…talking animals…what the blazes *are* you creatures?!"

"Just people," the male said sniffily. "Special, mutated animal-people. And I'll thank you not to be rude about it. Not everyone gets to be fully human, you know."

"They don't?" George was utterly bewildered. He didn't know a single place on earth where animals could talk like this. He was beginning to suspect that either the time travel was messing with his sanity, or he'd learned to translate animal grunts into something intelligible.

The female started bouncing in the cart, and the male said, "Just get started, and we'll tell you the story on the way."

"What story?"

"*Our* story. Come on!"

It was probably the shock of it, but George didn't question them any longer. The rodent-hogs wanted a ride home, he'd give them one. Feeling rather like a cart horse, he bent to pick up the wooden handles of the small cart.

As he set his hand down, he felt a slight touch, and imagined that he saw something like a smoky purple thread lash around his wrist. But a moment later the thought was gone. He shook it off and began to pull the cart up the hill, the whole time wondering if he was really seeing these creatures or if he'd lost half his good sense in the last travel. But no, he'd been insane before (briefly but memorably) and it had been quite, quite different.

As he climbed the hill with the creatures riding smugly

behind him, they chattered about their house at the very top, and how George should come and visit them for supper. But they were yet to give any information about their origins, or even their names. Perhaps if he could get them to stop for breath he could ask if they'd seen the ladies. After all, in the last few travels they'd ended up some distance apart. It was only a matter of time, surely?

The nameless male was chattering on, "…And if you run into the big ones, be sure to roar. If you make 'em think you're scarier than they are, they'll run. But whatever you do, don't show your fear!"

"Pardon? Fear of what?"

The two of them suddenly huddled into each other, and the male pointed behind George's shoulder, its glass-like eyes bright with fear and something else. "That!"

"That's quite a tale," Ash said to Bera, trying to work out whether she believed it or not. "So you're saying that we're still on Earth," thank Deias, "in another dimension that's very hard to access, one with lots of alter-power."

"Right."

"Sort of like…the supernatural. Magic. A realm full of every-thing that defies the usual laws of nature."

Bera shrugged. "That's a very simplistic description, but close enough."

Wow, Ash's alter-power obsessed father would feel so validated to learn about this…if it was true. She looked around her with interest, but she didn't see the sort of supernatural, almost-magical things she would expect from such a place.

"I don't know," she said doubtfully. "This place…it feels a bit strange, but I don't see anything out of the ordinary." And she'd seen *all* kinds of weird and wonderful in the last year or two.

"Do you feel like you're somehow more solid, and yet like everything could change in an instant?" Bera asked.

Ash nodded.

"That's the main thing that separates the Other from the normal, that there's so much *potential* here. Anything can happen, and that's why The Works is centred here rather than in the normal, because our reach is so much further." Ash wanted to ask what Bera meant by that, but the woman continued on. "Everything in the Other is what you'd see in the normal world, but *more*. In its true form, and with tremendous effect on the normal, and to a degree, the normal has effect on the Other too."

"Like these things you're making?"

"They'll be conduits soon enough," Bera explained. "Eyes and ears for the Creatures who are trapped in this realm, but who still wish to see and even influence what happens in the normal."

Ugh.

Ash's feelings must have shown on her face, because the older woman raised an eyebrow. "You're not sure what to think of that? Yet here you are in the Other with us, and you haven't imploded yet. What part bothers you? The idea that we're in an entirely different realm just bursting with alter-power, or that there are beings that only live here *and* impact on the normal world?"

"Both," Ash admitted.

The first part meant that her father was right – again – and perhaps explained how the Nobles back in Iversley had managed to command such power at all, but it blew her mind to hear that it was *real*. They'd been trying to get to Amaranthus, and they'd ended up in a place you couldn't even reach by plane, train or automobile. Or she had, anyway.

"The second part, about things that live here…" Ash continued. "Are they people like us?" Deias forbid there really *were* elves in this place, because then Anne would have been right all along, and that would be too much to bear.

Bera laughed. "Oh, bless you, dear. No, they're rather more than that, and it's a story that goes right back to the beginning of our concept of time, to when the two realms were joined. I'll tell you about it, and then you can tell me what brought you here. There's no doubt that it was one of the Creatures, because people can't reach this place by accident."

"Alright," Ash agreed cautiously, thinking of Amaranthus again and trying to fit the label 'Creature' onto him. But Bera had said the Creatures couldn't leave this realm at all, and he'd *definitely* left at least once, when he met George, hadn't he?

Ash didn't know what to think about the flying house, though.

"So," Bera said briskly. "We've now got the two realms. The normal – made up of the three dimensions of height, width and depth, and with all those things you can hold in your hand, that you can feel. We include the realm of thought in the normal, by the way, although it's close to the Other. You understand?"

Thought was a realm??? "Uh…sure."

"And then there's the Other realm," Bera continued, "which is where all the alter-power is, and where all the truly significant things happen. But once they were parts of the same realm, like skin over flesh, or paint on one of those toys there. The same. And living in this complete realm were both humans and the Creatures of the Other, who were more powerful in every way but lived with humans in peace. They were not human, but immortal beings far, far more powerful than the highest king."

"So what happened to break the realms apart?"

"War. A huge war between two factions of the Other, over the safety and freedom of all the world's inhabitants. See, one of the Other Creatures ruled as king, but he was a tyrant, so rebels rose up against him. The power thrown around was so intense that it seemed like it would destroy all living things, so the leader of the rebels made a decision. He selflessly used the last of his strength to create a spell that would separate the realms, take the alter-power somewhere it couldn't harm the normal any longer. That was how the Other was created, and all the Other Creatures good and evil were trapped in it forever, unable to move to the normal realm and interact with humans any longer."

"Wow," Ash said, equally hoping that it was and wasn't true. "Good and evil still both trapped in here, right?"

"Mmm...well, the Rift was only the first part of it," Bera replied, leaning comfortably back in her seat. "The worst part comes next. After the rebel leader had given everything to separate the realms and protect the humans, the tyrannical king had enough strength to do a terrible thing. He ordered every last one of the captured rebels killed, and their hearts torn out and burned."

Gross. "So they're dead, then. Long gone."

"No." Bera shook her head firmly, wagging a finger for emphasis. "I said they were *immortal*, girl, not long-lived. You take life away from an immortal being, and it becomes eternally dead. Their minds and souls could never die, but their bodies displayed some of the symptoms of death, and their minds were twisted by the horror of what had been done to them. They became a sort of living dead, sent away from their people. And now they roam the deserts of this place, maddened by pain and avoided by even their own kind..."

Ash leaned forward with interest, waiting for the punch line to the joke, but it never came. Bera just looked at her expectantly, and finally Ash burst out, "You're saying that the Other has *zombies*?"

"Nah," the other woman said dismissively. "Not really. It was all a long time ago, you realise. There *are* some dangerous Creatures out there, but they're not lumbering, mindless creatures out to eat brains, with all their bits rotting and falling off. They're just...different, without that spark that all living things have. They never change, and they never grow. They simply stay nasty and vicious, and they resent every living being as if they are personally responsible for their pain."

Urgh. Better than zombies, but barely, and Ash desperately hoped it wasn't true. "How do you know?"

"Gerak told me, and he should know. He's one of the Creatures that fought for the old king out of fear, but regretted it. Later he and some others escaped and made their own community here in the Other, and they're the ones who are good, who still try to help humans in the normal world."

"What about the king? Where is he, then?"

Bera shrugged. "Gerak says he hasn't been seen in millennia. Crawled into a hole and hid, I suppose."

"Oh. That's sad."

"It's less than what he deserves, for what he did."

"I guess so," Ash agreed, but she was wondering about the accuracy of the tale. It sounded like a fairytale or myth, but then some true stories grew so old and were repeated so often that they took on the ring of simplistic fairytales.

"So how *did* you end up here?" Bera asked curiously. "Come on, you can tell me. I've just told you everything about us here at The Works, after all. Did a Creature bring you through and then forget to wait for you at this side of the Rift?"

"Ahh..." It occurred to Ash then that perhaps Amaranthus could be one of these Creatures who'd abandoned the king after the realms separated and who now helped humans, but that wouldn't explain the house in the clouds where they'd first met. *That* was in the normal realm, although certainly not 'normal', and Bera had just said that the Creatures couldn't come through to the normal anymore.

"I don't know," she replied finally. "There's someone who's been helping us – my friends and I – but I don't know what he really is. Not normal, I know that much, and time doesn't seem to bother him at all. We were looking for him when we- *I* arrived here."

"Definitely a Creature," the older woman said decisively.

"Although he erred in pulling you through and leaving you in the desert. Outside the cities is always dangerous ground, and things can move faster than you realise out here in this atmosphere. Well, at least you can stay safe behind our walls until your Creature comes for you."

"Thank you." But Ash thought again of those four-foot-high walls surrounding the complex, and wondered. "So the undead Creatures can't jump, right?"

"The walls are warded," Bera explained. "So even if one could jump the fifteen feet required to make it over, they'd be knocked back."

Ash paused awkwardly. "Fifteen feet? You mean most of the wall is invisible?"

Bera gave her an odd look. "No, I mean there's a giant wall right out there. You came in through the gate, did you not?"

"Actually I just stepped over the wall," Ash admitted. "But maybe it doesn't keep me out because I'm just human."

"Then we're not talking about the same wall. You must have arrived inside the complex, if you don't know which one."

"Oh no, I definitely arrived outside. I walked almost half an hour to reach this place, but only saw a really little wall, going all the way around these buildings. I stepped right over it."

The two looked at each other in confusion, and Bera in growing suspicion. "There is no little wall that I know of. There is only one, the one I spoke of. The guard did let you in, I assume?"

Ash shrugged helplessly. "I didn't see a guard."

For a moment they just stared at each other.

Then the older woman's eyes narrowed and she stood, gesturing for Ash to follow her. "Come with me." She headed briskly out of the room and then out of the building, walking forward until the low wall was before her. She pointed at it. "What do you see there?"

Was it a trick question? No matter how Ash squinted, she still saw four feet of wall, and couldn't spot the high, protective wall

Bera had mentioned. Surely that was something that couldn't be easily missed?

"I see a low wall, and the desert behind. In the distance are mountains, but I can only just see them." Looking around a little further, she noticed a man sitting in a booth by himself by a dip in the wall, a stick of some kind in his hand. "I, ah, think I see the guard now."

Bera looked at Ash suspiciously. "Who are you working for that the wall seems nothing to you? Veritus? Evangeline?"

Ash spread her hands out helplessly in front of her. "I'm not working for anybody. I really don't mean any harm! I was just lost, and-"

"And tricked your way into finding out our secrets by pretending to be a worker," Bera finished icily. The friendly, gingerbread-baking grandmother was well and truly gone, and left behind was someone without an ounce of compassion. "You've shown your true colours. I think it's time for you to leave."

"I didn't-" Ash began to say.

"BEGONE!"

As the woman spoke, it was like an invisible force pushed up against Ash and sent her skidding back towards the low wall, then stumbling over it to land on her butt on the other side.

"What did I do?" she cried out, but the woman didn't seem to hear her or see her.

Bera was watching the place she'd fallen over with a blank, suspicious glare, and finally turned to the distant guard. "Did you see that?"

The guard nodded, calling back, "Infiltrator. If I see her again, I'll send her off."

Infiltrator?! Excuse *them*?!

Ash stared at the two of them in stunned dismay, then when it seemed like they really couldn't see her, stuck out her tongue. She was insulted, but also scared. There was power here in words and in objects, no matter how true or untrue the other stories, and she'd felt Bera's word like a blow. She hadn't felt power like that since Iversley, 2155. Or ever. What else could be lurking in this empty, dry place?

Lions and tigers and undead bears, oh my…

Ash shook off the tingle of unease, lifted her chin, and set off for the green haze in the distance. Better there than here.

The beaver-hogs were huddled together, staring beadily at something behind George. Staring *up* behind him. *The big ones*, the male had said…

In that too-slow manner one always had when one knew something dreadful was behind, George turned.

There, not ten feet from him, was 'a big one'. It was rather like a bull, if only a bull had huge, muscular forearms rather like an ape and enormous antlers sprouting like winter trees from above its ears. Its fur was half-grey, half-gone, its eyes were malicious and pink, and its smell… by Jove, he should have smelled that before he saw it.

"Er…good day to you, sir." (It had worked for the little ones, hadn't it?)

The bull-beast roared, and George now knew that the half-decayed grey matter went all the way down. There was also what looked like a large bone stuck in that hollow throat, and the beast cared not at all.

"Scare it away!" The little female hissed, huddling into her mate.

Scare *it* away? Was the thing serious?

"Act bigger, louder!" the male ordered with a fearful, almost laugh-like chitter. "Shout at it! Wave your arms!"

The antlered beast moved closer, and George didn't think. He dropped the cart and threw his arms in the air, roaring like he used to when playing monster games as a child with his brother. But unlike his brother, this thing did seem startled. It stepped back.

Using all of his courage (*oh please Deias, don't let it come charging at me!*) he roared again, stepping toward the creature and feeling rather like he was either committing suicide or under-taking the bravest act of his life, but either way unable to stop himself.

The bull-beast stepped back again, then sideways, looking at him with its piebald head on a quizzical angle. George roared, and it sidled around him a few times with that same startled, curious expression, then finally it seemed to have had enough. It shook its giant head, glared at him pinkly one more time, then turned and disappeared over the rise into the dry trees.

"You can stop roarin' now," the male beaver-hog said flatly. "It's gone."

Had he still been roaring? Feeling a little silly – but also like he'd quite been out of control – George lowered his arms. "What, by Jove, was that precisely?"

"One of the big ones," the female replied. "Playin' with you, it seems. Go on then, take us away before another comes."

Feeling like he was acting out the scenes of a play, George immediately bent to take the cart, heading on up the hill at as fast a pace as he could manage. "Who knew," he managed to get out in-between wheezing breaths, the air up here seeming thinner and his strength having been used on the roar/wave act. "Who knew that such a great lumbering beast would be frightened by a few loud noises." Well, these two had. "Thank you for your help."

"Oh, we're good help," the male said from behind George. But there was something in its tone George wasn't sure of. "Wasn't expectin' it to work so well."

"They're herbivores, I suppose," George commented. "But territorial, no doubt."

"Herbivores?" he heard the female whisper to the male.

"Ain't no herbs around here."

That was true. For a giant creature that no doubt needed a great deal of nutrients, there was very little to sustain it. And there had been that bone in its throat…and this hill was just growing steeper by the moment. "By Jove," he said again. "How far away are we?"

"Not far," the male answered. "Move faster."

Rude. "I'm going as fast as I can," George said with a bite in his voice.

"Too slow," the female said, and it was like her words pricked him, made him want to walk faster even though it was really the last thing he'd intended.

How had he got here, anyway? How had *they* got here? "You could be more helpful, you know."

"How's that, exactly?" the male asked. "Told you we can't walk the hill. We can't help push, what would be the point?"

"Well, you could at least stop telling me to speed up! It's not going to make me go any faster."

"Isn't it?" the female sounded disappointed. "Oh. I'd thought it was. We'll stop then. Terribly sorry."

And then they sulked in silence while George pulled, wrestling between wanting to comfort the little beasts and being very irritated with them. He settled for silence as well, and kept moving. He didn't know what that antlered creature had been, but he didn't want to meet another one.

It was several minutes later, where the hill was terribly steep (and George was becoming increasingly aware of his unfitness) that he began to notice the smell. It was enough to make his nose want to crawl back into his face. One of the little ones had passed wind, no doubt.

By Jupiter, what *was* he doing here? The hill had no end in sight, and he was acting as cart horse for two unknown creatures, who had not an ounce of good manners.

Abruptly George set down the arms of the cart. "I do believe my journey stops here," he began. But as he turned, he saw two things. One, the two beaver-hogs were disappearing into a cleft in the nearby cliff face at high speed. Two…well, the smell was less likely gas, and more likely another of the 'big ones'.

And there it was, standing on two legs like an oversized human – if a human was nine feet tall, with a long, straggly mane around a snarling leathery face. George was reminded horribly of a badly stuffed lion that he'd seen once as a child, the figure far more frightful in death than it ever could be in life.

The lion-thing roared at him, and George saw a glimmer of intelligence in its yellow eyes, but that was outweighed by the pure malevolence evident there.

A wash of cold fear rushed over him. His throat constricted, and just like Ashlea with the terrible lizard, he almost froze into place. But then miraculously he was able to move, and he pulled himself up to his full five foot ten, and roared as loudly as he could.

The lion-man made a face like laughter, or perhaps like biting its own inner-lip, and then it scowled and roared back. Not quite what George had planned. The fear was almost crippling him now, but he forced himself to roar once more as he carefully backed away, moving for the cliff. His voice seemed pitiful and weak compared to the other's, though, and it knew it.

As if able to smell his fear, the lion-man advanced. Behind him, George saw a second one sniffing at the air.

Go. Go go go go go or he was dead-

Forgetting the roar, George turned and flung himself towards that narrow crevice in the rock. It turned out to be the entrance into a small cave, the back of which grew so narrow that he couldn't see or reach into it, and where the beaver-hog couple were nowhere to seen. He scrambled in as far as he could, shaking with fear. The lion-man was scrabbling at the entrance, but as hard as it tried, it was too big to get in.

Or so it seemed, because as many swipes as those arms took,

they never touched him. George, mindless with fright, began grabbing loose rocks from inside the cave and shoving them at the gap, right into the thing's face. Much better if he smacked it in the head while he was at it.

His breath was loud in his ears as the gap slowly filled, and the lion-man's horrible face was blocked out. But the air in the small cave was getting thinner and thinner, and George felt as though he was suffocating.

He was on his belly, facing out at the now filled in entrance, and he realised that at some point there must have been a rock fall, because his chest was being squeezed, and he couldn't see, and he couldn't move, and the last thing he thought before he lost consciousness was: *damn it, not again!*

DISTRACTION

The horse was smelly and its back bony, but 'twas large enough to carry Anne, Elspeth and the old man Tray, although hardly comfortably.

Within a few minutes the horse reached the sandy-coloured house sitting in the sandy-coloured dirt. Without any instructions from Tray, it veered around the side of the house towards an open stable where another horse stood, placidly watching as they approached.

"Get yerselves into the house when yer ready," the man said. "I'll go let Mother know yer here." With that, he vaulted down off the horse with agility more fitting to a man decades younger and strode round the corner into the house.

Anne translated, and Elspeth looked at her curiously from where she sat side-saddle.

"Mother? I thought he said 'twas his wife."

Anne shrugged, looking down from their great height on the horse to the ground, which seemed very far below. "Some men call their wives Mother, because that's what they call them in front of the children."

"How odd."

"Indeed," Anne agreed, feeling distinctly irritable. "And he might have at least helped us down. This horse is enormous!"

And she couldn't get it to stop moving. Every time it got near the side of the stable where she *might* have been able to get a foothold and climb down, 'twould veer away again. It happened so many times that it almost seemed intentional, but no horse could be that clever or malicious. Even worse, it had no reins. In hindsight Anne had no idea how Tray had managed to steer it in the first place…

"OOF!" The horse abruptly sat down on its hindquarters, sending both girls tumbling off its back to the dusty ground. Then as if satisfied that its work was done, it stood again and ambled over to stand next to the other horse, and the two of them stood together and watched the girls pick themselves up.

"Z'wounds," Elspeth exclaimed. "What a beastly horse! I swear it did that apurpose."

"Don't be silly," Anne began, then stopped herself. She had known a horse or two that delighted in kicking or biting unwary humans, mayhap as their revenge for being forced to be beasts of burden. Why should this one be any different? "Oh, never mind. Mayhap it did."

She took a step towards the side of the house where the old man had disappeared, then stopped when she realised her sister wasn't following. "Elspeth? Are you coming?"

The younger girl was standing there anxiously, biting her lip. Finally she muttered, "'Tis not as though there is anywhere else to go."

'Twas true, more's the pity. Anne liked very little the idea of visiting a stranger's home, even a helpless old man, but 'twas his home or the wide desert, and she liked very little that idea also.

The voice had spoken in her mind and told her not to fear, so she'd determined not to. But sometimes her feelings would not bow to her will, because the hairs still stood on the back of her neck…

The old man stuck his grizzled head back around the corner,

interrupting her anxious thoughts. "Are ye gonna stay out here all night then?"

Anne took her younger sister's hand. "We're coming."

They'd thought Tray was old. 'Mother' – his wife introduced herself only as that – was the most ancient, hideous woman Anne had ever seen, and Anne had not even looked directly at her.

Bent in half like a chicken wishbone, with sparse white hair, almost-blind eyes rheumy with age, and her skin so full of lumps and wrinkles so that the features were almost lost underneath. Almost, but not quite.

From what Anne had seen of her before looking away out of sheer self defence, she had to be the ugliest human being Anne had ever set eyes on.

That sounded rude, but 'twas simply the truth, and was saying a lot considering some of the beggars Anne had seen in the village and in Lunden. Mother looked like an ancient troll, with an enormous hooked nose covered in warts; uneven, faded eyes and a mouth set in a permanent, toothless scowl; and that whole face as saggy as a Saint Bernard's jowls. Even Elspeth wasn't looking at the woman directly, and Elspeth wasn't one to hold back from staring.

"Well aren't ye lovely wee lasses?" Mother crooned, her voice rather nicer than her face, thank the Eternal One. Thankfully she didn't try to touch them or cosset them. "Poor wee lasses caught alone in the desert. Not wise. No, not wise at all."

"We didn't mean to be," Elspeth said defensively. "We were-"

"Lost and left behind, w'out a trail of breadcrumbs," the woman finished. "Poor, poor wee lasses."

Something about that put Anne's teeth on edge, especially once she recognised the folktale being referred to. "We're hardly babes in the woods, goodwife. And our friends will return for us anon. But in the meantime we thank you for your hospitality."

"But you've seen nothing at all! Here, have some stew. Have

some ale, some bread. Anything ye like, my dears."

Surprisingly the food was good and almost familiar. It made Anne wonder what year 'twas that they were cooking in such a way, but 'twas too odd a question to consider asking. They ate, and the whole time Mother crooned over them rather like they were children, although mayhap in her eyes they were.

Finally they finished eating, and although the sun was still high in the sky Anne found her eyes heavy. Across the table she saw Elspeth doing the same, and Mother clucked her tongue. "Poor wee lasses," she said for what must have been the twentieth time. "Tired from our hard day out, are we?"

Now, as Ash would say, that was really starting to bug her. They were *not* children, and while the food was appreciated, a little respect from adult to adult would also be appreciated-

"Here we go," Mother offered, pulling back the covers of a neatly made double bed. Elspeth was already snoring on the other side, and Anne wondered absently how they had arrived in the bedroom so quickly, as she did not recall even walking this far. "Sleep, my dear, and we shall wait for the nice trader to come in the morning, yes?"

And in spite of everything that had happened that day – or mayhap because of everything – Anne found herself obeying.

Ash walked slowly away from the low stone wall, occasionally glancing over her shoulder in bewilderment over what had just happened. Bera hadn't waited around for long after she'd made Ash leave. She and the guard had stared at the place where Ash had gone 'through' the wall, then after a minute they'd turned and strode back to the buildings, very serious expressions on their faces.

"I'm going to contact Gerak," Bera had said to the guard.

Ash wasn't sure who Gerak was, but she didn't think she

wanted to meet him, not when his employee had taken such unreasonable dislike to her. So now she walked alone through the ruins, out towards the flat expanse of desert, and the hopeful strip of green in the hazy distance.

Were there really horrible creatures out here? If Bera wasn't just a nutjob and had been telling the truth...

Oh Hades, Ash hoped not. She shivered (more from fear than cold, as it was quite temperate) and wrapped her arms around herself, moving a little faster towards the hills in the far distance as if that would keep phantoms away. If there *were* unfriendly things out here, she consoled herself, then surely far-sight would warn her. It always seemed to turn up whenever she was about to be injured or die horribly, so she didn't doubt it would this time too.

Really.

It would.

Remembering the book at the last moment, Ash pulled it out and studied the back cover once more, trying to make sense of those odd words scrawled around its centre.

Water is life. Well, duh. Who didn't know that?

All green does not mean growth. Ash knew that too, although she *was* heading towards some green hills-

She paused, taking a second look at the direction she was heading. She'd been walking maybe half an hour or so, and the hills didn't seem any closer, but they were very distant. And it wasn't like there was anywhere else to go.

Water.

I don't know how to find water! Ash argued with herself. *It's a bloody desert, and I'm not a rain man or whatever you call people who can find water!*

There was the sense of faint laughter, and Ash felt the edges of her lips curling up too. Rain man was a movie character, wasn't he? Nothing to do with actual water. But... "Amaranthus, I know you can hear me," she said to the empty air. "We came to find you, but we're lost. Or I am, anyway. Some help, please?"

There wasn't an answer, but Ash got the urge to glance down once more at the book's back cover. But no new words had appeared. Still the comments about water, and about green not meaning growth (which might or might not refer to the distant hills) and... *A gift once given is never rescinded.* And there was a little shape like a crudely drawn bird in flight.

Ash stared at it, and an idea ticked into her mind. If it was true, it would be so, so, so amazing. But it couldn't be, because Dr Walker had told them the flight ability only last two days. *Everyone* told them that, and she'd tried so many times after those days passed to fly, even just to hover a bit. She was certain that George and Anne had as well, without success.

But that was what the book said. So Ash took a deep breath, and decided. "If that's you, Amaranthus, then I'll believe you. I'll go look for water, and I won't get distracted by green in the distance, and..." Well, she'd see about the rest.

So Ash changed her course slightly. Instead of heading directly towards the distant green patch, she headed towards a closer, lower area. Water always ran towards the lowest point, right? And because she didn't look down, she missed seeing the fine shoots of grass work their way out from the dry dirt of the desert floor, spreading like a starburst from where she'd been standing.

Anne dreamed she was in a garden while the sun set, and the low light made it hard to see anything properly, casting it all into sharp silhouette. A shadowy figure was standing in front of her, comforting her, and while he looked like Amaranthus, she couldn't quite see his face. He was telling her to relax, to sleep in peace, because she would be taken care of.

Don't worry about anything. Sleep...

But in the dream her sense of unease was even sharper. "I do not know you," dream-Anne muttered. "I wish I did, but I do not."

Of course you know me, the shadowy figure said warmly, his green eyes glinting in the half-light. *I'm your friend. You can trust me.*

Even in the hold of the dream, Anne had felt her eyelids grow even heavier and her sleep grow deeper. She didn't need to wake up. She could rest right here in this garden, and Amaranthus would watch over her. All would be well.

But then something odd happened. 'Twas like Anne took a step away from her slumbering self and saw the world of the dream drawn around her small red-haired figure like a sketch, the shadowy figure still bent over in front of her, whispering words of rest and comfort. But now, even in the dream, she watched it happen and she knew with a certainty that 'twas not right.

All voices in your head don't come from me, Anne.

She turned and Amaranthus was standing next to her, his deep brown eyes bright, and his features clear even in this dim setting. 'Twas as though he carried his own light with him, and his face would never be hidden from her.

The other, shadow-figure was still whispering to the dream-Anne now sound asleep in the dream-garden, and Anne – the real Anne within the dream – watched them in confusion. "How can we be in two places at once?"

Freedom from time opens limitless possibilities, Amaranthus answered without moving his lips. *But you must learn to distinguish who I am. Do you not remember from your time with Seyen Johannis that there are many who can speak into your mind?*

"She never spoke into mine," Anne said a little defensively. "I did not drink that water." But the Queen had spoken to both Ash and George, and had controlled them both for a time.

That was in the normal realm. Here, in the Other, there is much power for those who know how to find it. You have a special gift; you and

Elspeth both. You see through illusion in a way that most cannot. He tilted his head on the side and smiled at her. *You have a great purpose for your life, and it doesn't end here. You are being equipped as you go.*

"What do you want me to do?"

Be brave, Anne. And remember to look people in the eye. If you wish to, you will see their heart.

She remembered the ancient Mother's hideous face and how she'd deliberately turned away from it. She couldn't stand to look for too long; it had offended her eyes. But mayhap that had been the purpose.

"Did you save me when I fell from the bailey wall?" she asked curiously. Of course she had wondered how her bones had not all broken, but there had been little time to consider it deeply.

In a sense. In another, you saved yourself.

And then 'twas as though Anne relived that moment when Edgar had pushed her off the bailey wall, except this time she saw that she'd reached for that place where the power for flight came from, and she'd grabbed hold of it just enough to reject gravity's pull…right before she hit the ground.

"I can still fly!" she exclaimed in amazement, and within the dream she felt enormous glowing wings unfold from her back, their span twice what her arms could reach, and as they rose and fell she began to leave the dream-garden and her slumbering self behind…

Chaos, the old woman cursed. He'd ruined it again, broken the hold of the dream that she had been spinning over her little guest, the one which told her to rest and never question her surroundings.

It had seemed to be going so well, just like it had with the other, littler one, but then suddenly Anne had snapped free of her hold and the old woman had sensed the distinctive feel of her enemy's power.

Lying in the large bed next to her younger, easier to control sister, the redhead began to stir. The old woman pulled her hand away from the redhead's face just in time as the redhead's eyes opened, and she stared up in confusion. "What are you doing?"

The old woman smiled, knowing her heavily distorted features would keep the girl from looking too close. "Poor wee dearie, old Mother was just checking on ye. Ye don't need to worry about me." *Trust her*, she added mentally, knowing that the silent voices tended to be more effective than any spoken word.

The girl didn't look comforted, though. She just stared up at her, staring her right in the eyes until the old woman grew nervous and moved away. And what a joke was that! Her, nervous? Gathering her composure, she smiled at her guest again and turned away. "Well, I'll be to bed myself then."

Anne sat up and looked after her. "'Tis still daylight. What time is it?"

She'd noticed that, had she? "Oh, it never really gets dark here."

"Why?"

"Asking a lot of questions, are we?" the old woman snapped, her voice sharper than she intended. The smaller girl stirred in the bed, and she quieted her voice. "Because it's…very high, near the poles, and it's summer. The sun never truly goes down at this time of year."

That should have been enough for this ignorant Tudar girl, but the old woman was surprised again.

"But aren't the poles very cold? 'Tis warm here, and dry."

"Only in winter is it cold," the old woman answered, then cut off any reply with another smile. "More talking in the morning, dearie. Now *sleep*." She added a little power to the last word, tapped straight from their surroundings, and seemingly against her will the girl slumped back to the bed, her eyes closing.

The old woman added for good measure, "And *forget this conversation.*"

Good…*heavens*, the old woman thought in irritation, quickly heading down the hall away from the spare bedroom. That girl was very persistent, wasn't she? But that should come as no surprise, since when had the enemy ever bothered with people who gave up easily?

In fact, as far as the old woman could tell, that was the only quality he ever looked for in his lackeys. They were rarely particularly beautiful or intelligent or powerful, tending to be very ordinary, but as long as they were tenacious and obedient the enemy seemed to snatch them right up.

Well, if he wanted them back, he would have to trade for them. It would have been better to get hold of the other two as well, the Regency man and the millennial girl, but Janeus was still out there hunting them down. Not very effectively, though, if he still didn't have them.

She couldn't believe her luck when Troilus had spotted those two girls in the desert outside their little house. It was like a cat making plans to raid the bird cage, only to turn and see the bird sitting, wings clipped, on the ground next to it. Too easy.

For a moment that thought held her, and she wondered if this was, in fact, a set up with *her* as the target. How had the two girls got through to the Other in the first place? They clearly didn't know what they were doing here.

Then she brushed off her concern. The enemy was clever, but he couldn't control everything, even if he liked to think so. He couldn't control the Creatures, could he? And she had made a bargain with them, one that kept them all here safely for the time being, along with fresh access to the almost unlimited power that made up the Other.

Outside, in the normal world, she had almost died. She hadn't been able to gather power, even though she'd tried several times…and for a very old woman, subduing *anyone* wasn't easy. She hadn't even had enough power to summon up a basic illusion! But then she'd overcome her horror of the Other realm enough to go through again, and she'd wondered why she hadn't done it earlier.

Here, she could cloak herself in illusion as easily as she had in the height of her power, just like she had today for that little performance with their 'guests'. And with every day she spent here – in as much as 'days' passed – she aged less and less. Perhaps in a year or two she'd merely look middle-aged rather than ancient, she thought sourly.

But she wasn't going to wait a year, was she? No, regardless of what she'd told the others, she had a rather more sophisticated plan…

"Seyen, Jenessa says-"

She turned on him. "*Tray*, call me *Mother*. I am your mother, am I not?"

"Of course," Troilus said sulkily. He hadn't liked the false name she'd chosen for him, saying it reminded him of when Jenessa (or 'Jenny', if the guests happened to see her) used to tease him as a child. But he'd accepted it, naturally. "But they think I'm your husband. Isn't it strange for me to call you Mother?"

Chaos, he was such an idiot. How someone could get to almost four hundred and still be so wilfully ignorant… It was his birth mother's fault, of course. She had been stunning, just like the twins both were, but she'd also been as thick as two short planks. Jenessa might be a cunning little witch, but at least she wasn't stupid. Mind you, that just meant that Seyen had to work harder to manipulate her.

"You introduced me as Mother, did you not? It would be strange for you to suddenly change that. Oh, and there's the fact that *Anne knows who Seyen is!* She'll only need hear that name once to be suspicious!"

"Sorry, Mother," he muttered.

It was strange to see his expressions on that aged face, especially as his eyes were now brown instead of their usual clear blue. Only he and Janeus were able to change their eye colour along with their form, but that was because they were both true shapeshifters. All the others in her old pantheon, even Seyen herself at the height of her power, had been unable to do more than slightly dull their eye colour. But people didn't usually look at that.

"I see you've stayed in your shifted form as I told you," Seyen said more gently. "Make sure you change back before you use the gateways. I don't want you losing your memory like your fool of a father."

"That's what Jenessa told me," Troilus babbled suddenly. "Not about him losing his memory. But about him."

"What about him?" Seyen asked in a low tone. This didn't sound good. Jenessa had been set to watch Janeus at the scrying pool in the nearby lowlands, since Troilus was both too slow and too precious to be used on such a thing.

He looked nervous, since no one wanted to be the bearer of bad news.

"Well, come on then! I'm not going to shoot the messenger. As you see, I have no weapon."

They both knew she didn't need a weapon, not here, and her joke fell flat. He licked his lips nervously, then said, "He's balking. Jenessa says he's had plenty of chances to find the other two now we know they're here, but he keeps slowing down or stopping or going in the wrong direction. It's like he's not even *trying*."

Seyen was silent a moment. She'd felt Janeus's reluctance to obey, but had thought that her directive had overridden that. She scratched distractedly at the rose on her chest, thinking. She'd set him after the Eternity Stone, or second best, after the travellers. "Or they don't have the Stone, and he's confused."

"Maybe," Troilus allowed. "But when we arrived here, he seemed fine." He frowned. "He did seem a bit guilty, though. Must be because of what he did to you."

He looked at Seyen so hopefully and transparently that she would have laughed, had he not been trying to weasel the story about Erastus from her. "Must be," she replied neutrally.

Clearly disappointed but unsurprised by her silence, Troilus rallied. "So what will you do about him? About Janeus?"

"I'm still debating the best option."

"Oh."

Troilus finally left, and Seyen sat down in her chair in the small library. Like all the furniture that the Creatures had produced for them on arrival, this one's origins were suspect. It was leather stretched over smooth, dark bone, but it was where the materials had come from that bothered her. Not because she felt sorry for them, but because she didn't want to be someone else's chair should this go wrong.

Seyen shuddered. There were still things that could frighten her, and that Tiger-Creature was at the top of the list. Things like that were the reason why she hadn't come to the Other sooner, among other things. It wasn't *actually* a tiger, but it wasn't like a human, either. Almost beautiful, but completely horrible.

Thankfully the Creatures had accepted Jenessa's use as a carrier as enough to pay their rent to stay here. Seyen didn't know how long that would last, but she didn't plan to still be here when they lost interest.

That was where the 'guests' came in. And if things went the way they were supposed to, then soon enough she'd be able to gather again and would be gone from the Other, never to return again. But if Janeus didn't pull through...

Seyen sat on that dubious leather chair, setting her fingers on the worn bone handles and closing her eyes. Here, she could feel the connection stretching from her rose mark to Janeus as strongly as if it had been an actual physical cord. In spirit she followed it out of the house and across myriad miles of Other desert, through a couple of portals, and then to where Janeus stood, half-leaning against a boulder with an expression of extreme unease.

What are you doing. She said it like a statement, and she knew he heard it in his ear as though she'd been in the same room with him.

He jolted, then shook his head. *Feel ill. The atmosphere of this place is killing me.*

Don't be a drama queen. You're just not used to it. Pull on the alter-power same as we all do; you'll feel better soon enough.

Can't. I tried, but it's not working.

Souls, he really was being pathetic. But Seyen could sense that he was feeling off. Weak. Weaker than she'd ever felt him since their very first meeting in Ciria, back when she'd been almost young, and definitely stupid. *I could take him*, she realised.

Well, well, well. It looked like the Other *really* didn't work well for shapeshifters – and that medallion wasn't doing its job here either.

But that was plan B. Plan A still remained that he would do his job and find what she wanted him to find. Kill what she wanted him to kill.

So Seyen drew on the power humming around her like taking in a deep breath, and forced it along the connection until it hit Janeus. It was like he was hit by lightning (and yes, she had experience of that), bending almost backwards with the power shock.

Now, Seyen said smugly once he'd managed to settle himself. *Go, and do what I told you to do.*

And because she was powerful and in control, and because she was the QUEEN, he went.

Anne woke with the sense that something momentous had happened, but it danced tantalizingly out of reach of her waking mind.

"Anne, have you seen the privy?" Elspeth queried. "'Tis the oddest one I've ever seen."

The privy was the next best thing to a flush toilet, Anne realised once she blearily hauled herself out of bed, although she knew not where the waste went to. In Ash's time there'd been pipes, but this one simply made the waste disappear. Elspeth seemed rather wary of it, and Anne had to convince her 'twas safe to use before she left the girl to do her business.

'Twas light once more. They must have slept a whole twelve hours… Oh, yes. Now Anne recalled waking up in the night, only it had not been dark. And the old woman had been there standing over the bed, and she'd said something about being near the poles so the sun never set. That had been creepy, to borrow a word from Ash's time.

But there had been something else, something which Anne felt was imperative to remember. A strange dream?

Anne heard the privy make its odd flushing noise, and Elspeth came bounding out of the bathroom with a mix of fear and excitement on her face. "It ate my doings!" she said in an excited whisper. Then she looked worried. "It won't eat *me* next time, will it?"

Anne couldn't stop herself smiling. She assured her that the privy didn't 'eat' people, only 'doings', and that Elspeth would be fine.

"Oh, good. 'Tis truly less smelly than the castle garderobes, do you not agree?" the girl chattered. "Although that means that 'twould be little use for keeping moths off gowns, I'd vow. Not that I saw any gowns in there at all, so I suppose that Mother and Tray already know that."

"Mm." Something about Mother…

Elspeth lowered her voice. "Isn't she ugly, though? The ugliest woman I ever saw!"

"Bethie! She might hear you," Anne chided. "And remember,

she has been so kind to us, even though we're strangers. You wouldn't want her to become offended and make us leave."

Elspeth looked shamefaced. "I know," she admitted. "But I cannot help myself. 'Tis like the time little John broke his leg and the bone was sticking out. 'Tis dreadful, and I cannot look away. But I think what makes it worse is her eyes."

"You mean that they're uneven?" Rheumy, almost blind-looking, although the woman appeared to see well enough-

"Are they?" Elspeth looked surprised. "I thought so at first, but then I was just struck by how very green they were, like leaves, or jade. And they look *clever*, Anne. I vow that Mother must be a very, very clever person, just looking at those eyes." She frowned. "I don't know if she's very nice, though. She frightens me."

That's because she looks as though she should be living under a bridge, Anne was about to say, but then she realised what Elspeth had said. Clever eyes…

Be brave, Anne. And remember to look people in the eye. If you wish to, you will see their heart.

"Saints preserve us!" Anne groaned as the memory of that dream came rushing back in. Then she crossed herself, just in case. She'd looked at Mother's eyes in the dim light of the room a few hours before, when the old woman had come into her room and they'd had that strange conversation. They *hadn't* been crooked after all, had they?

"What is it, Anne?" Elspeth asked worriedly.

"It couldn't be," Anne muttered. "Oh, but it could, but I would rather that 'twas not. 'Twould be the most dreadful, dreadful luck. Out of the frying pan indeed-"

"Anne!"

Anne looked up at her sister, the memory of sharp green eyes echoing in her mind. Plenty of people had green eyes, Elspeth too, but not that shade of green. Not with that expression.

Too easy, too clean that they'd come through here, but then

they'd already been warned that they were being pursued, had they not? And to come here, right outside the lair of the one they most wished to avoid…

The only question was why they still lived, and the answer was clear. They still had some kind of use…for now.

"I'm so, so sorry," Anne said quietly, "but I do believe I've made a dreadful mistake. We need to leave this place at once."

Elspeth's face went pale and her eyes wide, but then she proved what Amaranthus had said. She *did* have a gift, and she was no fool. She nodded, opened her mouth as though to speak, but that was when the door opened.

Mother was standing there, a welcoming smile on her face. "Oh, yer up. Good. I've got ye some breakfast, if ye want it."

Anne forced herself to look the woman in the eyes and smiled back, noting the shock on the other's face when she did so. And when she focused on those eyes, they seemed not at all rheumy. They were green, jade green, and sharp. "That's most kind of you, but we're not hungry. The meal last eve was most filling."

"Are ye not?" Mother looked over Anne's shoulder to where Elspeth sat on the bed. "Not even ye, little one?"

Elspeth shook her head, still wide-eyed, but didn't say anything.

"Well, last night's meal didn't poison ye, I hope. But if ye don't wish to eat, then verra well, don't. Perhaps ye'd like to come sit with me in my library instead? I've a fair few books and trinkets, but seldom anyone to share them with."

Books and trinkets. Could Anne have been wrong? But as they followed the old woman down the hall the sense of wrongness grew stronger and stronger, and she wondered why she'd ever thought to come here in the first place. 'Twas not a clean place here; not in terms of dust and mildew, but in spirit. She knew now that the power was unclean, and they needed a way out.

The library was down the other end of the house, in a small

dark room. There were no windows at all, and the origin of the little light that was there, was unclear. Down two walls were enormous bookshelves stacked with volumes of different colours, their titles embossed in tiny text that Anne would need to get far closer to in order to read. One large chair took pride of place between the shelves, and a closed chest sat in the last empty corner.

"Oh, dear," Mother said sweetly. "There aren't enough chairs." Then she turned for the door and bellowed, "Tray! Bring the benches!"

Anne heard footsteps, and not thirty seconds later the old man brought in a couple of small stone benches and sat them down by the chest. Anne marvelled at his speed and obedience, and noted again that although he was old, he didn't seem *that* old. In fact, he had seemed older the day before. Now he was more like a handsome middle-aged man who just happened to have white hair and a beard.

Elspeth was staring at him like he had a bug on his nose. "I thought your eyes were dark," she mused aloud. "But they're blue."

A light, clear blue, in fact. Almost pretty, if they'd not been in a possible-murderer's face.

Mother turned and gave her husband a filthy look, and the man looked panicked. "Um…they are," he said, ducking his head. "They're dark blue." He looked up again, and what did she know, his eyes were dark blue.

Anne just stared, and as if knowing he'd done something wrong, Tray turned and almost ran from the room, the door shutting behind him.

"Excuse him," Mother said again, her voice once again syrupy sweet. "He has trouble with incontinence. His eyes go darker when he has an accident."

"How unfortunate," Anne murmured. And how unlikely.

There was a long, awkward silence, then Mother said

abruptly, "Poor wee lasses. Yer bored, and ye wish to read a book. Or ye, wee lass. A puzzle."

Actually Anne did *not* wish to read a book (and she suspected Elspeth was ten years too old for a puzzle) but if it meant that she could pretend to be distracted, she'd do it.

She smiled tightly then moved over to the bookshelf, sure to keep Mother in her peripheral vision. Not so twisted after all, was she? In fact the woman seemed not half as old or as ugly as Anne had first thought. From the corner of Anne's eye she seemed almost ordinary; tall and straight and mayhap only three score and ten…

Help, Anne thought again, focusing as intently as she could on the idea of Amaranthus. *Hear us. If you're nearby, hear us.* He'd done it before.

The bookshelves on the other hand… By the Rood, what strange titles there were. *Dragon's bane and the Secret of Youth, You and your Shapeshifter,* and *Grecian, Reman and Norwygian Gods through the Ages.*

"Found something ye like?" Mother called across the room. She was sitting in the large chair with a blanket over her lap, and now those sharp green eyes were set right on the book in Anne's hands. When had she pulled it from the shelf? "Ah, shapeshifters. A verra good choice."

Anne shivered. "Yes…shapeshifters." 'Twas quite a coincidence, considering who was supposedly chasing them. "But I was just browsing, and now I can't see where to put it back." She still couldn't even recall pulling it from the shelf, in fact, but now 'twas in her hands.

"It won't let ye, not until ye've read it."

Anne had to actively stop herself from dropping the thing in disgust. "Is it alive?"

"Not precisely. But it wants to be read, dearie. In fact, it insists on it."

Anne would burn it first. "Oh," she said lamely. "Well, there's so much to choose from, and I'm not really in the mood for reading now." She placed it carefully on the nearest bench, then smiled awkwardly at Mother. "Are these all yours?"

"Not all, no. Some belonged to my dear late husband." Anne's eyes widened, and Mother quickly added, "I mean my first husband. Tray is quite alive, isn't he?"

"Yes," Anne replied. But she was barely listening to her own words, instead carefully watching the woman's eyes. Amaranthus had been right, hadn't he? They were the window to someone's heart, if you looked properly. And then, like she couldn't stop herself, the words came tumbling out. "I know who you are."

REVELATION AND THE THREE-LEGGED RACE

Mother stopped her smiling and looked at Anne curiously, her head tilted to the side. "What

do you mean, lass?"

Elspeth stopped studying the puzzles and turned to look as well.

But Anne had spoken now, and she couldn't take it back. "I said, I know who you are," she repeated, her voice shaking just a little. "Your eyes have not changed."

Mother shook her head. "Still lost, dearie."

"You do know what I mean," Anne persisted, whether bravely or foolhardily she was not certain. "Your manner of speech changed just now, as Tray's did. And he grew younger overnight, and you're much less hideous than you were, too. Do not think I have not noticed."

"Well, well," Mother replied, her voice soft and menacing. "Don't hold back. Just say what you mean."

So Anne did. "You're Seyen Johannis."

Elspeth gasped, and just like that, Mother's illusion dropped. But she certainly wasn't the Queen that Anne had known, that young, raven-haired classical beauty. No, this one was *old*. At least sixty, Anne thought, although she was no longer ugly.

"Anne of Covington," Seyen said. She didn't move from the chair. In fact, she looked quite relaxed. "How did you see through the illusion?"

"I…I know not," Anne lied. "I looked at your eyes, I suppose."

Seyen sighed. "Ah, yes. The eyes – always the weak point in an illusion, since they're almost impossible to disguise. Even for me, even here. But not for 'Tray'. No, he's just forgetful." Turning her head towards the door, she bellowed. "Troilus!"

Ten seconds later the door opened, and the old man was standing there again.

"Drop the shift," Seyen ordered. "Our guests have worked out our little secret."

Tray/Troilus looked dismayed for a moment, but then realised that Seyen wasn't bothered, so he wouldn't be either. He smirked, then his features melted into those of a younger man. This one was beautiful and golden with clear blue eyes, similar to how Seyen had made herself look when she wanted to impress people as the Queen. Anne suspected that this was natural, though.

The young man went to stand at Seyen's side, and she put her hand on his with a matching smirk. "Isn't my son handsome, Anne?"

"I thought he was your husband," Anne said neutrally. Any other time she would have been stunned by his fine appearance, but now she simply felt ill. "I'd vow that's illegal."

"It was a trick," the young man said with a sneer. "We're not really married."

Anne sneered right back, her tone dripping with sarcasm. "Truly? I had no idea."

He glanced at Seyen as if he was confused, and the woman rolled her eyes. "Handsome, yes, and a good son, but I don't keep him for his brains, as you see." At that Anne saw anger race across his face, but 'twas almost immediately hidden. Troilus didn't like the way Mummy spoke to him.

"You know," Seyen continued in that same conversational tone, "I wonder if you're any better. Here you are, at our mercy, and you blurt out that you 'know who I am'. You would have been better to keep that to yourself. Is there anything else inadvisable you'd like to tell me?"

"If you kill us, Amaranthus will know and he will avenge us," Anne answered quickly. "So I would not, if I were you."

"Ah," Seyen replied. "But why would I kill you when you're so much more use alive?"

Seyen knew without a doubt the other time travellers would come to find the little Tudar girls. She had been working on bringing them all here, but these two were better than nothing.

Back in Iversley the time travellers had used the Eternity Stone to get close enough to steal her earrings. Those weren't just jewellery: they'd been her entire collection of objects of alter-power, shrunk to a size that could be easily carried and easily hidden in plain sight. Seyen had never thought that anyone could get close enough to take them, but then she'd never anticipated she'd lose the Eternity Stone, either.

'Lose', ha. It had been stolen, and while she still didn't know *how* it happened, she knew she could lay the blame squarely on Amaranthus. As for the earrings, she'd never once taken them off her body. Once they were stolen, the objects would have scattered themselves back across time to their original locations, just as Seyen and her Nobles were returned home.

Well, *she* hadn't been. But never mind. If Janeus didn't manage to find them first, the travellers would eventually make their way here to free their little friends. And because Seyen was a whole new kind of powerful here, and because the Eternity Stone and most other objects of power refused to work in the Other,

Seyen and the twins would be able to overcome them and take the Stone, then leave the Other behind.

But that was plan C. Plan A being to simply find the Stone and then kill the girls, plan B being to kill the now weakened Janeus, cut out that medallion and *then* kill the girls… And if that didn't work, she could always try a little bartering. The Creatures were always happy to have a new toy, and especially toys that had belonged to Amaranthus.

There was an old hatred there, one that went further than anything Seyen was aware of, and quite frankly she didn't care except for one thing. The enemy of her enemy was her friend…

Except no one was truly friends with the Creatures. They'd said earlier that the twins weren't gift enough to restore her gathering ability, but Seyen had had nothing more to offer. Perhaps now she did…at last resort.

"What do you want me to do with them?" Troilus asked, scanning the two girls with an uninterested eye. Not like his philandering father, this boy of hers; there were far better things you could get from another person besides sex, with far less damage to your own person. Troilus showed little interest in either gender as anything except a gathering tool. She'd taught him that intentionally at a young age.

"Go get Jenessa. I'll watch them."

Troilus nodded and left the room, and it was just the three women, Seyen still ensconced comfortably on her leather chair. She said to the girls, "I suppose you think that because I'm old, I can't stop you from leaving."

They exchanged glances. It was clear that the younger one wasn't quite sure what was going on, and the older wasn't sure what to tell her. Anne ventured, "Yes?"

Pulling a little power from the sodden atmosphere of the Other, Seyen threw it at her. "Sit."

Anne sat, and Elspeth slumped back on the ground where she'd been sitting.

Seyen pointed at the shapeshifter book (horrible; she'd only read it once herself) and said with another burst of power, "Read it right through till the end."

Although clearly reluctant, the girl picked it up and she began to read. It was a small thing, this exercise of power over these weak servants of her enemy, but how good it felt. Hiding her satisfaction, Seyen glared at the younger girl. "You. Finish those puzzles."

She did, and Seyen smiled.

George woke to dust-filled lungs and the horrible feeling of weight holding him facedown to a hard surface. Something lumpy and hard was packed so closely around his nose and mouth that he could barely breathe. Panicking, he struggled to move, and was rewarded with a sound like a tiny rockslide and the pressure on his back and legs easing.

Then he realised where he was. In a cave, in the middle of nowhere, chased by talking animal-people… It was hard to believe that had truly happened, but by now George knew that anything was possible.

There was absolute silence, which he took to mean the lion-creatures out to devour him had gone. (Well, if they hadn't been set to devour him, then what? Shake his hand and bid him good day?) Those small furry creatures were either dead or gone, too. It was most unlikely that they would stay so quiet without being forced to.

He moved again, pushing himself up on to his hands and knees, and felt the gravel cascade off his back as he did so. He blinked, and his eyes felt gritty. There was a strong stream of light coming through a gap in the cave entrance. He'd filled it up with rocks, but someone, most likely those rodent-hog things, had cleared some away. And left him here, the little beasts.

Shaking himself off, George crawled his way to the gap. Outside, the light was too bright for him to make anything out at first, but he squinted, waiting for his eyes to adjust.

Finally he could see that there was nothing but dry ground and dry trees. Nothing living in sight (except for the trees, barely). He waited quietly for a few minutes, listening for any sounds that would indicate *something* was waiting outside for him. But it was as silent as the grave, without even the sound of wind in the trees or birdsong.

George briefly considered that lack of birdsong meant a predator in the area, then realised he'd *never* heard any birdsong while he'd been here. He didn't know for certain that he was alone, but he couldn't stay here indefinitely. His whole body ached, and he had a terrible dry throat and itchy eyes. He wasn't going to solve that here either, was he?

That last bit of reasoning was good enough for him. He scrambled painfully to his feet, as much as was possible in the small space, then clawed his way out through the small exit, staggering in the sunlight. He was cold. It shouldn't be possible here in this dry place, but now he was shivering.

There was nothing living in sight, not counting the sparse trees that littered the slope. So George forced himself to walk back down that steep path, and then as gravity pulled him faster, to run. The sooner he was away from here, the better.

Anne sat on the bench as she'd been ordered to, her eyes systematically scanning the words on the pages, but her brain trying to revolt against what she was taking in. Soon she worked out a system where she read, but saw nothing. In one ear and out the other…er, *eye*, more like. 'Twas how she was able to ask, "What are you going to do with us?"

She still wasn't able to look up, but she saw out the corner of her eye Seyen jolt in surprise, then her eyes narrow. "Anything I like."

"I see why you're angry at me," Anne said carefully. "But Elspeth has caused you no harm. You don't need to hurt her."

Down on the ground her sister glanced up at them, but her hands kept moving, placing the pieces together. Anne couldn't see what she was making, but it appeared to be three-dimensional.

Suddenly the compulsion to read left, and Anne looked up to see the former Queen glowering at her, her face twisted with rage. "You little thief," she snarled. "You have no right to ask me for anything! After the way you and the other two stole from me, took everything that mattered to me and left me like this? You're lucky I haven't peeled the skin from your hide!"

Anne swallowed. "We did not," she disputed. "At least, 'twas not intended." The Eternity Stone had ended up in their laps quite by accident. *'Twas* true that they had intentionally taken Seyen's power-filled earrings, but even that had been in self-defence, and out of fear of the woman's power and wickedness.

"No, you were used by *him*," Seyen spat. "But that doesn't take away from your crime. It's said that the hand that holds the gun is responsible for the crime, but I'll still destroy that gun, along with the hand."

Mayhap they might hit her very hard with one of those puzzle blocks Elspeth was using. Was it morally wrong to strike an old woman on the head, if that old woman was in fact a very bad person? A witch, even?

"Who is the hand?" Anne asked, although she already suspected the answer.

Seyen tilted her head on the side. "You don't know?"

"I only know that an old man gave me aid when others tried to kill me, so for that he has my loyalty."

The old woman laughed, a dry cackle. "Your loyalty is misplaced. That man – my enemy – is using you, and has been the whole time. He has his own plans and he'll use whoever he can to achieve them, and if you think he cares for you, you're a fool." She laughed again. "I'll admit he has a certain charm, but then the best of us always do."

Or mayhap they should not hit her on the head, Anne amended. They could tackle her to the ground, and tie her hands and feet together. Or tie her to her chair. But with what rope?

Her hair, Anne decided. She'd rip the old bat's hair out by the roots if it meant Elspeth would be safe. They *had* to get out of here.

Anne realised in pleased surprise that she could move once more, and dipped her head to hide her expression. She would attack, she decided. Ten seconds, she had to catch the witch by surprise. Ten, nine…

The old woman was staring at Anne with that little smile on her face, and the horrid thought occurred that the woman could still read minds.

Oh, help us, Amaranthus! Anne cried out mentally.

And then she felt he was there, so strongly 'twas almost like a tap on the shoulder.

Just wait, he whispered.

Anne looked at Seyen to see if she'd noticed, but the old woman was still sitting with that same wicked smile on her face. But her eyelids were drooping.

Anne watched her with bated breath, giving up her idea of attack when Seyen didn't move or say anything else. Her eyelids drooped lower, then suddenly snapped open again, glaring malevolently at Anne. Anne snapped back to attention, not daring to move a muscle.

She knew not how long they sat there, the two of them, but it could not have been more than five minutes when the former Queen lost the battle with sleep and her eyes closed fully.

Anne watched a minute longer, but the old woman didn't move again.

Most, most odd. She had simply fallen asleep. Anne knew

that old people slept more than young, and Seyen was certainly old. But to go to all the trouble of catching them, of sending her consort Janeus after them, and then to *fall asleep*? Right there in front of them, while she was supposed to be guarding them?

Anne felt a smile creeping over her face, and soon she was grinning widely. *Thank you, Amaranthus.*

Elspeth was watching from the floor. She was almost entirely surrounded by the blocks – she had been building herself a cage. Anne put a finger to her lips, then stood, gesturing for Elspeth to follow her. The younger girl stood too, stepping carefully over the block pile, but her long skirts caught the low wall and knocked it over with a resounding crash.

Seyen stirred, and they froze, staring in horror as the old woman stretched, then finally mumbled something unintelligible and went still again.

They hurried from the room as quietly as possible, moving around to the stables where they'd arrived. There wasn't much there, just the smaller, cranky-looking horse, and an elaborately woven blanket in shades of red and orange hung over a wooden rail. In a way it seemed too colourful to belong there, while the surroundings were dry and bland as week-old manchet bread.

Their next choice seemed obvious.

"The other man must have taken the larger horse," Anne mused. "Bethie, we must ride without a saddle."

"If the horse will allow it," Elspeth replied, looking at the creature doubtfully.

Like most things in this place, 'twas not ordinary, and it had a decidedly malevolent gleam in its eye. It curled its lip at them, showing yellow teeth, but allowed them to climb on with a minimum of fuss, both of them seated side-saddle on the repur-posed blanket.

"Ah, that wasn't so dreadful," Anne said.

Then the horse bucked, knocking Anne off onto her well-padded backside. Thank heavens for thick skirts. Elspeth managed to hang on, but she looked worried.

Anne scrambled to her feet, shaking off the dust, then looked the horse right in the eye. "If you will allow us ride you, I vow I shall get you something nice. Oats?"

It simply stared at her.

"Sugar lumps. Horses love those, do they not?" she said more desperately. "Come now, don't be difficult! This is what you're *for*."

The horse stared at her a little longer, then shook its head and nickered quietly. But it did let her climb on again, and this time it didn't buck.

Three minutes later, the two of them were sitting on the blanket, on the back of the cranky horse, riding quietly away towards the green hills. Yes, 'twas theft on two counts, but when one was stealing from a murderer in order to facilitate one's escape, that was surely permissible.

After a few minutes, Elspeth said, "I don't like this horse."

Anne agreed. Although the horse hadn't thrown them again, it had to be the bumpiest ride she'd ever experienced, with or without a saddle.

As if on cue, Elspeth said, "I do not like riding without a saddle. I want a saddle."

Sitting behind her as they trotted bumpily along the dusty path, Anne rolled her eyes. "Bethie, what else did you expect to do? Go back into the house and ask for one?"

There was a grumpy silence – Anne couldn't see her face, but she could *feel* the bad temper – and then her sister asked, "Where are we going?"

"Somewhere safe." At least, Anne hoped that the green hills were safe. Where else could they go?

"Are you certain? Have you been here before?"

"Of course not."

"I know you said that there is no such thing as elf-land, but if there was, that Tray would most certainly be an elf, he was so beautiful." Elspeth sighed and leaned back against Anne, and it suddenly struck Anne that her sister was of an age to notice males.

How very odd, especially as back in 1556 they'd tried to keep Elspeth *separate* from males, as her illegitimate status and injury made her vulnerable to those with ill intentions.

Oof! Just then the horse jolted extra hard, and the back of Elspeth's head snapped back into Anne's nose. She muffled a cry of indignation.

"Are we there yet?"

Anne looked at the bumpy green strip in the far distance. It hadn't seemed like 'twould take more than a day's ride, mayhap even half a day if luck was with them. But now the green seemed to grew further away the more they rode towards it, if such a thing were even possible.

They rode another hour or so, interrupted by occasional questions by Elspeth and the horse's equine mutterings. But cranky beast or not, it had taken them well out of sight of the house, and for that she would be grateful.

'Twas a very clever horse, Anne thought. Shame 'twas such a reeking brute. Not that it had *done* anything, mind, it had simply looked as though it wanted to…

And she was being irrational. Just like with the distant hills.

"Anne?"

"Yes?"

"This might seem foolish, but it seems like those mountains draw no closer. They seem just as far away as they always did." Elspeth turned to look Anne in the eye, looking just as worried as Anne felt.

"Mayhap not such a foolish thought after all. But where else would we go?"

They were approaching a small wooden bridge over a gorge, right next to a high, steep cliff, the same dusty brown as the rest of the landscape. The horse reached the bridge, a sturdy-looking affair over a deep ravine. On one side was a guardrail, and on the other the bridge was set right up against the cliff. Still, the rail was low enough that Anne felt nervous being up on the horse's back, well and truly higher than was safe.

"Hold on Bethie," she said. "I'll lead it over this part."

'Leading it' meant grabbing a hunk of its coarse mane and pulling it gently in the direction she wanted to go. They walked out into the middle of the bridge (which was about three horse-widths wide, and two horse-lengths long as Anne measured it) and then Anne could hear it; the sound coming up from the gorge they crossed. 'Twas a rushing, gasping sort of noise, a cross between a fast river and a death rattle. Gathering her courage, she looked over the edge of the guardrail.

There was naught to see. Simply blackness, and that horrid noise that grew louder as she leaned over. What on earth was down there?

She shuddered, moving away. "Come along, horse. There's nothing good down there." The horse dug its hooves in stubbornly, and she pulled. "Come on! Now is not the time to be stubborn!"

"Look, Anne!" Elspeth gasped. She was pointing at the cliff where the gorge emerged from it, right by the bridge. Above them was a gap in the cliff echoing that of the gorge, and through it was a glimpse of different, smooth, steeply sloping rock, going up higher than they could see.

Startlingly, the hidden rock was streaked with beautiful colour. 'Twas in deep royal blue and emerald green, ruby red and pale gold, smooth and bright as glass. And all those colours streaked the partially hidden rock face like cooled wax where it had run down a candle, or the like pictures she'd seen of volcanoes pouring out lava.

"'Tis beautiful!" Anne was spellbound. She forgot that she was holding a stubborn, clever horse by its stinking mane and standing on a little bridge over a terrifying gorge, because all she saw was the colourful rock's beauty. "It cannot be natural."

Elspeth climbed off the horse's back and moved cautiously closer to the wooden guardrail. "'Tis just like the stained glass window in the chapel," she said in awe.

Anne glanced at her sister's entranced face. "I wonder…"

"What?"

"'Tis the only true colour I've seen here, besides the blanket and the distant mountains. And the mountains don't seem to be getting any closer."

Elspeth looked worried. "Surely that is not possible."

"But mayhap *'tis*. I just cannot tell with this mad place. Forsooth, anything is possible here. I've had some strange experiences in the past year, and I know that things aren't always what they seem."

"What do you think we should do?"

Anne glanced back at the horse. "You wait here with that, out of sight, and I shall climb up to see if I can find anything."

"Climb up there? But what could you possibly hold on to? And what do you think you'll find?"

"Well, I must look first, mustn't I?"

But it happened so suddenly there was no chance to question further, let alone climb the cliff face. There was a rumble from deep in the coloured rock, and it echoed throughout the blackness of the gorge, slightly shaking the bridge.

Anne quickly grabbed Elspeth's arm to pull her away, and then without the slightest warning, the stupid horse rammed its whole body into the both of them. The thick guardrail snapped like a twig, and the both of them tumbled down into the blackness.

Anne could swear the last thing she saw was the sneer on that damn horse's face.

Ash trudged along, thinking. She thought about George, Anne, and Elspeth, and wondered where they'd ended up and why they were taking so long to find her.

She thought about the back cover of the photo-book and the vast promises it seemed to be making, and about the story Bera had told her of the two realms breaking apart, and how this place was supposedly full of resentful not-quite-alive beings.

Then she thought back over the last few months and about how she'd dreamed so vividly, and wondered if it had been far-sight all along, just like she'd had a couple of times since leaving her own time.

Nah. Those dreams couldn't be far-sight, because far-sight showed you what was about to happen, not what might happen sometime down the track.

Like here. This desert might look a lot like that dream where she was chased by horrible mummified creatures, but that had been months ago and obviously hadn't happened…

Creatures…? Wasn't that what Bera had called some of the beings living out here?

Ash stopped abruptly, the imagery from that vivid dream flooding back to mind in fast forward, fitting itself to this environment. She turned and *saw a cloud of dust kicked up by running feet, and then a creature – no, two creatures – that looked like they were doing a three-legged race, joined at one leg, and weren't happy about it at all. They were racing towards her at great speed, and they looked very intelligent and very, very angry. Deias, they move fast, Ash thought, and then they were on her.*

Huh, now that *really* had felt like far-sight…

The hairs on the back of Ash's neck prickled, and she turned. There, in the distance, was a little cloud of dust just over the desert floor. It was rapidly growing bigger.

Oh Deias oh Deias oh Deias oh Deias- She didn't wait to see what it turned into, or wait to see the forms make themselves clear, because once that happened she had mere seconds.

"Eeeeeeeeeeeeeeeeeeeeeeeeee!" She turned and ran, flapping her arms frantically like a demented chicken and desperately hoping to get off the ground, but the whole time she was thinking that if she could have flown then she would have done it already!

A gift once given is never rescinded…

Never taken back. The gift was given, and it hadn't been taken back. But if she could fly, she would have done so. This was life or death. Was it? Maybe the things just wanted some live company?

The follow-on from that thought showed Ash clearly that anything in their company didn't stay live for long, and fear spurred her into the fastest sprint she'd ever done in her life, faster than she knew she was capable of, and she knew it was from the power that filled the air around her.

But it wasn't enough, and she could hear them gaining on her, hear their rapid footsteps coming closer behind, hear mutterings and snarls that came from mouths shaped unlike anything she'd seen before-

Deias, dead things weren't supposed to move. They were supposed to sit there at the side of the motorway, two inches thick. But if these were dead immortals, the resentful undead, then she'd better quickly learn how to fly again.

It was then that Ash realised fear had never been her friend. Fear had always held her back. Believing she could fly had helped her before, and the arm-flapping hadn't been necessary.

BELIEVE you can, and DO IT.

Ash scrunched her eyes shut, shot her arms in the air, and began to chant, "I can I can I can I can I can…"

On about the seventh 'can', when she could hear the footfalls right behind her and smell the rank stench of whatever pursued her, she realised her feet weren't touching the ground anymore.

"I CAN I CAN I CAN I CAN…!" Ash stretched her arms upwards even further, clawing for the sky, and the ground grew farther and farther away, and she just about wept with relief.

But then they were right below her and as fast as she flew, they were keeping pace as if it was easy for them. They weren't even puffing – oh Deias did they even breathe? They better not be able to *jump*…!

Ash pushed herself higher into the dry air. Far below her now, the little dust cloud kept steady pace with her. Although they couldn't follow her into the air, those creatures weren't giving up easily.

She swerved and shot in the other direction, heading for a cluster of mountains that looked as though they'd break up the creatures' run.

Finally – it could have been one hour or three, George couldn't tell time here very well – he made it back to flat ground. The exercise hadn't helped with his aches and pains, not at all, and he was beginning to get very tired and uncomfortable.

And hungry. *And* thirsty; he hadn't had anything to drink since he'd left his own time, and he hadn't seen any more water after those acid pools he'd arrived next to.

There was something very wrong with this place, he thought, something that went beyond the obvious talking animals and acid water. It felt fundamentally broken, like a teacup that had hairline fractures all over it but still held its shape. You had to handle it very carefully, not put any pressure on at all, but no matter your care it would sooner or later shatter, and you'd end up covered in hot tea.

Mm, tea. George could really do with a freshly steeped cup of tea. Or even an old one, the sort left so long that the milk went a bit scummy.

He wouldn't mind. Truly.

George swallowed in another dry, difficult movement, deciding it was worse to think on the tea he couldn't have than the lion-men who he'd barely avoided. He shuddered at the memory. The worst thing about them, he decided, was that they'd been neither animal nor human. An animal's bestial nature and appetite along with a human's intelligence…and those horrible faces. Ugh.

He *was* upset, of course, but not as much as other people might be in the same situation. Strange, life-threatening things seemed to happen every time he'd time travelled, and the last time he'd lost his *mind*. This wasn't nearly as bad as that, and to be honest, he expected that this wouldn't be the last time he ran into trouble. Someone or something wanted to kill him/ enslave him/ do unspeakably hideous things to him? Ah, nothing new there. Get in line.

He thought of it as the price for living what had become a fascinating life – bizarre, unbelievable and occasionally terrifying, but still fascinating. And he would be severely displeased if he died here in this barren place.

George distracted himself as he trudged along by playing the alphabet game. He used to play it with his brother on long carriage journeys, when they were extremely bored and couldn't get away from each other.

First he went through the A's, listing all the animals he could think of that started with A. Anteater, aardvark, artichoke – oh wait, that wasn't an animal.

Antelope. Axolotl. Afrecan elephant.

He'd found that you could add the word 'Afrecan' to the start of almost any animal, and go on indefinitely. His brother wasn't here to complain, was he?

Thinking of Edward… George had never really had a chance to reconcile in his own mind what they'd talked about that last evening, before he'd most recently left. About Alice Bonney, and fidelity within marriage, and then with Olivia overhearing… Oops. Although it hadn't truly been George's fault, had it? If

Edward had been faithful in the first place, then there would have been nothing for his wife to overhear and get angry about.

It must have been a shock to his brother that seemingly overnight George had turned from the usual view that faithfulness in marriage was old-fashioned and unnecessary (for men, anyway) to the idea that if one had made a vow to physically cleave to no other, then one ought to bloody well stick with it. It now seemed evident that unfaithfulness would hurt the wife terribly if she loved him, and even if she didn't, it was a mark of a man's character to control his own desires.

Those were strange and strict views for his time, but they made so much sense. If you were going to marry, then *mean* it. No marriage of convenience or half-hearted affection for George now. Not anymore.

He didn't think that the people of Ashlea's time had it completely correct either. They had no concept of real commitment, and they mistook lust and infatuation for real love. Not that that was new to their generation, of course. But they did have one thing right that the careless upper class of his own time could have learned from.

They should love the one they were with. Spend time with them. Spend time with their children, rather than passing them off to some poor, harassed nursemaid or governess or tutor who wouldn't and couldn't be a parent to them. For surely once the children were grown and their characters formed, they would have missed their chance.

George had loved both his parents, but for much of his childhood they had been distant figures who he saw briefly in the lobby as they passed ways, each in their own separate lives. The twenty-first century ideal of small, close-knit families had seemed very odd to him at first, and he had wondered if it was merely the common people who lived that way.

Perhaps so, but there was something very appealing about

that. A small house, no servants, not owning anything he couldn't look after himself. A day's work for a day's pay, and nothing but respect from his peers because he actually got off his backside and worked like a man.

And then at the end of the day, to come home to a beautiful wife, who wore tight trousers that left nothing to the imagination, and had loose flowing dark hair, and a wide knowledge of physical love from those fascinating women's magazines…

Sigh.

But that could all stay where it belonged, in fantasy. For now he would focus on staying alive. And the B's.

Bear, baboon, blue-bottle…

Later, somewhere between earwig and Frencine poodle, George glanced back into that wide, unforgiving desert and saw something different.

A cloud of dust, tinier than his little fingernail, but growing. And there was a black speck in the sky above it.

What the…?

He squinted, trying to make out the details. It was growing larger, and he could see now that the speck in the air was actually ahead of the dust cloud. It almost looked like someone flying. A bird, most likely. But what kind of bird was that big? And if George were being fanciful, he would almost say that the cloud was *chasing* the bird.

Heh. A dust cloud chasing a giant bird. He really did need a drink. Water would be fine, although he wouldn't object to something alcoholic. It was happening in the wrong order, though. Mostly he had the odd visions *after* the whisky – hence his usual avoidance of the drink.

Then both the giant bird and the cloud drew closer, and defined themselves into what looked like a celestial, minus the wings and wearing a familiar two-piece seraglio-style outfit, and then what looked like two men doing a three-legged race.

Two ugly, ugly men...*things*...

A shudder of fear and revulsion worked its way down his spine. Suddenly, it didn't seem so funny anymore.

THE DOOR IN
THE MOUNTAIN

Ash was coming up to the foothills of the brown mountains, trying to lose the Creatures chasing her, when she saw the small figure. As brown as its surroundings, it almost blended in with the background, but like a camera suddenly focusing, clarified itself into the form of George.

He was standing there, staring up at her with a rather stupid look on his face. If Ash hadn't been in such a panic, she might have worked out that it was due to exhaustion and lack of food and water rather than actual stupidity.

But she *was* in a panic, so she shrieked, "Fly, you fool! Fly!" just like a character from a classic film. Except unlike in a classic film, she didn't mean 'run away', she meant *fly*.

But he didn't respond, and Ash knew that he couldn't hear her, and the gap between them was rapidly diminishing. She'd reach him in less than ten seconds, and the Creatures were still following right behind her. She kept screaming and screaming for him to "*Fly!*"; to get off the ground, because otherwise he was done for.

But she could see he was only just comprehending the danger, and desperation made her reach down and grab his wrist, dragging him behind her – but his weight only pulled her down for half a second before he was as weightless as her.

He swung up behind her, lighter than air, and as she stretched her arms forward to gain more height, the dust cloud was upon them, and something leapt and caught at George's heel. He shrieked and kicked it off, losing his shoe at the same time. But who cared? Better his shoe than his foot.

And then Ash saw he was catching on to what they needed to do to escape, so he waved his free arm as they gained altitude (much in the same way that people think leaning forward in a car will somehow make it go faster).

But this time it worked. Up they went, until they were well and truly free of the dust cloud, and the Creatures shrunk to the size of those useless toys you got with a children's fast food meal, although a fair bit more hideous.

Ash and George were still firmly linked arm in arm, and had just kept going up and up. No one had said to stop, and panic was a great motivator for getting somewhere fast. 'Somewhere' being very high in the air.

Ash glanced briefly downwards and almost wet herself. They were so high up that if there had been any clouds in this sky, they would have long passed them by now. The fluffy, low-lying sort, that was. Not the streaky sort. Anyone who knew anything about clouds knew that those ones formed really high up, where the air was cold…

She lowered her arm, trying to stop their ascent, but George was still waving his free arm so they spun gently sideways. She pulled gently at his arm and he finally turned to look at her, slowing down his movement. Their faces were very close, and they stared at each other for a long moment before Ash let out a nervous laugh. Then George laughed, and then she laughed some more because it was either that or cry, and finally she rested her forehead on his shoulder.

"George," Ash said into the dusty fabric of his coat, "that was too bloody close. I thought you were dead for sure."

"*I* thought I was dead for sure. I thought *you* might have been dead." He paused. "And I forgot to use the binding cord. Again."

"Do you think it would've worked?"

"I don't know. It seems like I ought to have tried."

Just then Ash made the mistake of breathing in, and collapsed into a coughing fit. This was a whole new level of dusty, and it seemed to be right inside the fabric of his coat. "George, what *have* you been doing?"

"Funny you should ask…"

Anne did not consider herself particularly afraid of heights, but even she felt justified to scream when pushed into a deep, dark, horrible chasm with apparently no end. That is, she would have felt justified if she could summon up the thoughts.

As 'twas, her mind was filled with something like this: !!!

She was just gathering some air for a truly good scream (Elspeth beside her apparently having no such trouble) when she fell *bump* onto a strangely rubbery surface. She felt herself fall into it, sort of like a really soft, thick mattress, but then it pushed her out again and became hard and smooth and slippery, and then she was shooting across its surface in the dark as though she was on the world's biggest slide. Considering that she'd only ever used the ten-foot-long children's slide at the park near Ash's house, 'twas enough to take her breath away.

Anne couldn't see anything at first, and as she felt herself speeding up, she managed to summon up a scream at last. Behind her she heard Elspeth scream again, and then she could see a pinprick of light ahead of her, growing quickly larger and brighter, coming up faster and faster…

And then suddenly she slowed right down and fell out of the end of the slide with a gentle *bump* into a patch of thick grass. None the worse for wear, just rather stunned.

There was a group of tiny yellow flowers growing right by her nose. Anne stared at them in surprise, unable to move or talk. Then there was an *eek!* and Elspeth came shooting out next to her. And even though their fall seemed to have happened in slow motion, it couldn't have taken more than five seconds from push to final landing.

With a consummate effort Anne turned her head over to face Elspeth. Her sister had a small grass stain near her nose, but apart from that looked fine. "Are you harmed, Bethie?"

There was a pause while Elspeth considered the question. "Nay, I do not believe so."

"Good. I do not believe I am harmed either." Anne pushed herself into a sitting position and looked around her. "Forsooth, Bethie, I thought we were dead for certain!"

One would think that when one fell from a great height into a chasm, one would end up staring at pearly gates. Not going down a slide into a lush garden, surrounded by flowers and trees of all kinds, and with birdsong in the air.

"But can you not fly?" Elspeth asked. "Your friend Ash said that you could. You could have saved us."

"I do not *know* that I can fly. Regardless, it happened rather too fast for me to react, and it does not seem as though we need saving any longer, does it?" In fact, now Anne had time to think about it, she supposed they must have reached that 'safe place' that Amaranthus had spoken of a month before. Wonderful. Wonderful. Wonderful-

Elspeth had got to her feet. Now she stood, her mouth rather unflatteringly agape, staring at a vision in silver and white. 'Twas a youth, a celestial, with palest blond hair, white skin and an incredibly annoying smirk on his handsome face.

"You should have seen yourselves," the vision said, barely holding back laughter. "When you came shooting out of that hole, the looks on your faces – it reminded me of a stunned mullet. Two stunned mullets, rather."

Anne scowled at him, her awe rapidly replaced with irritation at that nonsensical greeting. To be so afraid, and then to be mocked so? She deliberately turned to study the wall they'd apparently come out of. She didn't see any holes in it at all – 'twas smooth as glass.

"I do not even know what a mullet looks like," Elspeth said breathlessly. Clearly *she* wasn't bothered by that greeting.

The youth made a grotesque face, with staring eyes and a dropped jaw. "Like that."

Elspeth's eyes widened, and then she laughed along with the boy. Anne, on the other hand, suddenly felt less than impressed by his looks. She'd like to give him a swift kick on the backside, shiny silver suit or nay. "And who, sirrah, might you be?"

He looked her up and down, taking in her dirty gown, mussed hair and the fact that one of her shoes had disappeared on the journey down. Embarrassed, Anne tucked her stockinged foot under her skirts, and the youth raised a supercilious eyebrow, the smile still plastered on his face. "I have many names. Which do you wish to know?"

"The highest ranking one," Anne snapped. "You are speaking to the Countess of Longford, twice over." Although possibly widowed twice over, also.

The boy's face suddenly took on a serious mien, and he moved into an elaborate bow. "My birth name was Jayel Jon DeLuca, I have been betrothed to a comtesse of Frencia, but as for my highest rank – my people called me Prince of the Air."

Anne wrinkled her nose, and Elspeth looked worried. "What shall we call you, your highness?"

He laughed, and winked at her in a most annoying fashion. "You can call me Jon. Forget the others. What's your name, little girl?"

"'Tis Elspeth of Covington, and I am not a little girl. I am sixteen."

'Twas true. She was but six months Anne's junior – although

the time spent with Ash meant Anne might have her seventeenth birthday twice over as well.

"Isbets?"

"Els-peth."

"Iss-bets."

Anne stuck her hands on her hips. "Are you truly pretending not to know how to say my sister's name? Your Anglish has been perfectly good up until this moment."

Jon – or whatever they were calling him – turned a little pink in the cheeks, but grinned annoyingly at her once more. "We're not speaking Anglish, Countess. I hear you in Mesianth, but here in the Mountain, we all speak the same language." He shrugged. "I struggle with some sounds, like little Bets' name here."

"So we are *inside* a mountain?" Anne queried, ignoring the rest of what he'd said. She looked up above them to where a vast glass roof seemed to separate the garden from the bright blue sky, and she admitted it – her jaw dropped. But without rain, how would this place be watered? And another idea occurred…

Meanwhile Elspeth was saying to Jon, "You might call me Bets if you wish, I do not mind at all."

"A small name for a small person."

"I'm not so small, sir, you are very tall!"

"Please, call me Jon. We don't need to be formal here."

And now Elspeth sounded breathy. "Oh, but you're a prince, are you not? And I vow you wear the finest garb I've ever seen outside of- anything at all."

"They're just clothes, little Bets," Jon said solemnly. "And I'll let you in on a secret. It's-"

"Stop dallying with my sister," Anne cut in absently. "She is too young for you."

"I'm not dallying," possibly-Prince Jon answered defensively. "And I'm only seventeen. Eighteen. Maybe."

His uncertainty regarding his age was a definite sign of a time traveller (or an orphan), but forsooth, Anne cared little. She'd thought of something rather more important. "We came seeking a man by the name of Amaranthus. Do you know of him?"

Now he looked like he was about to laugh at her again. "*Everyone* knows Amaranthus. How could you have come here otherwise?"

"Where is *here*?"

"I already told you, it's-"

"The Mountain of Glass," another voice cut in. This one was a few years older and considerably less annoying, and belonged to a man who seemed Jon's opposite. Where tall, slender Jon wore ornate white and silver, this man wore brown on his middling height, middling build form. Where Jon's fabric was embroidered and the cuffs and collar were cascading white lace, this man looked plain as a monk.

And where Jon wore knee-high white socks under buckled black shoes, this man's feet were bare in the thick grass, and his skin was even more browned that Ash's had been after spending weeks under an Anglish summer sun. 'Twas as though a sparrow stood next to a white peacock.

Are you ready to say hello yet, Anne? The man looked at her with patience and mayhap a little humour in his familiar dark eyes, and Anne felt both a rush of familiarity and a little embarrassment.

It's easy to judge by looks, the man said silently, then he smiled. *But I'm not so easily offended.* "I'm so glad you made it," he said aloud. "You and your sister both."

"Thank you," Anne answered, feeling her cheeks flush pink. "But I fear that you seem to know us, where we have not met you, sir."

The man just looked at her with a raised eyebrow. *I'll give you a moment to think that through.*

One moment ticked by, and then another, and then something clicked in Anne's mind. She broke into a wide grin, as wide as annoying-pale-Jon's, as she suddenly made the connection. "So you *don't* always look old! But you might have told us at first!"

"I was waiting to see if you would recognise me," Amaranthus replied. "Most people don't know who I am in my human form, you know."

Now that was an alarming thought. "Are you usually not human?"

"Not at all," he replied. "Few people here are."

Now that was something to ponder. Also, why would he choose such a plain form when he could look like anyone? Why choose irregular brown features when he could have been as beautiful as Seyen's son, or even pretty like pale-Jon? But even as Anne thought that, she knew the answer. He preferred to be overlooked, at least until people might know his character.

Elspeth was staring at him with a sort of interested confusion, and Amaranthus smiled at her. "Hello, dear Bets. How is your leg feeling?"

Her eyes widened, but she didn't object to the nickname. It appeared the shortened version would stick, at least here in this place. "How did you know about *that*?"

"I know about a lot of things," he replied mysteriously, which Anne thought was most in character for him. "But I *do* know that you're both hungry and thirsty. Come with me, and we'll get that sorted, shall we?"

They began to follow, and it seemed as though Jon would be left behind. But Amaranthus called back, "Jon, let's show them the Hall of Treasures."

The boy brightened, and Anne felt her heart race. Treasures, eh? Mayhap 'twas worth the fall to come to this place, after all.

"What bothers me," George said, "is that the other ladies are nowhere to be found."

They were probably a mile high in the cool, Other air, having left the twin-mummy-thingies far behind in the dry mountains. It was low enough to be able to see details down on the ground, but still high enough to avoid a running jump…hopefully.

He'd told her what happened upon his arrival, complete with bossy hog-people and cave-fall in, and Ash had told him about the wall that wasn't there, and they'd tried to appreciate having flight back while being pursued by new, more creatively horrible enemies, and not worrying about the possible death of some dear friends.

"They'll be fine," Ash said, trying to convince herself of it at the same time. "They've got the Eternity Stone. Besides, if I know Anne, she'll have already worked out how to fly. There's something in this atmosphere that makes it easier."

At least that was what they'd concluded, because why else would they have tried so many times before and failed, and yet only now succeeded? (Except for how they'd had to flee the earlier-mentioned horrible pursuers. That was new.)

George didn't look convinced, but they'd already covered all the possibilities, and there was no point in rehashing them. "Anne's book," he said suddenly. "Do you still have it?"

Ash brightened. "I'd forgotten to tell you, Amaranthus has been sending me new messages." She got it very carefully out of her pocket, careful not to drop it, since there was a long way to the ground. Besides, they were still arm in arm, as though if they let go then one of them would plummet to their death or float away. "See, here on the back there are some cryptic messages. Or not so cryptic now, I suppose."

He studied it curiously. "And what about this one here?"

"Huh. That's new."

"Follow the pillar of cloud," George read aloud. "Safety is through the second door."

"But there are no clouds at all," Ash pointed out. "I was looking earlier."

"Oh, but there is one," he countered. "Over there. Look."

She looked, but it was less of a pillar and more of a fingernail-sized spot of smoke. "Seriously?"

"It's not as though we have any better options."

That, unfortunately, was true. But it was a direction, and they began to head in it, moving from arm in arm to hand in hand. It was more comfortable, and felt safe as they began to speed up to almost superhero velocity (and yes, Ash *was* enjoying that).

"What gets me," she commented now she had some time to think about it, "is that you actually obeyed those little pig things. You, George?"

"They reminded me more of tailless beavers, from the Discoverable channel," he corrected. "But yes, it was most odd, as if once I put my hand on that cart, I couldn't help but do whatever they told me to." His eyes narrowed thoughtfully. "I thought I saw a wisp of smoke at one point, but it quickly disappeared. I say, do you think it's possible to *see* power, Ashlea?"

She thought back to the factory in the ruins and the doll that moved on its own, and the way Bera's voice had acted like a physical force. "Maybe here. I don't see why not."

"Hmm." He was staring at the rapidly approaching pillar of cloud (looking more like a pillar now, and less like someone's burning garbage) and the dust from the cave-in had left creases around his eyes and nose. He looked dreadful, but Ash felt a rush of affection. Maybe almost losing someone would do that to you.

Just then he turned to look at her, and this close she could see the golden green ring around the centre of his iris, the thing that stopped his eyes being merely blue. He didn't say anything about her staring at him, just smiled, and Ash smiled back.

And it must have been the craziness of their circumstances or maybe the near-death experience – again – but she founded herself blurting out like an idiot, "I really do love you, you know."

George's jaw dropped, and Ash felt heat rise from her neck to her hairline. How could she have said such a thing? "Like a brother, I mean," she quickly amended. "And I love Anne like a sister, too. Because I really have missed you both, and I was afraid you had died. And you do have a good sense of humour, you know. When you're around, you can be quite entertaining."

He made a strange face that she couldn't quite read, looking down with an awkward smile. "Thank you, Ashlea. And I care for you, too. Also like a sister." Then he added, "And Anne, of course. And my sister-in-law Olivia, if only I knew her better, and my brother Edward, except of course *not* as a sister. Although I daresay he isn't too keen on me at the moment, but I am obliged to say that I love him as well."

Ash laughed, and he laughed too, and the awkwardness of the moment was broken.

A second later his attention had been caught by something in the distance. "D'you see that, Ashlea? That cave there?"

"Where?"

"That tiny black hole by the base of the mountains. The cloud comes from above it."

"I don't know…"

But as they drew closer she saw he was right: the black hole looked less like a squashed fly and more like a crevice.

No, not a crevice, an actual cave entrance. It was squarish and carved-looking, and probably large enough for them both to walk through side by side.

George looked very pleased with himself. "I daresay that's door number one."

Like ducklings following a mother duck, Anne and Elspeth followed Amaranthus through the garden and towards the Hall of Treasures. Jon came too, talking to Elspeth and still utterly mangling her name, but after a while Anne became so caught up in what surrounded them that she no longer cared.

'Twas more than just a garden inside its glass covering,

Amaranthus had explained. And yes, while 'twas most odd that he now looked so different, Anne found she was able to reconcile the two figures with the same name – once she heard his voice in her mind, she knew he was clearly the same person.

He told them how the vibrant colours they had glimpsed at the bridge were actually part of the *outside* covering, although it mostly couldn't be seen from above. From outside it seemed to be just another brown, dry mountain, unless one was fortunate enough to see the colours as the sisters had been.

But from inside…

The doorway/slide they'd come in through in the rock wall had vanished as suddenly as it had appeared. It had been created only for their rescue, Amaranthus had explained, because otherwise they'd have ended up in pieces on the bottom on the ravine. 'Twas the second time Anne had been snatched away from such a death, and really, she ought to be getting used to it by now.

But now the wall 'twas just solid rock which rose above them to form a dome high, high above their heads. By the time it reached a point at the top, the rock had become almost as clear as glass, and the sun shone in unimpeded. The hollow mountain covered the whole garden like a protective casing, smooth and even translucent from the inside, allowing in enough light that the whole place seemed bright as day.

Most of the inner mountain was filled with lush garden. Not the sort with very neatly regimented flowerbeds, but the wild and real sort that made one think that the Eternal One had reached down to earth and touched this one piece of land, filling it with spectacularly vibrant life. And 'twas a large area – it must have stretched several miles to the other side, Anne guessed.

Amongst the foliage were buildings, at first barely noticeable because they blended in so well with the surroundings, but once Anne had seen them she wondered why she had not noticed them earlier. They were made of some beautiful marbled stone, but somehow managed to look as though they belonged amongst the rambling trees and flowers.

And in the middle of it all, as bold and beautiful as the largest jewel on a crown, was the Mountain. The *true* Mountain of Glass, Amaranthus had said, since the outer one was merely a casing. The inner Mountain was *alive*.

This one was small as mountains went, but incredible. It rose up above the trees and other buildings like a king amongst kneeling peasants. When Anne had first seen it, she had noted its strange shape: 'twas a perfect cone, but rippled with a thousand tiny carved patterns, so perfect it could not be possibly natural.

At first she had thought 'twas blue, but then she realised that was just the reflection of the sky onto the moulded glass. The whole thing was made of glass, and the colours of the mountain wavered and changed and blended, much like moving water had no true colour but simply reflected its surroundings.

Elspeth was the one who had realised the truth. "I vow 'tis a waterfall," she had said, and she had been right.

Their host explained that from the very tip of the Mountain, where it almost touched the ceiling of the dome, came a spring of water. It rushed in a thousand streams over the humps and crevices of the translucent glass, creating the moving colours that so fascinated them both.

"But what are those tiny things crawling on it?"

People, Anne had realised as they drew closer. She had mistaken them for reflections in the water at first, but now she saw that the Mountain of Glass wasn't only an enormous water fountain. 'Twas also a city, and what she had taken for patterns shaped in the glass were in fact doorways and roads and balconies and windows, somehow still useable in spite of the water flowing over them.

Thousands of people lived here, Amaranthus had told them, but many, many more than that came to drink the water that flowed from the Mountain. It might seem like just many tiny streams running through the Garden, but the water continued far further than any of them could see, and became many mighty rivers, covering the world. There were many places the water could be accessed, even out in the normal realm, if one knew how to look for it.

"Oh, I should like to see that," Anne had said.

Amaranthus had smiled. "I'll take you some time."

Hearing that had thrilled her. She'd planned to take Elspeth to the twenty-first century with Ash, but mayhap there was an even better place to stay.

Only the People can live here, Anne. All others must pass through eventually.

People? She was people, was she not? They all were.

My People, Anne. The unfading ones. This place exists outside of time, and you and your sister and even Jon are beings trapped in time. You could not comprehend what it means to live here.

Oh. With that, Anne felt an incredible sense of rejection, although mayhap Amaranthus had not meant it that way. But then he had always seemed to take such an interest in her, that she'd mayhap overreached by even considering that she might stay here… At least he'd extended it to Jon as well.

"I didn't say that I didn't want you here," he said aloud, but quietly enough that the other two didn't hear. "Just that you cannot live here permanently, not as a mortal being."

"I cannot see how I can change that," Anne said stiffly. "I am what I am."

"Mmm."

Amaranthus didn't say anything else, but there was something in his tone that made her glance up at him quickly. "What is it? Is there a way to change?"

"There is a way, but it's a high price to pay."

Anne waited for him to finish, but that was all he was going to say, and then they'd reached a door. 'Twas an odd thing, a frame standing freely in the grass under the shade of a large fruit tree, and without even a handle.

Anne checked the other side curiously. "There's naught here but wood," she said. "A door on its own."

"And yet we'll go through anyway," Amaranthus replied. He lifted one hand and knocked on the wood; once, twice, three times. The door swung open to reveal…absolutely nothing different, just the garden still visible on the other side.

"Was it supposed to do that?" Elspeth murmured worriedly, and Jon laughed.

"Come see for yourself."

Just then Amaranthus stepped through what looked like a plain wooden frame – and disappeared. Jon shrugged and headed after him, and after a wide-eyed glance between the sisters, they followed.

Much like using the Eternity Stone, moving through this doorway felt like stepping from one scene into another.

But where Anne had imagined the Hall of Treasures to contain vast piles of gold, 'twas but a hall: narrow and high roofed and so long that it faded into darkness at the other end. The floor was tiled and displays were set into the walls, like at jewellery shops or museums she'd seen in Ash's time, but without the glass casing.

If she wished to, she might have reached right in and taken the 'treasure'. But in truth, it seemed without value at first glance, like someone's discarded junk. In Anne's brief experience of all things alter-power, that most likely meant 'twas precious beyond price.

Amaranthus led them down the hall some way, past bottles and chests and lamps and in one case, an eating fork – until suddenly he stopped. "I think you might be interested in these," he said, gesturing at a series of small, dull glass vials. They sat in a long row against the gleaming wooden casing, all different shapes and sizes, but none bigger than Anne's palm.

"Oh, they sparkle," Elspeth said in excitement.

"Do they?" Anne asked. She couldn't see it. In fact, they looked dull, dull, dull-

"Some people overlook them, but if you take the trouble to really study them, you'll see it," Amaranthus said in an offhand manner.

"What are they?" Jon asked curiously. "I can't read the script."

"That's because they haven't been gifted to you. If so, you'd be able to read them. They are the Gifts: peace, fire, growth, wisdom, joy… Oh, and here are a couple you might know. Here is flight," he pointed to a small, familiar-looking vial, "…and here is far-sight, also known as knowledge."

Suddenly much more interested, Anne looked closer. She recognised the shape of the flight vial immediately, and her hand itched to take it. She had a *little* flight left, so just a top up would be marvellous and not even missed, surely? "Do they all last two days, then?"

"No. They're all permanent gifts."

Anne paused. "If one drank the whole vial, 'twould be permanent?"

"Even a taste bestows the gift permanently," Amaranthus elaborated. His eyes were crinkling in a smile. "But it's inextricably tied with belief. If you don't believe it will work, then it won't."

Oh. *Oh.* So she *did* have the ability to fly? But she'd kept trying and trying after the two days had passed, without a jot of success-

And the whole time believing in your heart that the ability was gone, until you needed it too desperately to think.

Just like being pushed from a great height and having bare moments before meeting death. "This is most excellent news," Anne said finally, after thinking it through for a long time and deciding to accept his words at face value. "But did not Dr Walker drink the vial before giving it to Ash?"

"Did he?"

Anne thought about it, then suddenly laughed. The man could have been the flying doctor, had he but known it. Ha. Dr Flyer rather than Dr Walker.

'Twas a fitting punishment for what he'd done to them, that he not know what could have been…and she certainly would not return to tell him. Mayhap he'd find out for himself, in time.

Elspeth stared at the tiny glass vials with a new appreciation, especially the one Amaranthus had called 'flight'. Close up she could see a glimmer of colour through the thick glass, and the more she stared, the deeper and brighter the colour became. The vial still seemed to shimmer depending on which way she studied it.

"Oh, if I could but fly, I would travel the whole world," she breathed.

"It's not all it's made out to be," Jon said from beside her. Or beautiful Prince Jon, as she was now thinking of him, with his pale, pale skin, handsome features and silver blond hair. And those eyes, far darker than one would expect in such fair skin. He'd been friendlier than she'd imagine a prince to be, but mayhap 'twas because he did not know she was baseborn.

Elspeth held back the blush that had constantly threatened since meeting him, focussing on what he'd said. "You've flown? Like a bird?"

He smiled crookedly. "Maybe not quite like a bird, but yes. You just end up with bugs in your face and a fear of-" Then he stopped himself from whatever he'd have said next.

"A fear of what?"

But Jon had already moved away, avoiding the question and pretending to study some suit of armour. Elspeth didn't follow, instead moving to stand near the other two.

"I vow, peace must be the most valuable Gift," Anne was

saying. "Imagine, you could use it on anyone, and they'd do what you wanted without argument."

Amaranthus laughed. "I don't think you quite understand the nature of peace. It's not for getting your own way. But the vials must be gifted to you or they won't work. In fact, if you were to steal one, it would give you the opposite of what you sought."

Elspeth felt her eyes widen almost painfully, imagining the dreadful effects of such a thing. One would try to steal peace and find war, try to steal knowledge and find confusion, try to steal flight and find…she knew not what, but no doubt 'twould be dreadful. "That would stop any thieves for certain."

"You'd think so," Amaranthus replied, "but it hasn't always."

"But how would anyone even get in here to steal?" Jon asked. Elspeth had almost forgotten he was there, he'd been so quiet. "Surely you'd know the moment something was taken. Don't you have some kind of alarm system?"

"No one can get in here without the Keeper of the Garden's permission." Amaranthus winked at the girls. "That being me, of course. But an exceptionally long time ago – in your years, anyway – several of the Gifts were stolen by someone who ought to have known better. That, however, is a story for another day." He tapped his finger on a tiny, flat silver pot on one of the higher shelves. "This one here has just been returned to its place. I believe you might recognise it, Bets."

And then she did. "Is it the one used to heal me?" she asked in awe. It had healed more than just her fever, and she marvelled continually at her straight, pain-free foot. Amaranthus nodded in agreement, and Elspeth expounded happily, "What a wonderful power. I should like that Gift very much, I believe. I would never have to worry about losing anyone to illness, ever again. What a shame it only has a few uses."

Anne's friends had told her quite clearly that her own healing had been the last. 'Twas hard to tell from where she stood, but the little jar did not *look* empty…

"It won't stop anyone from dying of old age," Amaranthus said gently. "And it won't raise the dead. But nothing ever stays empty here. This has only a limited number of uses – for each user, not forever – for the sake of those who use it."

"I do not understand. Why would anyone not wish to heal the sick?"

"For most of you trapped in time, it would be more of a burden than a blessing. Think of how many sick people you knew back home."

Well, there was John the Baker's wife, who was crippled from a wagon running her over, and then there was Alfreda who'd been born unable to see, and Simon's twins, they'd never been quite right from what Elspeth had seen. That wasn't so many…

But then she thought about how many she'd known who'd died from a sudden ague rather than any long-term sicknesses, including her own mother, how she herself had almost died from a mere cut, and of the many women who caught childbed fever…

But Anne said it first. "The whole world is sick. How could one person ever do enough, even if they did have the ability to heal any disease?"

"'Twould consume their life," Elspeth realised. Because she would always know that every moment she spent sleeping, people were dying that she could have saved. *While you sat on the privy, five children died of the sweating sickness…*

Amaranthus nodded. "You are compassionate. All of you are. You might not think so now, but even if you were restricted to your own time, the sick would greatly outnumber your ability to heal – within the boundaries of your weak mortal bodies. The responsibility would be far too great, and it would destroy you."

By the Rood and all the saints, 'twould be a disaster. "Then thank you for limiting the uses," Elspeth said fervently. She couldn't be anyone's saviour. She just really wasn't built for it. But still, there was a part of her that wanted to ask if she could borrow just a little, keep it with her in case of sudden illness…

Or even worse, just slip the thing into her wide pocket. But she knew that while Amaranthus had his back to her, no evil deed went unpunished, and she wouldn't risk spreading death in place of life.

She turned her back resolutely on the vials and followed the others down the hall.

Up close, the cave entrance *did* look just like a doorway, but was too dark for Ash to see what was inside. As George had said, they'd met enough horrible creatures here not to check before wandering in.

So he'd gone in ahead with the binding cord, and she waited outside nervously, checking repeatedly over her shoulder for any resentfully undead company.

"A little far-sight would be useful, please," Ash muttered to herself.

"Pardon?" George called from inside the cave.

"Nothing!" she called back. There was nothing new written on or in Anne's album, but Ash did have the thought that with far-sight, she would know when she *needed* to know. She'd just have to trust that Amaranthus had their backs for when she didn't know what she was doing – like now.

Out of the blue, a chill went up Ash's spine. She turned to look behind her suspiciously, but there was nothing out of order.

Just then, George came out of the cave. "What an interesting cave. It's rather lighter on the inside, even though I couldn't see where the light was coming from. It's also much bigger than you'd expect, and clearly not naturally formed, but the most interesting thing is that on the far side there *is* another door…"

…and then Ash missed the rest of his words as she *saw a dragonfly, the size of her hand and dripping venom from its inch-long stinger, drop down from above and jab George on the back of the neck. He swatted at it but missed with clumsy hands, and it darted straight for Ash, stinging her on the arm through her clothes.*

The burning started at the point of entry and spread up her arm, and numbness quickly followed it. George stumbled, then fell to the ground. She took a halting step towards him, reaching for the binding cord, but her legs were like rubber and wouldn't hold her up.

Then the dragonfly fell onto George and morphed into a young man, olive-skinned and handsome, and the man was holding George's throat and staring into his horrified face, leaning forward as if to kiss him, just as the fake-George had done to Ash back in 1818. But there was no romance intended here…

…Trouble incoming.

CARRIER

Ash screamed, "Look out, George!" and shoved him out of the way, barely moving aside in time herself.

The dragonfly-thing veered towards George and he ducked, swatting at it with the loose cord. He missed, and the dragonfly turned, speeding straight at her instead. She reached into her pocket, pulled out the first thing she touched, and swung it at the bug.

Smack.

The dragonfly hit the little book with an audible crack, then bounced off, flying somewhat shakily now. She went after it, whacking it again, then George was getting into it, and he rather impressively gave it a solid kick where it buzzed in the air. *Finally* the thing fell to the ground, stunned, and George lifted his boot to crush it-

"NO, DON'T!"

He stared at her in shock. "Why in blazes not? Haven't you seen the stinger on that thing?"

"It's not a bug. It's a man, probably Janeus."

George frowned, looking down at it. "Are you sure?"

"*Yes*, I'm sure. I saw it with far-sight." Because who else could that man have been?

George didn't look appeased, and Ash suspected he would

have happily stomped on it anyway.

"Use the binding cord," she suggested.

"How am I supposed to put this cord on an insect?"

"It's a big insect. Try."

But while they were arguing, Janeus was regrouping. Ash turned and saw that the broken dragonfly *had shifted into something that looked a bit like a mermaid, if a mermaid could have a snake's body on the lower half. A lamia. It looked at George with its wide, rainbow eyes and said sweetly, "Give me the cord, my love," and his eyes widened and dropped to its generous, feminine chest (were three breasts really necessary?). Then as he was distracted, it whipped around its razor-tipped tail to grab for the cord and…*

…Ash threw herself at George again, knocking him out of the way, and the binding cord went flying. The lamia's whip-like tail tore a long cut in Ash's loose trousers, but she picked herself up and threw the little book as hard as she could.

It caught the lamia on the side of the head, stunning it briefly, then the two of them dove for the binding cord. Ash got there first, but was body-checked and knocked aside, and then *the lamia morphed into a komodo dragon and went right for the cord. It swallowed it and then George jumped on its back and…*

"ENOUGH!" Ash screamed just as the lamia shifted into the komodo dragon, and it was like the word had the impact of a blow.

The dragon fell over on its side as if stunned, and leaping into action, Ash grabbed the cord and flicked it out to its full circumference. And like a game of horseshoes, the cord looped over its head and around its neck. It immediately tightened, and there was a shift in the atmosphere – one she felt rather than saw – then the dragon shifted into the young man she'd seen in the earlier vision.

Janeus…?

Yes! They'd finally got him, and what a fight-

"Damn it to Hades!" George shouted, picking himself up off the ground. "Can't you give me some warning when you know that something's going to happen, instead of pushing me aside and saving me like a damsel in distress? I have weapons, you know! I could help!"

Ash stared at him silently until he quieted. "I do beg your pardon," he said. "I didn't mean to lose my temper. It just all happened very fast, and…well, I'm the man here, and I do have some dignity."

She sighed and patted him on the back, not bothering to argue that his 'manliness' wouldn't stop her from reacting to danger when it arose, rather than leaving him to deal with it instead while *she* acted the damsel in distress. "Just proof that you're human. And by the way, if I had time to tell you, I would have. Far-sight is actually very stressful. I get barely any warning at all, and I see any manner of awful things."

In unison they turned to stare at the man lying on the ground outside the cave entrance. He had his arms and legs sealed against his body as though they were glued, and he was quite naked.

Awful thing – case in point. There was a reason classical statues wore fig leaves.

George seemed to agree. "Good Lord! Ashlea, turn around. You don't need to see this." Then to back up his words, George slapped a hand over her eyes. It ended up hitting her in the nose, and she shoved him away, partly annoyed, partly amused.

"George, I see worse on Saturday night television," Ash said, trying to hide her smile. She was only exaggerating very slightly. "Did you forget what my time is like?"

He actually blushed. "Well, you shouldn't. It's indecent!"

She sighed, possibly in agreement, or out of tiredness. She couldn't tell at this point, but was feeling cheerful over how easily Janeus had been captured. Really, she'd expected it to be much harder. "Yes, it is. And so was that three-breasted mermaid thing, but you don't see me complaining about that, do you?"

George frowned at her mightily – with those thick, arched eyebrows he did it very well – so she sighed again, this time in resignation. "Fine. I'll turn my back. You can cover him or whatever."

She turned her back, taking the chance to pick up the book while she did so. Behind her she heard shuffling, a little light swearing and then silence. The last was suspicious. She turned enough to see that George was trying to work out how he could wrap his jacket around Janeus enough to make him decent. It wasn't going to work.

"Hold on, George. I've still got something that might work." Who knew that a many-layered skirt would come in handy? She fumbled for the last fine piece of cloth that she'd shoved into her pocket, shaking out the item with satisfaction. "See? This'll keep him decent enough."

"But it's a- a petticoat!"

"Your great-grandmother's petticoat, to be exact."

There was a pause, and then an expression of unholy glee came over George's face as he realised that while it was probably morally wrong to beat a prisoner (even one who'd tried to kill you), there were other, more interesting forms of revenge…

George had to wrestle their prisoner into the petticoat, not because he was uncooperative, but because he couldn't move at all, except for his eyes. Anyone who tried to dress a surprisingly heavy inanimate figure would soon realise it was harder than it looked.

But finally they had him all dressed up and ready to go inside the first 'door'.

"There, don't you look pretty," George said in vengeful triumph.

"Doesn't he just," Ash agreed with a smile. Janeus did *not* look impressed, not that he could say so. But those big brown eyes could be very eloquent. "One problem. How are we going to move him?"

"Let's see," George murmured. He bent down and grabbed Janeus by the leg and began to pull, but that merely dragged the petticoat up his body and made it rather less than modest. "Hmm. I'll try an arm then."

"I'll grab the other one," Ash said helpfully.

Together they managed to drag their prisoner through the wide doorway and into the cavern within. Ash found it a little daunting at first, like the yawning mouth of some vast being, but she found George had been right. It was definitely lighter on the inside, and she couldn't see where the light was coming from.

The cavern had a sharply carved dome ceiling of perhaps ten feet high at the edges, fifteen at the top, and nothing really much else to recommend it. Ash noted absently that flight would be no good in here – there was nowhere to go.

Dumping Janeus on the ground, she took a closer look. About twenty feet away, on the other side was a small door in the wall. This one was only large enough for one person, and was made of what looked like solid silver. A picture of what was either a city, a hill, or a water fountain that *looked* like a city on a hill, was carved into the centre of the door.

There was text etched into the silver, and it swirled and formed words as she watched. *All seekers of truth are welcome here.*

How nice – but there was no door handle.

"I suppose that would be the second door," Ash said aloud. She suddenly felt nervous, like waiting for a long-awaited date to arrive. She wanted to go in, but she was also a little scared to. "How do you think it opens? A push?"

"I didn't get to try it before," George replied, dragging Janeus closer then dropping him like a sack of potatoes.

Ash would have felt a little sorry for him, but…well, she didn't. He didn't deserve her pity. "Let's do it then."

"Very well." Clearly excited, George leaned in and pushed gently against the door, on the left where a handle ought to be. But it didn't give, and he frowned. "It's stuck."

"Try harder," she suggested. "Maybe it's just rusted shut. It looks old, after all."

"Silver doesn't rust."

"Well, it does tarnish, and this hasn't, and I can't see someone cleaning it, so it can't be silver."

George ignored her and pushed again against the door, then harder, slamming against it with his full body weight. "Ouch," he said, rubbing his hip ruefully. "Well, that was pointless. I would say we need a key, but where is the lock?"

Ash was beginning to feel anxious. "I can't see anything like that. Let me check the book..."

Down at their feet she saw Janeus shudder and look up at her with intense eyes. He was trying to tell her something, she knew, but she didn't speak Eyeball. "No way are we taking that thing off you," she told him. "You'll just have to deal with it. You *deserve* this."

Janeus just stared up at her beseechingly with those surprisingly pretty brown eyes, and she scowled at him. It reminded her of Sam back in 2155 Iversley. He'd also had pretty brown eyes, and he'd also been a massive d-bag. "*No.*"

But then his eyes widened urgently and flicked towards the cave entrance, and that was when it began.

Twenty minutes earlier

Jenessa couldn't believe they were here. Right here, on her doorstep.

She had seen them in the black water of the old city's scrying pool; those two time-travellers Seyen was so desperate to catch.

She also saw that they did not have the Eternity Stone. No, not at all.

She saw the girl capture Janeus as if it was no trouble at all, but then Janeus wasn't really trying, was he? It seemed like he was only trying just enough to make her *think* he was, so she would tell

Seyen that he was cooperating…but she knew better.

Janeus sat outside one of those vaguely labelled doors that Amaranthus shut himself behind, as though he thought he could make some sort of bargain with their enemy. Fool! Amaranthus was known for his absolute sense of justice as much as anything else. He'd say Janeus deserved death, and that was what would be meted out.

If Janeus made it through that doorway, that was. And Jenessa would do her very best to make sure he didn't.

She flicked a hand over the surface of the water, stirring it just a little, then whispered, "Troilus."

The images flickered and reformed until she saw her brother. He was riding the larger of the 'horses' that had been sent to keep watch on the family for the Creatures, and he was headed towards her. Excellent.

Bowing at the Creature gatekeeper with as much humility as she could muster, Jenessa made her way out of the walled area that held the scrying pools, then began to run. Here, in the Other, she wasn't limited by normal physics. As she'd seen the Creatures do many times, she pulled power from the atmosphere into her body, giving herself super speed until she left a high trail of dust behind her as she sped across the ground.

Troilus was barely a third of the distance to meet her when she passed him, slowed, then turned to join him.

"Jenessa!" he said in surprise, then switched into mind-speak. *I was coming to get you.*

"I know," she said aloud. "But something's happened. Something I need you for, now."

Ignoring the 'horse' which was quite deliberately listening in, Jenessa quickly recounted what she had seen. The Creatures would find out soon enough, anyway. After all, she was a carrier, and anything she saw, so did they. But maybe she could be fast enough…

"So we'll go and capture them and bring them back to Seyen,"

Troilus said, missing the point as always. "She'll be pleased."

No, Jenessa told him in mind-speak. *She'll only be pleased until it becomes obvious they're no use to her because they don't have the Eternity Stone, and then she'll be angry. And who do you think she'll turn it on?*

Troilus looked dismayed. *Us?*

Her, rather. But if it helped for him to think so… *Yes. Us.* Then in a blur of images and emotions, she forcefully sent across her plan. She showed him how Seyen was weak and powerless, how even though the two other travellers were doubtlessly juicy power-bearers, the power would be wasted; how Seyen was fooling herself if she ever thought that she could be what she once was, or regain the power that she once had.

Seyen's time was over, Jenessa told him in mind-speak. They'd faithfully served her for hundreds of years, and for what? So she could make snide comments and treat them both as if they were children?

They *weren't* children, and hadn't been for centuries. They were the ones who should be taking care of *her*, but she wouldn't let them…until they made her see it.

They had to work together, Troilus and Jenessa, and make a new life. A better one. A more powerful one. And they couldn't do that until they decided to stop following Seyen and go their own way, away from this unnatural realm…for her own good, of course.

"For her own good," Troilus echoed aloud, and Jenessa saw that he'd taken in every word. She could feel him thinking, *She does treat me like a child, a stupid one, and I hate it.*

"She won't anymore, not after this," Jenessa assured him. "She'll give you the respect you deserve. But we have to work together."

He stared at her with those clear blue eyes so much like her own, then nodded. "Together. We were born together, and we'll die together."

What…oh, he thought he was being poetic. Jenessa barely stopped herself from rolling her eyes. "We'll *rule* together," she said. "Now let's go."

The cavern

It began like a rushing wind, pouring into the small cavern and sending up dust in clouds. George called out a warning to Ashlea, grabbed his taser from his boot, and he just saw her fumble in her pockets as the rumbling sounded beneath their feet.

Then like a whip being cracked, a *thing* shot up from the ground, sending clods of earth everywhere. It looked like massive snakes, dozens of them, and then the base of the creature showed itself and George realised it was a massive octopus-like creature, one that dug rather than swam.

Ashlea screamed, and George bellowed out her name, aiming the taser at the tentacles that flicked against him and grabbed for his legs. The noise and chaos was terrible, though, and he could barely keep anything straight. Without warning, he felt something like a steel pylon wrap around his ankle. Then his leg was pulled out from underneath him, and he hit the ground hard, stunned. Another tentacle grabbed the taser out of his hand, then wrapped around his throat and held him in place.

"Ash-" George croaked, but then he couldn't speak. He could see her not five feet from him, held in much the same way, her face red.

A single tentacle rose from the writhing mass, thick as a telephone pole, and it began to morph and take shape into a handsome golden man's head perched obscenely on the end of that snake-like tentacle.

The head laughed, and bent down towards George until it was only inches from his face. He tried to head-butt it, struggling violently, but the other tentacles were grabbing his hair and holding him still, and the face was close to his for one interminable second…

…then pulled away.

"What are you doing?" another voice hissed: an angry, young woman's voice. "Gather, or I'll do it! We don't have much time!"

"I can't," the head said in obvious confusion. "I don't know why. He's blocked."

The woman's voice swore. "Try the girl, then!"

No. No, not the girl – but nearby Ashlea whispered something almost unheard.

"What did she say?" the tentacle-head asked again.

"Don't ease up on her-" the woman shrieked, but Ashlea spoke again. Very distinctly and quietly, her desperation clear.

"*Amaranthus.*"

Right then George felt the handle of his knife where it was tucked into his belt, and he pulled it out and stabbed blindly at the tentacle holding his throat. It could have gone terribly wrong – he could have cut his own throat – but instead he heard an inhuman scream, felt a trickle of something warm, and the tentacle immediately pulled back.

He followed it, stabbing blindly again and again, then chopping at the pieces that held Ashlea. Blood trickled thickly from the monster's wounds, too thick and too dark to be human, but he persisted, hacking like a madman with his little blessing of a knife.

The tentacle-creature screamed again and drew rapidly away, and George grabbed for Ashlea, pulling her back towards him and towards the door at the back of the cave. She stumbled with him, clearly injured but still standing, and in front of them George saw the scene change.

The tentacles pulled back and morphed into one massive bear, its golden head reaching the top of the doorway, and with dripping wounds on its paws. Beside it for a moment stood a beautiful blonde young woman, then she changed too, and there were two enormous, almost identical bears there in front of them.

"Are you Creatures?" Ashlea whispered hoarsely, and one of the bears laughed.

"Stupid girl. Don't you remember us from Iversley?"

"Nobles," George said in realisation. Although the faces were unfamiliar, the power wasn't. "You were with Seyen."

"But…all that power was just illusion, until the end," Ashlea said in disbelief.

One of the bears sneered, and the other rolled its eyes, which looked as odd as one might imagine. "You don't know anything," the male one said. Its wounds seemed to have healed already. "Our power is real, and it's even stronger since we came into the Other. And that little knife isn't going to stop us."

"I want the boy," the female said. "He looks juicy."

And then she laughed, and the two bears multiplied until there were four, eight, a dozen massive bears filling the cavern, and there was only a second's respite before the bears attacked, all of them. Ashlea and George both screamed this time and struck out at the nearest ones with their respective weapons.

George saw a flash of blue light and heard a crackle as the taser worked – Ashlea had clearly found it – and the bear that struck him sent him backwards with a jolt, but not before he swiped it across the forearm with his knife. It disappeared into nothing, and he realised in that moment that it *was* nothing. An illusion. The type that could injure you, to be sure, but the type that could be seen through.

In that moment his vision changed. He saw that the bears nearest them were insubstantial, and at the back was just one true bear, and also one woman standing within the transparent shell of a bear, holding a long, thin silver blade in her hand. One of the illusion-bears hit him again, and while it didn't have the power of a true blow, it still stunned him briefly.

Then the girl with the knife leaped for him. Her speed and

strength was inhuman, and George didn't have time or energy to leap out of the way. She knocked him to the ground, still in her bear illusion, and she raised the knife and brought it down violently into his chest.

Crack.

That was the sound the blade made when it broke on George's chest. Like it had been made of wafer rather than actual metal. The girl and George stared at each other in shock, then she looked down at the broken blade. "How-" she began to say, but the other bear/man interrupted.

"Creatures incoming!" Then the male – a true shapeshifter, it seemed – morphed into a massive eagle, took a few clumsy flaps, then crumpled to the ground.

Fool, the air is too heavy here for you to fly in that form, a sharp mental voice carried across, and George knew the girl was talking to the male.

She dropped the knife handle and leapt off George, sprinting for the cavern exit just as the eagle turned into a long-legged, stub-winged ostrich and raced from sight, leaving her behind.

The girl had almost reached the exit when *something* filled it, and she stopped as abruptly as if she'd hit a brick wall.

The thing spoke. "*Stay.*"

The thing advanced into the cave, ducking slightly to get through the entrance, and was followed by several others that looked just like it. George grabbed Ashlea again, the two of them stumbling back towards the silver door, but the things had no interest in them, not right now.

George stumbled on something and heard a squeak of pain – he'd stepped on Janeus. Their prisoner had somehow managed to get himself into a half-sitting position against the silver door, and he watched as they did.

The things looked like humans, but not quite, and some of them at the back were tall enough to fill the cavern. Not like animals either, although there may have been a few traits in there.

The first one had faint tiger stripes on its angular face which should have been inhumanly beautiful, but managed to be terrifying instead because of the cruelty evident in its expression. It wore armour of bone and leather, etched with embroidery in red and gold threads that looked like human hair. Shimmering ribbons came from its head and armour, moving in the still air as if they had a life of their own.

The Creature – for this was clearly what it was – looked down at the cowering girl at its feet. *"Carrier,"* it said, its voice as hideously beautiful as its appearance. *"Surely you weren't going to take such a tasty treat all for yourself?"*

The girl didn't answer, just cowered, and the Creature crouched down and placed a clawed hand on her head. Then she retched, and a shimmering ribbon of what George now understood to be a form of power poured from her nose and mouth to wrap around the Creature's arm.

"Of course you were," it murmured. *"And then you were going to escape this realm, and try to find a way to stop being my little cart-horse, weren't you? You don't like being my eyes and ears in the normal world, and you certainly don't like being fed off, do you, Jenessa?"*

The girl – Jenessa – didn't answer, and the Creature dug in its claws until a line of blood trickled down her forehead. *"That wasn't a rhetorical question,"* it said sweetly.

That was when George noticed the bite marks on the girl's neck and arms. He recoiled in revulsion. What were they, some sort of vampires? And as if to prove his point, the Creature swiped its finger through the trickle of blood, then popped it in its mouth as though it had been honey. Next to him, George heard Ashlea gag.

"No, I don't like it," Jenessa finally answered, her voice barely a whisper. Suddenly George felt incredible pity for her, even though she would have done much the same to them. How had she got involved with these things?

"Yet your adoptive mother sent you to us anyway in return for safe passage here in my lands, and for the use of our scrying pool, asking that your brother be spared." The Creature glanced slowly and deliberately behind him to where said brother had fled, leaving the girl behind.

Jenessa's voice was still a whisper. "Yes."

"That must make you very angry. Make you feel unvalued, uncared for."

"Yes."

The Creature stood abruptly. *"Then you will be pleased to know that your brother has also been used as a Carrier from the very moment your mother made the bargain, although neither of them knew it. We enjoyed the irony, although regrettably, we were unable to show visible feeding marks from him for that reason."* Beside it the other Creatures laughed, and the first Creature gestured at the cave mouth. *"You may go. We don't need you anymore."*

For a moment the girl stayed where she was as if frozen. Then suddenly she leapt up, moving hurriedly between the towering figures until she reached the door, then fled so fast she left clouds of dust behind her.

The Creatures turned their gazes to the trio at the back of the cave. *"Hello, there,"* the first Creature purred. George saw that its eyes were bicoloured with one blue, one yellow, and had slit pupils like a cat's. *"It's a pleasure to eat you, I mean, meet you."*

The line should have been unbearably corny, but George felt cold terror race down his spine. He backed further towards the locked silver door until he felt his back hit it, holding Ashlea's hand tightly as if that alone could keep them safe, with the other cold, sweaty hand gripping his small knife. They were practically standing on Janeus, but who cared?

Acting desperately, George lifted the knife and threw it with all the force he could muster. It was right on target, hitting the first

Creature in its exposed neck and burying to the hilt.

But the Creature just laughed. It grabbed the knife by the handle, pulling it out and throwing it to the ground. There was a small wound left behind, but no blood, and the Creature reached up and carelessly pressed the skin back together as if it was made of dough.

"Who *are* you?" Ashlea asked in a whisper. Her voice was shaking.

"Why would I tell you that, Ashlea O'Reilly? Names have power."

George leaned back harder against the door, pushing on it and praying desperately that it would open, but it still didn't budge.

Next to him he saw Ashlea audibly swallow, then say again in that low, terrified voice, *"Amaranthus."*

The Creatures didn't flinch. In fact, they took a step closer, and the first one laughed. It had sharp yellowed teeth like a predator, neatly matching its stripes, and the inside of its mouth was a sick blue-grey. *"Do you think you can call on him to save your-selves? He is the one who left you here; who gave you to us!"*

"Amaranthus," Ashlea said again, louder and with more desperation, if that was possible. "He wouldn't do that."

The Creatures didn't come any closer, but they were almost within arm's reach anyway, they were so tall.

The first one laughed again, its bicoloured eyes narrowing, then hissed with sudden malevolence, *"To let you come so close and shut you out of the door. How cruel, and how like him not to protect those who depend on him. Don't you know your other little friends are dead? One of our people in the form of a horse pushed them into a gorge, and he heard the splat of their bodies breaking."* It grinned, baring those vicious teeth. *"As for you, we're going to strip your bones clean, girl."*

George pushed more frantically at the door. He heard Janeus mumble something from underneath him, but he ignored it. Ashlea was shaking now, and she lifted her hand as if it would hold the Creatures back. "Gerak, go away!" she shouted.

They all stared at her, suddenly silent.

Who was Gerak, George wondered, and was Ashlea suicidal? But at this point, what could make things worse?

But then slowly, reluctantly, one of the bigger Creatures standing beside the first one took a step back. It was built like a tank, with tusks like a wild boar and its skin in an unhealthy mix of blues and leathery browns, and George would have said that nothing short of a sledgehammer could make it move.

But move it did. It turned slowly and took one step, then another, until it ducked from the cave and was gone.

"What do you mean?" Troilus asked in disbelief. "How could you have fallen asleep?!"

Seyen glared at him imperiously. "I have no idea. But the next thing to do is-"

Suddenly furious – and now convinced of the truth of what Jenessa had said about Seyen's general helplessness – he pointed one shaking finger at his mother, cutting across whatever she was about to say. "You let them escape! That redhead was a massive source of power; she could have kept us going for ages in the normal world!"

Seyen was clearly shocked. Troilus never argued with her or defied her to her face. In former days no one would argue with her because she'd turn them into a bug and step on them, or something equally fatal.

But now, Troilus didn't argue with her because she was just too bloody stubborn to ever give in. He could give a rational argument 'til he was blue in the face, and she wouldn't budge. Instead, Troilus would seem to comply, then sneak around and do what he really wanted behind her back, like a good son ought.

But today he didn't want to. He was so, so angry, so tired of being pushed around and overlooked and considered stupid, and perhaps feeling a very little bit guilty over leaving Jenessa with the Creatures. But what could he have done? Troilus reminded himself. Here in the Other, the Creatures ruled.

Seyen rallied, her hideous wrinkled face twisting with anger. "I'm almost six hundred years old!" she screamed back. "How in Hades should I know why I just fell asleep? Old people do that!" Then she shook her head. "No, no, it must have had something to do with Amaranthus. There's no way I would just fall asleep. I'm strong here."

"You said that he couldn't touch us here! You said the Creatures were in charge, and he wouldn't come near the house!"

"STOP QUESTIONING ME!" Seyen screamed. "Who are you to throw my words back at me, you who can't do anything without being given precise instructions? Chaos damn it, I should have fed you to the Creatures rather than Jenessa! At least she has a brain!"

The knowledge that the Creatures had been feeding off his sister jolted Troilus, but it was the last statement that stuck. Overwhelmed with fury, he bellowed back, "I AM NOT STUPID! You're the stupid one! You think you can get those objects back, and you think that you can return to what you were, but you never will! You can't even harvest power anymore! Jenessa was right, you are weak! Weak, and useless!"

Suddenly Seyen reached out, grabbing him by the ear and forcing that aged face right into his. "Listen here, you snivelling worm," she hissed. "I know exactly what you've been up to. You think you can ever beat me? You have no chance, because you *are* stupid, and I've foreseen everything you'll ever do-"

Crack.

Troilus pulled his hand away from her now limp form, the shock of what he had just done making him silent. Seyen's body slumped to the ground, the neck broken, and he didn't even bother to gather her life force. Anything she had simply came from the Other, since in herself she was almost tapped out.

"I am not stupid," he said finally, staring at the body.

CHOICES

Troilus was still there five minutes later when Jenessa came in.

I killed Mother, he told her without turning.

She didn't reply.

It was an accident. She kept calling me stupid, and she let the other ones escape. She fell asleep, Jenessa! Asleep!

"She wasn't our mother," Jenessa said finally.

Troilus turned to stare at her. "What do you mean? Of course she was."

"No, our mother was Aleda, a princess of Esparta. Seyen murdered her and took us as her own."

"I know that," Troilus repeated. "But she was still our mother."

Jenessa just stared at him with an expression he knew as disgust, and he grew angry again. "She raised us for almost three hundred years. What would you call that?"

His sister sighed. "Whatever, Troilus. Call it what you want." Then she turned and left the room.

Troilus stared back down at the still body. He wasn't...sad, precisely, but he felt something. There was a sense of loss, even if you disliked the person who was dead. But then he saw Seyen's eyelids flicker, and realised that she wasn't dead at all. Not yet.

Kneeling next to her and placing his hand on her forehead, he listened to her last thoughts.

Choices. So many choices – choose the right path, Seyen.

The words echoed through Seyen's mind as if they had been repeated many times, and he saw images of her life, moments when she'd had to choose, and she had chosen the path that led her right here to this moment.

As a young woman in the distant future, she had chosen to seek additional power in the Other, risking the Creatures, rather than accept the methods offered to her. Then, after she had been horribly injured and deformed through her experiences there, she had chosen to try to regain her old self through gathering, a previously forbidden activity, rather than going to her old tutor and asking for help.

Every single time Seyen had been faced with a human being and had decided to murder them and take their life force, she had chosen her path.

After she'd found the Eternity Stone, she'd chosen to use it to kill, steal and destroy. She'd used it to travel through time, finding more objects of power and collecting people for her pantheon, including Janeus. And when Janeus came to her, horrified because he had killed his brother, she had chosen to bring him with her and teach him her ways.

The most distinct choice had taken place in Erastus, in 2614 AD. Seyen hadn't been travelling that long, not more than eighty years or so, but then she'd discovered that the place she'd been born in eastern Europa was different. It had a weak point, a connection between the Other and the normal which meant that she could siphon power from the Other realm without having to interact with the Creatures anymore.

Of course, in her time, the weak point had long been broken open, having been damaged in the Great War of 2100. But if she went back to well before that, to the middle ages, she could use the power *and* convince the locals that she was a goddess to be feared. It would be fun, she'd thought, and easy, since they were very superstitious. All she needed to do to reach Lilluania, 1422 AD, was go through Erastus.

So Seyen had taken her small pantheon there, along with Janeus, of course. But then it had all gone terribly wrong. She wasn't the only one who was watching that weak point, and almost immediately after she'd showed up and attempted to establish herself, up turned the Creatures.

They'd pulled her through the weak point and into the Other, and they'd stripped her completely of her power. She'd been weak, twisted; more hideous than even the false form she'd worn here, but it had been real. She'd been completely humiliated, and everyone had seen it. The whole pantheon. Seen her weakness.

She'd barely managed to escape the Other with the help of Amaranthus. It wasn't the first time he'd made an appearance, but it was the first time he'd actively stepped into her life.

Now choose, Amaranthus had said. *Choose to turn from the path you're following, and walk a new path. I'll help you to leave this behind entirely.*

In all of her shame and fury, Seyen had spat at him. *Never*, she'd said. *I will never accept your help. I choose my own path.*

And she had. She had left Erastus for ancient Grecia of three thousand years earlier, and once she'd arrived she'd made another choice. She'd killed every one of her small pantheon, taking their lives to reclaim her old body, and out of love she'd left Janeus alive. But she'd told him with complete honesty that if he *ever* mentioned Erastus again, if he ever mentioned what he had seen, she would kill him.

He had listened, because in all this time Troilus had never known what had happened in Erastus. Until now.

And then there was the last choice. After the disaster at Iversley, Amaranthus had again spoken to Seyen. He hadn't let her go flying back to her original time, but he'd stepped in again and made sure she'd ended up in a quiet, empty place in the middle of nowhere. More choices, more offers of help: he'd told her she couldn't run free any longer. She could still change her course, and she had a few years left in that dirty little village where she could live a different life.

Ha. As if she would do such a thing. As she remembered that moment not so long ago, Troilus distinctly heard Seyen's mental voice repeat the same thought: *I choose my own path. Me and me alone.*

Then as resounding as a gong, he heard another voice: *So be it.*

He felt his mother's life truly leave this time, and after a few seconds her body crumpled into dust. Some stuck to his hand, and stunned, he tried to shake it off, but it wouldn't go. He ended up sitting there on the floor amongst the pile of ashes marking a six-century-long misspent life, and something struck him with absolute certainty.

This would be him. This would be his death, and it wasn't far away. He had lived more lifetimes that any person should fairly have, and he'd killed over two hundred people personally. He knew that to be true, since he'd stopped counting at two hundred. It seemed pointless.

Troilus knew he should feel guilt at what he'd done, but truthfully, he didn't care. They weren't really *people*, not important like he was. At least that's what he'd always thought. And he'd chosen, over and over again, to place himself over the welfare of anyone else.

Like how he'd left Jenessa. He didn't know why that kept bothering him, but it did.

The woman in question walked back into the room, standing before him with one arm loosely behind her back. She looked down at the pile of dust in front of her, and at him sitting in the middle of it. "Are you *still* here?" she asked in disgust. "And what is this mess?"

"It's Mother," Troilus answered. Jenessa rolled her eyes, not that he knew why, since he had just answered her question. "She told me what happened in Erastus. Or rather, she remembered it, and I listened in."

Now Jenessa looked interested. "Oh? Tell me."

He did, and she nodded slowly. "So the moral of the story is, don't piss off people more powerful than yourself."

Troilus frowned. "No, that's not it at all. It's about…choices. Making the right choice."

"The right choice for who?"

He looked down again at the ash covering his hands, then back at Jenessa's coolly arrogant face. "I don't know," he replied truthfully. "I've always chosen myself first. You know that. I wouldn't know how to do anything different."

"I *know*," his sister agreed, and he realised she was remembering that he'd left her with the Creatures.

"Like, I shouldn't have done that," Troilus continued. "I don't know how I know it, but I know I shouldn't have left you like that. Except if I hadn't, what would have happened to me?"

He frowned again. His head was hurting, and there was an uncomfortable feeling in his gut that he was afraid was guilt. He hadn't felt such a thing since he was a baby – or perhaps not even then. Seyen always said that guilt was for the weak.

"I want to…to be different," he continued thoughtfully. "But I don't know how, and I don't think I can do it. I don't want to end up like Mother, a pile of ashes on the floor, and unmourned by anyone at all."

Except maybe he, Troilus, did mourn her a little, but it was partly self-pity at knowing he would have the same fate. "You know," he said in sudden enlightenment, "I don't think I'm a good person. I might even be, well, *evil*."

Jenessa stared at him. "What is good and evil?" she asked. Then she pulled out the laser pistol she'd hidden behind her back, and shot him in the chest.

Troilus fell to the ground. He hadn't expected that, he thought muzzily, but then he never really expected his sister's actions. Perhaps he was a bit stupid after all…

It didn't really hurt, though. She must have been using one of the stun-laser pistols from the second half of the third millennium. Those things could pack a punch, and you wouldn't even bleed.

His sister bent over him, placing one hand around his neck and her lips close to his. She breathed in, and a shimmer of power that most people wouldn't be able to see passed from him into her. And then he couldn't see anymore, but he heard her whisper, "You deserved this."

He had, hadn't he? *But I wanted to make a different choice*, he thought plaintively.

And as the blackness rolled in, a gleaming light filled the centre of his vision. A flicker of hope.

And someone whispered, *You already did.*

Ash couldn't believe it when the Creature just turned and left; giant lumbering form, tusks and all. Just walked away.

In fact, she was struck silent – but only for the moment it took her to remember the other name Bera had mentioned. "Eve-Evangeline, go away!" she shouted. Then she added, "Amaranthus says go away."

Just like Simon says, Ash thought manically. But this time none of the remaining Creatures moved, and Ash realised that there was a very good chance that Evangeline wasn't even *here*. How could such a beautiful name belong to one of these horrible things?

The first Creature, the one with the tiger stripes, smiled at her again, but there was no humour on its face. *"Someone has been telling tales, I see, and they will be punished accordingly. But unlike Gerak, I have never been as foolish as to give away my true name. So you can order me all you like,"* and it leaned in, *"but I will do as I like."*

Ash felt dismay sag her spine. "You can't touch us," she said. "Amaranthus says you can't touch us. Any of us," she added, just in case they were thinking about grabbing Janeus.

"Oh really? And where are you going to go?"

The Creatures all laughed, and she thought that she'd never seen anything so terrifying. What could they do? Even if the Creatures *couldn't* touch them, they still couldn't get through the silver door to what Ash was desperately hoping was safety.

From behind her, she heard Janeus mutter, "Knock on the door."

"What?" Since when had he been able to talk again?

"Knock on it," he hissed.

"We won't just eat you," the Creature said, suddenly talkative again. And then it went into a detailed description of everything they would do to the three of them, most of which Ash hadn't had the imagination to think of before she'd heard it here.

Just then she heard George reach back and give the door a few sharp raps. The Creature's threats became louder and more violent, but Ash still heard the sound of invisible hinges shifting as the door swung inwards, then a *thump* as Janeus's slumped body fell in through the gap.

"We're going," George declared, his face intensely pale. "And you're not coming with us."

Together, without taking their eyes off the things in front of them, Ash and George bent down and grabbed Janeus under the armpits, dragging him into the darkness beyond the doorway. Ash didn't care where it went, she just wanted to be away from *here.*

"You can't get away from us," the Creature called, moving in towards the doorway until it filled it. *"We can follow you anywhere you-"*

Go, might have been the last word, but it was cut off abruptly as the door swung shut, sealing them on the other side of it in pitch darkness.

But the darkness only lasted a bare moment before bright light surrounded them – the exit a single step away – and they moved through it.

Light. It was all Ash could see, and it was so bright that for a few seconds all she could do was blink and try to recover. But then she could see she was surrounded by greenery, with a high rock wall behind her where the door had been.

They were safe. George was next to her, blinking in a baffled/pleased/relieved way she knew she must be as well, and for a moment she just grinned at him. But then his grin dropped, and she realised what had happened.

"Where's Janeus?"

"We seem to have a habit of leaving the villains behind," George commented. It should have been a glum situation, but he was feeling too bright at being in this place to worry overmuch. "He'll come after us again, there's no doubt."

"If the Creatures don't eat him first," Ashlea pointed out absently. She appeared to have taken on the same apathy that he had – but for good reason. "Look at this place, George. Have you ever seen anything like it?"

Seen it? No, but he'd imagined that the Garden of Aden might have been something like this. Even the air was wonderfully fragrant, a combination of fruit and flowers and something more, but not at all overwhelming.

Then he saw something he couldn't resist – a small stream running through the grass not ten feet away, shining like a diamond.

George had had his face in the pool of water for some time when he felt a tap on his shoulder. He looked up, face dripping and for the first time in ages *not* bone dry and painful from the rockfall, to see Ashlea's bemused expression. "Just checking you weren't drowning."

"Drowning? Have you *tasted* this water? It's so pure one

could almost breathe it." But even so, he wiped off his wet hands and face and sat up. "This must be where Amaranthus directed us. I suppose we ought to-"

Find him, he was going to say, but was interrupted by squealing. The very distinctive squealing of school-aged girls, which while he wasn't so much older, felt as though it belonged to another species. Then two petite, bell-skirted girls were running over and Anne was throwing her arms first around Ashlea, and then around him.

"Urgh, you're all wet," Anne said happily. "We've been waiting for you for an age! Where did you go?"

"Where did *you* go?" Ashlea challenged, although she was smiling. "We lost each other. We figured that since you had the Eternity Stone you'd come find us-"

"We do not have the Stone," Anne said. "*You* have the Stone. One of you."

"We don't have the Stone either," George replied redundantly. "Ashlea just told you that."

There was a long pause, then Ashlea sighed. "This isn't one of those times when it's actually been in my pocket all along, is it? Because I'll be *very* unhappy."

But when she emptied out her pockets, there were all manner of strange and useful items, but no sign of the Eternity Stone. The others all did the same with no result.

"I do not understand," Anne said unhappily. "How can we be present here if none of us has the Stone?"

"By the Rood," Elspeth murmured quietly. "*Edgar* doesn't have it, does he?"

"He was a mile away when we fled from that cave," Anne replied. "'Tis-"

"Wait a moment," Ashlea cut in. "You're saying that we left Edgar with the dinosaurs?"

The long silence told the answer, and George puffed out a deep breath. "It would be a quick ending, at least. And if we don't have the Eternity Stone, there's no way we could go back to help him."

"And he *did* try to murder me," Anne pointed out. "No doubt he deserved it."

'It' being to end up as a large pile of terrible-lizard excrement. Did anyone deserve that?

There was another heavy silence, broken by Elspeth saying, "But then where could the Stone be?"

"Oh, you can't bring the Stone into the Other," someone completely unfamiliar said. It was a boy, maybe a couple of years younger than George and a little taller, who looked as though he'd been dipped in white and silver paint. He'd been standing near the girls, overlooked until now. "Amaranthus told me that plenty of objects of power are supposed to be in the normal realm. So when they get brought through to the Other, they sort of bounce off the barrier and end up somewhere in the normal."

"Who," George asked, "might you be?"

That led to a round of introductions, and then a very hurried – and slightly panicked – recounting of where they'd all been since they were separated, and who they'd met on the way. It seemed George and Ashlea had been wrong to think it was only Janeus and those twins that was the issue…

"By the Saints," Anne said blankly once they'd finished speaking. "'Twas bad enough that the evil Queen and her Nobles still live, but you say there are creatures worse?"

"Creatures. That's what they're called," Ashlea explained. "Although they do have a strong weakness, if they can be sent away simply by knowing their *names*."

"'Twas a bit more than that, I'd vow," a small voice said. They all looked at Elspeth, who blushed at being the centre of attention.

"Well?" Anne asked finally, when her sister didn't speak any further. "What is it?"

Elspeth clearly wasn't used to being the centre of attention, especially because of something she had to *say*. She licked dry lips, looking at her feet. "Jon said that if you carry the Keeper's name or an object of his then you might hold some power over his enemies because the Creatures became what they are from lack of this water and this kind of power. That's why they've the weakness." She'd spoken so fast it took a moment to catch what she'd said, but then it made sense. Somewhat.

Next to her, pale-Jon shrugged. "Amaranthus told me."

"Wait," Ashlea said. "Are you saying that the Creatures are so nasty, are undead immortals, because they don't have *water*?"

The boy shrugged again, looking surprised. "Not just any water. *Living* water. What else would it be?"

"Bera told me…something else," Ashlea finished lamely. She'd recounted the story to George on their way here, and he'd thought it was an odd little myth, right up until they'd actually met the Creatures ten minutes earlier.

"Ah, the story about the hearts," Jon said knowingly. He seemed to do a lot of things knowingly. "Something like: the captured rebels had their hearts ripped out or stabbed or eaten, and so they're now technically the living dead. Or the dead living. And it's all Amaranthus's fault because he's the Keeper of the Garden."

George and Ashlea exchanged a surprised glance. "Amaranthus was never mentioned in the story," George said. "Just a fearful former king, hiding in a hole…"

There was a long, awkward pause, broken by a cough. "I'll have to disagree with that description," Amaranthus said pleasantly from where he stood behind them. He was a small man, brown-skinned and lined, with dark, dark eyes. They'd last seen him in a small cottage floating several miles above the ground – he was *not* ordinary. "But I'll leave you to draw your own conclusions."

He didn't seem at all offended, but even so George felt heat rise up his neck. "Ah. Good day."

"Isn't every day good in some way?" the man retorted with a

smile. "But I understand you've been looking for me."

Yes, and had taken a long route to get to him. "We are, and we're very glad to find you," George replied. "Somebody's trying to kill us again. Any help would be much appreciated."

"We did get the book," Ashlea added, "as you know. And it's been helpful…we think."

Amaranthus smiled, the expression making his eyes almost disappear in his lined face. "I did enjoy putting that together. Did you find the detours interesting?"

George felt his jaw drop. As he and Ashlea had flown here, they'd debated whether those detours had been intentional or just their own poor management of the Stone. Apparently it was the first. "So you separated us quite on purpose? You were making the Eternity Stone take us to the wrong places?"

"I may have encouraged it to alter destinations when the bearer didn't have something clear in mind."

"But we-" George exchanged a glance with Ashlea. Had they made a dreadful mistake? He really had no idea. "We had found some kind of healing object, and we used it. Because of the detours that you sent us on."

"Very good," Amaranthus said approvingly. "You used it for its intended purpose."

"But we didn't know the people that we helped," George said. "Ashlea even accidentally moved…some people from one time to another. We might've changed history!"

"Oh, you did," the little man said with a nod. "Every person does change history, some more than others." His eyes went blank, and he began to move his finger as though writing in the air. "Nerah daughter of Saruca, and Hasan the former eunuch, moved from here to here," and the distance was about two feet in the air. "And here we have consequences of that move…going all the way to *here*." He pointed at the empty air about three feet to his right. "Interesting the descendants they had. All manner of characters."

What on earth was he doing?

But Anne had worked it out. "Amaranthus," she said, sounding appalled, "Are you in the tapestry room at this very moment?"

"Just in spirit, dear. But I've seen this story before. Once they accustomed themselves to the change of language and scene, they did very well indeed. There are one thousand, two hundred and forty-three direct descendants of those two alone, and that's not even counting the five that were rescued from Iudea. Nicely done, don't you think?"

George was simultaneously amazed that the man could be in two places at once, and perhaps both proud and appalled that his and Ashlea's actions had had such dramatic consequences.

She clearly felt the same way. "But were they good people?" she asked, sounding a little panicked. "Did they change the world for good or for evil?"

"Do you mean, did their descendants include any tyrants, fraudsters or violent men? I'm afraid they did, my dear. But they also included a number of nice, ordinary folk who didn't impact the world at all except through those people right around them, for whom their existence made a wonderful difference. They all had the freedom to make their own choices, don't you think?" Amaranthus paused as though to let that sink in, then added, "But of course the fact they're related to four out of the five of you says something. In a way, you've ensured your own existence."

"Related?!" several of them exclaimed in unison, and George and the others exchanged shocked glances.

"I suppose we're nice and ordinary," Ashlea said, sounding stunned. "Which ones am I related to?"

"We left ordinary behind when we started time-travelling," George countered. He felt a smile curling the edges of his lips. Their own ancestors, eh? By Jove, his mother would have a fit to hear Moorish blood ran through their Anglish veins. "And which ones *are* we related to?"

"Descendants of one Eli bar Joseph moved to Europa, and then Italie," Amaranthus said, that far off look coming back over his face as his finger moved through the air. "Ah, here we are, the common point for you, Ash, as your grandfather is half-Italien. Elspeth, here is where we see the common ancestor for you through your mother, and you, Jon. And here, Anne, is where you were descended from the couple Ash inadvertently moved a thousand years back in time."

"We're related?" Jon said in surprise, looking down at Elspeth. "We don't look a thing alike."

"Elspeth was born in 1540," Amaranthus replied. "That makes her a rather distant relative, doesn't it?"

"Not that much," Anne commented. "I recognise your clothing from tee-vee shows, and would expect you've come from sometime in the eighteenth century, yes?"

Jon looked awkward. "Not originally." But he didn't say anything else.

"That's all very well," George interrupted, a little disappointed that none of the rescued ones were related to him. He quite liked the idea of ensuring his own existence. Well, Ashlea and him both. "But the fact remains that we've lost the Eternity Stone – again – and there's a queue of villains waiting to murder us once we do leave here. Quite frankly we've no idea what to do, except to look for you." And a safe place. This *was* a safe place…but it wasn't home.

"Never mind the Creatures," Amaranthus said dismissively. "They won't be able to bother you much once you leave the Other realm. They can't time travel, you understand, and so any connections they'd tried to make would have long fallen off – even if you didn't have the protective medallion to keep you from fatal harm."

"I beg your pardon?"

Ashlea bent down to pick up one of the items from when they'd emptied their pockets; the odd little metal disc George had found out in the desert. "Is it this one?"

"That's it," the little man said happily. "I'd recognise it a mile away. Once we had a hundred of them in this place. That's number sixty-seven."

"So that was why the blade broke on my chest," George said in dawning amazement. No doubt it was why he'd not been killed by either the lion-man or stag-person either – that rather than his own roaring ability. But then the beaver-hogs had looked almost disappointed with the first run-in, hadn't they? "By Jove, what good luck!"

"I'm starting to think luck has nothing to do with it," Ashlea said dryly, handing George the medallion. "Finders keepers – this one's yours."

He looked down at the small, plain object in his hand, which still remarkably resembled a coin with a hole in it. "I expect it could be worn around the neck," he commented. "But I can't take it. You have it, Ashlea. You're in as much danger as I. More, perhaps, because of your history with Seyen Johannis."

"*Our* history," she corrected, pushing his hand away. "She already stabbed you in the neck once, remember?"

And he'd somehow been healed. He vaguely recalled a bright light and then the sudden sense that the wound was closed, although he'd not understood what to make of it at the time. It did seem rather like the times they'd used the healing pot, although he didn't recall ever seeing anyone.

George looked at Amaranthus, who managed to look completely innocent and devious at the same time, and he found himself closing his fingers over the medallion. "Thank you," he said fervently. "But that's only one of us, and if you don't mind, I'd rather not risk my friends being murdered by a family of Nobles."

"Last I checked," Amaranthus said, "The family of Nobles had reduced significantly. A shame, really, as they could have been a wonderful force for good, had they just made different choices along the way. And yes, Anne," here he cut off the redhead, whose mouth was open to speak, "I know you just saw Seyen a few hours ago. Things can change quickly."

"Oh my Deias," Ashlea exclaimed. "Are they all dead? That's just too easy. Are you saying we're safe?"

"I daresay they didn't find the going easy at all," he replied mildly. "And whether they're dead depends on when you look. But you must realise that you will always have enemies. Some will come because of your friendship with me, and some you'll make all on your own. Be constantly vigilant, whether you know of the enemies or not."

"But most people don't need to dodge time travelling, power-using murderers," George said dryly. He felt irritated, in truth, because they'd come seeking aid, not apathy.

I know, Amaranthus whispered. Then aloud, "But of course most people lack the abilities that you lot have, hmm? Now I understand that you've had a long day, but I do this for your own good."

"Do what?" George began, but Amaranthus had already lifted his hands and suddenly it was as though they were being blasted with a high wind. Just very briefly, and then George blinked and the scene around him had changed once more to that small, tidy room in the upper parts of his brother's home.

"Dem me," George swore, feeling baffled and a little put out. "After all of that, he's just sent us back, Ashlea."

There was silence. He may as well have heard crickets chirping, except that he was inside.

"Ashlea…?"

Amaranthus had sent *him* back home. Just him.

Ash didn't swear when she realised she was standing alone down the road from her car, instead of in the Mountain of Glass with her friends. She didn't even make a fuss, because the change had been so quick that it took several moments to realise what had happened. Was that Amaranthus's subtle way of asking them to leave?

Except there were still the gateways...

Ash stood there silently on the road for a few more minutes, feeling crushing disappointment war with relief. Then she very quietly walked the twenty metres to reach her little blue Corolla where it still sat in the ditch where she'd left it.

But here was some kind of miracle. The car wasn't on its side like she remembered, instead on a slight, awkward angle that'd probably be moveable. The window was cracked but not smashed – although Ash *swore* she remembered glass flying – and still unlocked. Her phone was in there, showing that it was just after midday on Saturday. It seemed time had passed normally when she was away, and she hadn't lost or gained any.

Ash sat in the front seat feeling numb, but the numbness only lasted a few moments before being taken over with a sort of tragic hilarity: when you feel so shocked by what's happened that you can only laugh.

"Damn it all to Hades," she muttered finally, wiping the strange wetness from her eyes. The air around her seemed too warm, seemed to tingle and shimmer around her. "Stupid. Just stupid." She'd been sent right home, and she'd guess the others had been too.

So because there didn't seem to be anything else to do, she turned on the car (secretly blessing whoever had walked past and left it be) and with the minimum of effort, pulled out of the ditch and drove home.

Back at the Mountain, Anne watched as George and Ash both looked very surprised for a moment, then blinked out of sight.

Elspeth let out a little gasp, and Jon looked bored.

"Will they be alright?" Anne asked finally, moving to avoid a large butterfly flapping its way past her face.

"Of course," Amaranthus replied, sounding as surprised as the other two had looked. "I wouldn't send them through otherwise."

Which led to the next question, but Elspeth asked it. "Will you send us back now too?"

Amaranthus didn't answer at once, instead lifting his finger for the persistent butterfly to land on. It sat, waving its black and orange wings gently. "Your kind can't live here in the Mountain, little Bets. The outside world moves differently in time, and it would do you more harm than good. Ash and George couldn't stay for that reason, because there are things they need to resolve quickly back in their own homes." He paused, and just as Anne's heart sank, added, "but that's them, not you two. And while you will leave this place, it doesn't have to be today. Not unless you want to leave."

"We'll stay," Anne and Elspeth both said very quickly, then laughed.

"But what about you?" Anne asked Jon. "I'd vow you're not one of these immortal people. Why are you still here?"

He blushed– barely visible through his very white skin – and looked uncomfortable. "I haven't been told to leave yet, I suppose."

"Yes, but where are you *from*? What troubles might there possibly be in Frencia to bring you here?"

Jon laughed. "Not Frencia." Then he was silent.

But when Anne looked at Amaranthus for elaboration, he'd vanished, leaving the butterfly fluttering off into the nearest tree. They might as well have said 'none of your business', and she sighed. 'Twas true, 'twas none of her business. "Where did he go?"

Jon shrugged. "Who knows. He just does that sometimes. Do

you want to come see the city?"

"Oh, I do!" Elspeth said eagerly.

Well, 'twas not as if they had anything else to do. Feeling brighter, although trying not to show it, Anne followed the other two through the garden.

Eighteen

JUSTICE AND MERCY

The darkness was so complete that Janeus felt like he'd been swallowed by it; swallowed by some vast, empty monster and all he could feel was some kind of ground beneath his feet. No sound, not even the slightest wind.

And that feeling he would usually get when someone else was nearby, and he could sense them in some way even though he couldn't see or hear them, precisely? Well, he didn't even have that. He was alone; more alone than he knew it was possible to be, and despair overwhelmed him.

So this was it. This was what happened when you were snatched away from the physical realm and given what you deserved. In truth, it ought to have happened centuries ago, but he'd avoided it up until now. Maybe now it would be *worse*.

At least Tai isn't here, Janeus thought, but even that didn't give him much hope. Even if all those people he'd killed were here in some way, at least he wouldn't be so alone-

You're not alone, someone said very quietly. *There's me.*

Janeus jolted in place, looking around to see who'd spoken. For a moment there was nothing…but then the slightest hint of grey appeared in the darkness. Just ahead, like the light of a weak, distant candle. "Who's there?"

The unseen person didn't answer, but the light grew a little brighter. Janeus tried to move towards it, then realised he was still bound and couldn't walk. Meanwhile the light clarified itself into the shape of a man facing away from him. They were working at what looked like a patterned wall – or perhaps some kind of tapestry – and in the faint light Janeus couldn't really make out their appearance. Tall, short, thin, stocky – who knew.

"Are you Amaranthus?" he called out.

Yes.

Oh. Janeus hadn't met Amaranthus before, for all that he'd heard so much about him. He'd seen a few of Amaranthus's people, and some of them more than once, but things had never worked out well there. He still couldn't make out what the man looked like, but if he was as powerful as Janeus suspected, he could likely take any form. Many of the Creatures could, after all.

I'm not a Creature.

Had Janeus offended him? But the man still hadn't turned from what he was doing. "But they're like you, aren't they?"

Once they were. Now they've chosen not to be.

Oh. "Are you going to kill me now?"

There was a silence, and then, *I don't kill my enemies, Janeus. But I do send them away.*

"Away to where?"

Away.

And that was the most unhelpful answer, but a sense of dread was coming over Janeus. If this place, empty and awful as it was, was not 'away', then how much worse could it be to be sent further?

He'd made a mistake. He should have fought harder against Seyen, or even against those stupid travellers. But he'd decided to just let things happen, thinking it would be better than what he had now. It seemed he'd been wrong. But even as he debated his certain demise, the person spoke once more.

Why did you come here?

Because the two travellers had grabbed him and dragged him through the door, obviously.

Why did you really *come here?*

That question cut through the lies Janeus had told himself. He'd secretly wanted to end up in this place, and for one reason. "I want to forget," he blurted out. "I want to forget everything I've ever done, because I'm scared to die but there's nothing to live for anymore. I want oblivion, and I can't find it on my own."

And you think I'll give it to you.

Janeus raised his hands helplessly, realising his bonds had disappeared. "If you can't, then who can?"

Then Amaranthus turned around, and Janeus recognised him with a bolt of shock. "*You.*"

Me, the man agreed mildly. He was… actually rather average in appearance, with irregular features and a gentle manner in spite of his unsmiling face. *Were you expecting someone else?*

Janeus shook his head, frowning. "But we've met…many times. How can you be *him*? You're…you're just an errand boy." Met while Janeus had been doing less than lovely things with less than lovely people, in fact; pretending to be a god and such…

He didn't know whose idea it had been to pretend to be gods (although naturally Seyen claimed it was all hers) but they had all loved it. They'd gone to somewhere with a set mythology and beliefs about gods, and they'd flashed around a few lights and said, 'Hey, we're your gods!' and the stupid locals had believed them.

Janeus had never lost sight of the fact that it was a big con, but some of the others had. Especially Seyen. She would laugh and say that the regular humans were all idiots for believing so easily, but he had known how much she loved the power and the glory.

After all, she used to say, what was a god but someone or something that was worshipped? She was worshipped; therefore she was a god. Goddess, rather. She'd even borrowed from the Creatures the idea of taking giant forms to impress the humans, and it had worked. There was nothing like looking as if you could stomp someone flat to make them respect you.

Every now and then, they would run into one of Amaranthus's people. Some were regular humans like the time travellers he'd been captured by, mindless hacks who only blundered their way around instruction by instruction, but the others…

They were like Amaranthus, Janeus thought. They looked ordinary but they could do things that even Seyen couldn't, and they would all seem to disappear without any warning. Those ones were hard to kill, and until this moment, he had thought this *person* was simply one of those – he'd seen him around a few times doing menial tasks like feeding people or the occasional healing.

And he looked so ordinary! He didn't even have *hair*!

As for the regular humans when they ran afoul of Seyen and her pantheon…they weren't always so well protected. Janeus had to admit he'd helped get rid of a few of that sort. For gathering, they were usually a goldmine.

Oh Hades, Amaranthus had *definitely* heard that part. Janeus could feel that his thoughts were as open as a book, and reminiscing over the murders of Amaranthus's people wouldn't help the situation at all. Not when he'd just insulted the man by calling him an errand boy.

I've been called worse. But you let yourself be captured; you let yourself come to me thinking you'd obtain mercy?

Mercy, probably not. Justice, almost certainly. At least it would be an end of some kind.

Justice, Amaranthus said thoughtfully. *And you think that being turned into some lesser animal and having your memory removed will be a kind of justice. A whale?*

"Maybe not a whale," Janeus admitted. He'd always thought whales were peaceful – when not being hunted pre-2100, that was. But he wasn't only asking for justice; he was asking for mercy too. Maybe too much mercy to be allowed to be something as impressive as a whale, although that was a form he'd chosen to take on his own before. He'd carried his human mind and memory along with it, though, and that was the problem.

"A dolphin would be alright. That's not as big, is it?" There was a silence, and he added a little desperately, "A tuna?"

You appear to have some kind of fascination with fish, Amaranthus said finally. *Any particular reason for that?*

"Whales aren't technically fish..." But that wasn't the question that was being asked. Not really. And it wasn't about the fish, either.

"It doesn't matter what I'd turn into," Janeus said finally, his tone dull and eyes fixed on a point in the darkness. He didn't want to look the other man in the face. "Anything. Anything, as long as I don't have to carry this *guilt* anymore. You must know I've lived a long life; we've met enough times. And you probably know it hasn't been a good one either, what with all the messages you sent me asking me to switch sides.

"I killed my brother. It was an accident, but I had provoked him to attack me by stealing a very precious medallion that had been his birthright, because I was jealous that he had it and I didn't. And when I killed him, I also took on his ability to shapeshift. I was sorry for his death at first, but after so many years of using the power I'd stolen from him, I found that I couldn't completely regret it.

"I am a bad person. But I'm sick of my life. I've done anything and everything I could possibly do to entertain myself, but life is still dry and tedious and...not worth living." He finally looked up at Amaranthus, the errand boy, or whatever the being was calling himself. "I want justice. I want to face justice finally, and know that it's done, and I don't have to keep dreading it. And I want to drop the weight of guilt that I've carried ever since I started to get my memory back. I want death – and I know that's what's coming – to be final."

There was a long silence. *Death is extremely final,* Amaranthus said. *You don't want to ask for an extension of time, a chance to be better?*

Janeus shook his head. He didn't think he *could* change; after all, he'd been the same arrogant, selfish, uncaring person since he had killed Tai. Probably before that, actually. One didn't change the habits of a lifetime just because they felt *bad* about them.

Come with me.

Janeus shuffled over to where Amaranthus was running his finger over what looked like a big, grey wall, almost hidden until now by the darkness. Images flashed in fast-forward as the man moved his hand, some familiar, some not at all, and after a while Janeus realised what was happening.

Twins. Dark-haired infant twin boys. "That baby. That's me."

Yes. And then Amaranthus did a strange, horrible, terrible thing. He took Janeus's hand and set it where his own had been, and then it wasn't just images flashing in front of their faces. It was memories running through Janeus's mind, and not just his own: also those of every person he'd ever interacted with, starting from Tai in the womb.

"Do we have time for this?" he asked in growing panic. He did *not* want to know…he just didn't.

Oh, we have time. All the time in the world.

It could have been a millennium later, or maybe only an hour, but finally Janeus reached the end of his life's thread and Amaranthus finally let his hand fall. He was already sitting, though: in a pile on the ground that now seemed so much lighter than when he'd first come in. Now he could see everything, and what he saw most clearly was that he was scum.

"I should never have hurt them," Janeus said remorsefully, talking about every one of those people he'd met and treated like things. "I should have been the one to die, not Tai. Me."

Yes. It was clearly the answer to both statements.

"Well, do it then!" he shouted suddenly. "I can't stand the suspense! You said to me once that if I live by the sword, I'll die by the sword. So kill me! Gather, do what I deserve! I don't care anymore."

Then he ruined that whole announcement by beginning to weep. How was it possible that after seeing all of that, his heart's desire was still for mercy? He was stupid, that was it; chronically, wickedly stupid-

You throw yourself on my mercy?

That wasn't actually what Janeus had asked for. It was what he *wanted*, but he knew it wasn't going to happen in a-

You throw yourself on my mercy, Amaranthus repeated patiently. *Yes or no?*

Janeus shrugged dully. If there was any for him, then yes, he did.

Justice will be served, the man announced, with a tone that rang like a bell. Finality. *Justice, with mercy. You will take one last form, as you asked.*

And then in the moment of change Janeus finally understood the wonderful correlation between justice and mercy, and the crushing fear and the guilt washed away in one last, oblivious *change...*

Ash pulled up in her driveway, then got out of the car and went to sit in her tiny lounge, on the overstuffed couch that had come with the cottage. She sat staring blankly at the dark television screen for several long minutes before finally shaking her head. "My Deias," she said flatly to herself. "Did that really just happen?"

A moment later when her head bumped the ceiling – because she'd carried the ability to fly back here as well – she realised it had. She floated back down with a distinct thump, feeling her heart lift, until she realised the thump was the sound of her mobile phone bouncing off the couch onto the carpet.

It wasn't damaged, luckily. But then mobile phones were replaceable, weren't they? People just got rid of them when they got a new one. That was how Ash had been able to get George one; she'd just given him her last model. Except she hadn't seen his phone since he'd left…

Curiously she picked up her mobile phone and dialled his number. This time it rang almost immediately, and she began to walk around the house, listening out for the familiar, annoying *beep beep* melody. He'd hated it, but the phone had been too old-fashioned to upload a proper song, and it was probably out of battery anyway…

The familiar black plastic brick was nowhere to be seen, and she couldn't hear it either, even though the phone kept ringing. She'd made it out to the garden when he picked up.

"Ashlea? Is that you?"

George. Fuzzy-voiced but still recognisable. "You're in the twenty-first?" Ash exclaimed in shock. "Where are you?"

"But I'm not! I'm in my room back in 1818! I only just turned on my phone. I'd been saving the battery, you know." There was an excited pause, then he continued, "But I *am* above the library where you made that new gateway."

"I can't believe it," Ash breathed. "We've got reception through the gateways!" And not even the same gateways, at that. The one they'd made out here led to somewhere outside his manor home, if she remembered rightly. Then another thought struck her. "George, you took your mobile phone to 1818!"

"It's alright," he said, sounding a bit guilty. "I hid it in a snuffbox. No one knows; they'll think I'm just speaking into an old metal tin- ah, yes Nancy, I did ask for warm water. Just here, thank you. No, I'm quite well, I don't need- lemon cakes, yes please. But knock before you come back in, will you?"

A moment later there was the sound of a door closing, and he added sheepishly, "If the staff didn't think I was mad before, they do now. I'll bet you ten quid that the maid tells half the household within the day that I was talking-"

"Into an old tin?" Ash could barely hold back her laughter. It wasn't just the situation that was funny – although it was – but it was the fact that he was talking to her. He was there, and she was here, but they were still in contact. "Shame we never talked Anne into getting a mobile phone."

"Mm. Something tells me we'll be seeing her soon enough." George paused. "Speaking of which, will you be here in time for that walk to the village? Only about a quarter-hour has passed since we left, would you believe."

If Ash counted the night and morning she'd spent in George's time, then perhaps about the same had passed for her. "Do you want me to come?"

He sounded surprised. "Of course. I can't have my 'wife' disappearing on me, you know. Not after you'd arrived in such odd circumstances."

"Of course." But she couldn't help sounding a bit flat.

George didn't seem to notice. "So might you be able to come within the hour? Mother can probably find you another of those old mourning gowns-"

"No! No," Ash said in a more normal tone. "I…I actually have something here." Something she'd bought but never thought she'd have the chance to use.

"Perfect," he said happily. "By Jove, it's been a corker of a day, hasn't it? Not even half over yet at that. I'll wait for you at the gateway at the edge of the estate – that's the one in your garden, by the beech tree. Not the oak; that goes to 1556."

The beech, not the oak. Ash resolved to Oogle it before trying to go through just in case her botany wasn't up to the test. "I'll see you in half an hour, then."

"One last thing… Might you be able to bring me a new taser?" George sounded sheepish. "I've lost mine somewhere through the centuries, and after all that's happened I rather miss the thing."

Ash laughed. Tasers were *not* something she just had lying around the house. "I'll see what I can do."

Half an hour later Ash had discovered the difference between a beech and an oak tree (a useful skill for an apprentice landscaper), and had also worked out how to locate the remnant gateway on her own.

It looked like the shimmer of heat from a hot road, and it tingled when she got too close. Rather like the front seat of her car, in fact – which was something to remember for next time. That gateway to George's library was conveniently located in her car, not on the road where she'd been when she'd used the Eternity Stone. She'd have to be careful driving!

Ash took a deep breath, pulling her online-purchased cloak around her shoulders, and stepped through.

The other side of the gateway was in a copse of trees, off any marked path. She would've thought it quite isolated if George hadn't already been standing there.

He was wearing a slightly nicer version of what she'd last seen him in, and he brightened to see her. "You found…" But his words petered into nothing and he just stood staring at her.

Ash began to feel a little awkward in her previously unworn gown. It felt like going on a date for the first time, all dressed to impress and hoping she didn't disappoint him. She hastily handed over the small metal tube she'd found in her bottom draw, and he took it without blinking once. "No taser, sorry. You'll have to get that next time you come over."

George finally looked down at what he held. "Pepper spray?"

She grinned. "Seeing as you know how well it works. Aim for the face – and make sure you're pointing the nozzle the right way."

He shuddered, but grinned back. "I won't make that mistake twice. But Ashlea…where did you get that gown?"

"Is it so bad? I bought it online months ago when you were

still staying with me, but I didn't know if it was historically accurate, and if it's just not right I can go and change-"

"It's beautiful," he cut in. "You look...simply lovely. Like a lady ought to look."

"It even has a matching hat," Ash pointed out, trying to hide her flush of pleasure at the compliment. As though he couldn't have seen that she was wearing a hat – or a bonnet, as the online store had called it. It didn't fit quite right, sitting on her hair rather than over her head, but it looked pretty enough.

George held out his crooked arm, grinning. "So it does. Would you and your hat like to escort me to the village?"

"Do I have a choice?"

"Not really. I'm being polite."

But Ash took his arm anyway – because that was what you did here, apparently – and tried not to feel so excited about a simple walk to a village. *In 1818!*

The day was looking up. The sun was out, George had Ashlea on his arm (who was looking astoundingly pretty in a frilly blue thing that looked as though it belonged to this time period, barring the zip at the back) and no one was even trying to kill them.

Up ahead he could see the other members of the house party, chattering as they strolled towards Iversley village. Their concerns and conversations seemed so petty now George had seen what was beyond this realm.

The Other.

"You said you saw toys and mirrors being made," he said to Ashlea, thinking aloud. "Intended to aid the Creatures seeing into the normal realm. It's hard to believe such a thing is possible out here in this ordinary place. Perhaps it was simply for a different time period."

"Perhaps," she answered doubtfully. "But that wasn't the impression I got at all. I think they've always been there in some way or another. Just think of all the old stories out there about monsters – and yes, elves – maybe even ghosts. Maybe that's all just the Other filtering through to our world, except it's hard to prove."

George murmured his agreement, but his thoughts had turned in another direction. Up ahead was a small, fair-haired figure that could only be Miss Clarissa Margate, hanging off the arm of one of the other men. This one was a widower, perhaps? But as long as the girl got herself off the shelf, when George finally revealed the truth he wouldn't be thought such a scoundrel.

"Who am I fooling," he muttered. "I'll be a pariah."

"Pardon?"

"I was thinking about what happens when I tell the truth," he said glumly. "About you and I, that is. I'll be thought the worst kind of rogue, to lie about being married – then to bring a girl into my family home who isn't even my wife. They'll think you're my mistress no matter what we say, and neither of us will be welcome again."

Ashlea was silent a long moment, then sighed. "Will it be as bad as all that?"

"Most certainly. And we don't even have the Eternity Stone to create new pathways away from the estate so we could still visit." There was now one in the library as well as out here, but he wouldn't be able to access those. Neither would they be able to go back to 1556.

But there was one other option he'd been seriously considering. He'd hinted at it a few times, but still had no idea how she really felt.

"Of course," George said, making sure to keep his tone light, "we could always just make it the truth. Get married, that is."

As expected, Ashlea looked shocked for a moment, then turned away with a slight smile. "And here I swore I'd never have a marriage of convenience."

George knew he'd fumbled the question, but her response made him laugh and hurry to correct her impression. He might not have this chance again. "You're hardly *convenient*. In fact, barring the unfortunate lie I told two days ago, you're not convenient in the slightest. But-" *You're worth the trouble*, he was going to say, but they'd been seen by the others.

"Mr and Mrs Seymour!" one of the young men shouted, waving what looked to be an umbrella. "Slow coaches, much?"

"Hush," the girl next to him said coyly. Dressed in white – that meant unmarried – and perhaps a daughter of his mother's friend? Parsenne, that was it. "Newlyweds do like their privacy."

George saw Ashlea flush deep red, and the irony was that it wasn't at all true. Unfortunately. "Not at all," he said genially. "I was showing my wife the estate. There're some pretty spots around, if you know where to look for them."

"You'll have to show us later," the girl in white said with a laugh. "After we've bought our share of ribbons down at this village shop that the viscountess swears is quite well stocked. Will you be buying bonnets, Mrs Seymour? Perhaps one with a wider brim?"

"Why would I need a wider brim?" Ashlea asked innocently.

"The bonnet is supposed to shade your face, ma'am," the young man said. George recalled he was a lord something or other (Agglesley? Ellesley?), and that he had a snide sense of humour. "We suggest it out of concern for your health, only."

"The Anglish sun can be quite harsh," the girl added sweetly.

Ashlea turned and looked at George, and he could almost read her mind from that one expression. Confusion, then realization and a raised eyebrow. *Are they insulting- oh, they are.*

Finally she smiled. "How very kind of your friends to show such concern for the health of my skin," she said dryly to George. "Will you buy me a bonnet, darling? One with a nice, wide, healthy brim?"

He saw the houseguests' eyes widen at her use of the endearment (really not done in front of acquaintances, you know) but it felt rather good to hear it from her mouth. "I'll buy you a sombrero if you want," he replied, and they both laughed.

The others looked baffled.

"What's a sombrero?" someone plucked up the courage to ask.

But they never got to answer the question, because a clamour arose in the near distance.

"I say, what's that noise?" Clarissa's escort Mr Farnsworth asked from further up the lane. He was an older man, but surely not old enough to lose his hearing. They were waiting with a cluster of other guests – a couple of men, a couple of women, mostly younger – further ahead towards the village.

"Someone's saying 'pool, pool'," Clarissa said, wrinkling her nose sweetly. It appeared the story about her and George's interlude hadn't come out, judging by the lack of condemning words. Perhaps Mrs Coutts had kept the knowledge to herself after all. A miracle.

But the shouting continued, and it finally made sense. Several times during his childhood they'd had the same problem down this lane, and it had seemed like a wonderful game at the time. Except now…

"It's not pool," George said brusquely. "It's *bull*. One of the local bulls has escaped its field."

"I say," Mr Farnsworth said again. "Are we in any danger?"

"It really depends on how good you are at climbing trees!"

Then the big brown bull charged onto the scene, literally. There were a couple of youths running up behind it, trying to catch it (an almost impossible task because of the size of the creature) and it just ran right in, head down and charging about at the assorted houseguests.

There were screams and yes, a couple of people showed they *could* climb trees. Others leapt over the stone wall alongside the lane. The bull managed to ram Lord What's-his-name in the backside, sending him flying into a bush, then came at George and Ashlea. *They* didn't have any handy trees or walls to climb over, so they dropped their linked arms and fled in opposite directions.

The bull swerved after Ashlea. It hit her hard in the side, tossing her over its back, and then George got hold of the pepper spray. He ran back and sprayed it right in the eyes – it went mad, but at least it couldn't see anymore to target them. It shook its head, making a dreadful lowing noise, then ran directly into the thick brush behind them, the sounds fading as it went.

The two youths in farm gear ran after it, one stopping to yell, "Sorry, gov! We dunno how he got out this time!"

George didn't care how; he just cared about Ashlea, who was lying on her side on the ground, the pretty blue dress now marked with brown. "Ashlea! Can you speak!?"

She was alive, and awake, but her face was twisted with pain. She shook her head, eyes bright with tears.

Someone was screaming in the background, and he turned to shout, "The bull's gone! Might you refrain from making that racket?"

It had been Clarissa, and her pretty face turned bright red. "It's a wasp!"

"Oh, for Hade's sake," George muttered. "You'd think it had stung her in the eye. Ashlea, can you speak?"

She moved her lips just as he heard a buzz rush past his ear. "What? I don't know what you're saying. Is something broken?"

"*Wasp.*"

"Yes, I know it's a wasp, but there are rather more important things to be concerned about!" He took off his hat, swatting at the irritating insect as it buzzed far too closely past his neck, and got lucky with the second swipe. The wasp – which *was* a good size and virulently yellow-coloured – fell to the ground, twitching.

"*Squash,*" she mouthed. "*Quick.*"

"Very well, a mercy killing." George picked up a nearby rock and dropped it on the creature, squashing it flat. "There. Now, I need to ascertain if anything is broken-"

Ashlea was sobbing now, and he was horrified. "By Jove, it's worse than I thought. Wait, I'll send the others to fetch a horse. See, no one's really hurt-"

Even Lord Ellesley was now standing up, rubbing his backside irritably while the others either gasped or laughed.

A pleasant-looking older woman came up, crouching beside them. "Is aught broken, Mrs Seymour?"

"No," Ashlea managed to say. "Not broken." But she was still shaking, eyes bright with...something. She kept staring at the rock, the wings of the wasp still visible on one side of it. "Just winded."

"Winded," George said in some relief, but he still felt like he was missing something. They managed to sit her up, and he could see some embarrassment on her face along with the tears. A shame she hadn't managed to fly out of the way – but that would have taken some explaining later on.

"Five minutes," Ashlea wheezed. "I'll be fine."

Ash was just badly winded, but it was hard to get that across when she could barely talk. But once they'd finally managed to talk the others into continuing to the village she explained to George that she'd actually broken the fall with flight – had softened the blow. It could have been a lot worse. She was shaking with laughter, not with sobs.

"But why are you laughing?" George asked in confusion, helping her to her feet. "It's not hysteria from the injury?"

Ash was about to argue that she was never hysterical, but remembered her bad reaction to the dinosaurs. Almost never hysterical, she amended to herself. But as for the reason she was still giggling even through her tears...

She pointed at the rock that George had dropped so neatly on the 'wasp'. "You've got the medallion, right? The protective one?"

"I suppose I must. But what does that-"

"It wasn't a wasp," she explained. "It was one of those nasty insects with the stingers, from back in Reman Palestine, or wherever we were. A *shapeshifter*, George, and you swatted it after it tried to sting your neck. But it bounced right off…and then you *squashed it*."

He looked down at the rock, horrified. They could still see the faint, crumpled wing of whatever-it-was. Definitely dead, anyway. "By Jove. I killed the thing."

"After pepper-spraying a *bull*. I'm not sure that's the best idea you've ever had."

"Don't give me the weapon if I'm not to use it," he retorted, but his lips were curling into a smile. "Good Deias, I ought to be appalled, but all I can think is how glad I am that I didn't know I was doing it. Can hardly feel sorry, either. Did far-sight warn you?"

"Oh, yes. But not about the bull, so I think it might have been a real one. Bit of an odd coincidence, don't you think?"

"Perhaps," George agreed. "But those beasts have escaped half a dozen times from the local fields since I've been here, so I wouldn't think much of it. Er…shall we go back and clean your gown?"

Ash looked down in dismay. Her lovely faux-regency dress was now rather less lovely – which was why she ought to just wear jeans and gumboots, she decided. "Would I be expected to change for dinner?"

"Of course. But…" His face fell as he realised that even if her dress had been clean, it wouldn't have enabled her to sit with the others at a formal meal. "Oh. Perhaps my mother-"

Suddenly Ash felt deflated all over again. It wasn't enough to be able to speak the right way. There was so much more to fitting into George's time than she had imagined, and quite frankly, it seemed too hard, never mind too expensive.

"Never mind," she said in disappointment. "I'll just go home for tea. Might give you a call tomorrow to see how it's going? It'll be my weekend still." *If* he had any phone battery left, of course.

"I'll say you weren't feeling well after your fall," George said with a sigh. "Although it's likely people will come to their own conclusions."

They walked back to the remnant gateway Ash had arrived through twenty minutes earlier. Feeling an odd mix of emotions, somewhere between sadness and affection, she leaned forward and gave him a kiss on the cheek. "Thank you, George. I've had an interesting time."

"What with the veiled insults and the repeated murder attempts? I do hope I can offer a lady something more than just *interesting*."

"I'm not a lady, George," she said gently, and that made her feel sad too. She knew who she was, even if he'd forgotten, and right now the cultural gap between them felt tragically insurmountable. "I'm a peasant, remember? I'm just playing a role."

He scowled. "We're all just playing roles. I'm pretending that I'm a normal gentleman who *hasn't* spent six months in another era, and half of the houseguests here are pretending to be respectable human beings and hiding their vices. You *are* a lady to me, Ashlea. Ash." He paused. "When you go back…see if you can find the letter we wrote, back when we first left. You might find it interesting."

"Thank you." Because what else was there to say?

"One more thing." George pulled a small, coin-like disc out of his pocket. The protective medallion. He took her hand and placed the medallion into her palm, closing her fingers over it. "Keep this. If you had already held it, you wouldn't have been harmed today."

"And you would be dead from that insect's sting." Ash tried to give the medallion back, but he wouldn't take it. "Oh, come on,

George. I've got far-sight. You don't."

"It's not enough," he said firmly, putting his hands behind his back so he couldn't be forced to take the medallion. "I want you to have it, Ashlea."

She could see he meant it. "For now," she said finally, resolving to find a way to slip it into his pocket…next time.

She left.

The Mountain of Glass

The second time Anne visited the Hall of Treasures, it had changed from her first visit. The vials had gone, and in their place was a single bronze bowl, as large as a tabletop and full of water.

'Twas also set on its side against the wall, the still water ignoring the effects of gravity.

"'Tis jelly," Elspeth suggested. "Clear calf's foot jelly, or mayhap some kind of glass."

Anne frowned and looked closer. She could see the bottom clearly – the 'water' was shallow after all – and it shivered as she bumped the display case. "It moves, see. So not glass. Mayhap *'tis* some kind of jelly."

"Ah, you've found the portal," Amaranthus said over her shoulder. "And yes, that is water. You can touch it, if you like."

Anne tapped the surface with a crooked finger, and indeed it came away wet. "What purpose does this serve?"

"It's a direct link to our home world. There's another identical to it there, and the water is pulled towards it. That's why it doesn't fall."

"Home world?" Anne echoed in disbelief, recalling some of the truly odd tales told by Ash's people, rather like the 'elf' tales of the sixteenth century. "Are you saying that you're an *alien*?"

From her time with Ash, Anne now knew it didn't mean

'foreigner', but rather one who was foreign to planet Earth, if such a thing were possible.

But it must be, because Amaranthus replied with a grin, "Alien in the sense that the People did not originate on this planet, then yes. In the sense of little green men flying on a spaceship from far, far away, then no. Did you really think true immortals could originate in this world? Here, *everything* dies, even stars. My world isn't even in the same universe as this one."

"What isn't in the same universe?" Jon asked as he came up behind them.

Amaranthus pointed at the strange anti-gravity bowl. "The other side of this bowl. Put your hand in and see."

"Alright." Without hesitation, Jon stuck his clothed arm in the water almost up to his armpit…even though the bowl was only three inches deep.

"Jon!" Anne gasped. Was the rest of his arm truly in another universe? And how deeply must he trust Amaranthus to put his arm in without even testing the water.

He looked at her innocently. "What?"

She sighed. "Nothing." Then, curious now he wasn't screaming in pain, she asked, "What can you feel?"

"Not sharp teeth, if that's what you were worried about."

Anne flushed. "Of course not."

Then when Jon finally withdrew his arm, not only was his sleeve completely dry, but something more had happened. Something marvellous. His skin and the cloth of the shirt shimmered as though powdered with gold dust.

Jon held it to his face in fascination. "You know, I think that this hand actually looks younger."

"Let us see."

Anne and Elspeth crowded closer. And Anne saw that although Jon was only her age or a mite older, his skin on that hand was definitely smoother and fresher in appearance. More like the skin of a child, without spot or blemish.

"The effect will fade within a few hours," Amaranthus explained. "We rarely use the portal now, but it is only effective for transporting small goods, rather than enhancing one's beauty. It would be better to stay here within the Mountain for that. You'll eventually age to the best and healthiest time of your life, and it will last longer when you're on the outside."

Anne looked at around at the others. Jon looked…well, mayhap a little *darker* than when she'd first met him. Then, his skin had appeared white as snow. Now…mayhap closer to the shade of blancmange?

Elspeth, in contrast, stood straighter and taller, with a confidence Anne hadn't realised she'd previously lacked.

"Do I look different?" Anne asked.

Elspeth peered at her critically. "Your freckles are still there, if that is what you were asking."

Anne barely restrained herself from slapping a hand over her nose. As a redhead, no matter how much she hid herself from the sun, those dozen or so tiny freckles remained. They were the bane of her life, although Ash had told her she was being foolish. But then Ash had the oddest idea of what constituted beauty, so Anne had naturally ignored her. "Lemon juice, mayhap?"

"Or a wide-brimmed hat?" Elspeth suggested helpfully.

Or simply accept that your freckles are charming, Amaranthus said.

Really, 'twould be easier to wear the hat. But Anne did appreciate the gesture.

It's not a gesture. It's the truth. Simply because you see a flaw doesn't mean it's really that way.

Oddly enough, Anne believed him.

Ash had stripped off the now dirty dress, changing back into her more comfortable jeans and T-shirt. The house felt empty and small, and while she certainly hadn't wanted to hang around with George's 'houseguests', she didn't really want to be here either.

Well, there was always the TV – and warmed up leftovers. Hooray.

He'd asked her to *marry* him. Her, Ash. She couldn't stop thinking of how he'd asked, and how she'd desperately wanted to say yes, even though she'd known he couldn't possibly have meant it. They were friends, and there was some attraction, but it didn't mean he'd want to tie himself to her *forever*.

But then Ash remembered what George had said about the letter. She wandered into the entry hall again, checking under the wooden side table and even under the rug. She extended the search to the bushes outside the front door, in case a gust of wind had been *really* strong.

She'd almost given up when she pulled the side table away from the wall and saw a neatly folded piece of paper stuck in the seam of the wood. She could see the indents of handwritten text even from here.

Ash's heart skipped a beat. The famous letter that would have told her everything…had she read it a month ago. She pulled it out with bemused excitement, grabbed a cup of coffee and sat down to read it.

And read, and read…because when George had said it might be interesting, she hadn't realised it would tell her about more than just the gateways. Now, after everything they'd gone through, it seemed to say so much more.

George had rambled a bit while writing it, which seemed out of character, but then as he said, he'd been trying to write it quickly and hadn't done a draft. The start of the letter mentioned Anne several times, but then seemed to forget her existence. It went from *we* want you to come to the gateways, to *I* extend you my warmest hospitality.

Oh, it talked at length about what the gateways were, and about how they felt it imperative to leave at once. But it also requested that Ash come through as soon as she was able. It listed half a dozen possible times, then ended with, '*Or whenever you find yourself available. You will be most welcome…to see my world as I have seen yours*'.

The second half of the letter didn't mention Anne at all.

I fear that I have not shown you my best self, George continued. *If I had known there was a way to return to my own home, I would have displayed rather more good grace while I was a guest in your home. I shall make sure to improve for next time. :)*

Yes, he'd actually put a smiley face. Ash had told Anne about those (the girl being insatiably curious) but hadn't realised George had been paying that much attention.

But the last part made her laugh – a lot – and also want to cry a little.

For all of our disagreements, I do realise that there is no one else in this world who understands our experiences like the two of us. And Anne, of course, but somehow that is not the same. And here he'd crossed out a few words as though he'd made multiple attempts, but ended with: *You are quite marvellous as you are, Ashlea. I would have you know that.*

Maybe it wasn't a love letter, but Ash couldn't discount what had been written there. George had never been open with his emotions, and she'd have expected it to end with something like, 'my sincerest thanks for your kind hospitality'. Not comments about how no one else understood him.

Perhaps his claiming she was his wife hadn't been completely spur of the moment after all.

A flicker of hope rose in her, and she had to ask.

"But I just got changed," she whined to herself.

But that was what mobile phones were for, right?

THE LAST REASON

Iversley, 1818 AD

On a quiet semi-rural road, a large rock shuddered and shook where it lay.

Suddenly a woman lay there, battered and dust-covered with the rock now seeming much smaller where it sat on her stomach. She pushed it off, then groaned as she tried to roll over.

How could that have gone so badly? All she'd wanted was to take advantage of their stupidity and the strong alter-power they'd unknowingly gained while travelling (and yes, take revenge too) and it shouldn't have been so hard. She'd think that her enemies were particularly brilliant, but it appeared that they were just lucky.

Oh Chaos, in this moment Jenessa felt she was particularly *un*lucky. If she didn't have the power she had, she'd be dead. Even now she could feel her bones knitting back together. There was no way her rib cage hadn't been crushed; no way. In fact, if she didn't get out of here soon into somewhere more power-filled, she *would* be dead.

A moment later she focused on the ability stolen from her brother, morphing into a little brown rabbit that limped its way back to the gateway it had come in by. Jenessa switched back to human for the barest moment needed to move through the gateway, and then she was back in the Other. She hadn't planned to come back here, but what other choice was there?

Other or death. But if she moved too slowly, it would be Other *and* death, because the Creatures would be furious that she'd tried to leave them. Ironically, if she moved through a gateway in time and stayed there long enough, they'd lose their power.

She'd only worked that out after Troilus's death, after she'd left the Other and had determined not to go back no matter what. She'd aged and aged and – oh, *suffered*, but then suddenly she'd been fine, and it had all made sense. She'd understood that it was the Creatures who'd forced her and Troilus to age once they stayed away from the Other for more than twenty minutes or so, to prevent the twins from escaping their hold. If only Jenessa had known earlier, she'd have left long before.

But she couldn't take that back. It was done, same as Troilus and Seyen were dead, same as Janeus had been taken beyond her psychic reach. Funny, she didn't think *he* was dead…

Jenessa finally healed enough to stand upright again in the dry ground of the Other. The next gateway was some distance away. She focused on the long-legged running bird Troilus used to change into frequently, but by the third attempt, she had to accept that she was too weak to change.

Walking it was, and she moved as fast as she could manage, pulling power from the surrounding atmosphere to speed her journey so the Creatures wouldn't find her.

Oh please, please, don't let the Creatures find me.

She'd grabbed her laser-gun left at the edge of the gateway, but it wouldn't do more than just slow them down…

She was not scared, she was *angry*, she told herself in that moment, ignoring her now rapid heartbeat. Angry! Every bloody thing had gone wrong, and stupid Troilus had practically forced her into killing him, what with his muttering about morality and choices, and then he'd been the favourite for three or four hundred bloody years, much good had it done him.

Do you think this is going to help? A thought came quietly into her worried mind. *Finding a new place; killing new people?*

Duh. It wasn't like there was any other choice, was there? She had to live, and she was going to live *well*.

You'll never live well when others have to die to keep you alive. And you won't live at all if you don't ask for help.

That was a stupid thought. Jenessa pushed it aside, just like she always had when such random, ridiculous thoughts came to mind, and carried on.

She was striding up a hill littered with dusty, naked pines when the Creatures spotted her.

The tapestry room, Mountain of Glass

Amaranthus stood halfway up the tapestry, one finger lightly tapping an unusually long black thread where it almost reached its end. He hovered several metres above the ground, all his attention on the girl talking to the Creature.

Could she truly be called a girl at more than three hundred of her people's years? But to him, she was. That was why he had to watch this, even though he knew she'd made her choice and nothing further would be offered to her.

It was one of the smaller Creatures, who held little power now except to communicate with the other, stronger ones, and to make what malicious trouble it could. It wore a small, furry form with a little coloured jacket, and stood next to a small wooden cart where a female version sat in wait, paws in lap.

"Oi, Miss," it called.

Jenessa's thoughts exploded from her head in tiny text from the thread. *Oh, it's just a beaver-hog. I hate these little freaks, but they can't hurt me. Too small, almost no power.* "What?"

"The missus and I were wondering if you'd-"

"Forget it." *As if I would waste my time, and as if I would go near a Creature if I didn't have to, even one more beast than man.*

"But-"

More fear and anger poured off the girl, the anger winning briefly. "Trock off," Jenessa snapped at the thing. She kept walking, picking up her speed once more. She had better things to do than pander to pint-sized dead immortals that were too weak to even take a decent form.

"You'll be sorry!" The beaver-hog hollered after her. "You'll see!"

Whatever. Now, I know the gateway is around here somewhere. Higher up the hill perhaps, as long as there are no more turn-offs…

But she hadn't gone another two hundred metres when she heard a growl. She turned quickly, pulling the trigger of her laser gun just in time. The huge lion-man fell *thump* at her feet. Shaking her head in relief, Jenessa sheathed the gun. *It won't be permanent, but I'll have time to get away*, she thought in relief. *So that's what the beaver-hogs wanted. It was a set-up.*

But she didn't see the second one coming up behind her.

At least, Amaranthus thought sadly, the more bestial Creatures tended to make it quick. It was the others, the ones that ruled, that would have truly made her suffer.

He lowered his hand from the end of the thread and tucked it carefully in with the others nearby, then turned and left. Every thread came to an end, and some of those ends were tragedies.

But they did have choices, and she'd chosen freely.

Amaranthus resolutely pushed that thought to the back of his mind where he kept all the other similar, painful thoughts – because nothing could be truly forgotten – and headed for the Garden.

Iversley, 1818 AD

George hadn't expected Ashlea to call him again. Not after she'd been injured then had left so resolutely. He'd also accepted with quite some disappointment that she wouldn't…well, that perhaps she wasn't as interested in him as he was in her – as he hadn't *realised* that he was until it was too late.

So when his snuff box began to vibrate once more, he opened it almost incredulously, pressing the single button to 'answer' the call. His own mobile phone was much simpler than hers, but really, it was as much as he could manage – and he'd needed written instructions on how to use the thing.

"Hello, George?" Her voice sounded very clear, as if he was standing right next to her.

"Er…yes, it's me. Good evening, Ashlea. Are you well?"

"I'm fine! Where are you?"

"At a ball." He almost made a joke about her having a Regency era ballgown stashed away, but then realised she'd take it as more 'proof' that he only wanted her here so he wouldn't have to reveal his lie to his family.

"A ball at your brother's house? Are you in the ballroom now?"

"Er…no, I'm in the garden. Can't have anyone seeing me speak into a snuff box and thinking I'm mad, can I?"

"Can you come to the library?"

His heart leapt. "Most certainly!"

When George finally reached that room, Ashlea was standing by the bookcase in the same blue gown she'd worn earlier. It was a bit worse for wear, but she looked beautiful…and a little sheepish.

"I read the letter," she said.

"Oh." He paused, struggling to recall precisely what he'd

written, and wondered if he'd said a little too much. But then there'd been no time to write a draft. "Did you like it?" he asked, then wished he could take it back. Did she 'like it', as though he'd offered her a new flavour of cream cake.

"It made me think. About how we *do* have a lot in common, that other people can't possibly understand, even though our differences are so huge that they seem impossible at times. And because of the letter…and because you gave me the medallion, and because you said that you weren't a eunuch…"

What did *that* have to do with anything?

"…I have to tell you something. I lied to you earlier."

George's heart sank. Nothing was making sense except that she'd lied, and that was never good. "You did?"

"Back when we were flying in the Other, and I said I loved you like a brother. I really don't."

"Oh," he said again. "Oh. Well. That's…a disappointment, I suppose, but I do understand that although we've stayed together for so long, we're not truly family. We are friends – or I had thought we were friends-"

Ashlea put her hand on his arm, halting his speech. "That came out wrong. What I meant was that I do love you, and it's not very sisterly at all. Not platonic, either. And I wanted to know…" and here she looked tremendously nervous, "if you share the feeling? The not-platonic feeling, I mean. If you don't then let's just pretend this conversation never happened."

"I do!" he burst out, almost laughing in relieved shock. "By Jove, Ashlea, haven't I showed you in a hundred ways that I do *not* think of you platonically at all?! And I'm most, most relieved to hear that you might feel the same way."

"Oh, I do," she agreed earnestly.

He grinned. "Could you say that again, but in front of a priest?"

And that was how he made the world's oddest proposal – but

it was accepted this time. Perhaps because the bride-to-be was as odd as he was.

"You know my parents will go mad," Ashlea said some time later, when they'd become better acquainted. "They'll say I'm too young to be married."

"Bosh. In some cultures you'd have five children by now."

"Five?"

"Three," he amended. "But I promise I will do everything in my power to be amiable to your family. They will be mine too, after all."

She sighed ruefully. "I suppose I ought to become better acquainted with yours, too. After we've been shopping."

"Shopping? Why?"

"I can't stay here when I've only got one suitable dress."

"We'll sort it out," he said comfortably, his arm around her shoulder. "But we'll have to have the wedding in your time, because everyone here thinks we've already done it."

"Interesting choice of words," she said mischievously. "Is this my cue to say something about not buying the trousers until I've tried them on?"

George's jaw dropped as he realised what she meant, then a moment later that it had been a joke. He exclaimed in mock horror, "Ashlea Jane O'Reilly! Are you trying to take advantage of me? I'll have you know you can't have the milk without buying the cow!"

She turned adorably red, then she realised *he* was joking. And two seconds later, he was kissing her.

Several minutes later, the contents of which were nobody's business except their own, Ashlea suggested, "Six months at each home?"

"Maybe three. We'll see how we feel."

"OK. But if this era drives me mad, I can always escape to my cottage and watch TV."

George paused, then decided she meant it in good humour. Still, divorce was rampant in her own time… "You can have as much space as you need, just remember that marriage is for life."

She retorted, "And remember that if you cheat, your life will be that much shorter."

Pause. "I won't cheat, Ashlea. Not ever."

"Good. And neither will I."

And that, Edward Seymour thought wryly, was why one ought to close the door before revealing incriminating secrets. He ought to know.

But he recognised the extended silence for what it was, and gently pulled his wife away from the library door and down the hall. They'd come out for a private conversation, but had heard something rather unexpected.

The moment they were out of earshot, Olivia burst out, "I can't believe they're not married! How horribly, dreadfully scandalous."

"For all of us." Edward looked at her lovely profile, lit in the faint glow from the candles set along the hall. "If anyone found out…"

She pulled away from him where he gripped her arm and dusted herself off as if his touch was dirty. But then ever since she'd found out about his mistress two days before, she had acted as if he was a leper in private.

In public, she'd been merely cool, and after how lovingly they'd begun, that hurt. He'd only brought her out here so that he could apologise, try to put things right.

"I'm not going to say anything," she snapped. "Good grief, Edward. I would think you would be more worried about the fact that he seems to think her a time traveller of some kind. A *time traveller*, Edward. What sort of charlatan must she be? And your mother tried to befriend her!"

Olivia was probably right, but he felt the need to defend his brother anyway. "Let's not leap to conclusions just because of one overheard conversation. Let's give them a chance to explain."

"Give you a chance to explain about 'Alice', you mean?" she said acidly.

"Yes, that is what I meant," Edward argued. "I didn't think you'd *care* so much, Livvy. I don't love her, not at all, and I've already sent her a letter ending our…connection. If I'd known it mattered to you, I would have been done with it long before our marriage."

Actually, he hadn't yet sent the letter. It was half-written, and he was just waiting for the chance to finish it and send it. There were legal ramifications, of course. He and Alice had a contract, and he wouldn't just discard her and leave her on the street with nothing.

"It does matter!" Olivia hissed. "It matters because now I know what kind of man you are! I told you that Felix was the same, that he was unfaithful to me, and you acted so sorry for me, saying how wicked he was! Yet here you are doing the exact same thing!"

"It wasn't the same," Edward contested hotly.

Her first husband had been a real philanderer who'd slept with anyone who'd have him, from their servants to her married friends in the ton. He hadn't been discreet about it, either. Compared to that, Edward had felt like a saint.

If only he'd known she would care so much… If only he hadn't let her hear about Alice.

"It *is* the same thing! Adultery is adultery!" She looked furious, and Edward realised that it was likely in part because of what they'd overheard, how George had sworn fidelity to his 'wife'. Then Olivia's eyes widened in horror. "Is it Alice Woolsten?" she choked. "Did you bring her *here*?"

"No, no, no," he hurried. "For Deias' sake, *no*, Livvy. It is *not*

Alice Woolsten. I'm not Felix, and I would never *ever* be unfaithful with anyone of our own class." She looked even angrier, and he hastily modified, "Or anyone else! I swear it!"

"You swore it before the Eternal One on the day we married, and look how much that counted for," Olivia said bitterly. "I can't believe I fell for your lies, and came to live here with you and your mad family. Time travellers and false marriages! I-"

But whatever she would have said was silenced as another couple came around the corner, and the two of them gave them pleasant nods. By then they'd made it back to the entrance to the ballroom, and Olivia swept inside.

He had no choice but to go with her and keep up the front that they were a unified couple, as much as any of their class was, anyway.

But he was going to fix this if it killed him, Edward swore. Right after he asked George what the blazes he thought he was up to…

The Mountain of Glass

"I want to be immortal," Anne announced baldly. In the silence of the glass-filled washroom her reflection squinted back at her, and she sighed, imagining Amaranthus's response. *Sorry, dear, but only very good, kind, special people get to be immortal…*

"Like Janeus?" Elspeth said, and Anne just about leapt out of her skin.

"By the Rood, Bethie! You might've made a little noise before coming in!"

"I did," her sister argued. "I spoke."

Anne rolled her eyes. "Oh, very well, you did. But- what did you just say about Janeus?"

Elspeth stood next to her, studying her reflection in the mirror. They were the same height now, Anne realised in some shock, and her half-year of seniority hadn't lasted. Elspeth had also taken to wearing what the People did; a long brown tunic over loose trousers. She looked rather like Amaranthus, in fact, only much prettier. "Jon said that Amaranthus made him immortal."

"Don't be silly," Anne scoffed. "Amaranthus would never do that. Janeus kept trying to kill us."

"Jon says that was mostly his children, and they're dead now, same as Sane. And he said something about…justice and mercy going hand in hand?"

"It's Sey-en," Anne corrected, looking at her sister narrow-eyed. And she thanked the Eternal One for that death, because the woman had been too dangerous to leave alive.

Jon *did* have a lot to say, didn't he? She'd worry about her sister more if 'twas not for their location, because the two were spending a lot of time together. Too much.

"And 'tis hardly just to reward a murderer with eternal life. What kind of mercy does that show to his victims? You must have heard wrong, Bethie."

Elspeth shrugged. "If you say so. I'm going to the top of the Mountain again to watch the viewing-pool with Jon."

Anne watched narrow-eyed as her sister pranced away, then sighed heavily and followed after her.

She was stopped shortly after by one of the People, a pleasant-looking older woman in a white dress and trousers. She looked just like any other ordinary woman, except for the faint glow to her skin and the easily overlooked markings on her palms. "Amaranthus wants to see you."

Anne brightened. "He does? Why?"

The woman shrugged, smiling. "Find out." She waved a hand to her right, and a shimmering doorway opened in the hall. That was how they seemed to move around here, rather than flight or other shortcuts – they just went from one place to another. Almost like the Eternity Stone, but without limitations.

The doorway led to a room she'd never seen before. 'Twas brightly lit, and tall, narrow glass doors covered every wall. Amaranthus was standing staring intently into one, and as the image behind the glass changed, he beamed suddenly. "And there we are. Just on time."

Anne felt a little nervous in this unfamiliar place: very small and clueless, as Ash would have said. "You summoned me?"

"Ah. Yes. You wanted to talk to me."

She paused. "*You* summoned *me*," she said again, slowly.

His dark eyes crinkled into a smile. "Because you wanted to talk to me, dear Anne. Shall we talk?"

Suddenly Anne's throat was dry. He knew; of course he knew. There probably wasn't a word spoken in this place that didn't go past his ears. But the sooner she asked, the sooner she would be turned down, and she couldn't bear it-

"Yes," he said simply. "There is a way for you to become immortal, but it will mean giving up everything you've ever known or ever held dear. That's a very high price to pay, and most are unwilling to pay it. Do you still want it?"

He'd clearly taken the information from her mind. Anne frowned slightly, debating what 'everything' might mean, and whether 'twas worth more than living in this place, being like these People.

Finally she decided that it did not matter. "Yes," she said simply. "I do."

There was no sound, but her statement felt as final as the sound of a gong.

Amaranthus smiled widely. "Wonderful. Let's get started, shall we?"

"I told Anne about Janeus," Elspeth told Jon, "and she did not believe me."

He looked up from the swirling images in the foot-wide pool at the inner Mountain's peak. "Sorry, what?"

"Janeus," she repeated patiently. "I told my sister about how Amaranthus made him immortal, but she did not believe me."

"Of course she didn't. Why would she?"

Elspeth blinked, studying his handsome face. "But I believed you."

Jon grinned, and as always, the smile made her both want to smile back and to blush. She did both.

"But you're you," he said. "She's her. I think she'll have to see this one for herself to believe it."

Mayhap Jon was right. He'd told her about this odd, wonderful, dreadful loophole in Amaranthus's rules, where if a soul went through a certain gateway, their slate was wiped entirely clean, as though they'd lived a perfect life when in truth 'twas not at all. Some kind of plan devised by Amaranthus, who truly didn't like people dying, but one that made sense only to himself, mayhap.

It had something to do with another odd, wonderful, dreadful word – repentance. Janeus had regretted the life he'd lived, and he'd taken the chance offered to live another way.

Saints' bones, the man had been lucky. Elspeth wondered what Ash and George would think, considering that he'd very nearly killed the both of them.

And then she thought about how differently she was treated here where her foot was straight and her birth unknown – and then she looked at Jon, and felt again like a liar. But she'd keep this lie for as long as she could, to keep his friendship.

"I have some wonderful news," she said instead, thinking of the *other* excellent opportunity. "Amaranthus needs someone to run some errands for him, someone who is not one of the People, and he has asked me!"

"That's great, Bets," Jon said absently. He was still staring down at the dancing images on the viewing-pool's surface, but when she looked over curiously, he swiped a hand across the surface to clear them. "Did you say errands?"

Elspeth shrugged, blushing a little the way she always did around Jon. "'Twas his word, not mine."

"Sounds fun," he commented lightly. "But if you don't have to go already, we could visit the Great Hall. There's a dance starting in a few minutes."

It sounded lovely, but… "Oh, but I'm sure I won't know the dance."

"Neither will I, so we can learn together."

Jon got up to leave. Elspeth went to follow him, with a curious glance over her shoulder at the viewing-pool. The surface was as still as when they'd arrived, but still she knew he'd been hiding something.

She wasn't the only one with secrets.

Epilogue

In the Mountain of Glass there was a gateway. It was low and rough and easily overlooked, but Amaranthus had put a vast amount of effort into creating it.

But it wasn't what it looked like that mattered. It was what it *did*.

He could call it the great cleanser, or the balancer of the scales – but as far as he was concerned, if anyone walked willingly through this gateway (or crawled in some cases; it could be very low) then their scales would be balanced. Whatever wrong they'd done would be written off, and they'd have a fresh start. In his eyes they'd be as innocent as a newborn child....and they became one of his own, forever.

Others might think that was unfair, but he didn't care. It was his gateway, his rules. His house, his rules, said every parent ever: and his justice. But it was always justice with mercy, as Edgar LeSpenser was finding out.

Justice with mercy, and perhaps a sense of humour…

Many years before any calendar created by man

The creature appeared suddenly by the waterhole, scaring away the small prey which had been creeping up to drink, and well and truly ruining Og's hunt. Where it came from was a mystery, almost as much as what it *was*…

"What is it?" Nud hissed in a nervous whisper. "Is it a bird of some kind?"

Og lowered his spear and looked sideways at the strange creature. It looked like a man, except it was covered in these-…hanging things of all different colours, like petals from a drooping flower, and its hair and beard were cut so short they didn't even reach its shoulders.

But it wasn't *acting* like a man. It was whimpering and cringing away from them, and muttering noises like *Witchcraft* and *dontyouknowwhoIam* over and over.

"It's harmless," Og said finally. "And I'm pretty sure it's a man."

"We can't eat it, then," Nud groaned in disappointment. "I can't believe we're going to go back without even a bird to show for this whole day's hunting! If we take this thing back, we'll be a laughingstock, especially after the wolf incident."

That was true. The two friends had a record of bringing home strange creatures from hunts, and not easily eaten ones either. Last time it had been a wolf cub that was clearly alone and starving, and Og couldn't bring himself to kill it. Instead he'd taken it back to the caves as a pet and put up with the scornful response.

"I still think we can train it to hunt with us," he said instead. "Make it think it's human."

Nud stared at him incredulously. "What, use it as bait? If it's a man then it's clearly mad!"

"Not *that*," Og countered irritably. "I meant the wolf cub."

"Doesn't matter," Nud muttered. "You know that if we don't impress the Chief then he'll decide we aren't any use out here anymore, and he'll give us to Old Ebba." He glanced Og up and down. "Or *you*, anyway. You know she's been eyeing you up ever since her fourth husband died."

Oh stars, *anything* but that. Old Ebba should have been called 'Ancient, Hideous and Toothless Ebba', but she had an appetite for younger men (which meant *all* men) and she was the Chief's grandmother. He would never turn her down for anything, especially not a handsome young hunter who couldn't even hunt effectively.

Their strange find seemed a little less frightened now, and was approaching them with caution. It kept making those strange babbling sounds, but Og ignored them. The bird-man seemed taller and less pathetic when it wasn't hunched over, and that gave him an idea…

The birdman turned out to be good bait in more ways than one. Not only did Og and Nud manage to kill the two separate predators that tried to attack him after they staked him by the waterhole, but when they finally dragged him (plus hunting spoils) back to the main cave, Old Ebba took one look at Birdman and decided that his pale skin and colourful drapings were the sexiest thing she'd seen in decades.

"I'm going to call him Errl," she announced, "because that's the sound he makes the most."

They all looked down at the hog-tied birdman, still lying on his side on the dirt floor of the cave. He looked less scared now and more angry, not that that would do him any good.

"Now, one of you boys has to chew my meat. You know I can't do that anymore, now I've only got two teeth left."

"Oh, I would," Og said politely. "But I wouldn't want to take the job away from your new husband." Besides, Jissy was watching him flirtatiously, and being Ebba's official chewer wasn't exactly the image he wanted to portray.

Old Ebba seemed to accept that, and set herself to training the 'poor, mad thing' to masticate roast lion properly. It looked to be hard, hard training, involving a few slaps around the head and strangely enough, toothless kisses. That would work. A man would do *anything* to get her to stop.

"Stars," Nud muttered after they managed to slip away. "I wonder what he did to deserve that?"

As long as it wasn't them, Og thought. Aloud he said, "I guess we'll never know."

Not quite the end...

The story continues in *Across Time and Space book 3*

**Thousands of gateways, with
instant access to the whole of history.**

What could possibly go wrong?

With the discovery of the remnant gateways through time it finally seems like Ash and George can have it all – adventure, romance, and a steady paycheck. It seems to be working…until it isn't anymore. And then Ash finds a mysterious new gateway in the middle of an old Lunden street…

Meanwhile on the Mountain of Glass, Anne is chasing her dreams. She wants immortality, a permanent home for herself and her sister, and to finally find out what secrets Jon has been hiding. Her goals seem very close: just a single gateway away…

In a quiet corner of Europa, in the very distant future, Coryn of the Chosen is accustomed to danger. After all, that's what you get when you choose to live on the border of the inhospitable but power-filled Other realm. But then fire is found beneath the ice of the Other, and all Hades breaks loose.

Virtual reality meets alter-power meets some very determined immortals. Throw in time travel, and things are about to get messy…

Dear Reader,

Warning: contains spoilers.

Mountain of Glass was a natural progression from the end of *The Eternity Stone*, where Ash, George and Anne find they've all been dumped in the twenty-first century by the nefarious (and lazy) Dr Walker.

I had a lot of fun thinking about how George and Anne would react to various everyday objects, and how they'd handle living together. And then there were all the realistic issues – Ash would have had to support them all, and how could she afford to do so? Answer: Anne working under the table (don't do it!) along with 'Angland' being slightly cheaper than our England. Why? Because I said so.

But as always, the heart of the story came from a dream, or several dreams in this case. I dreamed very vividly that I was chased through a desert by these incredibly gross, scary beings that were stuck together as if in a three-legged race, and I couldn't outrun them. In fact, the whole scene from Ash finding the ruins to fleeing from those Creatures was based on this quite fabulous dream where I woke up and *knew* it was going to find its way into a book.

And it did. The scenes where Anne and Elspeth meet old man Tray, the stinky horse, the farmhouse and the colour-streaked mountain were also from a dream – however the underground Mountain of Glass exists only in my imagination.

Sigh. Now *that's* a place I'd like to visit.

As for you, feel free to 'visit' this series again with its next instalment, *Desert of Fire* (smooth advertising, right?) or check out my website, mmarinanbooks.com.

Not-horrible endings guaranteed.